WILLOW POND

A Novel

Carol Tibaldi

Willow Pond

Copyright © 2011 by Carol Tibaldi

No part of this publication may be reproduced, stored in a retrieval system, or transmitted, in any form or by any means, electronic, mechanical, photocopying, recording, or otherwise, without prior written permission from the author.

This is a work of fiction. Names, characters, places and incidents either are the product of the author's imagination or are used fictitiously. And any resemblance to actual persons, living, dead (or in any other form), business establishments, events, or locales is entirely coincidental.

FIRST EDITION TRADE PAPERBACK

March 2012

ISBN-13: 978-1468111729
ISBN-10: 1468111728

Cover designed by Jennifer Johnson, Sapphire Designs

Dedication

To my parents and to my niece Lisa. Always in my heart.

Chapter One

Laura Kingsley Austin was Jean Harlow beautiful.
Men first noticed the butterfly tattoo, its saucy wings peeking from her cleavage; it was quite the conversation piece. Unfortunately, that wasn't what Laura had intended. It had first appeared one crazy night when she'd gone with some friends to *Bacchanal,* her aunt's speakeasy, and had too much to drink. One of them dared her to get a tattoo, so she did. Ever since that night, she'd shied away from having too much booze.
Years later, everything in her life had changed. After separating from her husband three months earlier, Laura had moved into an apartment on Patchin Place in Greenwich Village. She loved the village and its diversity of people, and felt a kinship with the artists and writers living there.
Her whole apartment could have fit into one corner of Willow Pond, the huge colonial mansion she'd left, but it was all hers. She loved every cramped inch of it.
The front door of the apartment opened into a long hallway. To the left was a good sized living room, which she had decorated in the English country style. Her writing table sat in the northeast corner of that room, and it was there she often sat, surrounded by writing pads, pens, pencils and an old Remington.
Since she'd moved to the village, her life had changed more than she'd ever imagined it would. For the first time since her marriage, she felt her life was her own. She wasn't being

controlled by her husband or anyone else, and neither was her son, Todd. Like her, he smiled and laughed a lot more these days.

Each day she discovered new things about herself, both as a woman and as a mother. When she'd been living with Phillip, he'd always discouraged her desire to be a writer, saying she should spend her time and energy on more "important" things. Now she pursued her goal with zest; she'd already had a short article published in The Villager, a community newspaper. She felt as though she were coming awake after a long sleep.

The village offered excitement, with all its places to go and people to meet. Phillip had never encouraged her to make friends. He'd preferred to keep her to himself, though he'd never had trouble sharing himself with as many people as possible. Especially women. Laura had been afraid to confront him about that particular issue until the day she read about him and the actress with whom he was co-starring.

Almost from the beginning of their marriage, there had been rumors about Phillip with other women. She had tried to ignore them, tried to believe she could make her marriage work, but reading about his affair in the newspaper was just too much. She couldn't ignore it anymore. She and Todd deserved better. The day after the article appeared in the newspaper, she went to see a lawyer.

"Are you going to leave me?" Phillip asked a few days later. He'd just gotten out of the tub and stood in the middle of the bedroom, tying the sash of his white terrycloth robe.

She glanced out the window, then returned her gaze to him. He stood absolutely still, waiting. She nodded. "I can't live with myself any longer if I keep letting you treat me this way. Todd and I will be out of here by the end of the week."

Phillip scowled, bringing a crease to his handsome brow. "I'll never let you keep that boy from me. Do you understand?"

She sighed. "I would never do that to you or to him, Phillip. But tell me, just how much time do you spend with him now? He hardly knows he has a father."

"We know whose fault that is, don't we?"

Now Laura sat on the edge of her very own bed, weary of thinking about their petty arguments. She stretched her arms over her head, then smiled at the sound of tiny footsteps padding along the hallway. After a moment, Todd appeared in the doorway, clutching his favorite teddy bear in one hand and rubbing the sleep from his eyes with the other.

"How's my big boy today?" Laura asked, holding out her arms.

The child toddled to his mother's side, then climbed onto the bed and into her arms. She kissed both his cheeks, loving his little boy smell and the warm, reassuring feel of his body against hers. Todd was the best thing that had ever happened to her. She'd had no idea it was possible to love anyone as much as she loved this little bundle of boy. Now that his father was no longer a part of his life, Todd was blossoming like she'd always hoped he would. He hadn't been able to before, because he'd been too afraid of his father.

"Up," he said and tugged on her arm. "Me hungwy."

"Mommy is very sleepy," she teased, laying back down.

"No!" He peered down at her and very gently pulled the lid of one of her eyes back, then screamed when she popped up, saying, "Boo!" They both shrieked with laughter as they rolled around on the bed.

"Come on," Laura said eventually, taking his hand. "What do you want for breakfast?"

"Cake."

They wandered into the kitchen and she smothered a chuckle. "You can't have cake for breakfast, sweetie pie. How about cereal?"

He shook his head and pointed at one of the cabinets. "Me want cake."

Laura frowned and opened the cabinet, then realized he wanted one of the blueberry muffins she'd bought at a bakery a couple of days earlier. She took the box down and showed it to him.

"Is this what you want?" she asked.

He nodded. "Bippies."

'Bippies' was his word for blueberries. She lifted him and squeezed him one more time before settling him in his high chair. She set the muffin front of him, then pulled his bottle from the refrigerator. He rewarded her with a sweet, blueberry-stained smile.

"Good?" Laura asked, sipping on her cup of coffee.

He smacked his lips. "More cake," he said, and held up his sticky hands.

She was almost tempted, but not quite. "That's enough for now," she said.

When he stuck out his bottom lip she laughed, then handed him a small piece of the last muffin. After she drank her coffee and finished what was left of the muffin, she cleaned and dressed him, then dressed herself.

"Do you want to go to the park, Todd?"

He clapped his hands and headed right for his stroller. She caught up to him, helping him slip into a blue sweater with its matching cap. His little brow was tight with concentration as he climbed into the stroller by himself, and his expression made Laura think of his father. Occasionally she thought about Phillip and wondered if she'd done the right thing, taking Todd away. But all it took was one look to see how much happier their son was now. Even her aunt Virginia told her not to worry about Phillip.

"Go now!" he demanded, and she grinned. Every day he became more independent. She was torn between a mother's pride and the grief at losing her baby.

She headed down Patchin Place slowly, enjoying the sense of freedom that had recently become so important to her. Washington Square Park was only a few blocks away from her apartment, and when she got there she let Todd out of his carriage so he could play, though she always kept a close eye on him. He toddled onto the grass and sat next to a little girl playing with a pail and two shovels. Without a word, she handed him the second shovel and the two began to happily bang on the pail.

The little girl's mother sat next to Laura and introduced herself. "Isn't it wonderful how easily they can amuse themselves?"

Laura smiled and agreed. The two mothers talked for some time, until Laura realized it was time to go home. Before she left, they agreed to meet in the park at the same time the following week. Laura left with a smile on her face, hoping she had made a new friend.

***

The phone was ringing when she walked in the door. Before she'd even taken Todd out of the carriage she picked up the receiver, and heard Phillip's voice. She sighed. She refused to let him ruin what had so far been a wonderful day.

"Hold on a minute," she said. "I have to take Todd out of the carriage." She put the phone down on the table. Even when she was halfway across the room she could hear Phillip yelling about something.

"Out!" Todd demanded, holding out his arms.

Ignoring Phillip's ranting, she lifted Todd out of the carriage, removed his hat and sweater, then gave him a couple of animal crackers to nibble on.

"What took you so long?" Phillip barked when she picked up the phone again.

"Have you forgotten that I have a child to take care of? What do you need, Phillip? I can't talk to you very long because I have to give him lunch and put him down for his nap."

"I don't want you to forget that I'm picking him up tomorrow afternoon at one o'clock. Make sure you pack enough for two weeks. I don't want to run out of things like diapers or whatever else he'll need."

"You won't run out of anything, because you're not the one who's going to be taking care of him. Mrs. Nickerson will be there, and she knows exactly what he needs."

"Just do as I say, Laura," Phillip said, and hung up.

She gritted her teeth and pushed the conversation from her mind. While Todd napped she finished packing for his visit with his father. When she was done, she took out a writing pad and began jotting notes for the novel she planned to write. She'd start working on it while Todd was at Willow Pond. This was the first time she'd ever given a thought to writing a novel. Something she'd read had given her an idea, and she couldn't get it out of her mind.

After Todd awoke from his nap, she brought him into the living room to play. He went right for his alphabet blocks, spread across the floor in a mess of red, blue, green, and yellow. Virginia had bought them for him on his first birthday. Ever since then they'd been his favorite thing to play with. He plopped down on the carpeted floor, stacked one on top of the other until he had a tower of five, then knocked them down and started all over again.

Across the room from him, Laura was working on an article for `The Villager`. Every few minutes she looked up and watched him knock the blocks over, then clap and laugh with glee. His joy filled her heart. Once when she looked up he caught her eye, then knocked the blocks over again.

"Oops!" he exclaimed. "All gone."

"You little rascal," Laura said, getting up and scooping him up in her arms. "Is it time for dinner?"

She headed into the kitchen, put him into his chair, then began to prepare his favorite dinner: chicken broth with pastina. He ate heartily, finishing two bowlfuls of soup and smacking his lips between each spoonful. When he was finished, she put some grapes on his high chair tray and put the remainder of the soup in a bowl for herself.

"Did you have fun today, Todd?" she asked.

He pointed to the tray. "More gapes."

Afterwards, she bathed him, then carried him into the nursery where she sat in the rocking chair with him in her arms. This was their special quiet time together. It always had been. Even when they'd been living at Willow Pond, no matter what else had been going on, at bedtime she carried him into the nursery, closed the door and read one of his favorite books to him. Tonight she read `Tommy's Birthday`, but instead of using the name 'Tommy', she used the name 'Todd'. Every time he heard it, he laughed and kicked his feet.

By the time she was halfway through the story for the second time, she noticed he'd fallen asleep. Not wanting to let go of him, she sat a little while longer, watching her little angel sleep in her arms.

After a while she reluctantly gave him up to his crib. He sighed and rolled onto his side. She covered him then tiptoed out of the nursery. Tomorrow Phillip would come for Todd. She hated even thinking about it. If Mrs. Nickerson hadn't agreed to take care of him she would never have let him go.

Chapter Two

Phillip was never on time for anything. Laura had learned, over their two and a half years of marriage, that he actually believed no one else had anything to do that was more important than what he was doing.

By one o'clock the next afternoon, Todd was packed and ready to go. She hated the whole idea of his leaving and kept hoping the phone would ring, that Phillip would offer some lame excuse as to why he couldn't take Todd. Whatever the excuse was, Laura would have been happy to accept it.

It was nearly two-thirty by the time she saw the white Rolls Royce pull up in front of her building. She stared with disgust at the ostentatious car, knowing Phillip had used both it and his chauffeur to show off in front of her neighbors. It made her even angrier at him than she already was. Her neighbors had no idea she had been married to a movie star, and she liked things that way. Now they'd all want to know who had been driving the Rolls Royce.

When she opened the door, Phillip looked so annoyed she wanted to slap him. He strode into the apartment and glared down at Todd as if he were nothing more than a piece of property he owned. Todd blinked guilelessly up at him. It was past his naptime, and he had grown cranky. He tried to comfort himself by sucking his thumb.

"I thought we agreed that was a nasty habit, and you were going to break him of it," Phillip said. "Do you want him to grow up with buck teeth?"

"Oh, please," Laura said. "He's tired. You were supposed to be here an hour and a half ago. Where were you?"

Phillip shifted from one foot to the other. "We got stuck in traffic."

"I don't believe you," she said, narrowing her eyes. "Maybe I shouldn't let you take him. I doubt you're going to spend much time with him anyway. Is your new starlet at Willow Pond?"

He lifted his chin. "I don't have to tell you anything. After all, how do I know what goes on here?"

Ignoring her, Phillip walked over and picked Todd up. The little boy looked up at his father and sighed, then turned away from him. Seeing this, Laura became even less comfortable about letting Phillip take him, but she had no choice.

"I wish you'd brought Mrs. Nickerson with you. She'd know how to get him to sleep on the ride back." Laura removed a bottle of apple juice from the ice box and handed it to Phillip. "This might help. Give it to him if he starts to cry."

Phillip stared at the small ice box, incredulous. "My God, I never realized you had one of those ... *things*. Why don't you order a full sized refrigerator and send me the bill? I won't have my son living this way."

"No thanks. And your son is just fine. Better than ever, actually."

Laura watched them walk down the steps, climb into the car, and drive away. When they were out of sight, she wandered gloomily back into the kitchen, wondering how she was manage the rest of the day. The phone rang, providing a welcome distraction.

"Did Phillip pick up Todd?" Virginia asked.

"Yes, unfortunately. And he was late as usual. He's going to have a rough time with Todd and he deserves it. Thank God Mrs. Nickerson's there."

"I have a feeling Phillip's going to grow tired of these visits. They'll cramp his style. Do you have anything planned for this evening?"

Laura took a deep breath. "Not really."

"Why don't you come over and have dinner with me? It'll help get your mind off Todd."

Laura hesitated, craving solitude, but battling loneliness now that the apartment was so quiet. She accepted, and Virginia was delighted. She told her she'd put a bottle of champagne in the refrigerator to chill.

"What are we celebrating?" Laura asked.

"The fact that you're coming for dinner. The chef prepared Osso Buco, and I didn't want to eat it alone."

An hour later the taxicab pulled up in front of Virginia's West 77th Street brownstone and Laura stepped out. Whenever she went to her aunt's home she was struck by how opulent and yet homey it was, all at the same time. Somehow, despite her lifestyle, Virginia had managed to create a real home out of the four-story, fifteen room brownstone.

Virginia embraced her when she opened the door, then ushered her into the living room, which had been decorated in the Art Deco style. During a trip to Paris last year, Virginia had discovered Art Deco was all the rage over there. When she returned, she redecorated the living room and dining room to reflect that style.

"This room looks great," Laura said. "Is it the way you want it to be?"

"Pretty much, though you know I'm never completely satisfied with anything. I suppose you'd call that a character flaw. We could do the same in your—"

Laura held up her hand. "No, Virginia. Please let me live my own life and make my own decisions."

"Of course. I just want the best for you. But you're a very intelligent young woman. I know you'll do what's best for you and Todd. It's just hard for me to let go sometimes, you know?"

Laura leaned over and kissed her aunt's cheek. "I wish Phillip understood and felt that same way. He treats me like I have no idea what I'm doing."

Virginia snorted, waving her hand dismissively. "Does it really matter what he thinks?"

It took a moment before Laura finished pondering what Virginia had said. "I know what you're saying is right," she said slowly. "It isn't that I care what he thinks, but the reality is we are still connected through Todd. I don't want Todd to grow up thinking less of me because Phillip does."

"Believe me, Phillip knows how much that little boy loves you. He's jealous because Todd doesn't feel the same way about him."

Laura giggled as champagne bubbles tickled her nose. "You always make me feel better about myself. How can I thank you?"

"You can do that by being happy. That's all I want for you and Todd. Oh, and for you to remember that I'll always be here for you."

"Look at that," Laura said, pointing at the tears that had filled her aunt's eyes. "What would Dutch Schultz or Al Capone say if they could see you now?"

Virginia threw back her head and laughed, sniffing away the telltale tears. "I think they'd probably say I was an imposter, and the real Virginia Kingsley was dead. Whatever you do, make sure this never gets out. I have a reputation to maintain."

Laura placed her finger against her lips. "Not a word."

"So tell me. What you've been doing lately?"

Laura told her about the article she'd written, and the novel she was starting to put together. "I have no idea whether I'm ever going to finish it, but it's something I've thought about doing for several years."

"When you were a little girl you used to write short stories. After your mother and father died I found them in a box in your mother's closet."

Laura flicked an interested eyebrow. "Do you still have them?"

"Come with me."

They climbed two flights of stairs, and when they stopped they stood in a part of the house which was obviously in the middle of being redecorated. The walls were partially painted and the floor was crowded with painting supplies, drop cloths and piles of lumber.

"What's going on up here?" Laura asked.

"You know how much I always hated these four fussy little rooms. Well, I'm having them done over into two large rooms. I still haven't decided what I'm going to use them for, but I'll do that when they're finished." She took Laura's hand. "Come with me."

Virginia led her into the smallest of the four rooms. Inside was an old rolltop desk that Laura immediately recognized as having belonged to her father. She ran her hand over the top of the desk, imagining him sitting at it. He had died so many years before she felt only curiosity, not grief. Virginia left her to her memories, then climbed onto a chair and slid a box from the top shelf. She placed it on top of the desk then opened it and pulled out a sheath of papers.

"I remember this," Laura said, grinning. "I must have been around seven when I wrote this one about the two fairies. Have you read any of them?"

"Of course. I've read all of them. Your mother and father thought they were wonderful. They loved your imagination."

"They did?" For just a moment, Laura was a child again. She touched the papers lightly, as if she were afraid they'd crumble into dust. "Can I have them? For Todd."

Chapter Three

Virginia stretched like a sleek black cat in the four poster mahogany bed, trying not to purr as she gazed at Rudy Strauss' retreating figure. She'd bought the huge bed from a redheaded woman who owned an antique shop in Greenwich Village. The woman liked to tell tall tales, like the one she'd told Virginia about the Prince of Wales having once owned the bed. Virginia hadn't minded. She liked stories.

Rudy was patient where other men rushed, and that had made for a most enjoyable afternoon. Tired, spent and more thoroughly satisfied than she'd ever admit, she reluctantly slid off him and rested her hand on his chiseled abdomen.

"Never let anyone tell you that you aren't good for anything, Rudy."

A slow, stupid grin of male pride stretched across his dark features.

"Not for that, anyway," she said, smiling in spite of herself.

He looked at her blankly. She shrugged, then pointed to a bottle of champagne chilling in a wooden bucket on the bedside table. "Go ahead and open it. I'd say we've earned a bit of refreshment."

"The whole day's been great," Rudy said, heading toward the bucket. Virginia watched his big fingers pick at the foil on the top of the bottle. Skillful fingers despite their size, she thought. The foil peeled off neatly and he dropped it on the table before addressing the cork. "Your life's the bees knees, baby. You've got the greatest speak in the city." He took a deep breath and let it out slowly, looking at her from the corner of his eye. "Any regrets?"

She flicked an eyebrow in question. "Like what? Meeting you?"

"Kids, marriage, you know."

"What are you, a comedian?"

She lowered her feet onto the plush red carpet and reached for her dressing gown. The carpet was warm as summer grass under her feet and her toes curled appreciatively as she walked toward the window. Scooping open the red velvet drapes, Virginia peered outside. Central Park was busy in the late afternoon sun. Especially by the fountains. So far, 1930 had been the hottest summer anyone could remember.

The bedroom suite was enormous, having once been two rooms. She'd painted the top half of the wall white, the bottom a deep burgundy. From beside the table the cork popped and she heard bubbles hissing in crystal. She turned toward Rudy, who held two full glasses, one of them stretched toward her. Leaving the sun to flood into the room, she headed toward him, hand outstretched for her glass.

"How's your niece's kid?"

She sipped, then frowned. "Why are you so interested in him? You hate kids. Last time my assistant Harry brought his granddaughter in you looked at her like she had the clap."

"You can trust me."

"The hell I can. My family is off limits to you. Understand?"

Ignoring his indignant huff, she sat at her vanity and stared at her reflection. Since she'd turned forty, three years earlier, she'd begun to notice subtle changes in her skin she didn't like. With a sigh, she applied a layer of cold cream to her face, then gently removed it with a tissue. Rudy came up from behind and cupped her shoulders in his hands. Their eyes met in the mirror.

"You're gorgeous, baby, absolutely gorgeous."

She turned and looked at him. "Listen, Rudy. A rat is still a rat even if it has a smile on its face. I know perfectly well who and what you are. Don't ever try to fool me. Stay out of my personal life and my family's."

"Or else what?"

"You'll pay the consequences."

"You're worried about her, aren't you?" Rudy asked, unimpressed by the threat.

"Who?"

"Your niece. I see that worried look in your eyes whenever anyone mentions Laura."

"So now you're interested in my niece. What's going on, Rudy?"

He shrugged. "I've never met her."

Virginia glanced at him sideways, then shifted the clock on her bedside table so she could see it. "We have to get moving."

***

When Rudy heard the bathroom door close behind her, he slid open her bedside table drawer. It was empty apart from scattered Q-tips, a box of toothpicks and a razor. Kneeling down, he peered under the bed, then pulled out the large box there. Inside were six neatly folded cashmere sweaters.

He was about to get up off his knees when he realized the bath water had stopped running. She hadn't had time to fill the tub. He made a mad dash for the chaise lounge, then heard the click of a closet door. A few seconds later, the bath water was running again.

She probably had two address books, he figured. One for family and friends, and one the cops would love to get a hold of. He walked around the room trying to get a feel for where the mysterious books might be. She had two mahogany dressers, and he opened the bottom drawer of the taller of the two, then smiled when he saw the picture album. He flipped open the first couple of pages and stopped at two photographs of a little blond boy. The lad was playing in a pond that had to be on his father's estate. It wasn't exactly what he'd been looking for, but it gave him an idea. He flipped through the rest of the photographs quickly and found another, this one focused on the entrance to the estate.

The jingle of the telephone interrupted him. For a second he stood frozen, his hand poised on top of the album. Then he closed the dresser drawer, sat on the bed and waited for her to come into the room and answer the phone.

When it stopped ringing, he waited a few more seconds, then grabbed a couple of toothpicks from the bedside drawer to calm his nerves. Then he headed toward her walk-in closet and opened the double doors.

The old closet bubbled over with color, bright against the faded white walls. It wasn't until he pushed some of her evening gowns aside that he noticed a section of the back wall seemed to be freshly painted. He pressed his hand against the panel then stepped back in surprise as a rush of hot air hit his face. Peering curiously through the new opening, Rudy saw a room about the same size as her closet. He stepped inside.

The first thing he saw was row after row of champagne bottles. There had to be three or four hundred of them. To the left sat a couple of large boxes which he began to sort through. Finally he sat back, chuckling, and pulled out a small book filled with names and addresses.

Of course, he thought. He bought his booze from her.

***

Virginia strode back into the bedroom when she'd finished her bath, and flipped on the radio just in time to hear the opening music for *Amos n' Andy*. Rudy lay on the chaise lounge, smoking a cigarette and reading the racing form. He gazed up at her with deep brown eyes and she yanked the cigarette out of his mouth.

"If you had any clothes on, I'd make you empty your pockets."

He ignored her, standing to admire himself in the full-length mirror. Rudy was always fishing for compliments. He thought he was a dead ringer for Rudolph Valentino.

"What statue did you say I looked like?"

"David."

"Who's he?"

"Never mind. You don't need culture in your line of work."

She rolled a silk stocking over one long, shapely leg, then attached the garter in front. She felt his eyes on her as she stretched her leg out to reach the snap in the back.

"Some pair of legs, baby."

"What a cake-eater you are." She frowned and pointed at the floor. "Just look at that mess. Toothpicks all over my beautiful rug. Pick them up and put them in the waste paper basket."

"Don't have a kitten."

When they got downstairs he tugged open the refrigerator door and pulled out a bottle of champagne, shimmering with a fine coating of frost. Virginia took it from him and held the cold bottle to her temple, closing her eyes with relief. Mercy, it was hot.

"Ours?" he asked.

Her amber eyes snapped open, burning with warning. "Mine. Not yours. I don't need a partner, and if I did...."

"Oh, come on," he said with a dismissive wave of the hand. "You need me. Like it or not, you're playing a man's game. That sharp tongue of yours will only get you so far. Maybe it's time you start being more realistic."

"Silly, silly me," she said, batting her eyelashes. "How did I not realize I needed the guidance of a man like you?"

"You may not think you do, but you're wrong. Women aren't any good at business. You've just been lucky so far."

She laughed, but there was no humor in the sound. Anger bubbled like champagne in her veins. "You're a worthless punk who'd be out on the street if I hadn't given you a job." He chuckled, which only fed her anger. "You know what? I'm done. I'm sick of this. Get out."

"What did I say?"

Grabbing him by his shirt collar, she dragged him into the living room, toward the door. "You're a fool to think you can get a piece of my business, Rudy Strauss. You'll never outsmart me."

"Hey, you're choking me."

"I don't give a damn. Get out of my house."

He gave her a final, confused glance, and she shoved him out the door, slamming it behind him.

***

Two nights later, when Rudy showed up at Virginia's speakeasy, *Bacchanal*, she was surprised but not shocked. He was always doing things he shouldn't do. She figured the best thing to do was ignore him, so she did. He sat at the bar and ordered a drink, then tried to engage one of the hostesses in a conversation, but they weren't supposed to socialize with customers while they were working. What they did on their own time was their business.

Virginia couldn't help noticing how he looked her way every few minutes with a scowl of dislike. Then she realized he was looking past her and staring at Phillip. That was strange. Rudy was glaring at Phillip as if he wished the man were dead. In a way, she almost agreed with him. Phillip had annoyed her all night, complaining about Laura or eyeing every pretty girl who passed their table. Virginia didn't like the way he treated her niece. Even though she had once tried to bring them together, she couldn't help thinking Laura might be better off without him.

"Is she interested in some other guy?" Phillip had asked earlier.

"Laura?" Virginia poured herself more champagne and swept her dark brown hair behind her shoulders so it fell down her back, out of the way. "How would I know? I don't follow her around."

He indicated her champagne bottle. "How about me?"

She chuckled and sipped her drink. "I think you've had enough."

Out of the corner of her eye, Virginia noticed Rudy walking toward their table and braced herself for some unpleasantness. Though he'd only been there a few minutes, she could tell from his expression he'd already had far too much to drink.

Phillip was watching him too, disgust coloring his expression. Virginia began to wish she'd stayed home that night.

"Boss lady," Rudy said, slurring his words together. "Red sure as hell is your color."

Phillip looked as if he were going to be sick. "Oh, come on. Why is *he* bothering us? Doesn't he have hole to crawl into someplace? Why do you associate with such low lives, Virginia?"

Rudy put his hand on Phillip's chair. Virginia saw Phillip's back stiffen, and anger flared so hot in his eyes she actually felt slightly afraid. But his expression didn't come close to matching Rudy's.

"Get your hand off my chair," Phillip said.

Rudy removed his hand from Phillip's back then walked around so he stood in front of Phillip. "I'm not good enough for you, am I? You're a rich as hell hotshot movie star, and I'm a two bit nothing, right?"

Phillip shrugged. "You have no business with us, so why are you here? Go back to the bar with your friends."

"Sure thing, Mr. Movie Star." He gave Virginia a fleeting look tempered with a sneer. "You have no business with me, do you?"

She didn't answer, and he walked away.

Chapter Four

Laura lifted the damp hair from the back of her neck and stretched, hoping for some relief from the heat. Digging in a drawer, she found a barrette to pin up her hair, then glanced at the clock. It was almost noon. Laura stared at the paper in front of her, but the heat had made her as dull and lifeless as the two main characters in her novel. No matter how many times she rewrote the first chapter, the dialogue sounded flat.

What was Todd doing now? Probably playing in the water. She imagined the little boy splashing in the pond behind the mansion and smiled. Mrs. Nickerson would have taken him there to cool off.

Slumping to her room, Laura peeled off her robe and tugged on a much cooler pair of Chinese pajamas. The only possible place to sit in this heat was in front of the electric fan, which is where she went to attempt Thomas Wolfe's new novel, *Look Homeward Angel*. No use. She couldn't concentrate. She considered calling one of her girlfriends and going to a movie. One of those air-cooled theatres would feel good.

The phone rang, jarring her from her musings. Ordinarily, the sound would have irritated Laura. It interrupted her train of thought when she was writing. Today she welcomed the distraction.

"Hello?"

At first all Laura heard was someone breathing hard on the other end, then a muffled sob. She rolled her eyes. Not again. She'd gotten a crank call a couple of days earlier and was about to hang up when Mrs. Nickerson's hoarse voice crackled over the wire.

"Mrs. Nickerson? Is that you? What's wrong?" Laura demanded.

"Oh dear God!" The nanny's voice rose and fell as she sobbed. "The baby's been kidnapped!"

"What? Mrs. Nickerson, calm down. What are you talking about? Where's Todd? What's happening?" Laura said.

The nanny wailed, and all Laura could make out was "Dear God! Dear God! Oh, the poor little boy!"

A tremor began in Laura's fingers and spread like fire throughout her body. This couldn't be happening. The phone felt slick in her hand and fell through her fingers, landing with a soft thud on the carpet. When she bent to pick it up she was caught by a wave of dizziness, and let herself slide to the floor. Leaning against the wall for support, she reached for the phone and spoke as calmly as she could.

"Mrs. Nickerson," she said, fighting the wobble in her voice. The image of Todd's sweet face popped up in her mind, his soft blond curls bouncing under her hand. She squeezed her eyes shut. "What happened? Where is Todd?"

"Oh Laura," said the older woman. "We were at Willow Pond. He was having a wonderful time. You know how much he loves the water."

Panic set in. "You are sure he didn't go under the water, Iris?"

"No! No! I was watching him play. One minute he was laughing, and the next – Well, whoever it was, he hit me over the head with something heavy. I woke up on the ground and our baby was gone."

"But ... But ... Who could have done this? Why?" Laura's voice broke and bile burned up her throat. "Who did this?" she demanded. "Did you see who did this? Iris, please help me!"

"I couldn't see kidnapper's face. He was wearing a clown's mask."

"Oh dear God. Did you call the police?"

"Of course."

She fought nausea, thinking frantically. *Phillip. She had to speak to Phillip.* "Let me speak to Mr. Austin."

"He went to Washington D.C last night. He thought it would be better if Todd stayed here with me."

Laura blinked, incredulous. "He isn't even there? He wanted to spend time with his son and he *isn't even there?* Oh God. This is my fault. I should have said no. I wanted to, but I gave in."

"Laura, I'm going to call your aunt and tell her you need her."

"No. I'll call her. I have to get a hold of myself and be strong for Todd. He needs me."

Her hand was shaking so badly she had difficulty putting the receiver back on the cradle. *My baby, my baby ...*

A moment later, the phone rang. "Mrs. Laura Austin?"

"Yes?"

"This is Officer Albers from the East Hampton PD. I'm afraid I have bad news. Your ..."

"I know! My son!" Laura said. "Why are you wasting time on the phone with me? Find my son!"

"Of course, ma'am. Mrs. Austin, would you be able to come to East Hampton right away? Detective Wilson wants to question you."

"I'll get there as fast as I can."

Laura's phone conversation with Virginia was even shorter. "How am I going to live without him?" Laura managed to squeeze through sobs.

"You won't have to. I'm here. I'll help. Stay there. I'll pick you up."

"I have a taxi waiting outside."

When Laura arrived at Willow Pond, police swarmed the estate. No one seemed to notice her arrival, a fact which had her both surprised and relieved. She paused outside the huge white colonial house, recalling the little things she had once done to make the place into a home, when all Phillip wanted was a showcase. Her eyes traced the familiar lines of house and yard, and she remembered the trill of Todd's laughter skipping across the grass.

Will I ever hear that sound again?

If only she'd paid more attention that last morning they were together. It had only been one week, but it seemed like an eternity. Had she combed his hair? What had he worn? She hated that she couldn't remember. She knew she'd packed some toys: ducks and toys boats for the water, and one of his teddy bears to sleep with. So many details she wanted to remember and couldn't.

She went around to the back door and found Iris Nickerson sitting at the kitchen table, holding her silver crowned head in her hands. The large kitchen usually cheered Laura up with its patterned yellow wallpaper, oak table and chairs. Not today.

Laura's shoes tapped the wood floor as she walked in, and Mrs. Nickerson looked up. "Oh, Laura! You're here!" Her chair scraped the floor as she jumped to her feet. "Let me put on some tea."

Instead, Laura moved to the woman and embraced her. "Oh, Iris. Did he hurt you?"

"Never mind me. But the baby! Oh, Laura, I'm so sorry. But there's nothing I could have done."

"Where did he hit you?" Iris leaned forward and showed her the spot, right at the base of her skull. The large bump still carried traces of dried blood. "That looks painful. The doctor should take a look at it. Did you ice it?"

Iris nodded.

"I'll call the doctor," Laura said. "Then we'd better call Phillip."

"The police already have. He's on his way."

While they waited for the doctor, Laura busied herself, pouring tea for Iris, tidying the kitchen, doing anything to keep her mind off what might be happening to Todd. If she stopped moving, thoughts of him flooded her mind. She felt his warm little hand in hers, heard his belly laugh.

"I'm going down to the pond, Iris. I'll bring the doctor to you when he gets here."

She had always found the pond so peaceful. Now, as she wandered along the shore, she couldn't stand to look at it. She had never before noticed how close it was to the road. Those bushes were the perfect place for someone to hide. Was that how the man with the mask had snuck up and snatched her little boy?

When she felt more stable, Laura approached one of the dozens of cops wandering the estate grounds. She introduced herself and asked who was in charge.

"That'd be Detective Ben Wilson. He's just over there." The officer indicated a short man headed across the lawn toward them. "Looks like he wants to speak with you."

When Detective Wilson was close enough, he held out a hand for Laura to shake. "Good afternoon, Mrs. Austin. I'm sorry to have to meet under such circumstances."

"So am I. What's going on? Have you come up with any leads?" Laura asked.

Detective Wilson shook his head, then stuck a piece of gum into his mouth. "Not yet. If you don't mind, I need to ask you a few things."

"Certainly. Whatever brings Todd home sooner."

Ben Wilson squinted at her in what she assumed was his information-gathering expression. It was slightly unnerving. "Was the nanny with him when he was snatched?"

"Didn't you ask her? She told me you talked to her."

"Do you trust your servants?"

"Iris has been Todd's nanny since he was born. She loves him very much, and Todd loves her. I never worry about him when he's with her."

"That doesn't answer my question. Do you trust her?"

"She's never given me any reason not to."

Wilson sneezed, then wiped his nose with the back of his hand. "All right. We'll say for now that she's not a suspect. But whoever took your boy knew his routine well. We have to assume, since he is only a year and a half old, that this was done not because of him, but because of either you or your husband."

"*Ex*-husband," she said.

"Sorry. Ex-husband. Does Mr. Austin have any enemies?"

Laura shrugged. "In the movie business people either love you or hate you. He's a famous actor, so he has plenty of both."

"What about your aunt? Are you and Mr. Austin having any problems with her?"

"Why are you asking about my aunt? She has nothing to do with this." The line of questioning irritated her. "Why are you asking all these questions unrelated to Todd? Shouldn't you be investigating clues or something?" The doctor's car pulled up outside the front door and Laura stepped back from the detective. "I'm sorry. I have to bring the doctor inside. Can we continue this later?"

As she accompanied the doctor to the house, she couldn't help thinking about the circus the press would create over Todd's kidnapping. Their tragedy would entertain the world.

Chapter Five

Erich Muller leaned back in his chair, his feet propped on the city editor's desk. Tilting his head to the side, he peered across the desk at Daniel Spencer, who was busy editing an article about Mayor Walker and the corruption at Tammany Hall.

Muller sniffed to get his attention, but Spencer didn't show any sign of having heard.

"Phillip Austin's infant son has been kidnapped," Muller said calmly. "Bet the underworld's involved."

Spencer's head shot up. "What else do you have?"

"Not much. He was snatched from the Austin estate around eleven thirty this morning. Kidnapper knocked the nanny out and took off with the kid."

Spencer frowned and crossed his arms. "It's past one o'clock. Why is this just coming over the wires now?"

"Who knows? But my gut tells me this could be messy."

"What makes you think the mob's involved?"

"The mother is Virginia Kingsley's niece."

"Look into it, Muller. Bergen!" Spencer's voice cut across the newsroom. "My office. Now." He turned back to Erich just as Peter Bergen stepped into the room. "The two of you need to find out what's going on. Bring me back something I can sink my teeth into, chapter and verse. The unabridged, illustrated version. Now get out of here. East Hampton is way the hell out in East Jesus."

***

Erich whistled through his teeth as he drove the Model A along Willow Pond's long, winding driveway. The colonial mansion stretched over one hundred acres, with rolling hills in the back and a meticulously landscaped garden in front. Erich had never seen anything like it before.

Reporters, photographers and police officers roamed the grounds like ants at a picnic. There were so many cars there already he had to pull up onto the grass and park inches from a well kept flowerbed. He looked around for a familiar face but didn't see one, so he scouted for the youngest cop he could find. He was in luck. A freckle-faced kid who looked fresh out of the police academy stood nearby.

"Excuse me, officer, do you know if anyone's spoken to the child's nanny yet?" he asked.

"You'll have to talk to Detective Wilson, same as everyone else."

Erich sighed and nodded his thanks. It figured Ben Wilson would have caught the case. The man was as useless as he was uncooperative.

The pond for which the estate had been named was sandwiched between the East wall of the house and a thin thrust of trees and bushes that ran along the road. Phillip Austin had built it because one of his close friends had drowned in a swimming pool, and Phillip wanted his family to have what he considered a safe place to swim. Whatever the reason, it was a great choice as far as aesthetics went.

Peter Bergen stuck his camera between two trees and took a picture of a toy boat bobbing by the edge. He shifted position and snapped a couple of pictures of two plastic ducks floating toward the middle. Just a few hours ago the scene might have been idyllic.

Erich toured the circumference of the pond, looking for anything out of the ordinary. It didn't take him long to figure out how the kidnapper had come and gone. The grass on the far side of the pond had been flattened into a neat path between the edge of the water and the road. *It must have been so easy.* Upon closer inspection, he discovered a toy mouse on the grass a few feet from the pond; a squeaky toy that must have belonged to the boy. Good ol' Detective Wilson hadn't even noticed it yet.

An anonymous cop approached and warned him away from the crime scene. Erich headed for the house, but slowed when he heard muffled conversation coming from the garage. Since no one seemed to be paying attention to him, he veered closer to the building, ears wide open. The voices belonged to a man and an agitated woman, but he couldn't make out what was being said.

Suddenly the air around him was lit by a series of camera flashes. Voices called out as the door to the garage opened and Laura Austin slipped out. She managed to sprint into the main house before the reporters caught up with her.

Peter spotted Detective Wilson and stepped into his path, his own flash popping. Wilson glared and turned away, almost bumping into Erich, who fell in step behind him.

"Do you have any suspects, Detective? Any idea where the baby might be?"

"That's what we're here to find out. Having a bunch of jackass reporters all over my crime scene ain't helping."

"Have you considered a connection to the mob?"

Wilson shot him a sidelong glance. "If we turn up any leads that suggest that, you can be sure they'll be investigated."

"What about Virginia Kingsley? Are you going to question her?"

"At this point that's none of your concern. Now get out of here. I mean it."

Erich hadn't become one of the city's most respected reporters by doing what he was told. He stuck to Wilson like a fly on honey. "Honesty isn't your strongest trait is it, Detective?"

"And tact isn't yours, Muller. Go interview the maid or something."

Erich pressed on. "With the Kingsley family's connection to organized crime, it sounds like you'd better come up with something soon."

"Don't tell me how to do my job. Now get out of here before I have you arrested."

"Has there been any demand for ransom?"

"I mean it, Muller. Another word and all you'll need to worry about is your own bail."

Erich shook his head and jammed his notebook into his pocket. Maybe he should have gone after Laura Austin instead.

***

Virginia stopped just inside the kitchen and narrowed her eyes when Detective Wilson approached her. "Great. First the press harasses me and now you. I'm here for my niece."

"Yes, I'm sure you are, Miss Kingsley. I just have a few questions to ask you first."

"Don't you have a kidnapping to investigate?"

A mocking smile stretched over Wilson's face. "Maybe you could help our investigation along by telling us what you know."

She matched his expression. "What I know is my niece needs me. I have no idea what happened to Todd or why, but one thing we can be sure of is he isn't here. So I suggest you stop wasting time, Detective, and stay the hell out of my way."

"Take it easy, Miss Kingsley. Let's not overlook your role in this."

"My role? What are you talking about?"

"Don't tell me you haven't considered the possibility that this might be the doings of one of your so-called business associates. I'm sure you have a number of … friends who might, shall we say, reach out to you in this manner."

Virginia glared at him, but said nothing. Until now she hadn't considered that possibility, and she didn't like where her thoughts were leading.

The detective assumed a businesslike air. "The truth is, Miss Kingsley, you have a reputation that gets where you go before you do. I wouldn't be surprised—"

"We all have reputations, Detective Wilson," she snapped. "Now if you'll excuse me."

She started up the stairs, trying not to appear the slightest bit bothered by the detective's comments. She forgot about him altogether when she saw her niece. Laura was curled up on a bed in one of the guest bedrooms, clutching Todd's teddy bear.

"Laura, honey, I am so sorry. I got here as fast as I could."

Laura looked at her with swollen eyes, her pale cheeks lined by tears. "I … I don't understand this. He's just a little boy. Who would do this?"

Virginia sat quietly on the bed next to Laura and stroked her niece's silky blonde hair.

"I should have been with him," Laura said, sniffing hard. "I'll never forgive myself."

"Laura." Virginia cupped her niece's chin in her hand, turning Laura's face toward her own. "A criminal did this. Blaming yourself isn't going to help find Todd, honey. Getting through this is going to be hard enough without making yourself even more miserable in the process."

The words came out more sharply than Virginia had intended, but Laura brightened just the same, if only a little. She took a deep breath and told Virginia everything she knew, which wasn't much.

"Do the cops have a picture of him?" Virginia asked.

"I don't know. Maybe Mrs. Nickerson gave them one."

"I wouldn't be sure with these idiots."

Virginia regretted the words as soon as she spoke them. Laura needed hope, not cynicism. But Laura was already thinking along the same lines.

"That's what has me worried. I have spoken to two detectives and God knows how many policemen, and not one of them gave me any confidence that they know the first thing about what they're doing."

Virginia patted Laura's knee. "Come on. Let's find a picture to give them. See if we can get them moving."

Laura knew exactly where Phillip kept his photo album. After all, his bedroom had been hers as well. She pulled the book from the bottom drawer of his dresser and tried to control her trembling fingers as she removed a picture of Todd. The boy sat on the grass, squinting into the sun. He wore a train conductor's outfit and cap and the biggest smile in the world.

"This one?"

Virginia nodded. "That should do. How about this one, too?"

Laura stared at the picture her aunt held out, but Virginia didn't think her niece saw anything. When she spoke, Laura's voice was soft and slow, almost hypnotic. "You know, it's strange. I can't get the last thing I read to him out of my mind."

"He'll be reading to himself soon. What was it?"

Laura's thumb caressed the photo while she spoke. Her eyes were glued to the image of her son. "A poem by Milne. I read it once and it's etched in my memory."

James, James
Morrison, Morrison
Weatherby George Dupree
Took great care of his mother
Though he was only three.

"After I read it to Todd he ran around the apartment laughing and repeating it over and over again. He was so happy. You should have seen him. And now ..."

"Just think how happy you'll both be when you have him home again," Virginia said, patting the back of Laura's hand. "Meanwhile, don't torture yourself like this."

Laura sighed heavily and gave Virginia a smile that didn't quite reach her eyes. "Maybe torturing myself is a comfort in some weird way." She sat straight and took a deep breath, then waved the two pictures at her aunt. "Now let's go find that detective."

Chapter Six

A white Rolls Royce limousine raced along the extended driveway of Willow Pond, stirring up dust. At precisely six-thirty, Phillip's limousine pulled up outside the front door to the mansion. The car door hadn't even opened before throngs of early morning reporters and photographers converged on him.

"Is there a Hollywood connection to your son's kidnapping?"

"Is Virginia Kingsley ..."

"Do the police have ..."

Phillip said nothing, just smiled through the window as photographers snapped picture after picture. Before getting out of the car, he glanced at his reflection in the rearview mirror. Phillip had never met a mirror he didn't like. He would have posed for longer had Laura not knocked on the window behind him. She looked furious.

Phillip lowered the window and met her eyes. "How could you leave Todd here alone?" she hissed.

He looked away, then stepped out of the car and into the crowd of reporters. He gave her another quick glance. "He wasn't alone," he said in his defense, and marched toward the door.

When Laura stepped inside, she noticed he still stood in the middle of the room, wearing his hat. His expression seemed restless. As if he didn't know what to do next.

"What's with the long face, Phillip?" she snapped. "Feeling guilty for leaving Todd? You should."

Laura knew her words hurt him. She wanted them to. All Phillip ever wanted was to be the center of attention, and now she wanted him to suffer the consequences. He shot her a wounded look, but his eyes glimmered with a deeper pain. Her resolve weakened slightly.

"You know, if this hadn't happened," he said, "Mrs. Nickerson would be right here, feeding Todd his breakfast. Somehow this empty kitchen makes it all more real."

"Oh, it's real. Tell me, Daddy of the Year, what was so important in Washington?" Laura demanded, crossing her arms.

Something about Phillip always made her suspicious, whether it was warranted or not. But the tortured look on his face caught her off guard. The other hurtful things she wanted to say stuck in her throat. For a moment she saw him as the gentle man with whom she'd fallen in love.

They had met at *Bacchanal* during the spring of 1927, and their whirlwind courtship ended in marriage six months after that. Laura was seven months pregnant with Todd when they returned from their honeymoon. The next morning, Phillip slept with someone else.

Now he swept off his hat and raked his fingers through his hair, looking far less confident than in those days. "I'm sorry, Laura. I only planned to be away overnight." He sat down at the kitchen table and rested his head in his hands. "I should have—"

She sighed and swallowed her fury. "I know. Almost every thought I have begins that way. Never mind." She sat down next to him, but not touching. "All that matters is finding Todd."

The cook set a plate in front of Phillip, piled high with scrambled eggs, bacon and two corn muffins. Nothing ever affected Phillip's appetite, no matter how great the crisis. Laura sipped her tea and picked at a muffin, staring across the room at Todd's highchair. His favorite teddy bear lay on its tray, fuzzy limbs stuck out like a star. Laura clearly recalled the look of joy on Todd's face when she had placed the bear in his arms on Christmas morning.

Later on, Wilson walked in and headed directly to Phillip. The detective stopped at his side, then waited impatiently for Phillip to acknowledge him. When Phillip finally looked up,

Wilson glared down, arms crossed. "It's about time you got here, Austin. I need to ask you a few questions."

Phillip scowled, but didn't have time to answer before they heard a commotion outside. Laura got up and parted the kitchen curtains, peering toward the road. A cop was running toward the house, pursued by dozens of reporters and photographers. For a second she wondered if they had found Todd, then read the expression on the cop's face and knew they hadn't. He stepped into the kitchen and slammed the door in the reporter's faces, looking somewhat frazzled by the chase, then handed an envelope to Phillip.

"What is that?" Wilson asked, frowning.

"It's for Mr. Austin. We believe it's from the kidnappers, sir."

With Detective Wilson looking over his shoulder, Phillip read the note out loud. His voice was smooth and commanding, obviously comfortable with performing.

```
Dear Sir:
We have your son. If you follow our
instructions and do not involve the police,
he won't be harmed. We want $250,000. In two
days, you will receive another letter
telling you where to deliver the money.
```

Laura stared agog at Phillip. "Don't involve the police? Oh God. We never should have called them. But I didn't know what else to do. Oh God, Phillip. What are they going to do to him now?"

"Take it easy, Mrs. Austin," Wilson said, examining the letter. "They're just trying to throw a scare into you. Mr. Austin, two hundred and fifty thousand dollars is peanuts to you. What are these bums really after?"

When Phillip didn't say anything, Laura jumped in. "Phillip and a friend have been flying up and down the East Coast, looking for stills. Could that be it?"

"Huh." Wilson turned to Laura. "Did he get your aunt all steamed up?"

"My aunt? I already told you she has nothing to do with this."

"Oh yeah. She's a saint, I'm sure." He turned back to Phillip. "Which bootleggers are you messing with?"

Phillip cleared his throat and glared at the detective. "Bootleggers are not the issue here, Detective Wilson. My son—"

"Maybe you just answer my questions. Then I might have something to go on."

"I'm not the criminal here," Phillip murmured.

"I need names of anyone suspicious. Trust me, folks. This is no time to play it cute. What about former employees? Anyone got it in for you?"

A look passed between them and Wilson took out his notepad. "Out with it."

Laura got up and walked to the window. The sky was dotted by clouds, as if someone had tossed cotton balls and let them scatter across the blue. She gazed at the tulips, hands on her hips. She could only think of one employee episode, and it had happened the autumn before, when she had helped Brian Madigan plant the bulbs. Phillip had been angry and embarrassed when he learned she had been helping the landscaper. He would have fired Madigan had she not talked him out of it. She had to wonder. If she'd let Phillip fire him, maybe this wouldn't be happening.

While Laura, Phillip and five hundred guests attended Todd's October christening, Brian Madigan had broken into the safe in Phillip's office. He'd stolen twelve thousand dollars and Laura's diamond necklace. As Phillip finished telling the story to Detective Wilson, the cop shook his head with disbelief.

"Don't you have any security?" Wilson asked. "I mean, how careless *are* you people?"

"If cops did their jobs, we wouldn't have to live in an armed fortress," Phillip grumbled.

"Did you press charges?"

"Sure, but they were dropped for lack of evidence," Laura said.

"Wait a minute," Phillip said, squinting at the detective. "I don't like the way you're asking these questions. It's almost as if you think this is our fault."

Laura sat down next to him and put her hand on his leg. "If it will help find Todd …"

He glanced down at her hand, then studied her face. She held his gaze even when his frown twisted into a mocking smile. "All right," he said. "But I'm still curious about how Madigan got into the safe. Maybe he's some sort of master thief."

The most difficult aspect of that situation was Laura had liked Brian Madigan. He was bright and articulate, and she enjoyed talking with him. Could she inadvertently have said something which might have prompted Todd's kidnapping?

"You fired him," Wilson said.

"Of course."

"Can we find out if he has a criminal record?" Laura asked.

"I'll get one of my men on it right away."

"He swore he would get back at us," Laura muttered.

"What about his wife?" Phillip asked. "Wasn't she crazy or something?"

Laura and Madigan had been planting the tulips when he'd told her his wife, Gabrielle, was being released from Bellevue Hospital. Laura had felt sorry for the poor man. Now she wondered.

A rap on the door, then another younger cop walked in, looking for Wilson. The two men stepped outside for a few minutes and Laura tried to listen to what they were saying, but their words were muffled by the wall. When Wilson returned he sat down, slammed his hands on the table and looked straight at Phillip.

"Any of your bootlegger friends drive a dark blue 1925 or '26 Buick, Austin?"

"Your insinuations are annoying."

"No kidding. Listen. You are damn lucky I haven't asked you where you were between eleven and eleven thirty yesterday morning. Actually, now that I think of it, where were you?"

They stared at the detective.

"Are you accusing me of kidnapping my own son?" Phillip demanded.

"Just answer the question. Where were you?"

"Washington, DC."

"Uh huh." Wilson scribbled on his notepad, then waited, pen poised. "What about an alibi?"

"I was at a meeting with the film director, Richard Hamilton, among others."

Wilson shoved a cigar into his mouth. "Get me a phone number where I can reach him."

"What's this car you mentioned?" Laura asked.

"Your neighbor claims he saw a car matching that description headed this way around eleven o'clock yesterday morning. He said he'd never seen the car or the man behind the wheel before. We'll look into it. In the meantime," he said, snapping his notebook shut, "I have a few other leads to investigate. I assume I don't need to remind you to stay close while this investigation is underway."

"We're not going anywhere until you find Todd," Laura assured him as he headed outside.

Laura stood at the window, watching Wilson make his way past the reporters and photographers. When the familiar weight of Phillip's arm wrapped around her shoulders, she stiffened and moved away.

Phillip's expression was laced with contempt. "Oh," he said. "I see. So it's okay for you to touch me, but not for me to touch you?"

"I'm sorry, Phillip. It's just, well, I feel like we're in a fishbowl." She waved irritably toward the media outside. "Can't you do something about those vultures?"

"I will. Later. For now I just need some quiet."

"Quiet? Ha. There's a big difference between you and me, Phillip. I cannot stand all this quiet. This house should be loud with Todd's voice right now. Do you think we'll ever see him again?"

Chapter Seven

During the long days and nights of waiting, the press never left them alone. Fortunately, only one reporter managed to get into the house. A crafty reporter from the *Newark Star Ledger* climbed a tree and edged onto a particularly large branch, from which he managed to open Mrs. Nickerson's second story bedroom window.

After the police removed the man and Laura was satisfied the nanny was all right, she joined Phillip in the living room. They sat side by side on the white velvet sofa, feeling the awkward space between them. He stared at her, and she avoided his eyes, looking from the rose-colored walls to the double glass doors leading to the garden.

But before the police had ousted him, the reporter in Mrs. Nickerson's room had said something that clicked with Laura. What if they *did* cooperate, at least in part, with the media? An interview might uncover a new lead, or cause someone to remember something they had seen or heard.

Phillip looked uncomfortable at the suggestion. "I don't think that'll do much good. Plus, once one of those vultures gets into this house we might as well let him move in."

"We could choose who we want. I have someone in mind already."

That surprised him. He cocked an eyebrow. "Who?"

"The reporter who covered the shooting at McGuire's last year. I met him when I went to make sure nothing had happened to Virginia."

McGuire's was a small speakeasy on East Twenty-Ninth Street, and Virginia was friends with the owner. Two rival gangs had been fighting over whose territory held the speakeasy when the shooting occurred. Three men wound up dead, including the owner. Virginia had been on the premises when it happened, but had managed to stay out of the way.

"Why him?"

"I like the way he handled it. I think he'd be fair."

"Fair or unfair, you're just asking for trouble."

Laura felt blood rush into her cheeks. He was so stubborn. He seemed perfectly happy to sit back and wait for things to happen. Well, she couldn't.

"Phillip, please. You cannot expect me to just sit on my hands. I have to do something to get Todd back. The police don't seem to be getting anywhere. It's just another case to them. But ..." She swallowed hard and struggled to get the next words out. She hated appealing to his ego. "You are such a big star, Phillip. A reporter might take an active interest in helping. Who knows what he might be able to turn up."

"Yes, but a man in my position has to be careful."

Phillip didn't seem to realize a man in his position should be careful around her as well. Since Todd's kidnapping, there had been an unspoken truce of sorts between them, but he was about to find out just how fragile their truce was.

"That's a horrible thing to worry about, Phillip. You should be ashamed of yourself. How self-centered and egotistical can you be?" she demanded. "This is our son we are talking about. Don't you care about him at all? He is *missing*. We have no idea if he is still alive. And all you can think about is yourself. That makes me sick."

He pursed his lips, then closed his eyes in a rare moment of acquiescence. "All right, all right. I will see what I can arrange. Which paper does he write for?"

"The *Herald Tribune*, I think. I don't remember his name, but I know he won a Pulitzer for that series about gangsters."

***

Just before noon, Virginia pulled up in front of *Bacchanal*. She opened the door of her forest green Packard town car and extended a shapely leg from within. Stepping onto the sidewalk, she took a quick look around, then descended the short flight of stairs and went inside.

After the bright hubbub of Sixth Avenue, *Bacchanal* was as dark as a cave, its bar mirror shimmering like a mirage. Sawdust was sprinkled on the floor, gathering remnants from the previous night. The sickly sweet blend of gin and cheap perfume still hung in the air.

While she was opening the blinds to let in some light, Virginia spied a police car pulling up to the curb. Two men got out and made their way toward the speakeasy's entrance. At five feet eleven inches, Virginia was well aware of how her physical presence affected people. Especially men. Cops were just men with badges. She timed it so that when she opened the door, Wilson was just putting his fist up to knock.

"Oh." He looked confused for a moment, as if he didn't know what to do with his fist. Then he dropped it to his side. "Miss Kingsley. We need to ask you a few more questions."

"Fine." She ushered them inside then closed the door behind them. "We can go into my office."

"I'm afraid not. They have an interrogation room ready for us at the station house. Get your coat if you like."

Virginia stared straight into Wilson's small eyes and spoke with an icy calm. Her tight smile matched her voice. "Fine. I will let you play your game, Detective. After all, I guess even you have to find a way to amuse yourself. But you should be aware that the game will not last long."

Fifteen minutes later they led her into a small room at the police station, and Wilson pulled out a chair for her. She accepted it graciously, and he told her to wait as he headed out the door.

The walls of the windowless room were institutional green; the cracked linoleum was gray. There were no paintings on the wall, not a speck of color to break up the monotony.

Virginia was delighted. The lack of personality in the room was perfect. The other cop had remained in the room with her, and he couldn't take his eyes off her. She smiled coyly at him and placed her hands on the table. He stared at her long red fingernails as if he'd never seen anything like them.

She used her most sultry voice on him. "Boring job, huh?"

She rose to straighten the skirt of her red Chanel suit, and watched the young cop's hungry eyes travel down her body, then linger on her long legs.

Wilson returned and tossed a newspaper on the table in front of her. He tapped the headline with a stubby finger.

"Seen this?"

`Police question aunt about possible connection to Austin kidnapping`, it read.

"Not until now," said Virginia, scanning the article. "Why?" She glanced up at Wilson, a mischievous smile lighting her eyes. "Are you enjoying the spotlight, Detective? Pretty impressive case, this."

"Why don't you tell me about the bad blood between you and Phillip Austin?"

She looked away, accidentally catching the eye of her young admirer. He stared at her lips while she spoke. "I thought you had jurisdiction over Suffolk County, Wilson, not New York City. What are you doing here?"

"The N.Y.P.D. has been ..." He frowned. "Just answer the question."

"Ah." Her gaze dropped to her fingers, still flat on the table. "One of my favorite games: cops doing favors for each other. Now. What do you want to know?"

Wilson leaned toward her, thick brown eyebrows nearly touching in the middle. "You and Austin. What's going on with the two of you?"

She raised her eyes first, then her head. Their faces were no more than a foot apart from one another. For the first time, she looked straight at him. "You are crowding my space, Detective."

He glared back, looking so furious she wondered briefly if he might strike her. But of course he wouldn't. After a couple of breaths he backed away.

"That's better. Now, you were asking … oh, right. Phillip and I have no problems with each other."

"Not even after he reported three of your stills to the cops? That must have ticked you off. Maybe you decided to get back at him."

The bust to which he referred had been a publicity stunt set up by MGM studios to improve Phillip's image with his fans. The three stills in question were back and running within days. It was a weak question, and it made Virginia slightly nervous on behalf of her niece. The fact that the cops were focusing on her and Phillip must have meant they had no leads in the kidnapping case.

She lit a cigarette and the other cop slid an ashtray toward her. She flashed him a killer smile. "Water under the bridge, Detective. Let's not forget little Todd is my own flesh and blood."

"Those three stills were destroyed by prohibition agents. How much did that cost you?"

"Why do you insist on embarrassing yourself, Detective? Anyone who knows me knows I'd rather cut off my right arm than do anything to hurt Laura or Todd."

Wilson paced back and forth across the tiny room. "What about the shooting at McGuire's?"

She frowned. "What about it? Not an unusual thing in my business."

"Phillip Austin was the informant. He set up the hit for the Schultz mob."

Virginia sighed. This man would never find Todd. He was an idiot. "Am I a suspect in my nephew's kidnapping?"

"Not officially, but there's no doubt in anyone's mind that this is an inside job."

"Then what are we doing here?"

"Cut the crap, woman. Just because no one has taken you down yet doesn't mean we don't know what you do or the kind of scum you associate with. If you are as concerned about the boy's wellbeing as you say you are, you will quit being so evasive and answer my goddamn questions."

She took a long drag on her cigarette and blew a stream of smoke into his face. Her voice remained calm. "If I had any confidence that you were anything but a foolish, incompetent publicity monger, I might be more inclined to help you, Detective. But that's not the case."

"Get up," Wilson said, eyes narrowed. He tossed a set of keys to the younger cop. "Maybe a night in jail will change your mind."

"Don't be absurd," Virginia said. "On what charges?"

"Lock her up, officer."

She ignored the clang of the cell door as it slammed shut behind her and walked to the cot. They couldn't hold her for more than a night without bringing charges. She would wait until morning to call her lawyer. This was as good a place as any to do some thinking.

Chapter Eight

When rumors circulated among reporters that the Austins were going to do an interview, Erich had never considered himself to be in the running. Especially after Virginia Kingsley told them what he had written about her. He figured a reporter from the *New York Times* would do the interview.

But when he'd walked into his editor's office yesterday, Dan had greeted him with a glass of scotch and a wide grin.

"You got the Austin interview," he said. "Congratulations."

Erich stared at him, running Dan's words through his mind a second and third time, just to be sure he'd heard right. "Why me?"

"Must be those pretty blue eyes of yours. Laura Austin requested you herself."

"Huh."

It had been a year since he'd met the woman outside of McGuire's. She had made quite an impression on him, and not just because she was a knock-out. Something in her smile had grabbed him. Something he couldn't seem to forget.

The last time he had driven up to Willow Pond, Erich hadn't noticed either the water fountain or the two cherubs in front of the house. Extravagances for the rich. He parked the car, walked up the steps to the dark green double doors, and pressed the doorbell. From inside of the house he heard it ring like a chime.

A maid, complete with starched white apron and cap, admitted him into a white marble foyer and asked him to wait.

To the right of the entrance was a room. The sign over top declared it to be "The Powder Room". Curious, he peeked inside and whistled, impressed by the gold faucets in the sink. More extravagance.

The maid returned and showed him into Phillip Austin's office. Prominently displayed on a central shelf in the room stood Phillip's Academy Award, which he had won the previous year. Feeling slightly ridiculous, but unable to stop himself, Erich touched the little Oscar. Just to say he'd actually touched an Academy Award. How many folks could say that?

The office was entirely masculine, walled by dark wood and furnished in brown leather. When Laura Austin came into the room and sat on the oversized sofa, she looked out of place. She wore a light blue, expertly tailored dress and the curls of her blonde hair shone like spun gold. She didn't say a word, but smiled at him from time to time while they waited. She didn't seem to mind that he stared. She was absolutely the most beautiful woman he'd ever seen.

Phillip's arrival felt like a staged entrance. He looked every inch the handsome movie star in his tan silk shirt and brown slacks. Before he took his place behind his desk, he paused in the doorway to survey his audience.

"My wife thinks you will be fair with us," he announced. "She had better be right. If she is not, your editor will hear from me. This is a delicate situation, you understand. I have to consider how this will appear to my fans."

Erich made a desperate attempt to keep from rolling his eyes. Fortunately, he succeeded, but it was tight. This was going to be interesting. Erich was treated to another one of Laura's smiles, or at least to the hint of one, anyway. She looked down, staring at her hands in her lap and Erich had to peel his eyes off her. She was even lovelier than he remembered.

Phillip wanted to establish rules before they began. "We will answer any questions you ask about the kidnapping, but we will answer none about our personal lives. Do you understand?"

"Of course." Erich leaned forward in his chair. "You might be comforted to know that most of the calls we are getting are sympathetic. Everyone wants to know how you are coping."

"It is a very difficult time. Particularly for me, since my son was kidnapped because of my status as a major film star," Phillip said, as if it were obvious.

Laura glared at Phillip, then refolded her hands and directed her attention toward Erich. "Phillip is right. It is a terrible time for us both. I try to get on with every day things as much as possible," she said, her voice coming faster with every word. "But everything I ever did included Todd. I can't seem to …" She stopped and clapped her hand over her mouth. It was a moment before she was able to speak again. "I am sorry. I have to control myself better. It's just that I keep expecting to look up and see him smiling at me, or playing with his blocks, you know?"

"He liked to play with blocks?"

Austin had stipulated no questions about their personal lives, but she nodded. No one objected, so Erich went on.

"Tell me more about Todd."

"He's a very energetic little boy. At bedtime he likes to run and hide. It was like a game to him. But when I told him it was time for a story, he would curl up in my lap. Stories and the water were his two favorite things. Oh, and chocolate milk. Have you seen pictures of him? He is the most beautiful little boy."

She was looking at Erich now, but from the glaze over her eyes, he knew she hardly saw him there. "Yes," he said. "The paper ran a picture of him right away after the kidnapping."

She sighed. "When Phillip looked at Todd, he thought of the future. I looked at him and thought about how little and sweet he was. I love him so much."

Erich barely had to take notes. This was classic. Readers would eat this stuff up.

"Whoever had the audacity to walk onto my property in broad daylight and kidnap my son will pay for what he's done," Phillip declared.

Phillip Austin was a Hollywood cliché. So far, Erich had not heard him utter one word of concern for his child. He wondered why Laura Austin had ever married him. They seemed entirely mismatched.

"Mr. Austin, did you do an interview with *Time Magazine* a few weeks ago?"

Phillip scowled in Erich's direction. "I did not."

"It is my understanding that you arranged the interview."

"That is a lie."

"Not according to the reporter who did the interview."

Erich had been surprised that morning by a phone call from a *Time* magazine reporter. The man said he'd spoken with Phillip Austin for an earlier interview, and believed the kidnapping had been a publicity stunt. Erich hadn't agreed or disagreed, preferring to meet with the man first and see if he had any evidence to back up his claim.

Erich had to sort through some different theories now that he was assigned to this case. Some thought Virginia Kingsley or some member of her gang was responsible, others were convinced bootleggers had kidnapped the baby as a warning to Phillip Austin to stay away from their stills.

Phillip got up and stood at the window, his back to them. "Mr. Muller, you are getting on my nerves. I do not care for your tone of voice."

"I have a copy of the galleys. It's a fascinating read. You state all bootleggers should be put out of business, and you target Virginia Kingsley specifically. Do you think she might have done this to get back at you?"

Phillip clenched his fists and turned to face Erich. "That article isn't going to be published for weeks."

"It is on the newsstand tomorrow."

"Still," Laura said, glancing nervously between Erich and Phillip. "She couldn't have known he'd said that. Not yet."

Erich turned to a fresh page on his notepad. "She has connections all over the place, doesn't she?"

Laura glared at Phillip. She was frowning, and Erich was enthralled by the tiny creases in her brow. "Quite a phony, aren't you?" she demanded of Phillip. "When did you become a teetotaler? If you caused this with your big mouth, I will never forgive you."

Phillip returned her glare. "I'll be damned if I'll stand for this."

"Six days before the kidnapping, you and Virginia Kingsley had a violent argument," Erich said.

"What is he talking about, Phillip? What did you argue about?" Laura demanded.

"I will not stand for this in my own house," Phillip said, staring furiously at Erich. "Get out, Mr. Muller."

They were interrupted by a knock and Iris Nickerson appeared in the doorway.

"So sorry to interrupt," she said. "There's a call for Laura from Virginia's assistant, Harry Davis."

"Tell him I'll call back, would you?"

"I would, but he insisted I tell you it's important he speak with you right away."

"Oh." She stood and pointed deliberately at Phillip, the warning clear in her glare. "Don't say anything more until I get back."

When she returned, her cheeks were flushed. "Virginia was in jail overnight. I've already told them she had nothing to do with this. Why are they wasting time on her when they should be looking for the real kidnapper?"

"Have they charged her?" Erich asked.

"Of course not. Harry says they don't have enough evidence. They are releasing her later today. I have to go to her."

"No," Phillip said. "I won't let you go. It is too dangerous."

Laura gave him a bemused look. "Going to the police station is dangerous? You know what, Phillip? Stop telling me what to do. You've made a mess out of everything."

"I could drive you to the city," Erich offered, rising from his chair. "I need to stop in at the newsroom anyway. It would give me a chance to change clothes."

Phillip's eyes shifted from Erich to Laura.

"Give me ten minutes, Mr. Muller," she said. "And we'll be on our way."

***

When they arrived at the second precinct in downtown Manhattan, Virginia still hadn't been released. Erich stopped at the front desk to talk with a cop he knew while another one showed Laura to the holding cell. Virginia glanced up from a magazine, calm and confident as always. She smiled warmly at her niece.

"Laura, what are you doing here?"

"I had to see you, of course." Laura slid a hand down the cold metal bars. "How can you be so together in here? I would be climbing the walls if I was locked in a cage like this. Have you been here all night?"

"Yep. Since yesterday afternoon." She got up off the cot. "Who told you?"

"Harry Davis called."

"I told him not to bother you. I'm due to be released at five o'clock. What time is it now?"

Laura glanced at her watch. "Five-twenty. I'll find out what's going on."

Ten minutes later, the guard unlocked her cell door. Virginia collected her personal effects and walked into the main office where Erich and Laura waited. The women hugged each other and Virginia kissed her niece's cheek.

"Who is this?" Virginia asked, stepping back and frowning at Erich.

"Oh, this is Erich. He is a reporter. He was interviewing us when Harry called, and was nice enough to drive me into the city."

"How gallant."

"If you wouldn't mind, I'd like to ask you a few questions," Erich said.

"Ha! Not all gallantry, huh? Forget it. I need a bath and a good meal. Come on, Laura, let's go."

Laura turned toward Erich, wanting to thank him again for the drive, but he took a step toward Virginia instead. "Are you involved in the kidnapping?" he asked.

Virginia spun around. "What paper do you work for?"

"The *New York Herald Tribune*. Please answer my question."

"Leave her alone, Mr. Muller," Laura said, frowning with concern. "Can't you see she's exhausted?"

Virginia came face to face with Erich and poked an accusatory finger at his chest. "I know you. I've seen your picture with your articles. You're the one who wrote those lies about me in yesterday's edition. Tell your editor I am thinking of suing."

"There was nothing libelous in that article, just the facts. Do you deny arguing with Phillip Austin only days before the kidnapping?"

"It was a family disagreement, nothing more," Virginia said. She grabbed her niece's elbow and tugged her toward the exit.

Laura glanced back at Erich as they left. The pleading expression on her face was the only thing that kept him from pursuing them. By the time it occurred to him to wonder how they planned to get home, they were nowhere in sight. He looked up and down the street outside the police station for a few minutes, then grinned. The thought of Virginia Kingsley needing to bum a ride with him was too good.

But her niece ... Now she was something else. Something else entirely.

Chapter Nine

The second ransom letter arrived the following day. Detective Wilson was briefing the press when a young officer received it. Because Wilson was busy, the officer read it first, then passed it to Phillip, meaning Wilson didn't get a chance to see it. Phillip took the letter into his office, sat on the brown leather sofa and read it to himself.

```
Mr Austin:
Bring $250,000 to the entrance of St.
Catherine's School for Girls on Beach Street
in Great Neck tomorrow at midnight. Do not
try any tricks. Come alone. If you do not
follow these instructions, we cannot promise
your son's safety.
```

Phillip drummed his fingers on the desk, contemplating the letter. Two hundred and fifty-thousand dollars was nothing to pay in exchange for Todd's life. But could he trust the kidnappers? Would they do as they said they would? He gripped the paper hard, trying to keep it from shaking along with his hands. To anyone watching, it might appear to be an angry reaction, but in truth the adrenaline pumping through Phillip was more about anticipation.

Oh, sure. He was angry about Todd. But a thought occurred. What better way to win back Laura's heart than by being the one responsible for the boy's safe return?

He took a sip of Coke and released a long, reflective sigh. He'd played plenty of heroes on the screen. Could he do it in real life? The idea was exciting. And what great publicity! He smiled, imagining the headlines.

He recognized the sound of Wilson's shuffling footsteps approaching his office, indicating the press briefing was over. What an idiot the man was. Even the newspapers were saying he'd bungled the case. His questions were repetitive and unanswerable. And he still hadn't looked into the question of Brian Madigan. Both he and Laura had requested another detective be assigned to their case, but so far nothing had changed.

He didn't plan on showing Wilson the ransom letter. The detective would want to send someone to the meeting place with Phillip, and that would foul up his plan to become a hero. Just as he was opening his bottom desk drawer to hide the letter, he glanced up and met Wilson's eyes.

Wilson's arms were in their habitual position, crossed over his chest. "Excuse me, Mr. Austin, but I need a moment of your time. Your wife has tried to help as much as possible, but every time I want to talk to you, you're busy. If you could make yourself more available we might get somewhere."

Talking to Wilson was a waste of time. The most important thing for Phillip to do now was go to the bank and put the ransom money together.

Wilson was staring at the envelope in Phillip's hand. He lifted an inquiring eyebrow.

"What if I told you this was personal business?"

"Bullshit, Austin. Right now every time you take a leak it's my business."

"This is part of a script for a movie I'm supposed to start filming next month. It wouldn't interest you."

"Sure it would. Let me have a look at it."

Phillip coughed and took another drink. "Sorry. There's a confidentiality clause with scripts. Why don't you go and see if there are any new developments in my son's case?"

"I'm surprised you aren't a better liar, Mr. Austin. Listen, if you want to see your son again, give me the ransom letter."

Phillip sighed and grudgingly passed him the letter. Wilson's eyes flicked over it and he nodded briefly.

"We'll send a man with you in an unmarked car."

Phillip grabbed the piece of paper and stuffed it back into the envelope. "No. You and your cops don't get a part of this. You just want a spotlight. Arrest the kidnapper of Phillip Austin's son and you're a big man, right Wilson? The kidnapper told me to come alone and that's what I'm going to do."

"Maybe the kidnapper just wants to blow your brains out. Ever think of that? He can't do it if anyone else is around."

"Pay attention, Wilson. You're not sending anyone with me. I'm going alone. After we have Todd back you can do whatever you want."

Wilson pounded his fist on the desk. "By that time this guy could be in China."

"While you're there looking for him, you can learn Chinese."

"Listen, wise guy. I suggest you remember who has experience with criminals like this." Wilson glared down at him, hands now hooked behind his back. "We could arrest him on the spot."

Phillip shook his head and fixed a black stare on Wilson. "Maybe so. But if you do that, they'll kill Todd. I won't take that chance. I'm going alone."

Chapter Ten

Brown paper grocery bags crunched against Nancy's chest as she worked the stiff latch of the front door. It swung open and she stepped in, slamming it shut behind her with a shove of her heel. With relief, she set the bags on the table, then called out. No one answered, but she thought she heard a small noise upstairs.

The baby lay on his back in the crib, staring wide-eyed at the ceiling. Nancy huffed with affection, then reached for the little boy. She held his little body close, thinking furious thoughts. That man, she thought, breathing in the baby's honey curls. Unbelievable that he'd left the little one all alone while he went off to collect his blood money. He probably hadn't fed the baby either, even though she'd asked him to. Just assumed she'd do it, like she did everything else. If she didn't do it, he'd let the poor baby starve to death.

The whole thing made Nancy slightly sick. All he cared about was the money, not the lives he'd torn apart. He'd assured her he'd give the baby back after he got the money, but she didn't trust him.

He was a miserable bastard. Always had been. Why she married him, she had no idea. The three years they had stayed together had almost driven her insane. He never considered her feelings, never hesitated to beat her or cheat on her. The day she walked out was the smartest thing she'd ever done.

Then he called her with this crazy scheme. He made it sound like she could make some easy money, and since he already owed her so much,

The problem was that she had never expected to feel anything for the child. Instead, she'd fallen in love with him the moment she saw him.

She carried the baby to the bathroom, where she removed his pajamas, changed his diaper, then sponged him off with a cool cloth. All the while she cooed at him, staring into his big green eyes like a suppliant begging for mercy.

Afterwards, she brought him downstairs to the kitchen, talking to him as she went. The kitchen was enormous and badly in need of repair, just like the rest of the house. At one point the pine-walled farmhouse might have been beautiful, but someone had poked holes in the walls in the living room, kitchen, pantry and master bedroom.

When she put the baby in the high chair he fussed.

"Ah," she said sympathetically. "It's too small for you, luv. And that old meanie won't get us a new one."

Tears welled up in the little boy's green eyes and she wrestled him out of the high chair. "Don't need this nasty thing, do we?"

She sat him on her lap, facing her, and felt the rigid little muscles of his body relax. He took the baby bottle she offered and sucked on it, then put it down and stared at her.

"Don't you like it? Drink your milk and you'll grow up to be a big strong bloke."

The child reached toward her.

"Oh, you darling!" she said, then bounced him up and down on her knee. At first he looked startled, but before long he laughed. It was a contagious sound. She laughed with him.

"You're a right beautiful little bloke," she cooed. "Yes. Do you know how beautiful you are?"

He gave her a half smile. She leaned over the table and stuck her finger into an open jar of peanut butter. Using her finger as a spoon, she held it to his lips. He ate it quickly, cleaning her finger in no time. When he was done, he stared at her and smacked his lips.

She kissed his soft, round cheek. "Would you like some more?"

She hefted him onto her hip and wandered across the kitchen. From out of the cupboard she pulled a loaf of Wonderbread, then grabbed a knife on her way back to the table. He watched her carefully while she made him half a peanut butter sandwich. She handed it to him and he ate the whole thing, smearing most of it all over his face. When he was done, he smacked his lips again.

"All yummy in the tummy," she said. The little boy laughed, a deep chuckle that started in his belly and bubbled up. "Mommy's going to have some, too." She helped herself to a spoonful of peanut butter. "Mmm. Good."

"Mommy," he said.

She put her face close to his. "Yes, Mommy."

He frowned slightly, then held out his open hands. "More."

While she made another half sandwich, he picked up his bottle and drank.

Nancy hummed while she spread peanut butter on the bread. "Mr. Grouchy says you won't eat, but we know he's wrong, don't we? He's just a mean old thing. We don't want him around."

After they'd finished their snack, Nancy took him back upstairs. When they got to the landing he sniffled.

"Mommy," he said, round eyes filling with tears.

"Yes," she said, grinning. "I'm your mommy now. And I promise I'll love you just as much as your other mommy did. Maybe more."

Half an hour later he fell asleep in her arms and she laid him gently in the crib which had become his prison. For a few moments she stood watching him and couldn't help noticing how restless he was, how he couldn't seem to get comfortable. Once she thought she saw a tear hanging on his eyelash, then looked closer and decided it was her imagination.

By now Phillip Austin would have paid the ransom. Rudy would be on his way home. It chilled her to the bone when she thought of what he might do to Todd after he walked in the door. More than once she had seen him look at the baby with dislike. But the baby was hers now. She wouldn't let anything happened to him.

She needed to get Todd away from Rudy, but she didn't have much time. If she didn't leave, God knows what Rudy might do to them. She had been the victim of his violent outbursts more than once, and she couldn't let them happen to Todd. She didn't have much money and had no idea what she was going to do, but she didn't want to take any chances. She didn't want the blood money either, though it sure would come in handy.

A car went by and her heart pounded. She watched, relieved to see it wasn't Rudy. He would be there soon. She grabbed the suitcase she had brought with her and threw the few things they had for the baby inside, followed by a change of clothes for herself. Everything else she had brought for herself would have to stay behind. She needed room for the baby's things. When the suitcase was latched, she filled two bottles with the remaining milk from the icebox.

She went back upstairs to the baby's room. He was sleeping, his little rear end up in the air. He seemed so peaceful she hated to wake him up. When she lifted him, he opened his eyes, gazed sleepily at her, then went right back to sleep.

Even though it was over seventy degrees outside, she wrapped him in two blankets, then put a hat on him to cover his curls. The hat was too big for him and he looked silly, but she couldn't chance anyone recognizing him. That wouldn't be too difficult, since his picture had been on the front page of every newspaper over the last few days.

With the suitcase in one hand and the baby in her other arm, she walked to the nearest bus stop. The bus squealed to a stop by her and she climbed onboard, not knowing where she was going. All she knew was she had to get the baby as far away from Rudy as she could.

Chapter Eleven

At 8:30 the next morning, Virginia returned from a walk in Central Park. She picked up the newspaper from her front step and stared at the headline with disbelief.
`Austin Ransom Payoff Botched.`
What could have gone wrong? She clutched it under her arm as she opened the door of the brownstone, then settled in with her coffee, immersing herself in the article. Phillip had gone alone to meet the kidnapper. Amazing. The grandstander had actually stood up for his son. Her first thought was that for once Phillip had used his brain. Then she read on and discovered all he had gotten for both his money and his show of spirit was a bump on the head. She chuckled. That sounded more like the Phillip she knew. She blew on her coffee, smiling. The cops would be livid.

But something else concerned her. Phillip had brought the money, as he had been asked, but Todd had not been returned. Did the kidnappers intend to string them along forever?

The thought made her ache for her niece. Laura must be devastated. She'd expected to have her baby back in her arms today. Virginia dialed Willow Pond, but the line was busy. She tried again five minutes later, and it was still busy.

How would they ever find Todd now? According to the article, the kidnapper who had met with Phillip had worn the same clown's mask he'd worn in the initial kidnapping. Phillip was able to describe a few things, however, as vague as they might be. He said the police should be looking for a guy in his early thirties, about six feet tall, with a medium build and an olive complexion. Virginia rolled her eyes. That described half the men she knew.

She dialed her assistant's number. Dependable Harry picked up the phone right away. "I heard all about it," he said. "Call me if you need me. I'm fine to look after everything for now."

"I knew I could count on you, Henry. I'll call you in the morning."

She went into the library, already stifling hot in the midmorning sun, and sat at her desk. A photograph of Laura and Todd from the Christmas before caught her eye. He was dressed in a ridiculous little Santa Claus suit, and mother and son were laughing into the camera. She picked it up and gazed at it, absently tapping the back of it with one long finger.

"Where are you, little one?"

Setting the picture aside, she picked up her phone and dialed the police commissioner, Tony Jaeger. She was surprised when his deep tenor voice answered the phone.

"Is your secretary napping?" she asked, trying not to sound flirtatious. She hoped this conversation didn't end the way all their recent conversations had, with his proposing marriage and her gently letting him down. It would be so inappropriate for them to be anything other than lovers.

"She's filing her nails. Listen. What's going on with that crazy family of yours? Everyone's talking about how bad things went last night. I didn't know Phillip Austin had the guts, him being an actor and all."

"I'm as surprised as you are. But never mind him. Talk to me about the kidnapper."

"Well, he was smart enough to wear a disguise, so maybe he knows what he's doing. At least he knows that'll make him difficult to find. Thanks to Austin, he now has quarter of a million bucks. He can go anywhere and do whatever he wants. Only trouble is, no matter where he goes, folks are gonna recognize that baby."

"You think he's still holding Todd?"

"The kid's gotta be somewhere. He hasn't turned up anywhere else." He hesitated, then added, "Yet."

She shuddered. "Just thinking about the possibility that something's happened to him is killing me," said Virginia. "I can't imagine what Laura must be going through. I need to know where the kidnapper's hideout is, and I need to know fast."

"So do we all, sweetheart. We're working on it. Both ransom letters were mailed from a post office in Bayside, Queens. I've got men searching the area as we speak."

"Dammit, Tony, he can't get away with this." Her voice quivered and she struggled to control it. "I don't give a damn what we have to do. That little boy – Christ."

"I hate to hear you like this, Virginia."

"Does that mean you've had a change of heart since yesterday?" she said wryly, recalling the lousy dinner she'd had in the jail cell.

"I heard what that S.O.B. Wilson put you through. I gave him hell this morning. He'll go easy on you from now on. Otherwise I'll see to it he's out of a job."

"The man is an idiot. He has no idea what he's doing."

"Let's have dinner tonight. You pick the restaurant."

"Soon, Tony, I promise. Just … please get me the information. I promise I'll make it up to you."

"How long do I have to wait before you make an honest man of me?"

"Oh, Tony. You know damn well I can't marry you."

***

The farm was in a middle class residential community in Bayside, Queens. Traditional farmhouses shared the northern sections with generic-looking new tract homes; Tudor style mansions occupied the southern sections. After four days of searching the area, the police got a tip about a farmhouse on 28th Avenue and 201st Street. A man and a woman had recently been seen coming and going at odd hours.

Wilson interviewed one of the neighbors, a short, stocky man in his fifties. "What makes you think this house might be what we're looking for?" Wilson asked.

"Before this, the house had been empty for two months," the man said with a shrug.

"Are you positive about this?" Breaks in the case were few and far between. Wilson wasn't in the mood for a wild goose chase.

"I'm telling you, I know what I saw."

"In that case, why don't you describe these people for me?"

"Afraid I can't help you there. They never went out during the day, just at night. So nothing stood out about them."

Wilson sighed, drumming his fingers on the man's kitchen table. "So you know what you saw, but you didn't see anything."

"What I saw was a man and a woman who might as well have been vampires, Detective."

Wilson sighed. "What about the owners, then?"

"The Pierces? They retired and moved to North Carolina. Their son, Geoffrey, was supposed to take the place over, but he's a good-for-nothing bum."

"Can you get me an address for them in North Carolina?"

"Sure." He blinked at Wilson. "Right now?"

***

Ben Wilson climbed the three steps to the front porch, hearing the old wood planks creak beneath his feet. On the porch sat two wicker chairs, white where the paint hadn't worn off. He knocked on the door, waited a few moments, then knocked again. No answer. Wilson turned the doorknob, surprised to find it unlocked. He stepped into the foyer, turned right and entered an enormous kitchen, the kind his wife always complained she didn't have. The refrigerator held an empty milk bottle and three bottles of beer. He took all four items out and dropped them in an evidence bag.

Upstairs, the first three bedrooms were empty, apart from a few chewed up toothpicks scattered around the floor. He crouched and put the toothpicks in a smaller baggy, then opened the door of the last bedroom.

The crib and the can on the floor were empty, who knew for how long. But the sweet pink aroma of baby powder wafting through the room was unmistakable.

Chapter Twelve

The three weeks Laura spent in East Hampton seemed like three years. Hopes of finding Todd alive, or even finding him at all, dwindled. She was miserable and rarely slept. She forgot to eat. And every day she grew more irritated, living in such close contact with Phillip. They had limited, cordial contact, but his selfishness and philandering made her wonder what she could ever have seen in him.

One morning she woke up and realized she couldn't stand being near him anymore. It was time to go home. She packed her suitcase and found Phillip in the dining room, reading the latest police report.

"I'm leaving," she announced.

"All right," he replied, barely glancing toward her. "I'll call you. We'll find him soon."

"I'm not so sure anymore," she whispered, feeling her throat tighten.

Phillip said nothing. She wondered if he'd even heard.

Laura tossed her luggage into the car and started down the long driveway, purposefully keeping her eyes averted from the pond. Once she was on the road, she decided to stop at Virginia's brownstone. If anything, her time at Willow Pond had left her starved for decent company.

Virginia answered the door and greeted Laura with a broad smile. "Laura," she said, folding her niece into an embrace. "I'm so glad to see you."

They sat in the same living room where she and Phillip had been married. The beautiful room hadn't changed a bit. Its high ceilings, wood floors and original moldings dated back to the 1880s. Despite the sour memory of her wedding, Laura still loved the room.

"Is that Mozart I hear, Virginia?"

"Umhmm. Clarinet Quintet. Nice, isn't it?"

"The sound is so clear."

"I know." She gestured toward the other side of the room. "This phonograph's the latest from Victor. It plays all the 78s. Better than those old Victrolas any day."

Laura walked to the phonograph and ran her finger appreciatively over the dark wood. It was a beautifully crafted piece, just like everything else in the room. It always amazed Laura how Virginia came off so crass in one environment, so dignified and cultured in another. Here in this room she was in her element, surrounded by things she loved. For some reason, Laura was more comfortable with her here in this place than when they were anywhere else.

"The Chinese inlay is the latest thing too, isn't it?"

Virginia smiled wryly. "You know me ..."

Laura glanced at her, but Virginia was looking away. Ever since Phillip's bungled attempt to pay the ransom, her aunt had seemed preoccupied. She was more attentive than ever, but Laura had the strange impression she was keeping secrets. More secrets than usual, that is. Laura knew Virginia had people looking for Todd and the kidnapper, but when she asked, Virginia put her perfectly manicured finger to her lips and smiled. Laura took this to mean it was better if she didn't know.

They sat on the couch together in a comfortable quiet.

"You can stay here, you know," Virginia said after a few moments. "As long as you want. Now's no time to be alone."

Laura shook her head. "That's a nice offer, but I can't. I can't hide from life, you know? The best thing for me to do is face what's happened. That's what you always do."

Virginia nodded and patted the back of her niece's hand. "I understand. But Laura, remember. I'm here anytime you need me."

When she got to her apartment, Laura set down her bags and went directly to the nursery. She leaned against the doorframe, vaguely aware of particles of dust dancing in the shaft of late afternoon sun. She stepped quietly through the door, feeling like an intruder in the empty room. Her chair creaked as she settled into it, and she closed her eyes, rocking gently. She could almost feel him in her arms, practically smelled the powder, sweet on his skin. *Oh Todd.* The anguish of longing was so intense she nearly doubled over.

But when she was able to open her eyes, to look around the room, she knew she'd been right to come home. Painful as the reminder was, he seemed more real here. His things lay everywhere she looked, making it easier to believe he was still alive somewhere. How could he not be, with his little slippers waiting for him right there under the crib?

Chapter Thirteen

Laura was stretched out on the flowered chintz sofa, listening to the radio and daydreaming when the phone rang. It was early in the evening, and she was tempted not to answer. A week had passed since she'd left Willow Pond, and she was having trouble working up the energy to do just about anything.

"I hope I'm not taking you away from anything important," Erich said when she eventually picked up the phone.

"Not really. Just listening to *Fibber McGee and Molly*."

He chuckled. "That's one of my favorites. Hey, I was wondering what you were doing for lunch tomorrow."

She sighed heavily. "Oh. No more interviews, Mr. Muller. That piece you did was okay, but—"

"Please. It's Erich. Nobody but you calls me Mr. Muller. What do you mean it was *okay*? Should I start looking for another line of work?"

"No, I didn't mean that. Nothing dreadful was in it. About us, I mean. What you think of Virginia is your business, but she's my aunt and I love her."

"I know what you mean, Laura. I was kidding. And to be frank, I'm not asking for another interview. Just lunch. Nothing in it for me other than some good company."

She was surprised at how appealing the prospect of seeing him again was, and shocked herself even more when she agreed to meet him at the Pepper Pot Inn.

The Inn had been one of her favorite places since the day she spotted the poet, E.E. Cummings, sitting at a table and writing in a notebook. It turned out he lived a few doors down from her, at 4 Patchin Place. After seeing him there, she'd gone out and bought herself a notebook to jot down ideas for her novel, but at first was too embarrassed to take it out of her purse. What if he saw her copying his idea? It had taken a few weeks before she felt comfortable using it, and now she never went anywhere without it.

***

Laura set out the next day for her lunch date, thinking how beautiful the day was. A light spring breeze swayed the budding trees and the sky was like crystal blue water. Laura strolled down Patchin Place, past the one gaslight lamp left in the city and headed toward Waverly Place.

Walking alone helped her feel the pulse of a place. Helped her clear her mind. It also reminded her of the country road in Maine where she'd been walking when her sister had found her. That was the moment when she'd learned their parents were missing. She thought about them often lately.

The restaurant was crowded, but Erich had managed to get them a table by the window. He pulled out her chair when she arrived, and she smiled at him, then glanced out the window. She was grateful to have somewhere to look besides at him. His startling eyes, an incredible cornflower blue, never left her face.

"I'm so glad you decided to join me."

This was the first time she'd done anything social since the day Todd had been kidnapped. It felt strange. A little scary. She couldn't help thinking she should have stayed home in case there were any news about him. There wouldn't be, she knew, but her son was always on her mind. So she told stories about him to Erich.

"He sounds like quite a boy," Erich said. She'd just finished telling him about the time Todd climbed into the driver's seat of Virginia's Packard and refused to get out. He'd screamed and hung onto the steering wheel. It wasn't so cute at the time, but sweet to remember.

"He is. Smart and funny and …" She smiled. It felt natural, speaking with him about Todd. "I suppose all mothers think their children are wonderful." She took a sip of iced coffee. "Since I separated from his father I worry I won't be able to give him what he needs."

"My mother always said all children need is love. From the way you talk about him I'd say Todd's doing just fine."

She nodded with appreciation and swallowed hard.

"You know," Erich said. "I remember the day I met you. Todd was one of the first things you mentioned then, too."

She put her sandwich down, feeling slightly guilty. Her strongest memory of that day had been her concern about Virginia, not Todd. He'd been safe in their Patchin Place apartment with Mrs. Nickerson. If only he were in that lady's loving care now. She had to believe whoever had him was taking good care of him. To think any other way was only inviting madness.

Erich frowned and bit his lower lip, then lifted his eyebrows apologetically. "I know I promised you I didn't want an interview," Erich said, "but I can't help wondering. Don't the rumors bother you?"

She stiffened. "What rumors?"

"You know. That the police are considering the possibility that the kidnapper is part of your aunt's gang."

She glared at him. "I find that impossible to believe."

"Really? Think about the world she lives in, the people she does business with. Think about—"

"Stop it," Laura said tersely. "Please."

Ever since they'd sat down she'd been avoiding looking at him. Now, when she finally did, she was unprepared for the intensity of his gaze. She forced her tone to soften. "So tell me. Are we just here having lunch? Or are you here to grill me about my aunt?"

"I just wanted to take your mind off things for a while, that's all."

"By talking about my aunt? By telling me she could be responsible for kidnapping her own nephew? You have an odd sense of humor, Mr. Muller."

Why was he doing this to her? She had been enjoying his company until now. Despite the fact she knew he was a journalist, this felt like a betrayal. Maybe Phillip was right. Maybe all reporters were vultures who enjoyed the misery of others.

She tucked her purse under her arm and started to get up.

Erich reached across and gently laid his hand on her arm. "Don't go. Please. The truth is, well, the truth is I asked you here because I wanted to see you again."

She frowned at him. If he had any romantic interest in her he had a strange way of showing it. "Why?"

"It wasn't to talk about Virginia, believe me," he said, looking bemused. "Actually, in hindsight, I don't even know why I brought it up."

"Mr. Muller - Erich - if you considered this to be some sort of date, you need to understand I can't think about things like that right now. My life's in turmoil. All I do is worry and wonder about Todd. I wonder where he is, if he's all right, if I'll ever see him again. When I do manage to work, loss in one form or another creeps into everything I write."

"You're a writer? I didn't know that."

She sighed, defeated. "No, you wouldn't. I feel lucky to have been published in literary magazines. Nothing big."

"So you write ... what? Fiction? Non-fiction?"

She let herself to sink back down, but clutched her purse in case she needed to make a mad dash.

"I've tried both. I've had several non-fiction articles published in a community newspaper called *The Villager*."

"Really? I know the editor. Good guy."

"Yes, I like him."

"I tried writing fiction once and ended up tossing it in the garbage."

"I don't know how many times I've done that." He held her gaze with the bluest eyes she'd ever seen. "You should give it another try."

"Another try?" A faint smile crossed his lips and he returned the gaze. She knew where he was going with this. "Maybe you're right," she said after a moment. "I'm a big believer in second chances."

Chapter Fourteen

Laura had just hung up her coat when the phone rang. It was Ben Wilson, and something in his voice frightened her. He said he'd been trying to get in touch with Phillip, but no one had answered at Willow Pond. She could have told him that. Phillip had been staying in Manhattan. She was about to give Wilson his telephone number when the detective interrupted her.

"Mrs. Austin, I'm sorry to have to tell you this, but the body of a small child was found in a vacant lot in Jamaica, Queens."

The image shot through her like lightning. "Oh, God. No!"

"I'm sorry, Mrs. Austin," Wilson said. "Truly I am."

She hung up. She was unaware that she shook, that tears streamed down her face. Somewhere in the back of her mind she watched people walk by, and hoped none of them ever experienced the pain she felt at that moment.

Deep within herself, Laura's heart began to harden, but she refused to get angry. For her to become bitter would mean the kidnapper had won. She couldn't let that happen.

When Phillip's white Rolls Royce pulled up in front of 12 Patchin Place, Laura sat waiting on the stoop. Phillip sat beside her and she raised her tearstained face to his.

"Why does it have to end this way? I thought ... I thought I wanted to know if he were dead. But I don't. I'd rather keep on hoping."

He took her hand and spoke in a husky voice. "I won't rest until I find out who did this."

She tried to recite the Lord's Prayer during the ride to the morgue, but kept losing her place and finally gave up. Phillip held her hand the whole time. He didn't want her to see the body; he wanted her to remember their son alive. But she insisted it was something she had to do. She dried her eyes and vowed they would help each other get through this.

When they arrived at the door to the morgue, Phillip took control, as if he were playing the lead in one of his movies. He shoved the door open and strode toward a tiny lump laying on a table. No one else was in the room. Laura began to shake and Phillip put an arm out to steady her. They stood perfectly still by the body, saying nothing. Then, without waiting for permission, Phillip flung back the sheet.

Laura cried out, spinning away from the sight.

"Wait!" the coroner cried, coming in behind them. "Wait a moment." But Phillip had uncovered the little body and now stared down at it.

Phillip turned to the coroner, frustrated. "We weren't told the child was burned beyond recognition. We can't possibly identify this child. There may never be any way to identify these remains. There's nothing left of him."

The coroner looked at them with a vague smile, laced with impatience. "I know that. However, had you waited for me, I could have saved you the trouble. We took a measurement of the pelvis and have determined this is a female. This is not your son."

Laura's jaw dropped and she stared hard at the coroner. Tears hung on her eyelids like raindrops after a storm. "You're sure? Is there any chance you could be mistaken?"

"None whatsoever. The child was around the same age as your son, eighteen months to two years, but it's not him. There's still hope for you, Mrs. Austin. I wish I could say the same for the parents of this poor little girl."

Through her tears Laura took one last look at the horrible remains of the child's face, then turned and followed Phillip out of the room. She felt sick, twisted by grief for the parents of the other child, and relief for herself.

The first thing she saw when they stepped into the sunshine was Erich.

"Is everything okay?" he asked.

She blew out all her breath and explained what had happened, then dropped her chin to her chest. "So what do we do now?"

"Wait," Phillip said. "Just wait and hope."

"If there's anything I can do, let me know," Erich said. "Anything."

She nodded, unaccountably relieved to see him there. She noticed Phillip staring at Erich and didn't like the expression in his eyes.

Phillip took her arm. "The driver's waiting. We'd better go."

Once they were in the car he turned to her. "What's going on between you and that guy?"

She shrugged. "We're friends."

Phillip's narrow expression said it would take a lot to convince him of that.

Chapter Fifteen

Later that afternoon, Erich covered a five alarm fire in Brooklyn. When he got back to the newsroom he walked into Daniel Spencer's office, closed the door, and asked his editor for a couple of days off. Dan shook his head. He couldn't be spared. Several reporters who'd been hired during the last six months had been laid off, and the entire newsroom staff had taken a ten percent cut in pay.

"How long am I going to be covering fires like some cub reporter?"

"Connelly's mother died. Give the guy a break." Dan took a sip of what Erich knew to be at least his fifth cup of coffee of the day. "Why do you need time off?"

"To do some investigating."

"The Austin kidnapping? The trail's cold."

Erich propped his feet up in the same spot as always, nestled between the picture of Daniel's nieces and nephews and his press club plaque. "The kidnappers rented a car from a place on Northern Boulevard. I thought I'd snoop around Bayside, see what I can find out."

Dan squinted at him, tapping the end of his pencil against the desk. "Probably a waste of time."

"Maybe so, maybe no. I'd like to try. Be quite a story if I turned up something the police haven't."

"All right. But I may have to pull you back in if things get hairy."

***

Three mornings later, Erich left his apartment in the Bronx and headed to Queens. Spring was in full bloom, filling the air with the smells of freshly cut grass and budding flowers. He gazed up at the cloudy sky and spied a patch of blue. He smiled, hoping it was a good omen.

He found Walters Car Rental on Northern Boulevard and pulled his car into the parking lot. He sat for a few minutes, looking around. Then, instead of going inside, he headed down the street and started ringing doorbells. He'd developed a pretty good nose for figuring out who didn't want to become involved and who really hadn't seen anything. Out here people slammed doors in his face too fast to pick up anything. Obviously he was working ground the police had already strip-mined.

It was part of the job though, so he kept at it. He hit paydirt at about 9:30 when an elderly woman answered the doorbell. Her husband had been a reporter for the *Daily News* for thirty years. She was certain if he'd been around, he'd have been working on the kidnapping too, but he'd died a year earlier.

Erich expressed sorrow for her loss and said how much he appreciated her talking to him when so many others wouldn't. She wanted him to know how angry the residents of Bayside were that the kidnapper had chosen their community as his hideout.

"We don't like the publicity. Your being here just means we're going to have more. What was your name again?"

"Erich Muller. From the *Tribune*."

"Oh right," she said, waggling a finger at him. "You're the one who won the Pulitzer. Hmph. Well, I guess we can count on you to be accurate, anyway. But you're looking in the wrong place, dear. The farm is on the other end of Bayside. Take Bell Boulevard to 32nd Avenue, make a left and keep going."

He walked back to Walters Car Rental, situated between an empty lot and a Chinese restaurant. Erich had skipped breakfast and was hungry, so he thought he'd have an egg roll and some wonton soup when he was done. The owner of Walters Car Rental couldn't slam the door in his face, but was either too reluctant to talk or just bored with the subject. He recited his answers as if he'd said them many times before.

"Can you describe the guy who rented the car?"

"A woman rented the car."

That stopped Erich. He'd never heard anything about that. "A woman?"

"A woman."

"Can you describe her?"

"About twenty-five, average height, good figure, made me think of the lines of a good racecar."

"What about her hair, her face?"

"Her hair was dark, but I think it was a wig. She had big sunglasses on, so I didn't get much of a look at her."

"How come I've never heard this woman mentioned before?"

He shrugged. "How would I know? Ask the cops."

"Do you have a phone?"

"Remember who's paying the bill."

Erich dialed the Wilson's number. "Detective Wilson? It's Erich Muller. Got a minute?"

"What's the problem, Muller? Laura Austin turn you down?"

"Comedy doesn't suit you, Wilson. Tell me. What's this about a woman being involved in the Austin kidnapping?"

"Who told you a woman was involved?"

"Do the Austins know?"

"We're checking things out."

"Why are you withholding this information, Detective?"

"That's none of your damn business. We're in the middle of a criminal investigation and we'll do it the way we think is best."

When Erich got to the other side of town it didn't take him long to find the farmhouse. That was just about the same time as he noticed a dark green Packard town car parked in front of the house. He stopped across the street, close enough so he could see the farmhouse clearly, but far enough away so he wouldn't attract attention. About half an hour later a woman came out and got into the Packard.

Erich stared. What was *she* doing here?

Chapter Sixteen

Ben Wilson got off the elevator at the fourth floor. The tapping of his heels on the wood floor echoed as he paced the long narrow hall. He read the names on the doors to his left and right, then turned the corner and opened the door to the Ackles Employment Agency.

Typically, business people hate seeing cops, and when the young, blonde receptionist looked at him and frowned, he knew this time would be no different. Her frown deepened when he told her he needed to see Gina Ackles.

"Is Mrs. Ackles expecting you?"

"She will be when you tell her I'm here."

The look of confusion on the girl's face was replaced by one of relief when Gina Ackles appeared at her office door and motioned Wilson in.

Wilson smiled back at the receptionist. "See? That wasn't so hard."

Mrs. Ackles ushered him into her office and he sat in the leather chair she offered. "What can I do for you, Detective? Mr. Austin called and asked me to help you in any way I can."

"Then you already know this is regarding the Austin kidnapping case."

"I do. How can I help?"

"I'm here about Brian Madigan. I believe you have his records."

"Brian Madigan." She looked blank for a moment, then started thumbing through a box of cards. "Let's see. Oh yes, the landscaper. We usually handle household employees, not groundskeepers or anything like that, but he had excellent references. Too bad it didn't work out."

Wilson needed to see the employee records. Gina Ackles searched briefly through a filing cabinet, then produced a slim folder. She slipped two sheets of paper from the folder and began to read.

"He came here a few days after the Austins let him go, but we had nothing for him."

"Is that the last time you were in touch with him?"

She frowned and followed her notes with one slender finger. "No. It says here a nice family in Connecticut was looking for a groundskeeper and we recommended him. If we'd had any idea why the Austins had let him go we never would have, but at that time we didn't know what had happened."

She read more, then stopped. "That's odd."

"What is?"

"Brian Madigan's wife was hired as a maid by the same family, but fired a few months later. According to this, she had an alarming habit of hiding their little girl."

Ben Wilson reached for the folder. "Let me see that." He read a few lines then looked back up at her. "Is this the current address and phone number?"

"As far as I know. Oh dear, that doesn't look good, does it? Hiding the little girl, I mean."

Ben Wilson was out the door before she finished the sentence.

Chapter Seventeen

Virginia and Tony spent two days in bed, but when he tried to mount her for the fourth time the second day, she pushed him away. She sauntered to her walk-in closet and removed a black satin robe, which she slipped into, knowing his eyes were on her body. Seconds later she felt his hands on her shoulders. She chuckled. For a man his age, he was insatiable.

"No more cuzzy," she murmured.

"A bearcat like you never has enough."

"Maybe not, but right now all I'm hungry for is dinner. Come on downstairs."

They'd met four years earlier when he was appointed police commissioner, and they'd been seeing each other on and off since then, even though his divorce had only become final last year. He spoke of marriage often, and when he did, she laughed.

Virginia watched him dig into a bowl of mushroom and barley soup but had to look away. He had some distasteful habits which she tried to ignore because of all the influential people he knew. He was also an energetic lover who was always willing to try new things, and she definitely enjoyed that part of his personality.

She passed him the Italian bread. "I tried to call in some favors, but no one's talking."

"Favors? What favors?"

"You know better than to ask me that." She dipped a piece of bread into the soup. "Did the police find any clues at the farmhouse?"

"Next to nothing: an empty bottle of milk and some beer. They dusted them for prints and dusted surfaces around the house too, but didn't get any clear prints."

"That's it?" She waited as he slurped the soup.

He shrugged. "A couple of toothpicks. Dusted them, too."

Toothpicks?

Virginia's fingers tightened on the bread until the soup was littered by crumbs. Rudy. His interest in Todd suddenly made sense. Her mind spun. She would have to find him, but she hadn't paid much attention when he'd dropped out of sight, since he did that all too often. She should have picked up the signals.

"Virginia, what is it? You look sick."

She took a deep breath and waved a hand at him. "No, it's nothing. It's the stress of the last few weeks. Nothing matters to me but finding that baby."

He narrowed his eyes. "Are you keeping something from me?"

"How about a vacation sometime?" she asked. "Just you and me on a beach somewhere?"

"Vacation, my ass. You'd better tell me what's going on, or I'll toss you in the clink."

"For what? Feeding you dinner? I'm not that bad a cook."

"Out with it."

She sighed, then studied his expression, trying to figure out if she should play hard or soft. He looked all business, so she went with the truth. "Listen, Tony. I need your cooperation. I've gotta find Todd, and I think I have the best shot at doing that. You know I'm not gonna drop this. I'll devote the rest of my life to it, if necessary."

He shook his head. "What are you asking for?"

"Just some room, you know? Let me do what I have to do without having to answer all your questions."

"You can't just do this, you know, shove the law aside when it suits you."

Now was the time to play soft. She tilted her head just enough and lowered her chin so the light caught her eyes. It had to be perfectly choreographed, and she was the master. "Please, Tony?"

He frowned, looking unsure, so she leaned over the table, letting her cleavage beckon. She saw the moment when he surrendered, when his eyes gave up the fight and filled with lust. She stood and tapped her slender fingers on the back of her chair.

"Let's go back upstairs," he said, his voice a little rough.

Her lips puckered exactly the right amount. "If anything comes into the department concerning my nephew's kidnapping, you'll tell me. Understand? Only me."

He closed his eyes briefly and shook his head again. "I've got thousands of trained police officers at my disposal. This is one time you aren't going to get your way, Virginia. I won't call off the investigation no matter how many times you threaten me."

She glared at him. "Why should I trust the N.Y.P.D.? Look what that idiot Wilson did to me. Look what you *let* him do."

"Come on, Virginia. I knew nothing about that. As soon as I did, I told him if he ever tried those tactics again he'd be pounding the pavement out in Suffolk County."

Virginia played her last card. She crossed her arms over her chest and flicked up one sardonic eyebrow. "Tell you what, Tony. You give up that floozy you've gotten hidden up in Maine and not only will I tell you what I know about Todd, I'll even take your marriage proposal seriously.

Chapter Eighteen

Virginia racked her brain trying to remember what she might have said to Rudy to prompt him to kidnap Todd. She thought about everything they'd done and said. Then, all at once while she was putting on mascara, she recalled telling him Todd would be at Willow Pond that week.

So it was her fault. It was all her fault. She sat on the side of her four-poster bed, dropped her head into her hands and let the tears come, feeling sick with guilt. But she had to pull herself together. Indulging in self-serving emotions was a waste of time. The only thing that mattered was finding Todd.

She went to the one-room dump in lower Manhattan that Rudy called home and took anything she thought might give her a clue as to where he might be. Though his address book was full, all the names except for two had been blackened out. It was time she paid a visit to these men whom Rudy had mentioned to her a few times. The first was named Eddie.

After she finished dressing, she took a long look at herself in the mirror. The navy blue silk dress accentuated her tall, slim body to perfection. Slipping on her best pair of black heels, she headed downstairs to where the cook had breakfast waiting for her. She wasn't hungry, so she had one cup of coffee, then stepped outside. She glanced up and down the tree-lined street, making sure she didn't see anyone suspicious, then drove her dark green Packard town car away from the curb.

The fine car hummed as it rolled down the streets of Manhattan. When she reached the Park Slope section of Brooklyn, she turned onto Seventh Avenue and drove past Woolworth's, the A&P, a gas station and a school. She made a left onto President Street and slowed the car, trying to get a feel for an unfamiliar section of Brooklyn. She stopped in the next block, near three girls playing hopscotch in the street. Further ahead, a group of teenage boys were playing stickball. Unlike the girls, they didn't budge after she honked the horn several times.

She rolled down the window and told them to get up on the sidewalk. One of the boys ran his hand smoothly over the Packard's hood, then poked his head in her window and asked her to take him for a ride.

"Not too friendly with soap and water, are you?" she asked.

He stared at her. "A fine lady in a fine car like this is out of place here. You sure you want to be telling me what to do?"

She shrugged. "Are you sure you want to mess with Virginia Kingsley?"

His eyes bugged out in a satisfying manner and he backed up as soon as he heard her name, but she smiled and motioned for him to come closer. He took a few steps toward her, but now he kept his head down. She wanted to know where 320 President Street was. He pointed toward an old couple sitting on a porch.

"That's the house you're looking for."

The old man had evidently been reading a magazine, but it had slid out of his hands and onto the sidewalk when he'd fallen asleep. As Virginia approached, the woman nudged him awake.

"What you after?" the old woman asked without lifting her eyes from her knitting.

"I'm looking for someone." Virginia glanced around to make sure no one was near enough to hear. "His name's Rudy."

The old man came to life and waved her away. "You need to talk to my son. If he doesn't hear the bell, ring it again and wait. He don't hear too good."

A man in a filthy undershirt opened the door and peered out at her. She watched with disgust as his bloodshot eyes traveled the length of her body and a crooked leer settled on his face.

"Hot damn," he said after a moment. "Been way too long since I seen a broad like you on my doorstep."

Of that she had no doubt. "Listen honey, why don't you keep your eyes where they belong and answer a few questions for me. You know a guy named Rudy Strauss?"

He opened the door wider and reached for her hand. "Who wants to know?"

She avoided his hand and sidestepped the rest of him, stepping into the hallway and using her foot to block the door from closing behind her.

"I'm a friend of his. Do you know him or don't you?

"A guy like Strauss has no friends. You one of his broads or something?"

"Maybe so. All you need to know is I need to find him. Have you seen him around?"

He shook his head, assessing her. "No way. You got too much class for a clown like that guy. Tell me why you're looking for him and I'll decide—"

He stopped short and took a step back, a nervous expression settling on his bristled face. "Wait a minute," he said, shaking his head. "You're that bootlegger broad." He took another step away. "Damn, I should have kept my mouth shut."

"It's too late for that, isn't it?" She leaned forward and put her face right into his, careful not to inhale. "So where is he?"

"Beats me. It's been over two years since I seen the guy."

She jabbed a finger into his gut. He winced, but made no move to retaliate. "What's your name?"

"Eddie? Why?"

"Well, that's real strange Eddie, because I was talking to a waitress at the diner around the corner and she said she'd seen a two bit sleazebag who looked just like you in there not two weeks ago. And the funny thing is, this punk in her coffee shop wouldn't shut up about another guy named Strauss and how pissed off he was at him. Sound familiar to you?"

She straightened and looked him in the eye. "You'd better tell me, Eddie, because if you know anything about me, you probably know I can make life real hard on you. You're not going to make me do that, are you?"

"Jesus, lady, I'm sorry. I hadn't seen him in a while, just like I told you. Then he shows up a few weeks ago, says he needs a place to stay for a night and he's calling in a favor. I don't owe that guy nothing, so I told him to get lost. That's when he hit me."

Eddie lifted his undershirt high enough to reveal the remnants of an ugly bruise on the upper left side of his abdomen. "I think the fucker broke a rib. That's why I didn't wanna say nothing."

Virginia shook her head and let out a long sigh. "Did he say where he might be headed?"

"Just that he needed to get out of town the next day. I know he's got some people in Detroit and Chicago, though."

"People, huh?" she said. "How do you know that, Eddie?"

"He was always bragging about his so-called business associates. You know, like he's connected to important people or something."

"Did he mention any names?"

"Sorry, lady. If he did, I sure don't remember." He looked her up and down. "And if he'd mentioned you, I would have."

She considered him for a minute. Instinct was what she lived on, and her instincts told her Eddie was telling the truth.

"Tell you what," she said. "You seem like a decent guy, Eddie. Maybe you could be a sport and ask around. If he didn't stay with you he had to stay somewhere. Maybe it was in the neighborhood?"

"I don't know. This guy's trouble. And one thing I don't need in my life is any more trouble."

Virginia smiled. "Suppose I make it worth your while?"

He might not have gotten what he'd hoped she'd offer, but it took him less than two minutes and one tiny favor to secure a promise that he'd do his best and contact her at *Bacchanal* if he heard anything. Odds were he wouldn't, but it was worth the two bottles of gin she'd offered if he were successful. In the end he was more than happy to cooperate.

Chapter Nineteen

Erich called Laura three times the following week and invited her to dinner. It wasn't until the fourth call that she agreed to meet him at *Bacchanal*, thinking she'd feel more comfortable on her own turf. She decided it wouldn't do any harm to see him again and was certain he'd stay off the subject of Virginia.

She arrived at eight o'clock, half an hour before the time they'd set. John Barrymore and about half a dozen friends were singing "Bye Bye Blackbird" so loud the young singer couldn't be heard over the din.

With steak dinners at two dollars and fifty cents, washed down with Pol Rogers champagne at twenty dollars a bottle, it was almost guaranteed there'd be a line of Duesenbergs, Lincolns, Packards and Rolls Royces all parked in the porte cochere every night. Virginia had designed every inch of *Bacchanal*'s décor, from the oak paneling to the red linen tablecloths on each round oak table. Laura fiddled with the white rose in a crystal vase in the center of her table and glanced around.

One of the hostesses appeared at her table carrying a glass of champagne. "I love the feather in your headband," she said to Laura. "Your whole outfit is hot."

The black silk hoyden dress was a perfect background for a long strand of pearls and the imitation jewel-encrusted headband set in her blonde hair. The dress, a gift from Phillip, had hung in her closet for months with the tags still on it. She blushed when she realized the care she'd taken with her appearance tonight.

She blushed again when Erich arrived. He was an uncommonly handsome man, a tad over six feet, with eyes so blue she was afraid it might hurt her eyes to look into them for too long. He stopped at the table and gave her a long look, then settled into the chair across from her, never glancing anywhere but at her.

"You look incredible. The most beautiful woman here."

"You sure? Have you checked out the hostesses?"

He snorted. "Could their chemises be any shorter?" He obediently watched one of the hostesses walk by. "Your legs are much nicer."

She cocked one eyebrow. "You should see them do the shimmy."

"W.C. Fields was up on stage with them a few weeks ago."

"Hate to see him in gold chemise."

He chuckled and spread blue cheese on a piece of French bread, then signaled to the hostess, whose sole job was to sell roses at two dollars each. Laura shook her head when Erich asked what color rose she'd like, but he stopped the hostess before she could walk away.

"I have some new information I want to tell you," Laura said.

Erich held up one hand, asking Laura to wait. "Hey, I know the rules. No man is considered a gentleman unless he buys his lady a rose. Yellow? Pink?"

She blushed. "Yellow's my favorite. Don't you think it's more unique than pink or red?"

He placed the rose in front of her and set it in the crystal vase. "To keep it fresh while we're here," he said.

"Thank you. You are now officially a gentleman."

He nodded. "Now. What's your news?"

She leaned forward, her expression intent on his. "The police interviewed that family in Greenwich, Connecticut yesterday and found out some odd things about Madigan's wife. Like the fact that she liked to hide their little girl."

"You have the most beautiful green eyes I've ever seen. Like emeralds."

She frowned. "Thank you. But I want to tell you about this."

"I'm interested. Go ahead."

"Okay. Well, apparently she'd hide the little girl in the closet, the garage, or in the woods in back of the house. Once she was missing for six hours before they found her."

"Sounds like there's something wrong with Madigan's wife," said Erich. "Do the police consider her a suspect?"

"They haven't said anything about that to me, but they did some digging and discovered she'd worked for three other families and done the same thing with their children."

"It sounds like she has problems. But I doubt she's a kidnapper."

"How can you be certain? She may have a psychological problem with children. One little boy she hid almost died because he was outside in below freezing temperatures for almost twelve hours."

He leaned toward her. "Laura, I asked you out so I could help take your mind off things. You deserve some enjoyment."

"I appreciate that."

"Now. The last time we saw each other you mentioned you were writing a novel. I'd love to know what it's about."

She picked at the yellow rose. "I don't want to be one of those writers who thinks other people are interested in listening to them drone on about what they write."

"That could never happen to you. Besides, you're allowed. I asked."

She gave him a grudging half smile, unaccountably pleased that he'd asked. "Well, all right. It's about a nun who has to choose between the church and the man she loves. Doing so almost destroys her."

"A priest in my home town in Germany had a wife and two children," said Erich, refilling their glasses with champagne. "Even after his parishioners found out they wanted him to stay. Of course that was impossible."

"I'm hoping agents and editors won't find it too controversial," said Laura, "but I can't write about anything I don't feel passionate about."

"Of course not. Then it wouldn't be too interesting to read."

She smiled at him, feeling like she'd made a friend.

"How would you like to go sailing next weekend?"

She grinned. "It sounds like it could be fun."

"Let's dance," he said, and led her onto the floor.

In his arms Laura felt safe. She closed her eyes. He smelled fresh, as though he'd just taken a bath. The band was playing one of her favorite songs, "The Man I Love," and she found herself yielding to the skill and tenderness with which he led her. They were on the dance floor for two more dances before she realized the song had ended.

When they got back to the table, she took a pack of Pall Malls out of her purse and he lit her cigarette for her. She half turned in her chair so she was facing a couple who had been staring at them. As a result, they busied themselves looking anywhere but at Laura.

"Maybe they've seen my picture in the newspaper and wonder what I'm doing here with you."

"Maybe they think we drink gin out of flasks and dance the Charleston all night."

"I've done those things."

"I wish I'd been there with you. I wish - what's the matter, Laura?"

She'd been smiling and happy one minute, but a sprinkling of dust floating in the sunlight triggered an almost unbearable sense of guilt.

"I shouldn't be here. I can't go sailing either."

He put his hand on her arm. "Please, Laura, don't do this to yourself. I want to be there for you if you'll let me."

He suggested they have dinner someplace else. Somewhere they could hear each other without shouting. After a brief discussion, they agreed to go to Marta's, where they served some of the best Italian food in the city.

She smiled and picked her purse up off the chair. "Being with you does make me feel better."

"I'm glad. I plan to be there whenever you need me."

Chapter Twenty

A few days after her encounter with the dirty undershirt, Virginia drove to the Hell's Kitchen address of Rudy's other friend, Kevin Butler. The Butlers lived in the grimmest section of the city, on Thirty-eighth Street, just off Eleventh Avenue. The streets were lined with tenements, factories and rundown churches. Garbage cans overflowed.

Virginia checked the mailboxes in the hall for his apartment number, then knocked on the appropriate door. It creaked open a crack.

"Mr. Butler? I need to talk to you."

"I'm real puzzled about what you're doing here."

"I found your name among a friend's things and I need to find him. I'm hoping you know where he is."

A young girl came up from behind her and barged through the door. Virginia followed in her wake and stood in the entryway.

"I thought you were with your mother and the other kids," Kevin said to the little girl. "Why don't you go to the playground and see when they're coming home?"

"I want a snack first."

Virginia smiled at her. Something about the girl reminded her of Laura at the same age.

"This won't take long," Virginia assured Kevin. "I'm looking for Rudy Strauss." She tried to gauge Kevin Butler's reaction but saw none. "It's urgent that I find him."

He bent over the kitchen counter, spread peanut butter on a slice of Wonderbread and offered it to his daughter. Frowning a bit, he turned his gaze back to Virginia.

"Haven't heard Strauss's name in a long time. What's he got to do with you?"

"Has he been in touch with you?"

"Not since I decided to go straight and settle down."

"You're sure?"

"My wife would have my head if I had anything to do with the likes of him."

Virginia shook Kevin Butler's hand and left him eating a peanut butter and jelly sandwich with his daughter. Her instincts screamed that he was lying. But she had no way to prove it.

***

"A couple of hours ago a woman came home and found her husband and twelve-year-old daughter murdered," Daniel said.

Erich glanced up at his editor and shook his head. "The poor woman."

"I know, I know. It's terrible. See what you can find out. Go easy on her. The cops say she's in bad shape."

Erich's eyebrows rose with offense. "I'm a heartless reporter when it comes to criminals and politicians, not innocent victims."

After two hours with the woman, Erich returned to the newsroom and wrote the story for the evening edition. The numbing desperation of the poor woman and her children had gotten to him, and he could feel tension in his neck and shoulders as he turned the corner for home.

He was halfway up the cement steps when he heard a car door slam behind him, followed by the sound of someone breathing hard behind him. He turned around and looked into the face of an overweight man of about fifty-five, then past him to the Packard parked across the street. One of Virginia Kingsley's men? That was just fine. He'd be glad to talk to her. He'd love to tell her what he thought of her.

The man tried to grab his arm, but Erich yanked it away and strode over to the car without any prompting. He was about to knock on the back window when the door opened.

"Get in the car, Mr. Muller," Virginia said, then watched him slide in beside her. She smiled.

He met her gaze. "So?"

"I can see why my niece is interested in you."

"I'm glad to hear she is. Sometimes I'm not so sure. Is that why you hauled me in here? To check me out?"

She looked down her nose at him, as if she were bored. "Stop writing lies about me. I told you the other day I'd sue the newspaper if you continued, yet this morning another story ran, filled with inaccuracies."

"What article are you talking about?"

She frowned. "The one on the front page."

"Never write anything not based on fact."

She crossed her long legs and continued to stare at him. "That may have been true in the past, but now you've sunk to the level of yellow journalism."

"What was in that article that you think I made up?"

"Seeing me at the kidnapper's hideout and deciding I know something about Todd's kidnapping." She took out a cigarette. "You're wrong about that."

"Prove it."

"I can't."

"Then my story stands as is."

"Don't make this more difficult than need be. I can't lie to you and say I wasn't there. But I wasn't there for the reason you think."

"Laura knows you were there."

Virginia punched the back of the driver's seat. "You talked to her about it?" Virginia asked.

"What difference does that make?" Erich said. "She deserves to know the truth."

"I've always been there to take care of Laura," Virginia objected.

Erich opened the car door. "She's stronger than you think," he said, climbing out and looking back over his shoulder at her. "In time she'll find out you know something about her son's kidnapping, and she'll realize you've been keeping it from her."

"You've made a big mistake, Mr. Muller. I want you to leave her alone, or I swear I'll teach you a lesson you'll never forget."

"I hope for Laura's sake I'm wrong. What I really hope it you haven't made a much bigger mistake."

Chapter Twenty-One

The following Saturday evening, Erich and Laura went to see *All Quiet on the Western Front* at the Rialto Theatre. Afterwards they strolled down the moonlit Manhattan streets to Erich's car.

He was quiet, but it was a comfortable quiet. She gazed up at him. "What are you thinking about?"

Erich put his arm around her and she thought it felt like the most natural thing in the world. "Well, I was thinking about how well the movie portrayed the worst time of my life, and here I am with you on one of the best nights of my life."

"You … went through all that?"

"I was sixteen when I wound up in the trenches of Verdun." He took a deep breath. "When I came home things were even worse. My brother had been killed … and … oh well, we survive all kinds of things."

She stopped walking and took his hand in hers, and he watched her, looking puzzled. His hands were long and slender, with fingers her mother would have called piano fingers. They didn't look like the hands of a man who had seen the horrors of war. But she knew he was telling the truth. He'd never lied to her, unlike Phillip. Phillip lied all the time.

"I'm so sorry, Erich, so very sorry."

He ran his fingertips down the length of her face. "You don't have anything to be sorry about, *liebchen*."

"No, but, I just felt someone needed to say it."

He drew her face close to his and kissed her lightly on the lips. When he drew away they gazed into each other's eyes, savoring the moment, and something electric passed between them. Neither of them had to say a word. After a moment they turned and resumed their walk, this time hand in hand.

Laura didn't want the evening to end. "I have a vague memory of hearing my parents talk about the son of a friend of theirs who'd been killed in the war," she said.

The news had come Thanksgiving morning, 1915. Laura and her sister had been rehearsing a play about the first Thanksgiving, and their mother was watching. The phone rang and moments later their father came into the dining room with tears streaming down his cheeks. Their mother was on her feet immediately, taking him into her arms and comforting him the best she could.

When she'd gotten got older Laura had understood it was fitting her parents had died together. They were much too close to have spent any time apart.

"I tried to write about my experiences," he said, "but Remarque did a much better job than I ever could."

They continued down the street, her high heels clicking on the sidewalk. After a few steps Laura stopped and glanced around.

"What is it?"

"I think someone's following us."

He squeezed her hand. "Don't worry. It's just your imagination," Erich said.

"No, listen. Don't you hear that?"

He tried to distract her, telling her a rather risqué joke Peter had told him the day before, when they heard the screech of a car's tires and were caught in the glare of the car's headlights.

Erich grabbed for her hand, but it was too late. Three men jumped out of the car. One thug grabbed both his arms and even as he flailed at the other two with his legs and feet they were wrestling him to the ground. Laura tried to jerk one of them off Erich, but she was shoved onto the sidewalk. Before Erich could react, the same guy took hold of his ankles and the third pummeled him in the chest and face. He managed to get one arm free and swing at the man who'd gone after Laura, but he missed.

Laura jumped to her feet, trying desperately to think of some way to help. Her hands flew to her head and she removed the hatpin from her cream-colored cloche. She jammed the hatpin into the back of one of the assailants. He shuddered and clawed at his back, trying to remove it, but she'd pushed it all the way in and he couldn't grab hold of anything. He stumbled toward the curb and she felt a kind of wild elation when she saw the back of his shirt turning red.

After a fierce blow to the left side of Erich's head and a couple of kicks to his ribs, the three men made a mad dash to the black Cadillac and sped away before Laura could see more than the first letter of the license plate number.

She turned her attention to Erich, who lay unconscious and bleeding on the sidewalk. She sat next to him and cradled his head in her lap, gently cleaning his bloodied face with a handkerchief. She nodded when a man ran into a nearby store, signaling his intent to call the police. When Erich opened his eyes, she felt a rush of tenderness.

His voice was a whisper. "Did they hurt you?"

She shook her head. "I'm fine. Now don't talk. Save your strength." She clutched one of his hands, the one that didn't look too badly hurt. "A nice man just went to call for an ambulance."

Each time he tried to take a deep breath his face contorted in pain. Laura leaned forward and kissed his forehead, praying he'd be all right.

***

Waiting areas outside emergency rooms are not designed for comfort. Even though she'd only been there a couple of hours Laura was weak from exhaustion. She couldn't help thinking about the time she and her sister had held hands in the same kind of room while they waited for word on their parents' condition. Virginia had arrived at the hospital moments before the doctor told the girls their parents were dead.

Now she was here again, waiting. It was a terrible place to be. She glanced up quickly when the doctor called her name, then jumped to her feet.

"How is Erich?"

"He'll be all right," the doctor assured her.

He had suffered three broken ribs, a couple of broken bones in his hand, and a concussion. One of the ribs had just missed a lung. They had set his hand, and a couple of the lacerations on his forehead had needed stitches. She wanted to see him and was told he was groggy from painkillers, but had been asking to see her.

She wondered if he were asleep when she walked into the room. A sheet covered him up to his chin, and his swollen eyes were closed. Seeing him like this made her want to cry. His handsome face was purple with bruises. She slipped her hand under the sheet and covered his hand with hers. The moment he felt her there, his eyes blinked open.

"Oh, Erich. How do you feel? Are you in much pain?"

He tried to smile, but she could tell it was painful. "It still hurts like hell, but not as much as it did when I first got here. But I'm worried about you."

"Why be concerned about me? You're the one who was beaten up. I'm worried about *you*."

"Just be careful."

"What happened tonight could have had something to do with your investigation into Todd's kidnapping. After all, it obviously wasn't a mugging. They didn't take anything from you. Those bootleggers you were talking to earlier this evening may be responsible."

"Maybe." He sighed. "Let's talk about it some other time."

She frowned. It wasn't like him to avoid a conversation. "Are you keeping something from me, Erich?"

He closed his eyes and didn't move. For a moment she thought he might have passed out. Her heart picked up its pace.

"Erich?" Not knowing what else to do, she peeked out into the hall and yelled for the nurse.

"I'm okay, Laura," he said groggily. "I just need to rest. I'm very sleepy. Probably all the meds." He yawned. "The guy who held me down was driving the car the other night when I saw your aunt."

"You saw Virginia?"

A nurse came in to see if anything were wrong. She adjusted the transfusion apparatus while she was there. Erich waited until they were alone before he said anything more.

"She told me she'd teach me a lesson if I kept seeing you."

"She did *what?*"

"And I recognized one of the guys from when I saw Virginia the other night." His eyelids fluttered. "I can't stay awake, Laura. I'm sorry. Will I see you tomorrow?"

"Of course, Erich." She kissed him lightly on his cheek. "Sleep well."

Chapter Twenty-Two

She took a cab straight to Virginia's brownstone. She had never been so furious with her aunt. She tried to control her anger, but it threatened to overwhelm her. Every time she felt herself begin to relax, she thought of Erich and his bruised face. The fury inside her simmered even hotter.

This wasn't the first time her aunt had disapproved of someone she was dating, but it was the first time she'd tried to harm one of Laura's boyfriends. They'd argued about it in the past, and when Laura was younger Virginia sometimes got her way. But that hadn't happened in a long time. And it wasn't about to start. Laura intended to keep seeing Erich whether Virginia liked it or not.

The cab pulled up in front of the brownstone and she paid the driver, then stepped out onto West 77th Street and climbed her aunt's cement steps. Just before she tried the door, she heard the wail of an ambulance siren. It reminded her of how frightened she'd been on the way to the hospital earlier that night.

Laura stormed into the brownstone without knocking. A light was glowing in the kitchen, and the teakettle had just started to whistle. She barged into the room and glared at her aunt.

Virginia spun around to face her, her beautiful face twisted with a combination of welcome and concern. "Do you have news about Todd? Have the police—?" She held out her arms, but

Laura didn't move into them as she usually did. "What have you been doing?" she asked. "My goodness! You look exhausted."

"Exhausted? Yes, I suppose I am."

"I know what will help. I bought a new blend of cinnamon tea yesterday that tastes just like the one your mother liked so much. Would you like a cup?"

Laura stood without moving. "Three men beat Erich up tonight. You're responsible, aren't you?"

"That reporter?" Virginia turned and took two mugs from the cabinet, then looked back at Laura. "You do know how to attract good-looking men, Laura. But looks aren't everything." She lifted her chin a little higher. "I don't approve."

"He's in Lennox Hill Hospital in so much pain he can barely talk. He told me he recognized one of the men because he'd been with you when Erich saw you the other night. Is that true?"

"Is what true? And why would you think I had anything to do with what happened?"

Laura's anger reached the boiling point. "Don't take me for a fool. I'm talking about whether you saw Erich."

"He wanted to confront me."

"He told me you threatened to teach him a lesson if he kept seeing me." Laura's lips curled into a mocking half smile. "What happened to him tonight is a bit too much of a coincidence, don't you think?"

Virginia turned away and picked up the tea kettle, pouring tea into two mugs. "How do I know how many enemies he's made? He's a ruthless reporter who doesn't care who he hurts with his lies. Many people may be out to get him."

"That's a lie. He's a well-respected journalist."

Virginia set the tea kettle down and focused hard on her niece. "Laura, you know I'd never do anything to hurt you or anyone you care about. And I'd have to be blind not to see that you care about this man."

Laura shook her head. "There are two inescapable facts." She lifted one finger. "First of all, Erich was beaten up tonight by a guy Erich saw with you." A second finger joined the first. "Second, you had threatened him. Why shouldn't I believe you're responsible? It makes perfect sense to me."

"I'm telling you I didn't. I've never lied to you."

"Neither has Erich."

"You haven't known him that long."

Laura's green eyes softened. "That doesn't matter. I feel like I've always known him."

"I've always been there for you. I'd *never* do anything to hurt you," Virginia said irritably. She sat and sipped her tea. "I don't trust him, Laura. He could be using you to further his career."

"He isn't."

"How can you be so sure? You're too trusting."

"Don't change the subject. You haven't answered my question about Erich yet."

Virginia gave a half snort. "I've disapproved of some of your other boyfriends and never harmed any of them. Why should things be different now?"

"It is different this time because I love Erich. Do you hear me? I love him. I won't let you do anything to hurt him. Stay away from him."

"Laura, we're both telling the truth. I won't deny threatening him, and, though I'm sure you don't approve, I did it to make sure he knows that if he doesn't treat you right he'll answer to me. But I didn't have him beaten up. With all you've been through do you think I'd put you through that, too?"

"No, I honestly didn't think you would. At least I'd hoped you wouldn't. But it just seems like too much of a coincidence. I want to believe you," she said. "I do." She glared at her aunt, who sat quietly watching. "All right. Let's leave this for now. I'm tired. I'm going home to get some sleep."

She walked out without even looking at the cup of tea.

Chapter Twenty-Three

When Laura stepped outside the next afternoon, the weather had changed. Heavy, gray clouds now loomed overhead, and it had been so windy during the night the sidewalk was littered with leaves and twigs. She walked toward Fifth Avenue where she hailed a taxi to the hospital.

She unbuttoned her coat as she got off the elevator on the fourth floor and walked past the nurses' station to Erich's room, hesitating to stare at a closed door across from Erich's. Behind it she heard a woman sobbing, and almost cried herself. Only the loss of a loved one could cause that much pain. Laura knew that kind of pain. She had lost Todd; she had almost lost Erich.

Erich looked even worse this morning, covered with bruises and bandages. She handed him a box of chocolate-covered caramels and leaned in to kiss him. It was a gentle kiss, but more than a friendly peck. When she pulled away, he reached up and stroked her face with his left hand.

"You've never kissed me like that before. It's worth getting beaten up for."

"Don't say that."

"Well, all right. *Almost* worth it. You're better for me than any of this stuff," he said, gesturing at the hospital room. He patted the bed and she sat on the edge.

"I talked to Virginia last night," said Laura. "I don't think she had anything to do with what happened to you."

"I'd rather have another kiss than talk about your aunt."

Of course he would, but his attitude was frustrating. Laura wanted to explain. She wished he'd at least try to understand her feelings about Virginia.

For years Laura had been trying to convince people that Virginia's work life had nothing to do with her personal life. A friend had once asked her if she approved of what Virginia did for a living, and she hadn't been able to answer. She still wouldn't be able to if she were asked today, but she had always been able to separate the loving aunt from the other. Now it was getting more difficult.

"Well, I think you need to find out who's responsible," she said.

"I will, Laura."

"Did the doctor say when you could go home?"

"If I'm still alive in another week, the doctor will give me my walking papers. Unless I run away with the nurse before that."

She raised her eyebrows at him. "You'd better not."

"She's going to be disappointed." He winced as he tried to find a more comfortable position.

"Erich, I ..." She hesitated, suddenly shy. "Last night when I thought you might die, I realized how much I care about you." She avoided his eyes and played with the hem of the pillowcase instead. "I'm angry with myself and at you for the way I feel, but I can't do anything about it."

"I like the sound of that, except the angry part."

"How else can you expect me to feel? My son is missing and I have no business getting involved with a man." She got up and began buttoning her coat.

"Do you have to go already? I like to have you here so I know you're safe."

"I am safe. I'm just not sure how safe you are."

Chapter Twenty-Four

A couple of weeks later, Laura sat outside, holding the Willa Cather novel she was reading, *Death Comes for the Archbishop*. She glanced up when she heard Erich walking toward her. They'd spent almost every day together since he'd left the hospital and she looked forward to every moment they shared. He was like no man she'd ever met before.

"Oh, there you are." She stood up, book in hand. "I was starting to worry."

He smiled and reached for the small cloth satchel she held.

"Are you sure you should be carrying things? What did the doctor say?"

He looked at the bag with its delicate floral print and chuckled. "He said I'll live to be a hundred, and I can manage this pretty little thing." He took her hand. "Must be something going on around here, because I had a real problem finding a place to park. I hope you don't mind a bit of a walk."

"On such a beautiful day? How could I mind?"

She felt her optimism soar as she walked hand in hand with Erich, enjoying the perfect day. When they found Todd, how would he react to the new man in her life? He'd need his father, obviously, but Phillip hadn't needed Todd. A new film or a new woman had always been more important to Phillip. Erich could fill that void in her little boy's life.

Erich chatted happily as he walked beside her, filling her in on what he'd been doing. "I interviewed those two French aviators yesterday and they were as sick as dogs. On Thursday they stood in the rain for hours posing for photographers. If I start sneezing or coughing, send me home."

"If you say so. What was it like to interview them?"

"It was fine after we got an interpreter. They were so exhausted they fell asleep before it was over. I'm going to finish it on Monday."

"Phillip and I took several airplane rides last year. I love flying. Have you done it yet?"

"No."

"Oh, you must. The feeling of freedom is exhilarating. When I find the time, I'm going to take lessons and get my pilot's license. Phillip didn't want me to, but now that we're separated I'm going to do what I want to do."

On Tenth Street they discovered a dozen evangelists singing praises to God.

"Hallelujah, brother! Hallelujah, sister! Praise the Lord," one woman called, then stretched out her hand. "A contribution for Jesus?"

Laura reached into her purse and produced a dollar bill. Even after Laura gave her the money, the woman continued to stare at her and Erich.

"I feel like a fool," Laura said. "I hate that everyone knows what I look like."

As they crossed the street, hand in hand, a woman walking two poodles bumped into them. The woman was only interested in Laura, so Erich got no help freeing himself from one of the leashes, which had wrapped around his ankles.

"Laura Austin, you poor thing. I pray for that beautiful little boy of yours every night."

"How kind of you," she said, wishing she could escape the woman's attention. Her intention was well meant, but the woman was a complete stranger and Laura craved privacy. Phillip was the famous one.

Not all the streets in Manhattan were sunny. Further ahead they found a man selling apples. She took one and handed him a five dollar bill. Erich took another and gave him a dollar. The man thanked them with tears in his eyes. At the next corner two emaciated children in tattered clothes stood staring at passersby. Laura and Erich handed their apples to the children, and Laura folded several bills into the older child's hand. The two looked up at them with blank expressions.

Laura looked at Erich. "Something has to be done. I've always wanted to take in a couple of foster children, but my selfish husband wouldn't hear of it. Now I'd like to find a way to do it myself."

"I'll tell you this much. If this keeps up, Hoover can kiss the White House goodbye in a couple of years."

"I think you may be right about that."

"Things are going to get a lot worse before they get better."

They eventually arrived at Erich's parked car, then continued uptown in the green Buick. As they approached East 32nd Street, the sounds of construction made conversation difficult. At the corner, Erich stopped for a light and they craned their necks to get a better look at the city's latest skyscraper, the Empire State Building. The building rose incredibly high, looming over what had been farmland a hundred years before.

"Never seen anything like it," Erich said. "They say it will be a hundred and two stories high when it's finished."

"Look how high it is already. It's amazing to see how much progress they've made since I was here in March. If you think about it, it's just a pile of glass and steel. I hated it when the Flatiron Building when up, but at least it has some character."

The light turned green and off they went. Laura looked back at the monstrous buildings and wondered if construction would keep advancing toward Fifth Avenue till these new buildings replaced even the quirky intimacy of her beloved Village.

Seafood restaurants dotted City Island Avenue. Looking at them all filled Laura with nostalgia. "This reminds me of the little town in Maine just north of Bar Harbor where we spent our summers. We had a cottage on a lake."

"You and Austin?"

"No. Me, my parents and my sister." She thought of her parents and the summers the family had spent in Maine. They'd gone boating and swimming, and bought lobsters in Blue Hill from an old man named Seth whose eyes were about as blue as Erich's. She and Elaine never ate lobster because they didn't like the way they smelled. Phillip had been trying to get her to eat it for years with no luck.

"Has Austin ever been there?"

"Are you kidding? It's too rustic for him. No servants, you know. My sister and her husband still go every year for a couple of weeks." She looked away. "I'd planned to take Todd this summer."

He stopped for a light. "I don't think I've heard you mention your family before."

"My parents were killed when I was nine. Another car went through a stop sign and hit them head on."

He glanced quickly at her, then focused on the road ahead. "How sad they never got to see you grow up. I'm sure they would have been proud."

"Having Todd helped me understand what they felt for me and my sister. They would have been devastated by what's happened, so in a way I'm glad they aren't around." She inhaled deeply then let her breath out. "My sister and I were lucky Virginia took us in and gave us a home."

"She raised you?"

"Yes, and I'm sure it was difficult at first. She had no children of her own and wasn't used to having two young girls around."

"I guess she's been good to you."

They stopped at a diner and ate clam rolls, French fries and vanilla ice cream and laughed about how it could be called 'homemade' at a diner. After lunch they walked to Simpson's boatyard on Beach Street and Erich asked her to wait while he went inside to speak to the owner.

She stretched her legs out in the sun, watching a couple of ducks cross the road. When Erich and a balding middle-aged man emerged from a rusted out trailer, Erich pointed to a twenty-five foot cabin cruiser bobbing in the water, all white save for a thin line of azure blue around the hull.

"When can we take it out?" she heard him say.

"Half an hour."

They wandered the streets for a while, then turned the corner onto a tiny private beach.

"What do you think of this?"

She looked at him, his blue eyes searching hers, and she smiled, feeling more peaceful and tranquil than she had in ages. "It's wonderful."

"A few years ago I was looking for a place to fish and stumbled onto it by accident."

They held hands, walking along the water's edge until it was time to board the cabin cruiser.

Once they were in open water, Erich dropped anchor while Laura spread a blanket on deck. He lay on his side beside her, looking down at her, and it felt wonderful when he kissed her. She shivered when he pulled the top of her bathing suit down and caressed her breasts, but she felt warm and secure. He was a different kind of lover than Phillip. Her pleasure seemed as important to him as his own.

When the heat and the sun and their desire for each other became unbearable, they went below deck and showered, kissing passionately while water cascaded down their bodies. They took turns drying each other off, though she tried to hide her body with the towel at first. He took it from her.

"Don't. You're so lovely."

They collapsed onto the cabin bed and made love with a kind of intensity Laura didn't think existed. Afterwards they lay naked in each other's arms, and she traced the outline of his face with her fingertips, noticing the yellow remnants of a bruise under one eye. He picked individual strands of her hair and held them up to the light.

"I love your hair. It's like holding sunshine."

Something raced through her chest. "Oh, boy," she said. She was sure he felt her body stiffen, because he began gently stroking the tense muscles. She took another deep breath. "What am I doing here? Nobody's ever made me feel the way you do. I wish I could be sure I'm making the right decision."

"Shh. Stop worrying for once, Laura. I want to make you happy." He stroked her hair and she closed her eyes. "Just be happy."

She lay quietly, wishing the day would never end, waiting for the apprehension and worry to return, and finally drifting to sleep. When the sun filled the cabin with a rosy glow, she nudged Erich awake. Dusk was upon them, so he pulled in the anchor and they headed back to shore.

Chapter Twenty-Five

"Are you still planning to go ahead with that crazy scheme?" Daniel asked a few days later.

Erich ran his hands over the stubble on his cheeks and smiled, thinking of Laura. She complained his beard scratched and wanted him to shave, but she'd have to put up with it for a while. Unfortunately, he had no intention of telling her the reason why he was growing a beard.

"I'm meeting Bill McCoy in Montauk tomorrow night. If anyone can give me information, he's the one."

"Why the hell are you willing to risk your life for this?" Daniel asked. "If they find out you aren't who you say you are, your life won't be worth a dime."

While he'd been in the hospital recuperating from his injuries, Erich had decided to do something to find Todd. Something more substantial than reporting on the latest developments.

Since his initial interview with Laura and Phillip, he'd wondered if bootleggers might be responsible for the kidnapping. He hadn't said a word to Laura about his suspicions. He hadn't wanted to get her hopes up before he'd even begun to investigate. His first and only idea was to infiltrate the gang of bootleggers operating on the East End of Long Island. It took him weeks to come up with an idea and figure out the details. He knew it would be dangerous.

"The last guy they got suspicious of got three bullets in the head." Peter slammed the door behind him. "Dan, get him to stop. Tell him you'll fire him if he goes ahead with it."

"No. I told him I'd help him out this time, and I will." Dan turned to Erich. "But just this one time. If your work suffers one iota because of this, you're out on your rear. Understand?"

"Such gentle, caring friends. If I don't come in on Monday you'll know I'm a lousy actor."

"You're a fucking jackass," Peter snapped. "I asked around like you wanted. My brother-in-law and a neighbor are interested. They'll take a few bottles off your hands, but I won't have all the cash until next week."

"As long as you're sure they'll come through."

Daniel stood up. "Listen, Muller, be careful. Those guys don't fool around. If you even begin to suspect they don't believe you, get away from them."

***

The drive to Montauk took four hours. It was ten o'clock when Erich pulled his rental truck into the parking lot and entered the main office of the Malibu Motel.

"Just one night?" The woman curled her lip. "Most people stay longer than that."

"I'm here on business." He looked out the window. "It is beautiful out here, though. I'll be back."

She handed him a key. "Don't wait to make reservations. At this time of year we get booked up fast. You got lucky tonight."

He left the motel and walked toward the beach, which was dotted by boats. The bootleggers called the Long Island coastline 'Rum Row', and William McCoy, the man he was meeting, was the most notorious and successful rumrunner of all. Instead of selling watered-down liquor, he sold quality stuff at fair prices. Erich hoped he'd be straight with him, too. He watched the schooner ease to shore. The man he assumed was McCoy stood on deck, leaning against the mast with one hand.

"You must be the new guy," McCoy said. "Where did you say you were from?"

"Connecticut. Guilford, Connecticut, along the coast." He hoped he sounded convincing.

McCoy jumped off the boat. "Never heard of it."

"No? Well, you will. Lots of people up there want booze and don't want anyone to tell them they can't have it."

McCoy laughed. "Amen to that. I didn't catch your name."

"Kohl. Hans Kohl."

McCoy pointed to two small boxes. "The goods are over there. Gotta unload them by yourself. My guys don't like to waste time on the small stuff."

Erich picked up both boxes. "If business goes the way I expect it to, I'll need more the next time."

"You small time bootleggers are no match for guys like Schultz. You'll be lucky if he doesn't take you for a one-way ride."

"I heard some guys plan to lay low for a while because the cops are too damn noisy for their own good."

McCoy looked him up and down. "Whoever you heard that from was telling you a story."

Erich laughed. "Yeah, right."

Chapter Twenty-Six

Virginia had grown weary of all the revelry at *Bacchanal*. She slipped out and headed toward the couch in her office so she could take a nap. About an hour later someone opened the door to deposit the mail onto her desk. She woke up when the door opened but didn't open her eyes in time to see the visitor. She was glad whoever it was hadn't spoken, because he wouldn't have liked her response. It could have been Harry, and she really didn't want to see him. He'd already voiced his concern about her bad mood and the fact that she never wanted to join in on the fun anymore. He was right, and she knew it was bad for business, but she was too angry with Rudy to care about *Bacchanal*.

Unable to sleep, she sat at her desk, pushed the mail aside and stared at the front page of the *New York Daily News*. After a few moments she took a good look at the headline, **Police Find Few Clues in Double Homicide**. The photo of the victims was front and center, and Virginia stared in shock. The black and white faces of Kevin Butler and his daughter stared back at her. She turned to page three and started to read the article, gasping when she learned the murders had taken place on the same day she'd been to the Butler apartment.

The only conclusion she could think of was that Rudy had been hiding somewhere and heard everything they'd said. After she'd left he'd shot them to death. But then why hadn't Kevin given her some kind of sign to let her know something was wrong? Maybe Rudy hadn't been there. Maybe he had just seen her leave the building and guessed why she was there, then shot them.

Had Todd suffered the same fate as the Butlers? No. She couldn't let herself think that way. She had to find Rudy, but it wasn't going to be easy. She needed all the help she could get. For the rest of the evening she made a list of all the friends Rudy had told her about, then studied the list, hoping one of the names could give her a clue as to where he might be.

He'd mentioned Dan Molloy to her in passing. When she'd pressed him, he'd explained that Molloy was in Sing Sing serving a ten to fifteen year sentence for armed robbery.

Virginia slumped at her desk, already feeling defeated. If a chest cold hadn't sent him to a sickbed, Tony would have been at *Bacchanal* with her like he was on most nights, and she missed the attention he lavished on her. His phone must have rung a dozen times before he answered it.

"Were you sleeping, Tony?"

"Dead to the world. What's on your mind, beautiful?"

"I need information about an inmate at Sing Sing by the name of Dan Molloy."

"I'll get one of my men on it and get back to you."

"I'm on my way home now. Call me when you find out anything, no matter what time it is."

At 5:15 a.m. she picked up the phone in her bedroom suite.

"Molloy's served four years of a fifteen years sentence and is a model prisoner. A guy named Rudy Strauss fingered him. The cops knew Strauss was in on it too, but he testified for the prosecution and was given a suspended sentence. A crook and a snitch all rolled into one."

"When did this happen?"

"The robbery? February 1926. Why are you so interested in this, Virginia?"

"It wouldn't interest you," she said and hung up.

As soon as she got off the phone, Virginia decided to visit Molloy in jail. The next morning she drove to Ossining. After about an hour in Sing Sing's waiting room, Virginia followed a guard to another room and was ordered to strip. She was shocked.

Did they think she'd be dumb enough to hide a weapon on her body?

When the body search was done, she was taken back to the waiting room. Another hour passed before the same guard escorted her into the visitor's area and told her to sit behind a screen. A few minutes later the prisoner arrived, shackled and in handcuffs. It seemed excessive for a model prisoner who was in for grand larceny.

"Who the hell is she?" He looked at the guard. "Are you sure she's here to see me?"

The guard shrugged.

Virginia leaned forward. "You don't know me, Mr. Molloy, but there's someone we both ... Well, let's say the information I need could benefit both of us."

She couldn't tell him why she had to find Rudy, but he deserved some sort of explanation. She just wasn't sure what that would be.

He leaned back in his chair. "Don't know anybody. In here you got to watch your back every second."

This wasn't going to be easy. "I can imagine. The man I'm looking for is a friend of yours from the outside."

He threw back his head and laughed, then set cold, gray eyes on her face. She wondered if she could trust him. He'd been Rudy's friend, and Rudy was a talented liar. She had no idea if Molloy was as well, but she had no choice but to follow through with her plan.

"Think about it, Mr. Molloy."

He turned to the guard. "How about a smoke?"

The guard lit a cigarette and put it between his fingers.

Molloy inhaled, long and deep, then blew the smoke straight up. "I got so much time to think I'm damn sick of it. I don't want to think and I don't want to play games. What do you want?"

"What makes you think I want anything from you? Maybe I'm here to help you," she said, trying to sound convincing, though even she didn't believe that.

"Who are you, Santa Claus? Stop wasting my time. I got a beautiful woman waiting for me back in my cell."

"Rudy Strauss."

Molloy's lips tightened into a thin line and his eyes darkened. "That bastard. When I get out of here his good times will end."

"He was the trigger man, but you took the rap for him, didn't you?"

He narrowed his eyes. "He'd be dead if that was true."

"You're lying to me." She smiled. "I also know he's been looking for the big touch and not long ago he found it."

"Did he send you?"

"No one sends me anywhere. I came here to tell you Strauss is going to pay, and he's going to pay big time. I'll see to that." She looked him in the eye. "I hope that makes you happy."

"There's no such thing in here."

"I need to know if he's been in touch with you."

"What's in it for me besides happiness?"

"I have some influential friends. Just try to be patient."

Molloy tapped his fingers on the table, thinking, then he took another drag of his cigarette. "A friend of his wrote me with some bad news." He snickered. "Then again, maybe it's good news. One of Capone's thugs shot Strauss."

It couldn't be. If this were true, how would she find Todd?

Molloy continued. "Strauss had planned to go to Detroit to join the Purple Gang in their poker game. Guess he never made it."

"He's dead?"

"It's a sad story, ain't it?'

Fear slithered down her spine. "It could turn out to be a lot sadder than you could imagine."

Chapter Twenty-Seven

The card game had been going on for seven hours. A single lightbulb hung from the ceiling and two bottles of whiskey, one empty and one half full sat on the round, wooden table. Virginia thought it looked like a gangster movie set. She concentrated on not laughing.

The man to her right turned to her. "You in?"

"I'm up four hundred dollars. What do you think?" She looked at the cards in her hand and decided to stay in the game, even though she had nothing. Money meant nothing to her, and information about Rudy was worth whatever she lost.

She placed her hand facedown on the table and studied each man, wondering if any of them would tell her the truth. It was becoming clear that in the circles Rudy traveled, it would be difficult to find anyone to trust.

"I heard someone won big here last week," said Virginia.

"What rat you been talking to?" asked a guy the others called Rossi.

She sniffed with disdain. "I make it my business not to talk to rats. They carry all kinds of diseases." By the look on his face, she knew he hadn't understood a word she'd said. Virginia glared at him. "I know what I heard. Last week a new guy sat in on the game and lost thousands."

Rossi tossed his cards onto the table. "Game's over."

He motioned toward Virginia and she followed him into an adjoining room where a large man stood up and pointed a gun at her. Rossi dismissed the fat man with a casual wave of his hand.

"Bigboy would do anything for me, Virginia. Even kill someone. Now. It's time you tell me what you're up to."

"It's a shame I don't have a killing machine of my own." She smiled. "I need information about the guy who played here last week."

"There was no game last week."

She sighed. "Bullshit. This is a running poker game, four nights a week, and even if one of you dropped dead the others would play. You had another player last week and I want to know what he said and did."

"Why are you so interested in a boring poker game?"

"It couldn't have been boring to whoever won this guy's money."

"Can't help you."

"No? You know I'm going to find him, with or without your help. Remember, I never forget a favor."

She watched the thought sink in and decided it was time to let him know how important it was to her.

"He may know something about my nephew's kidnapping."

"That punk."

"Is your memory improving?"

"He was going to Houston to see about a horse. That's all I know."

She took the gun out of her handbag and aimed it at his chest. "You sure?"

"Jesus, Virginia. Put that thing away. You can ask the other guys and they'll tell you the same thing. He said he was going to Texas to bet on a horse he knew. Claimed it was a sure thing."

Rudy hadn't changed. A million dollars or ten million dollars, he'd never have enough.

***

The temperature in Houston, Texas was about a hundred and ten degrees, with a humidity that settled like a layer of wet towels. By the time she got to the racetrack, Virginia felt like she might pass out. The man in the front office brought her a glass of iced water and told her to sit down. Manhattan was hot, but Texas felt like hell.

Virginia drank the water and asked for another glass. "I called last week," she said.

"Mike's at the stables taking care of his new foal."

She finished the glass of water and stood up. "Thanks. That helped."

He took a sun hat from a hook by the door. "Here. This will help, too."

The man she'd come to see was feeding oats to a chestnut foal whose spindly legs looked as wobbly as she felt. She could tell by the way he was looking at the horse that he loved animals. Personally, she thought the thing stank.

"Beautiful thing, a newborn foal," he said.

"I'm not much for animals, but I can see what you mean."

And she accused other people of lying.

He took a brush and stroked the foal's mane. "Are you here about Strauss?"

"So you know him?"

Mike had lived in New Jersey until a few years earlier. He and Rudy had been good friends, even though Rudy was always borrowing money from him. Then one day Mike hit it big at the racetrack and bought a ranch in Texas.

"How do you know Strauss?" he asked.

"He did some work for me."

"Good thing you put that in the past tense. You're better off without him."

"You aren't telling me anything I don't already know. Is he still around here?"

He laughed. "No way. He got roughed up pretty bad."

"Roughed up? Someone told me he was dead."

"That wouldn't surprise me. He showed up here with some money. Don't know how he got a hold of so much, but he had it and wanted to show off, I guess. Paid me back some I'd pretty much forgotten he owed me. But a couple of guys who weren't as forgetful as I was followed him here from Detroit to collect what he owed them. With interest."

"How bad was it?"

"I'm not sure if he made it. He should have gone to the hospital, but he refused. Couldn't understand that."

"When did this happen?"

"Yesterday. I'm on my way to see him now. Do you want to come with me?"

She couldn't believe her luck. But her anticipation was held back by one thought: why hadn't Mike mentioned a child?

Chapter Twenty-Eight

Virginia followed Mike out of the stables and down a dirt path to his brand new Lincoln. He opened the door for her and she climbed in, winding her window all the way down. The people they passed seemed happy and had a spring in their steps, giving Virginia the impression Houston was an exciting place. If only it weren't so damn hot.

Mike made a right turn onto 27th Street and a left onto Avenue N and drove a mile until stopping in front of the Charles Adams House. He parked and they both stared up at the building.

"Pretty ritzy, isn't it?" he asked.

"That bum sure has come up in the world." She stepped out of the car and moved toward the door. "Come on. I'm kind of anxious to see him."

"So am I. And I can't wait to see the look on his face when he sees you." Mike chuckled as he opened the hotel door for her. "This should be interesting."

They approached the front desk and the clerk smiled. "Good day," he said.

"Hello. I hope you can help us. A friend of ours is staying in Suite 221, and I think he needs help. He wasn't feeling well yesterday," Virginia said, flashing her biggest doe eyes. "If you'll just give us a key to his room …"

The clerk frowned. "Why don't I call him and tell him you're here?"

"I tried calling him before I left my house and there was no answer," Virginia said. "We're both worried about him."

Mike took her arm and they walked toward the elevator. The clerk followed, rattling a key. When they arrived, he stuck the key in the lock of Suite 221 and turned it, but just before the door opened Virginia took a deep breath. This was a big moment. Not only was she about to confront Rudy, she was also about to learn what had happened to Todd. In a short time the little boy might be in her arms again. A swell of emotion went through her and she shivered. Mike looked at her but didn't say anything.

They stepped into the room and all three gasped. The place was in shambles. The bedspread was soaked with blood and ripped into pieces. The mattress had been dragged onto the floor and cut open, the stuffing strewn around the room. One of the bedside table lamps had been broken and lay next to the radiator. The other one had been smeared by a bloody handprint.

"I have to get the manager," the clerk said quickly and slipped out of the room.

"He looked scared to death," Mike commented.

They checked the bathroom. "Rudy's not here," said Virginia. "Damn!"

Mike shook his head. "I don't understand how he could have gotten out of here. They must have come back and finished the job."

She glanced at him, then opened the top dresser drawer to see if Rudy had left anything behind. She didn't find anything until she looked under the bed. There she saw the gleam of a gold card. She recognized it as one folks used to gain entrance to *Bacchanal* until she'd discontinued them at the end of last year. Had someone gotten word to Rudy that she was looking for him?

"Hey! There he is!" Mike cried, banging on the window while he struggled to open it. "He's getting into a taxi."

She spun around. "What? Stay here and keep trying to get his attention." She threw off her heels and dashed out of the room in her stocking feet. The cab had just pulled away when she got down to the lobby.

Mike met her at the front desk, carrying her shoes. The manager didn't look happy. "What do you know about the man in suite 221?" he demanded.

"He just left in a taxi," said Virginia. "I need to know where he's going."

The manager snapped. "Yeah? Well, I need to know who's going to pay his bill."

He pushed a stack of papers toward Virginia. She picked them up, inspected them, then tore them into pieces and flung them in the manager's face. "I don't give a damn who pays them. You can pay them for all I care." She turned to Mike. "We should have followed him in your car."

"I doubt that would have done much good. He took off pretty quick."

They left the building, ignoring the manager's ranting. He followed them outside, waving wildly at them, but Mike had already started the car. She couldn't have cared less about Rudy's hotel bill. She had other priorities.

There had been no sign of a child in that room.

Chapter Twenty-Nine

Phillip was sitting in his trailer trying to cool off, but perspiration dripped off his face. That morning the temperature had reached ninety-seven degrees in Washington D.C., making it the hottest May 26th in the city's history. Phillip was certain that by now it was over a hundred degrees. The bustling capital moved languidly amidst the waves of heat.

He removed his shirt and went back to reading the script, which had already gone through at least a dozen rewrites. It still needed work. The screenwriters he'd worked with on his last two films had no idea how to write good dialogue, and he'd rewritten many of his own lines. What disgusted him more than anything was the fact that this was only the second day of filming. He saw nothing but problems ahead until the filming was completed.

A couple of hours later Phillip received word that Louis B. Mayer wanted to see him. It didn't take him long to figure out why. Ever since Phillip had separated from Laura, Mayer had been warning him his philandering was getting out of hand. He'd told Phillip if the studio had to pay for one more abortion, they wouldn't renew his contract. Phillip hadn't paid attention to such foolishness. He had the right to live his life they way he chose. The studio also claimed his last three movies had lost money, which he didn't believe. He figured that was just a ploy to get him to behave. Women loved him. They dragged their husbands and boyfriend to all his movies. As far as he was concerned,

MGM owed him money, and when it came time to renew his contract he'd ask for twice as much as he was getting now.

Today's message from Mayer was curt and to the point: Phillip was to come to the old man's office during lunch break. No ifs, ands, or buts.

***

Phillip arrived ahead of schedule and waited half an hour before being called into the office. Old L.B. was nowhere in sight. All Phillip saw was some kid trying to look important.

"Mr. Austin, thank you for coming."

"I thought I'd see the man himself."

The upstart grinned. "Mr. Mayer is too busy to attend to minor details. That's what he hired me for."

Louis B. Mayer was busy counting his money. That's what this was all about. He was afraid one of his pictures might not make enough to keep his wife and mistress in diamonds. Phillip struggled between relief and irritation. If the old man hadn't come to the meeting himself, it couldn't be that important. But he hated to have to sit and listen to this kid.

"Let's get this out of the way so I can go back to learning my lines."

"I'm sorry, Mr. Austin. It's not quite that simple. Mr. Mayer is quite upset with you."

"Why?"

"The fact is, your reputation has gotten out of hand. Mr. Mayer says something has to be done about it."

"What are you talking about?"

The kid smiled blandly and held out his hands, palms up. "Too many allegations about you and this starlet," he said, lowering one palm then the other as if using a scale, "or that model. A few rumors can be squelched, but when they're in the dozens there isn't much we can do."

Phillip laughed companionably. "What would you do in my position? They throw themselves at me."

"This has to do with your fans, the people who go to your movies and pay for the opulent lifestyle to which you're accustomed." He opened the top desk drawer and took out a sheet of paper. "Your last two movies lost money."

He held out the sheet, and Phillip took it from him. "Numbers don't mean anything," Phillip spat. He tossed the paper onto the desk. "How do I know these haven't been tampered with? I'm still the biggest star in Hollywood."

"Not any longer. Your popularity has been dropping since you separated from your wife."

"What's Laura got to do with all this?"

"There was a lot of sympathy toward you when your son was first kidnapped, but that stopped when you and your wife didn't reconcile. There's a rumor some people may picket the opening of your next film."

"Bunch of crackpots."

"The public likes unblemished heroes, not ones who cheat on the young, beautiful mothers of their kidnapped children. They don't expect you to find your son by yourself, most of them anyway, but our information suggests they'd feel a whole lot better about you if you went back to his mother."

Phillip frowned at him. "So ... so I go back to Laura and everything's fine?"

He could think of worse things. Give the people what they want. Laura was beautiful and looked great on his arm, and though she pretended to be hurt by his affairs, he didn't think she cared much about what he did anymore. Besides, she had Erich Muller to keep her happy now. It could work out fine for both of them.

The young man pulled the papers back and tapped them into a neat stack. "That's about it. Otherwise we may have to release you from your contract after you fulfill the three picture deal you have with us."

Chapter Thirty

Laura and Erich were enjoying a spaghetti dinner at his apartment a few nights later, when she asked him if he would like to go with her to Washington, DC the following weekend.

"What's the occasion?" he asked.

She chuckled. "Occasion? Let's see. First off, I want to ask Phillip for a divorce. Other than that, well, I'd also like to see my sister. It's been months since I've spent any time with her."

"I'm in," Erich said.

Before they left, Laura called Phillip and told him she was going to be coming to visit her sister for a couple of days and she wanted to see him. When they spoke she noticed some hesitancy in his voice, but wouldn't be dissuaded.

When she and Erich arrived, they checked into the Jefferson Hotel. Not wanting to put it off any longer, Laura left immediately to see Phillip. An hour later she arrived on the set. Phillip was in the middle of a scene where he played a senator. He and the actress portraying his secretary were handling a phone call from the president.

Laura caught his eye but knew to keep out of the way. Even though she'd visited him on many sets over the years, she was always amazed by the number of people and the amount of time it took to film even a simple scene like this one. When they completed the scene he ushered her into his trailer. They sat side by side on a small sofa and though it wasn't even noon yet she could smell liquor on his breath. For several moments, they sat and stared at each other, not knowing what to say.

After a what seemed like an eternity to Laura, he broke the silence. "I'm not happy with that Detective Wilson and his haphazard investigation."

She shook her head. "Neither am I."

"I think we should hire a private investigator. What do you think?"

She was surprised at his enthusiasm. "Yes, definitely."

"Good. I'll take care of that."

They stared at their hands without speaking for a few minutes. Then he cleared his throat and started up again. "So. You're staying with your sister? How is she?"

"She's three months pregnant. She didn't tell me when she first found out, but Erich says she was probably just thinking of me and what happened to Todd."

Phillip frowned. "That reporter is with you? I didn't know you and he were that close."

She hadn't expected him to be jealous. "It happened suddenly."

He dropped ice into a glass and filled it with scotch. When he offered her a drink she shook her head. She didn't remember him drinking this early in the day. What was troubling him? Whatever it was, it made her uncomfortable. She couldn't wait to leave. Had it always been this way and she just hadn't noticed? The only connection they had to each other was Todd. Without him, they had nothing to say to each other.

"Would you like a cup of coffee?"

"No. I've already stayed longer than I meant to. I'm meeting Erich at Old Ebbitt Grill for lunch."

He raised an expressive eyebrow. "After what he wrote about Virginia, I never thought you'd have anything to do with him."

She swallowed hard and summoned all the courage she could muster. "I want a divorce. It's what's best for both of us."

"Not me."

That wasn't what she'd expected. She stared at him, mouth slightly open.

"I love you more than ever," Phillip declared. He took both her hands in his. "Muller can never understand what we've been through."

She was confused, and her frown said so. "I love Erich in a way I've never loved you."

"You'll fight about Virginia until it destroys what you feel for each other."

She stared at him, shaking her head. "I don't believe this, Phillip. How can you believe things will ever be right between you and me?"

His gaze was so intense she couldn't take her eyes off him. "I want to try. We were happy once, remember? It can be that way again. I know it can. We need to be together for Todd when he comes home."

"Don't say any more."

"Laura—"

"No more. I mean it." She got to her feet, shaking her head. Then she lied. "I'll think about it, okay?"

Chapter Thirty-One

The Pavilion Royale was one of the most popular speakeasies on Long Island, though Laura thought it lacked *Bacchanal*'s elegance. The clientele it attracted were a rowdy bunch, and they'd given the place a dangerous reputation. Laura and Erich were there was to see Louis Armstrong and his band perform, and they'd invited Peter Bergen and his wife, Dorothy, as their guests.

This was the second time the two couples had double-dated. They had a fair amount in common, and got along well. Peter and Dorothy had a little boy named David, who was six weeks older than Todd.

Like Virginia's place in Hampton Bays and Texas Guinan's in Jericho, the Pavilion Royale was packed every night. Competition was fierce, but in reality there was enough business for everyone.

"If your aunt finds out you were here, won't she be angry?" Peter asked.

"No. She's not like that." Laura laughed. "Besides, she doesn't run my life."

Two hostesses came to the table. One carried a basket filled with dolls dressed like French schoolgirls, and the other held a basket of fresh tulips. Erich asked Laura which she wanted. She and Dorothy looked at each other and giggled, then said they wanted both.

"Don't spend every dime I have tonight," Peter said. "We need to save."

"You? Save?" Erich laughed. "I find that hard to believe. Hang on a minute. Why are the two of you grinning like Cheshire cats?"

Peter took his wife's hand and beamed. "She's pregnant."

Erich shook his friend's hand. He got up and hugged Dorothy. "I knew something was up. Are you happy?"

"I guess we could have waited another year or two," Peter said, "but now that I've gotten used to the idea I can't wait. I'll have a soccer team one of these days."

"I hope this one's a girl," Dorothy said. She turned to Laura, her expression stricken. "I'm sorry, I shouldn't be so selfish."

"I'm fine," she said, but felt better when Erich took her hand under the table. "There's no reason for you to feel uncomfortable because I'm here. I'm happy for you both."

Laura got up and walked around the table and the two women embraced, then started crying. Dorothy drew back, wiping away tears. "Oh Laura. I'm sorry. I can't help it. It's just that I look at David and I think of—"

"No. You shouldn't do that," Laura said. "Your little boy is wonderful. Now there are two babies I have to look forward to: yours and my sister's."

"A little girl would be nice," Erich said, agreeing with Dorothy. He glanced at Laura. "Sometimes I wonder if I'll ever have children."

Laura turned away from him. "I wish you hadn't said that."

He shrugged, apparently not prepared to drop the subject. "I'm just saying it would be nice if you made up your mind about the divorce so we could get on with our lives."

Dorothy turned to Peter. "Let's go dance."

"But I—"

"Let's go dance," she insisted and dragged him away from the table.

Laura watched them go, then turned back to glare at Erich. "I can't believe you said that."

"Why not? You need to make up your mind."

"It's not an easy decision to make."

The hostess brought their drinks and appetizers to the table, then headed toward the next table. "I know it's not," said Erich, "though I can't understand why you're even considering going back to Austin after what you told me."

She picked up her drink and swirled it gently, staring into its contents. "Maybe I don't want to be with either one of you."

"Maybe not, I guess. I mean, compared to Austin, what do I have to offer you? Could you get used to living on a reporter's salary? And, of course, you and Austin have something else that ties you together. I think that's the reason you can't decide."

"I don't want to listen to any more of this."

"Fine." His attention focused on a man who'd come in and sat at a back table. "Hey, I'll be right back, okay?"

"What is it?"

"Sergeant Law."

Laura frowned. "Who's he?"

"One of my sources," Erich said. "I have to talk to him. I'll be right back."

***

The cop glanced furtively around when Erich sat next to him. He jerked his chin toward Laura, who was watching them from the other side of the noisy speakeasy. "I didn't know you were seeing her."

"Yeah, well, you don't know everything. What's up?"

The bartender placed a drink in front of Law, who nodded a quick thanks then frowned at Erich. "Two things came into the department today and I don't know what to make of either one of them." He glanced at Laura. "Christ, I wish you'd told me you'd be here with her."

"Don't worry about her. Do you have news about the kidnapping?"

"Yeah," Law said, still staring at Laura. "She sort of takes your breath away, doesn't she?"

"There's a lot more to her than her looks. Tell me what you've got."

"A child matching Todd Austin's description was seen in Maine. We're trying to pinpoint an exact location. We also got a tip that some bootlegging gang on the East End may be responsible."

"Anything to connect the sighting in Maine with the gang?"

"No."

"What about Virginia Kingsley?"

"We haven't come up with anything linking her to the crime. Her fingerprints weren't on any of the evidence."

"What about the fact that I saw her coming out of the farmhouse?"

"She's got good connections to the department and the victim is her nephew. We've got nothing to go on with her yet."

"Keep me posted."

Half an hour later, Louis Armstrong and his band took the stage and performed for more than two hours. Afterwards, the crowd in the speakeasy jumped to their feet, and Louis rewarded them with three encores.

After they'd left the stage, Laura pointed at a table in the corner. "See those two guys over there? One's from the Schultz mob. The other's from a gang in Detroit. They're rivals."

Erich smiled at her, looking impressed. "I thought you didn't know anything about gangsters."

She shrugged. "I know a little."

It didn't take long before the two gang leaders got into an argument. They shoved their table over and drinks slid to the floor with a crash. One punched the other and he stumbled backward across the room, knocking over tables and sending patrons scurrying for the door. The falling gangster landed at Laura's feet.

"Let's go," Peter said, tugging Dorothy behind him.

Erich couldn't take his eyes off the men. They were still going at it, rolling on the floor beside her pretty black shoes. Erich caught the gleam of a knife near her and jumped to his feet, lunging for it. Just as a third man was about to come at Erich, he was hit over the head with a chair by yet another gang member.

Peter grabbed Erich and dragged him outside. Laura and Dorothy had run out ahead of them and stood waiting on the sidewalk.

"Muller, are you nuts?" Peter demanded.

"I couldn't let them get near Laura."

Peter held out his arms in mock resignation, then rolled his eyes skyward. "He takes in stray kids and defends damsels in distress. What's next?"

"Leave him alone," Dorothy said. "I think it's sweet."

Laura laughed and took Erich's arm, sinking her nose into his jacket and enjoying his scent. Someday she would have to find out why people felt such a need to protect her.

Chapter Thirty-Two

Twenty years had passed since Virginia had called off her engagement to Paul O'Malley. At times she wondered what her life might have been like if she'd married him. But it would never have worked. Paul could never have reconciled himself to the fact that she was more ambitious and successful than he was.

"It's been a long time, Paul."

"Almost ten years. You look wonderful, Virginia." He smiled at her and she let herself enjoy the familiar twinkle in his eyes. "I've been reading a lot about you in the newspapers since the kidnapping. I bet you aren't too happy about that."

"It's terrible to be a suspect in my own nephew's kidnapping. The cops drive by here a few times a day looking for God knows what. They think I don't know what they're doing."

"How's Laura?"

"She's got a new boyfriend. He's a reporter who's convinced I had something to do with all this. I think he's using her. I've talked to her about it, but you know how headstrong Laura can be."

Paul glanced at his watch. "It's time we got going. Ready?"

He took her arm and they headed onto Central Park West, enjoying the cloudless sky. They walked toward Riverside Drive, and for a few moments the tapping of her high heels was the only sound they heard.

"Maybe you should talk to her some more," Paul suggested.

"I've tried, but I might as well have been talking to myself. And it's such a bad time for her. She's miserable without Todd."

He hailed a cab and they rode uptown to Yankee Stadium. It was good to get out and do something like this. Something out of her regular routine. With everything else going on, she sometimes felt like she might explode. She'd needed someone to talk to. Sometimes she wished she'd kept in closer touch with Paul, but the most difficult part of that was he had that annoying habit of always being honest with her. At times she couldn't handle that.

As they climbed the bleachers she turned and gave Paul a puzzled look. "What are we doing way up here? I have box seats behind the bleachers.

"I think we're better off here. We'll get some privacy in a public place. I wanted to talk to you about something that happened at one of Capone's hangouts."

She climbed the stairs ahead of him, calling out her question over her shoulder. "What's he up to now? Last time I saw him he tried to trick me out of a piece of my business."

O'Malley laughed. "Bet you were too smart for him. Nah. This is about another guy. Here. These are our seats."

When they were settled in, she tilted her head. "So? Go on. I never could read your mind."

"A guy from New York hit Chicago on the run. He went from one speak to another, buying drinks for everyone, trying to pick up any woman who would give him a second glance."

"Another Don Juan in Chicago. I've met dozens of them. What makes this guy different?"

"This nut bought from Capone's people *and* Torrio's people. You know what that can do."

She pursed her lips and gave a low whistle. "Start a war between the two gangs."

"He showed up at Capone's headquarters demanding to see him. When he was told he couldn't, he stormed into Scarface's office and started ranting about a machine he'd invented that would make more booze for less money."

Virginia laughed. Just the kind of stupid thing Rudy would do.

"Then he mentioned your name."

She stopped laughing. "What did he say about me?"

"Nothing that made any sense. But a guy spending money like it was going out of style and throwing your name around ... well, I thought you'd want to know about it."

"It might be something. You'll keep a lookout for me?"

"Always."

"Thanks." She kissed his cheek and sat back. "You know, it's kind of fun up here. Now where's that hot dog man? My treat."

Chapter Thirty-Three

Bill McCaffrey's first assignment for Erich was to make some deliveries to a few speakeasies on the east end of Long Island. Erich was as nervous as he was excited about talking to some of the speakeasy owners. He just had to remember to use the name Hans Kohl, which didn't roll naturally off his tongue. He felt bad about the excuse he'd given Laura about why he couldn't have dinner with her. He'd said he had an assignment he couldn't tell her about. That part was true, mostly.

The first speakeasy was in East Moriches, a pretty little town on the water. The owner, Otto Bayer, greeted him with a frown, but Erich thought it was probably because he'd never seen him before. Figuring he was also German, Erich laid his accent on thick. Bayer neither looked at him nor spoke to him, so he collected what he was owed and left.

His next stop was a popular speakeasy in Hampton Bays called The Canoe Place Inn. There were a few men and one woman at the bar, and he decided to have a beer and keep his eyes and ears open. He was trying to listen in on a conversation about Dutch Schultz, who had set up shop in Patchogue, when the front door to the place slammed open and two prohibition agents stormed inside, machine guns raised in the air.

"This is a raid! Everybody on the floor."

Erich shook his head. "Unbelievable," he muttered to himself. He'd heard these raids were often staged and wondered if Bill McCaffrey had something to do with this one. Could be the East End bootleggers were trying to find out what he was made of. He would play along. Not that he had much choice in the matter.

Within a few minutes the police had herded everyone into their van and taken them to the Hampton Bays police station. There they were fingerprinted and had mug shots taken. An hour after he walked into the Canoe Place Inn, Erich was sitting on a cot at the local jail like a common criminal.

As soon as the cops went through his personal belongings they'd find out he wasn't Hans Kohl. If the bootleggers found out, he'd be in danger. He had no idea how friendly the cops and the bootleggers were with each other, but he had heard stories.

"Guard, can you come here for a minute?"

A man sitting at a desk in the corner turned around. When Erich called him again he approached the cell.

"I need to make a phone call."

The guard laughed. "Who do you want to call?"

"My boss."

"Who's that, Dutch Schultz or Al Capone?" The guard laughed. "You'll pay a fine and be out of here by tomorrow morning. Relax."

Erich waved a dollar bill between the bars. "Just let me use the phone. It's important."

The guard slipped the bill from his fingers. "That's a pretty paltry bribe." With a sigh, Erich held out a five and the guard took that, too.

"Phone's on my desk. Two minutes, no more. I'll be timing you." Erich slipped out of the cell when it clanged open, then picked up the receiver from the guard's desk. He glanced up, meeting the bore of the guard's gun. The guard smiled patiently. "Go ahead."

Fortunately, Dan picked up the phone right away.

"I'm in the Hampton Bays jail," Erich muttered into the phone, out of the guard's earshot. "Drive out here as fast as you can and get me the hell out of here before my cover is broken."

"Jesus, Muller. You can get into more trouble than ten men. What the hell are you doing in jail?'

"I'll answer all your damn questions when you get here. Just do what I tell you."

"Are you on assignment? Don't remember anything happening out there."

"Don't ask so many questions. Just get out here before they find me floating in Long Island sound."

"I've got better things to do than save your ass."

"No, you don't. I'm your best reporter." He chuckled. "Oh, yeah. And bring cash. A fifty should do."

Chapter Thirty-Four

Police commissioner Tony Jaeger's phone call had shocked Virginia, and she'd packed in a hurry. It was mid-June and Tony was vacationing at his summer home in Cape Cod. He'd received word that a little boy matching Todd's description had been seen at the Draper Inn in Falmouth, Maine, along with a dark-haired woman in her mid-twenties.

Tony had begged Virginia to come to the Cape with him, but she had refused. She knew his mistress was up there too, and she had no interest in getting mixed up in all that. Besides, her priority was finding Todd. She tossed what she thought she might need into an overnight bag, wondering if she should call Laura. In the end she decided not to. No sense getting her hopes up before she knew anything for certain.

By the time she'd headed out of New Rochelle on Route 3, Virginia was positive someone was following her. It was a dark green Buick, never right behind her, but two or three cars back, sometimes in the same lane, and sometimes not. Where had she seen that car before? Once she slowed and tried to get a better look at the driver, but he pulled away before she could.

When she reached Bridgeport, Connecticut, she spotted the Buick parked outside a restaurant when she stopped for lunch. The driver was nowhere in sight. A few minutes later she spied Erich Muller leaning against the driver's door, eating a sandwich and drinking a soda.

She pulled out of the parking lot with him right behind her. When she stopped for gas he parked by the side of the road.

"I've had it," she muttered to herself. "That's enough."

The gas attendant looked confused. "Ma'am?"

"Not you. I'll be right back."

Muller's expression didn't change when she stuck her head through the open window of his passenger side window.

"Following me, Mr. Muller?"

"Why would I do that?"

"You've been tailing me since we left New York."

He shrugged innocently. "I'm on my way to visit my sister in New Hampshire."

"Bullshit. I'm surprised at you, Muller. By now you should know how dangerous it is to interfere with me."

"Trust me. I'm one of the few people who knows what you're capable of. But unless I'm breaking the law there's nothing you can do, is there?"

Just before four o'clock she pulled up in front of Tony's summer home. He greeted her with a kiss and a glass of wine and she disappeared from Erich's sight.

***

About forty-five minutes later, Erich watched them get into a Packard and pulled out behind them. Since Bridgeport, there didn't seem to be much point in trying to be inconspicuous. So he followed the car in plain view, staying there even though they were traveling inland instead of along the coast toward Portland.

After a couple of hours, they heading right onto a winding country road then turning onto a dirt road a few miles later. They made another right and pulled into the driveway of a New England colonial.

Erich parked and walked down the dirt road to a beach that was close enough to give him a good view of the house. A man and a woman came outside and headed down the road, followed by two school-aged boys. Another woman came out with Jaeger. He was holding a little blonde girl in his arms.

Where was Virginia?

He walked closer and watched the two boys splashing in the water. Jaeger put the little girl down and started toward him.

"Are you a peeping Tom? Show me some ID or you're under arrest."

Erich took out his driver's license. "What law have I broken, Commissioner Jaeger?"

"Trespassing, vagrancy, I'll come up with something." He studied Erich's driver's license. "So you know who I am. Your name's familiar. Where have I heard it before?"

"Where's your traveling companion?"

"Right over there." He grinned. "But that's not who you're looking for, is it?"

"Pretty slick. Virginia's well on her way to Portland by now, isn't she?"

Jaeger tried to grab Erich's arm as he walked away, but he didn't go after him.

The police commissioner and Virginia Kingsley. Very interesting. Just how close were they? Close enough to help her slip a tail. God knew how much more.

***

Draper's Inn was an eighteenth century Victorian house, situated off a well-traveled road and down a small embankment. Not the ideal place to hide the most famous kidnapped child in the world.

Virginia went into the office and rang the bell on the counter. She had to ring it two more times before a middle-aged woman emerged from a back room, rubbing the sleep from her eyes.

As she spoke, Virginia played noisily with a twenty-dollar bill between her fingers. "I'm looking for a man and a woman and a little boy about two years old."

The woman glanced from Virginia to the twenty, but shook her head. Virginia put the twenty down on the counter and slid it toward her.

"The child's blond, fair-skinned with curly hair," Virginia said. "The man's tall and dark haired. I'm not sure what the woman looks like."

The woman opened a file box, took out a card and handed it to her. "She's the only woman who's stayed here during the last few weeks with a child that young. No man, though."

Virginia studied the signature. Maggie Pierce. Round letters, neat and even. Then she looked at the date: 15/6/30. Europeans always put the date in front of the month. Even after living here for thirty years Virginia still found herself writing it that way at times. What did that mean? Was this just a mother and a child traveling, or had Rudy ditched them?

"When did she leave?"

"Around eleven o'clock last night."

"Did you see the little boy?"

"No. Told me she had a son and he needed a crib."

The woman reached for the card but Virginia pulled her hand away. "I must keep this."

"No, don't. My husband—"

"I'll make it easy for you." Virginia pushed the twenty dollar bill closer to her. "For your trouble. And a look at the room."

The woman stuffed the twenty into the pocket of her bathrobe and grabbed a key from the hook on the back wall. "Follow me."

They walked up a flight of stairs and the woman opened the second door on the right. "You can go in by yourself. I got stuff to do."

Virginia walked into the little white room and glanced around. The aroma of pine permeated the air. Centered on the wall facing the door was a double bed covered with a faded hand-stitched quilt. No crib. She searched the dresser and the night table and found nothing apart from a Bible. Nothing hid under the bed or dresser but dust.

There were a few unopened Band-Aids someone had left behind in the medicine chest, but nothing else. In the end, all she took away from crawling around on the bathroom floor were sore knees and an unpleasant odor that lingered in her nostrils long after she left.

Chapter Thirty-Five

    Ben Wilson was surprised to get a call from the warden at Sing Sing. He told Wilson an inmate named Dan Molloy had been asking to see him for weeks. The warden had ignored Molloy at first, but the inmate kept insisting it was important for Wilson to pay him a visit. Molloy refused to tell the warden why. He said he would tell them when Wilson arrived at the prison.
    At first Wilson refused to go, saying he wasn't interested in playing games with some two-bit con. He wanted Molloy to be be more specific about why he wanted to see him. Probably just wanted to squeal on someone on the outside so he could get his sentence reduced. The warden relayed the detective's message to Molloy, but the inmate insisted he didn't want any favors and refused to say any more.
    Detective Wilson finally relented. His meeting with Dan Molloy took place in the warden's office. When Molloy walked in, shackled and in handcuffs, Wilson was shocked by his gauntness. Something was wrong with the man.
    "If you need me, the guard stationed outside will know where I am," the warden said.
    He closed the door behind him, leaving Ben Wilson and Dan Molloy alone. Despite his thirty years on the force, Wilson was never comfortable around criminals.
    "You'd better not be wasting my time, Molloy."
    "Do I look like I have any time to waste?"

"No, but …"

"Doctor told me I'd be dead by this time next month. Cancer. I gotta tell you what I know now before it's too late."

Wilson looked him in the eye, suspicious. He was so jaded he couldn't even trust a dying convict. "Let's hear what you've got."

"The Austin kidnapping. Is that important enough for you?"

"What do you know about it?"

"I know who the kidnapper is."

Wilson saw the prisoner in a new light, but tried not to let his excitement show. If this were true, Wilson would solve the Austin kidnapping. One step at a time, he admonished himself. "Where did you get your information from?"

"A woman came to see me a couple of months ago. Just before I found out about the big C."

"Who was it?"

"You know who I'm talking about."

"No, I don't."

"Sure you do. Think about it."

It took a matter of seconds for him to realize who Dan Molloy was talking about. But was he telling the truth? He couldn't believe she was the kidnapper. No, it had to be someone else.

"Virginia Kingsley?"

Molloy just smiled.

***

A terrible thunderstorm knocked out power in Manhattan on the West Side the night before. By ten o'clock the next morning, when Wilson pulled up in front of *Bacchanal*, it still hadn't been restored. He wondered if anyone would be there and was surprised when a young man came to the door.

The detective pushed past him and headed for Virginia's office, but when he turned around the young man was still right behind him. Wilson ignored him and knocked on Virginia's door, waiting for her to respond.

"Let me in, Miss Kingsley. I'm not going away."

She flung the door open. "Wilson. Are you here to waste more of my time?"

He strode past her, into her office, and sat on the sofa. "I think you'll find what I have to say very interesting." They glared at each other. "Close the door," he said.

Virginia crossed her arms over her chest. "I should throw you the hell out of here."

"You know where that'll land you."

Harry Davis came to the door and she spoke privately with him. She patted his hand and he walked away, tossing Wilson a backward glance filled with warning as he went. A few minutes later Harry returned and sat in a chair right outside her door.

"Everyone sure is protective of you around here."

"Does that bother you?"

He smirked. "It's like you're one big, happy family."

"Tell me what you're doing here, Wilson. By any chance are you still investigating my nephew's kidnapping?"

"Sure am."

"You haven't told me why you're here." She chuckled. "A bit of socializing, perhaps?"

Wilson puffed on his cigar. "Is the name Dan Molloy familiar to you?"

"Nope."

"You never went to see him in Sing Sing?"

"That's right."

"Never told him you know who kidnapped Todd?"

She shook her head. "If I knew that I wouldn't be sitting here talking to you. I'd be out trying to find him."

"Been out of town a lot lately, haven't you?"

"Keeping tabs on me, Detective? I've always liked to travel. I'm not doing it any more now than I usually do."

Wilson scratched his chin, skeptical. "Why would Molloy lie about this? He has nothing to gain."

"How can you be sure of that?"

"I am. Let's just leave it at that."

Chapter Thirty-Six

It had taken time to become accustomed to using another name, but once she did, the transition from Nancy Evans to Maggie Pierce was much easier than anything else going on in her life.

In late July, she drove down a narrow road in Vandalia, Ohio with the radio on and the little boy sitting next to her, humming along with the music. He was such a good-natured child. Maggie was so tired of driving and being on the road. All she wanted to do was lay her head on a soft pillow and sleep for days.

While they idled at a stoplight, waiting for it to change, a couple of hobos shuffled into the street and knocked on her door. She waved them away. She didn't have a dime to spare. One of them stared in the window at the child beside her, looking puzzled. As soon as the light changed, she sped away. Everywhere she went, suspicious people watched her. She had to find a way to disguise the little boy's appearance.

Despite all the problems he presented, he was a delightful baby. He was sweet and loving, and she'd come to think of him as her own. He snuggled up to her while she read him a story or sang him a lullaby, and she realized even at his young age he understood her feelings. When he'd started calling her Mommy, it had filled her with love. She hoped he was young enough to forget he'd once had another mother.

At first, keeping food in their stomachs and a roof over their heads was almost impossible. She drove from town to town in upstate New York, searching for somewhere to go. Most of the time they lived in the car, which was hard on the child, and as a result he was cranky much of the time. She tried her best to comfort him, but most of the time he'd turn away from her and cry himself to sleep. Watching him broke her heart.

Occasionally she found a room for them where no one stared and they'd stay a few days, but never longer. Over time she began to wonder if anyone really was suspicious or if it was all her imagination. When she found an inn in Falmouth, Maine that she liked, she decided to look for work around there. But when she returned and was told a tall, dark-haired woman had been looking for her, she knew she couldn't let her guard down. They'd hit the road again and alternated living in the car with crashing in rooms in out-of-the-way places.

One morning they passed the border into Ohio and she knew she had to find a way for them to settle, at least temporarily. If she got a job and changed his appearance, no one would take much notice of either him or her. There was no way she could settle here for good because she had other plans, but in order for those plans to work out she needed to save some money.

When she reached Vandalia, Ohio, she knew it was the right place. Remembering the incident with the two hobos, she drove a short distance until she saw a sign for an employment agency. She parked the car and locked it, then went inside a brick building and was told to fill out an application. Less than ten minutes later a tiny woman in a dark blue dress called Maggie into her office.

"I'll take any job you have available."

The woman sniffed and shook her head as she looked over the papers in her file. "There isn't much. All I have right now is a job cleaning offices from seven-thirty in the evening until three in the morning."

Taking that job would mean the little boy would be alone for those hours and that frightened her. But what choice did she have? The money was almost gone. If she took this job, they might be able to stop running.

"I'll take it."

"Do you have any experience? You list experience as a salesgirl, not a cleaning woman."

"What woman doesn't know how to vacuum and dust and mop? I was seven years old when my mum got sick and I took over running the house until she got better, which wasn't for two years."

The woman nodded. "You can start tomorrow." She wrote an address on a piece of paper and handed it to Maggie. "You and another girl will be responsible for cleaning all twenty offices in this building. I wrote down the name of your supervisor and you are to report to her at six o'clock tomorrow evening."

Maggie beamed and extended her hand. "You have no idea what this means to me. Thank you."

She found rooms at Flay's Boarding House, which was within walking distance of her job. Their accommodations consisted of two rooms, a combination sitting room and kitchen, plus a large bedroom and full bath. The kitchen had a drop leaf table, hot plate and icebox. It suited her needs just fine. Apart from the nosiness of the owner, Mary Flay, she dared to hope her luck might be changing.

After a few days she settled into a routine. Even though she'd only slept a few hours, she forced herself to get up at seven in the morning and feed the child breakfast: cereal and fruit. Then she'd let him play until eleven o'clock, when she'd put him down for a nap and take one herself. At one in the afternoon they ate a big lunch, and afterwards she kept him as active as possible so he'd be ready for his bath, a quick dinner and bed by quarter to seven. By the time she left for work, he was always fast asleep.

One evening, just as she was leaving, she heard a knock on the door. Maggie didn't answer it in the hopes whoever it was would go away, but the knocking persisted. When she eventually opened the door to leave, she found Mary Flay standing there with her hands on her hips. Her expression was always haughty. That annoyed Maggie. Mary kind of reminded her of a stork, all skinny with legs almost up to her neck.

"On your way to work, Maggie?"

"Yes, and I'm late. I need to hurry."

Maggie headed down the stairs and Mary followed her. Another boarder, a middle-aged man, smiled at them and walked into the main sitting room where he joined some of the other boarders. They were playing checkers and listening to the radio.

"Maggie, I came upstairs to ask why you never join us for dinner and to insist you join us on Sunday. It's at six promptly and I'm serving lamb stew, everyone's favorite. Believe me, you won't be disappointed. Can I count on you?"

Mary was quite a busybody. Maggie didn't like people who thought everyone else's business was theirs. She also didn't like lamb stew. It made her think of some of the nauseating concoctions her mother had passed off as food.

"I eat early so I can shower and get ready for work."

"At least you can join us on the weekends."

Maggie closed the door behind her before Mary could get another word out.

Chapter Thirty-Seven

Erich was just tugging on his jacket, ready to leave for work, when he heard a ferocious knocking on his apartment door. He tugged the door open and found himself face to face with three men, all of whom he knew to be members of the gang of bootleggers he had been trying to infiltrate. He stood frozen for a moment, not knowing what to do. He was entirely aware they could just kill him right then and there.

The men pushed into the room and the youngest of the three kicked the door shut. The other two shoved Erich toward the sofa, and when he landed on it one of the men practically sat on top of him. In the next instant Erich flinched, feeling the cold pressure of a gun to his head. He squeezed his eyes shut and swallowed hard, certain he was about to die.

Then the pressure was gone. Erich's eyes popped open and slid to the right. The gun now sat patiently on the couch between him and the bootlegger.

"Hans Kohl or Erich Muller?" the bootlegger demanded.

Erich didn't answer, and the bootlegger sneered his displeasure. "Did you really think we wouldn't find out who you were?" The man chuckled. It was a low, nerve-wracking sound. "You know something? It just so happens who you are is gonna save your life."

Erich glanced up. The other two bootleggers were sitting at the kitchen table, drinking the coffee he'd just prepared. They were watching him and chuckling. He had never felt more inept in his whole life.

"I don't understand," he managed, hoping he hadn't said the wrong thing.

"You don't understand?" one of the men asked. He looked like the oldest of the three. He was stockier, with more gray around the temples. "Let's see if I can explain it to you. It would be so easy for us to take you for a one way ride and get things over with. Do you know what that means?"

Erich nodded, then realized he was no longer quite as frightened as he had been. Maybe it was because the three men who now surrounded him looked angry, but not murderous. Or maybe it was because the whole situation was nuts, just like Dan and Peter had said. Whatever the reason, Erich had to follow this thing through to the end. To do that, he couldn't show any fear.

"I've heard about those kinds of car rides. To be honest, I'd rather skip that," Erich said. "I really have to get to work so ..."

"You may be late," the bootlegger with the gun said. "But I got a feeling you'll come up with a good excuse. Remember what I said before about who you are being the one thing that saved your life? Well, here's the thing. You're also going to save your girlfriend's life and get the cops off our backs."

"Laura?" Erich asked, feeling suddenly sick. "Is she in danger?"

"She will be unless you do what we ask you to do."

Erich glanced from one bootlegger to the other, wondering whether he had ever seen any of them before. He had met others in Montauk and at the Canoe Place Inn, but no. These three hadn't been there.

"What do you want me to do?"

The man chuckled. "This isn't something we want you to do. This is something you *will* do."

"What if it's something I don't think is a good idea?"

This time all three men laughed. "You'll do it anyway. If you don't, well, it's sad to think of something so beautiful as dead. So sad."

A chill spread like ice through Erich's body. "What do I have to do?"

"We want you to get the cops off our trail. We didn't kidnap your girlfriend's kid, and you're a bigger fool than you seem if you think we did. We don't kidnap babies for ransom, and we ain't got no idea who did. We want you to put the heat on someone else. Virginia Kingsley would be a good choice. Everyone thinks she was involved anyway." The man narrowed his eyes and put his face right in Erich's so he couldn't avoid his hard stare. "So, Hans Erich, you have seventy-two hours to get the article in the paper and on the newsstands. If you don't, you won't get an opportunity to kiss your girlfriend goodbye."

When Erich walked into the newsroom of the Herald Tribune an hour later, he headed right into Daniel Spencer's office and told him everything that had happened.

"I told you you'd never get away with that crazy plan," Spencer said. "So did Bergen."

Erich glared at him. "Did you hear what I said? They threatened Laura. All I want to know is if they'll run the article. Well?"

Spencer tapped his pencil on the desk, thinking. "We can't run anything if you out and out say she's guilty. The best you can do is hint at it."

"What if that doesn't satisfy those bastards? They'll kill Laura. I have no doubt about that. And it'll be my fault." He slammed the back of one hand against his forehead and squeezed his eyes shut. "How the hell could I have been such an idiot?"

Spencer got up from his desk and gripped Erich's shoulder with one hand. "Just make sure you don't say she kidnapped the boy. You can say anything else you want, just not that. When you're done, bring it to me and we'll go over so it can be in tomorrow morning's edition."

Erich worked almost the entire day on the article. Every word had to be perfect. This was Laura's life on the line. He rewrote it a dozen times until he was convinced he had it just right, and even then he wasn't satisfied. When he was done, or as close to done as he'd ever be, he laid his work on Daniel Spencer's desk. Spencer stopped what he was doing, flicked one acknowledging eyebrow at Erich, then began to read.

"Did I go too far?" Erich asked.

Spencer shook his head, studying the paper. "No. Almost, but you skirted around things enough I don't think she can sue. However, I still think before we run this, you'd better get her side of the story."

"You know who we're dealing with. She's going to threaten us again."

"We can handle threats as long as she doesn't take any action."

Erich grabbed his jacket and laid it over one arm. "She might not want any more bad publicity, but Wilson's certain she knows something. I've been trying to think of a way to get her to talk. I guess this is it."

Twenty minutes later the door to *Bacchanal* was opened by a tall, distinguished-looking man who resembled a banker more than a hoodlum. Virginia Kingsley attracted all types of people.

The man extended his hand. "Good day, Mr. Muller. I'm Harry Davis. What can I do for you?"

Erich kept his hands at his sides. "I need a few minutes of her time."

"Not possible right now. She asked me to be of assistance to you."

"You're a lot more refined than most of the guys in her organization."

"And you're a lot less polite than most of the people who believe they need to see her." Despite his words, Harry smiled, and his manner continued to be mild and confident. "Now how may I help you?"

"Five minutes of her time, that's all."

"Mr. Muller, I dislike repeating myself."

"Suit yourself." Erich handed him a copy of the article. "This will be in the morning edition of the *Herald Tribune*. She has one hour to call if she has a problem with it. We go to press at six-thirty."

Harry scanned the article. "She isn't going to be too happy about this."

"Keeping Virginia Kingsley happy is your job, not mine."

***

By the time Erich arrived, Laura had dinner almost ready. He offered to help, but she'd already sliced the mushrooms and had the butcher cut the beef into strips for beef stroganoff, leaving him little to do.

When she went into the bedroom to freshen up he followed her. He took the hairbrush from her and began to brush her hair. "Your hair's like spun gold. So beautiful."

He put his lips to her neck and she closed he eyes but whispered, "Please don't." Their lovemaking filled her with such joy - and such guilt.

"How long has it been since we've seen each other?"

"It feels like forever."

They ate dinner and cleared the table together, and she washed while he dried. She enjoyed doing little things with him and knew he felt the same way. Phillip had never enjoyed little things like washing dishes. He'd said it was beneath him, and even after they'd separated he'd wanted to hire a maid for her. Every time he'd brought the subject up she'd cut him off because she knew he was trying to control her.

When Erich went to put something in the trash, he spotted an old bouquet of roses. "Where did those come from?"

She'd forgotten to put the flowers in the garbage can outside. *You're a damn fool*, she thought to herself. But she couldn't lie.

"They're from Phillip."

He scowled. "Why did he send them to you?"

"I'm not sure."

Erich hitched his hands on his hips, watching her closely. "He wants you back, doesn't he? And the fact that you didn't refuse the flowers makes me wonder if you're thinking of doing just that."

How could he think such a thing? She'd been very clear about how she felt about Phillip. And about him. "You know better than that."

He reached for her, but she stepped away and folded her arms across her chest. His expression barely changed, but he nodded slowly, coming to some conclusion. "Just a minute," he said, and headed outside. He went to his car and returned a few moments later, carrying a manila envelope which he placed on the table.

"I've avoided talking to you about your aunt because I didn't want to upset you. But this is too important not to mention."

Virginia? Why would Virginia's name come up now? Laura glared at him. "What now?"

He told her about what had happened when he'd trailed her to Maine, and all about the police commissioner's questionable involvement.

She shook her head defensively. "There isn't something sinister in everything Virginia does, you know. Why shouldn't she go to Maine? We have friends there."

"Laura, did you hear what I said? A child fitting Todd's description had been seen in at an inn in Falmouth, Maine. That's where she was going."

"Why wasn't I told?"

"Ask your aunt and the police commissioner."

"I will, but right now I'm asking you. You knew. You could have told me."

"I didn't want you to be disappointed again."

"Oh, sure." She tossed her napkin on the table. "You're more concerned about finding more dirt on Virginia."

His lips pulled tight and he shook his head, clearly irritated. He removed several sheets of paper from the manila envelope and handed them to her. "I wanted you to see this before it hits the newsstands tomorrow."

She read the article, feeling worse with every word. Why couldn't he stop? When she looked up at him, her vision was blurry with tears. "I thought you cared about me," she said.

"I do. I love you. You know that."

"I thought you no longer considered Virginia a suspect. I explained to you why it's impossible. I thought you understood."

"This is news, and I'm a reporter." His expression softened. She could tell he was having trouble seeing the hurt in her eyes. "Laura, I'd give anything for this not to have happened."

"Is it in this evening's edition?"

"No, tomorrow morning."

Laura got to her feet and gripped the back of her chair. "Virginia once stayed up all night with Todd. She rubbed him down with alcohol to prevent his fever from going above 105 so he wouldn't have convulsions. She would never do anything to hurt him."

"She knows something, Laura. I'm certain of it."

Her fingers hurt from squeezing so hard. "You know how much this hurts me. Why are you doing it? You wouldn't be doing this if you really loved me."

"I'm not trying to hurt you. I'm trying to help you. Why can't you see that?"

"Did you ask her where she was going?"

"Come on, Laura. Isn't it obvious? My source told me where she was going and he's always been straight with me."

She looked away from him so he couldn't see the tears in her eyes. "Maybe he wasn't this time."

"Eighteen years on the force, two years away from retirement and they cut him off without a dime," Erich said.

This was crazy. Why was he doing this? Laura sat back down and glared at Erich. "The N.Y.P.D. must have a reason for what they did. It seems unfair, but what do we really know?"

"Virginia Kingsley and the police commissioner did that to him. Why done you ask her what she's keeping from you?"

It was too much. Laura gritted her teeth, ignoring the tears rolling down her cheeks. "Why don't you ever stop?" she demanded. "What do you want from me?"

Erich's voice was soft, earnest. Almost pleading. "I want you to see the truth. Virginia knows something about Todd's kidnapping and she's keeping it from you."

"I trust Virginia." She refused to budge. "When we find Brian Madigan we'll find out what happened to Todd. You'll see."

"You and Austin are fooling yourselves. Madigan's a petty thief, but he had nothing to do with Todd's kidnapping."

She shook her head. "Talk about stubborn. You refuse to even consider that I might be right. Virginia is my aunt. I know her a lot better than you do."

They reached for the creamer at the same time and their fingers touched. She yanked her hand away, feeling her heart pound in the midst of all the confusion. Obviously, she had to stop seeing Erich. It would be a mistake for them to go on this way any longer. They didn't understand each other and probably never would.

"I'm tired. I would like you to leave when we finish our coffee."

"Okay. I'll pick you up at ten tomorrow morning."

"What for?"

"We're going sailing with Peter and Dorothy, remember?"

She'd forgotten all about that. It seemed strange to think of something like that when all this was going on. "I don't want to go. Apologize to them for me, will you? I'm sure the three of you will have a good time."

He blinked, looking as if she'd just slapped him. "They'll be disappointed."

She couldn't give in. It was important to be the strong one this time. She straightened her shoulders and shook her head. "There's nothing I can do about that." Her voice broke. "I don't think we should see each other for a while."

His cheeks flushed, his blue eyes practically sparked. "What? Were you lying a couple of hours ago when you told me you loved me?"

"I meant every word. But sometimes love isn't enough. You and I will never understand each other. I can see that now." She saw tears standing in his eyes, and it broke her heart, but she stayed strong.

The pain in his expression hardened and he got to his feet. "You're thinking of going back to him, aren't you? Is his money more important than I am?"

"What? After all the things we've talked about, how can you not know that money was one of the things that drove me *away* from Phillip?"

Erich grabbed his jacket and reached for the door. When he stood in the doorway he turned and glared at her. "Think hard about what you're doing, Laura. Remember how miserable you were with him."

The door slammed behind him and Laura stared at the spot where he had been. "And how happy I was with you."

She left the coffee things on the table, changed into her nightgown and cried herself to sleep.

Chapter Thirty-Eight

Laura was at her writing table, proofreading and making last minute changes to her novel, *Shattered Vows*, when she heard a knock on the door. When she opened it, she was handed a dozen long-stemmed yellow roses by a smiling delivery boy. After thanking him and giving him a ten cent tip, she closed the door and opened the card which accompanied the flowers.

My dear Laura,
The most beautiful flowers in the world for the most beautiful woman in the world.
Love always,
Phillip

For the past couple of weeks he'd been sending her a dozen roses every day. She knew she should ask him to stop, but hadn't bothered. It was his money, after all. Besides, fresh flowers always added happiness to a home, and God knew she needed some of that. She trimmed the roses and replaced the old bouquet with the new one.

When he'd first sent her roses she'd been angry. She didn't trust either him or his motives. However, when he called the next day, she sensed a change in him. Something more earnest, less showbiz. From that, she'd hoped they might manage to be civil to each other in the future.

She ignored the phone when it rang. She wasn't satisfied with a scene she was rewriting and didn't want to lose concentration. Later, when she came out of her writing daze, she realized the call could have been news about Todd, so she called Ben Wilson to make sure. He told her there had been no new developments.

Ten minutes later the phone rang again.

"Did you put the roses in the crystal vase we got as a wedding present?"

She smiled, glancing over at the bouquet. "They're beautiful, Phillip. But you can't keep sending them. I'll have to move if you do."

"Why not? If I send them often enough you might start to believe me when I tell you how much I love you."

She frowned and looked back at her writing. She had hoped he wasn't thinking that way. "It's a little late for that."

"I don't think so."

She sighed heavily, suddenly weary. "Phillip, we've been through this before. Things can never work out between us."

"Have dinner with me tonight. Give me a chance."

"I already have plans."

"I'll call you again in a few days." He cleared his throat, changing direction. "Oh Laura, I hired that private eye we talked about. You know I'll move heaven and earth to find our son."

"I hope you mean that."

Time wasn't easing Laura's anguish over Todd. She missed him more every day and was getting increasingly frustrated and angry at herself. Now, when she tried to remember something he'd said or done, the memory loomed just out of reach.

When they found him, whenever that day came, would he remember her?

***

Three days later Laura accepted Phillip's invitation to come to his apartment. She sat in a comfortable chair, her bare feet curled under her, and sipped the champagne he handed her, enjoying the bubbles as they tickled her nose.

It felt strange, being here. Even more strangely, being here with Phillip almost made her feel as if she were sneaking around Erich's back, which of course she wasn't. She hadn't seen Erich since she'd asked him to leave. Now she wasn't sure what to do. Everything was fine until she thought of him. Then the tears came. So she tried hard not to think of him.

"I like you much better here than when you're at Willow Pond," she said to Phillip.

Phillip nodded. "I'm glad I closed the place up last week. Without you and Todd I don't want to be there. Too many ghosts."

She held her glass between her hands, watching him. When she spoke her voice was sad. "We were happy when Todd was born."

He met her gaze. "It took what happened to him to make me realize how much I still love you."

She didn't believe him, but it felt good to talk about happier times. "Remember that tiny apartment we had in the Village? We were so happy and so in love."

He laughed. "And so broke."

"I didn't mind. It was exciting to see you blossom as an actor." She smiled. "I was so proud of you when you got your first part on Broadway."

"Then Hollywood discovered me and ruined our lives."

He grinned and she joined him, then nodded. "Yep, that's pretty much what happened."

From the table beside her, Laura picked up a photograph of Todd which had been taken a few days after his first birthday. How much had he changed over the four months since she'd last seen him?

Phillip took her other hand and she set the photo back on the table. "You must understand, Laura, that what's happened has changed me. I'm not the same man I was before he was kidnapped."

He was such a good liar, so convincing. Did he ever stop acting?

"You know, Phillip, I'll never understood why you needed all those other women. You never even gave us a chance."

He sat up straighter. "I've got something for you."

"No, Phillip, no more—"

Before she got the last word out he was already out of the room. She had objected when he'd bought her a new Rolls Royce. That didn't slow him down, and he'd shown up a few days later with a mink coat as well as a diamond and emerald necklace. A few days later he brought her the earrings that matched the necklace. Money meant nothing to him as long as he had it. It was funny that he thought she cared about that.

She looked around his apartment, thinking this place suited him better than Willow Pond ever had. Though enormous in comparison to most Manhattan apartments, and three times the size of hers on Patchin Place, it seemed more like a home than a showcase.

He returned carrying a large square wrapped in brown paper, and he set it against the wall. They sat on the floor together, and she tore at the paper. When she realized it was a portrait of Todd, she turned to Phillip with tears in her eyes.

He clapped his hands. "Finally! At last I've given you something you want."

"Yes. Oh, yes. Thank you, Phillip. You have no idea how much this means to me."

She tore the rest of the paper away and ran her fingertips over the rough oil paint that captured the sweetness of her son's face.

He smiled. "Seeing the look in your eyes is all the thanks I need."

"How were you able to have it done?"

"I gave an artist all the photographs I had of him. I think he did a fine job of capturing our son and that mischievous glint in his eyes." Phillip turned from the picture and faced her. "Have I made you happy?"

"Yes." She kissed his cheek. "This means so much to me."

He pulled her close and tried to kiss her with a little more intimacy, but she turned her face away.

"Have I done something to offend you?"

She held the laughter in, keeping her tone light. "I go to bed with you and that's it, right, Phillip? I forgive you all the other women and the lousy way you treated Todd and me? I'm sorry. I refuse to make it that easy for you."

His eyes held hers, their intensity a little too much. Like he'd over-rehearsed. "I won't pretend I don't want you back, Laura, because I do. Almost more than I've ever wanted anything. The only thing I want more is to get our boy back. I'll do anything to make that happen, spend every dime I have if necessary. I'd kill to get him back, do you know that?"

"Phillip!"

"Yes. I'd commit murder if I had to. I can't help thinking it's my fault he was kidnapped. I always had the deluded thought that I was more important than you and Todd because of my fame. But I was wrong. You and he were all that ever mattered. Come back to me, Laura, and I'll bring Todd home to you."

She stared at him, incredulous. All these theatrics just for her? Could she believe him? It was impossible to know. He was an actor, after all. She wanted to believe him. She really wanted to. It would be nice to have the old Phillip back, to bring Todd back to a whole family.

"I need time to think about it."

Chapter Thirty-Nine

On the September day that Todd turned two, Laura found herself missing him so much it was almost unbearable. She imagined he spoke in full sentences now and tried to remember what his voice sounded like. It was so unfair. Whoever had him was experiencing the joy of watching him grow and change, while she had been denied what was rightfully hers.

She rolled over in her maple double bed and blinked with surprise at the alarm clock. It was twenty to twelve; she couldn't believe she'd slept so late. She eased her feet into bedroom slippers and padded into the bathroom, hoping a good hot shower would wake her up. Unfortunately, when she'd finished she felt as lethargic as she had before. She pulled on a blue cotton skirt and white sweater, had a quick cup of coffee and half a cruller and headed outside for a walk.

It wasn't only Todd's disappearance that was tearing her up. It was Erich, too. When anyone mentioned him around her, she had to look away, force herself not to cry. She felt weak, as if with the two of them gone, all her support was gone. She'd lost them both: her baby and the man she loved, yet she was the one who felt lost. Nothing meant anything to her anymore, not even writing. Every time she sat at her typewriter she heard Erich's voice praising something she'd written, and she'd start to cry.

The Village was crowded on the weekends and this Saturday afternoon was no exception. She wandered down the street, pausing to look in shop windows or admire the artwork displayed on street corners. She ducked into B. Daltons, looking for a copy of Virginia Woolfe's *A Room Of One's Own*, but there were none in stock. The clerk told her they'd order one for her if she wanted. Instead, she bought a copy of *The Good Earth* that had just been released and was all the rage. A good book would get her mind off her troubles at least for a while.

On McDougal Street she stopped for iced coffee at an outdoor café. When she'd finished her drink she headed in the direction of Eighth Street, not knowing where she was going, just enjoying the fresh air and the chance to get her mind off things. She went into a couple of stores and was tempted to buy a new hat, then reminded herself she already had too many.

On the corner of Sixth Avenue she saw an intriguing dress shop, but was distracted by a sign hanging in the window of the store next door to it: *Tarot Card Reader and Advisor*. She had heard of tarot card readings and had once gone to a party with Phillip in California where a psychic had given free readings. It was all in fashion among the Hollywood set, but she wasn't convinced she believed in it. Still, it couldn't hurt …

She opened the door and stepped into a small room lit by candles and reeking of incense. A moment later a heavyset, middle-aged woman emerged from behind a red and gold patterned curtain. She looked at Laura, but didn't show any sign of having recognized her. That was good. It would be too easy for the woman to fake a reading if she knew who Laura was.

"Are you here for a reading?" she asked.

"I'm not sure," Laura admitted. She glanced back at the door as if she were looking for escape.

"You want the reading," the woman said decisively. "Sit down. I can help you."

Laura sat, smiling nervously. The woman sat across from her and shuffled a pack of oversized cards, observing Laura's expression as she did so.

"My name is Samara," she said gently. "The cards will reveal your life to you."

Laura frowned, but nodded, watching the woman's hands. She felt silly, but since she was there she figured she might as well see things through to the end. If this woman came up with anything concrete, Laura would be amazed. So far Samara still didn't seem to have recognized her, and she hoped that continued. She didn't want the woman to be influenced by anything she might have read.

Samara spread the cards in front of them like a fan. Two of the most visible cards were pictures of male figures. Laura thought of Todd and Erich and wondered if that were significant.

"Much has been lost to you," Samara said thoughtfully. "You are filled with sadness."

"People suffer loss all the time. You could be talking about anyone."

Samara nodded, a vague smile crossing her lips. "You are a woman who is not easily convinced and is not quick to trust. That is good. The man who owns your heart knows this as well as anyone. He sits alone and stares at your picture."

"What picture?" Laura asked.

"It was taken in some kind of restaurant. A tavern? There are others in the picture: a blonde woman who is with child and another man."

Laura swallowed hard, picturing the Pavilion Royale on that night, seeing again Dorothy and Peter as they announced Dorothy's pregnancy. She blinked, trying to think logically. This was all nonsense. Had to be. Samara sorted through a couple of cards and pointed at one in particular. What she said froze the blood in Laura's veins.

"The boy is somewhere in the deep south in a town that begins with the letter V."

"W-w-what boy?"

"Your son," she said, matter-of-fact. "At times he sees your face, but doesn't remember who you are. He cries, but he doesn't know why he's crying."

Laura couldn't stand anymore. With a sob she tossed a five dollar bill onto the table and bolted out the door, heading to the safety of home.

She went into her office looking for paper with which to make a shopping list, but ended up at her typewriter, writing much more than a list. It was a surprise to her, seeing her fingers fly. Since the kidnapping she'd had trouble getting started, but now the words poured out in a rush.

She began by describing the day she and Phillip met. She'd written more than five pages before she stopped and read her words. Should she turn it into an article and try to get it published? Probably not. She wasn't sure she wanted to share such an intimate part of her life with strangers. Everything that had happened during the first few weeks of her relationship with Phillip found its way onto the page. It was almost eleven o'clock at night when she finished. She had never felt either as tired or as exhilarated.

By the end of the week she'd written over fifty pages. It was too long for an article, and she couldn't think of what to do with it. Erich would know, but she couldn't bear to call and hear his voice. It would only make her miss him more. She wandered from room to room trying to decide what to do. When she finally gave in and dialed the *Herald Tribune*'s number, her hand shook.

"Erich?"

The silence on the other end didn't help. He finally spoke, his voice cool and impersonal. "Why are you calling me?"

"I need your advice on something I've written."

"That's why you're calling?" He laughed, sounding incredulous. "Publish it or throw it in the garbage. I don't care."

"Erich—"

"I can't talk now. I have to go over to City Hall. Mayor Walker is outlining his new plan to crack down on gangsters and bootleggers. Ironic, huh? Guess he knows your aunt pretty well, doesn't he?"

She hung up without saying goodbye.

***

Two nights later her phone rang. "The police have a lead," Phillip told her.

"What is it?" Laura asked, afraid to hope.

"Wilson just called. He said a little boy matching Todd's description was seen in Miami with a red-haired woman. I have a friend who'll fly us down there right away. I'll pick you up in a couple of minutes. Just stay where you are ... that is, if you want to come."

"If I want to come? Of course I'm coming. Oh God, Phillip do you think it's really him?"

"We'll have to wait and see."

"Do you think we'll need to stay overnight?"

"No idea. Pack a bag just in case."

Laura, Phillip and Wilson flew through a rainstorm, their plane bobbing and tumbling with the turbulence. Laura was oblivious to the pounding rain on her window. She spent the entire flight praying and imagining how it would feel to have Todd in her arms again. At two in the morning they landed on a Miami airstrip and waited over an hour for a taxi.

A huge grin spread over the driver's face when he got a look at Phillip and Laura climbing into his taxi. "Whoa. Wait until my wife hears about this."

"Oh, for Christ's sake," Ben Wilson said. "Take us to the Palm Breeze Tourist Court. And keep your eyes on the road, not the rearview mirror."

The driver didn't seem to mind the detective's gruffness, nor was he offended at being called an idiot every time he snuck a look in his mirror. Laura was relieved when they pulled up in front of the tourist court fifteen minutes later. By the time they woke up the manager, Laura felt physically ill with apprehension.

The manager shuffled in, his wiry grey hair mussed from sleep. "Do you people have any idea what time it is?"

"Since when is managing a place like this a nine to five job?" Wilson demanded, then flashed his badge. "We're here on police business."

The manager sighed, sounding resigned. "Now what did he do?"

"Who?" Laura asked.

"My grandson." He squinted at her, then glanced at Phillip. His eyes widened. "Say, aren't you ...?"

"Why the hell would we care about your grandson?" Wilson said. "We're here about some people who are staying here: a red-haired woman and a little blond boy."

"You've got the wrong place. There's nobody here. Business is so bad I'd sell this place if I could. The only guests we had here last week were two old men and three nuns."

"Not again," Laura said and sagged against Phillip. She buried her face in his shoulder and tried to hold in the tears.

Wilson frowned. "We got a call from someone at the Palm Breeze Tourist Court who said two people fitting those descriptions were staying here. This is the Palm Breeze Tourist Court, isn't it?"

"Yes, it is."

Wilson shoved a piece of paper into the manager's face. He wanted to know who'd called it in to the NYP.D. The manager excused himself and returned a few moments later with a sleepy-looking boy in tow. The boy couldn't have been more than ten years old.

"Tell them what you did, Sammy." He shoved the boy forward. "Go ahead and tell them."

"I was just fooling around. I thought it'd be a good joke."

"Do you know what these people have been through?" Wilson asked, shoving his bristled mug into the boy's face. "How would you like to spend some time in juvenile hall?" The kid bit his lip and Wilson turned toward Phillip. "Mr. Austin, you can press charges."

Laura cried softly into her hands. Phillip took her arm and shook his head, looking disgusted. "I just want to get out of here. I don't want to waste another minute in this place."

Chapter Forty

Almost overnight the heat was replaced by cool, crisp air, welcoming the early hint of fall. Fall was Laura's favorite time of year. For the next couple of weeks she managed to keep herself busy, taking a pottery class at a local community college. She decided in the spring she might take some literature courses.

Since that night when they'd double dated at The Pavilion Royale with Erich and Peter, she'd kept in touch with Dorothy and they'd had lunch together once. Dorothy was a tactful woman and never asked about Erich. Laura was grateful for that, though sometimes, in the back of her mind, she wondered if they ever heard from him. Did he miss her even a fraction of how much she missed him?

Walking became a way to keep sane. Laura walked all over the city, window shopping and picking up knick knacks for the apartment. One morning, as she came out of one cute little antique shop, she was forced to stop and grip the doorframe, overcome by a wave of dizziness. She sank onto the sidewalk, waiting for the spinning to stop, then hailed a cab back to the apartment.

She collapsed on her sofa when she arrived at the apartment, trying to figure out how she felt. A thought struck her and she got up to check the calendar, then felt another wave wash over her when she figured out what was going on. She headed back to the sofa and sat in shock for several minutes, then called the doctor's office for an appointment. She had to make sure before she panicked.

On the morning of her appointment, Laura sat nervously in the waiting room, clutching her purse to her chest. She followed a nurse into an exam room, where Laura sank into daydreams while she waited.

"The doctor will see you now, Mrs. Austin."

Laura's head jerked up and she stared up at the nurse, momentarily forgetting where she was. In her mind she'd been on the beach with Todd, watching him play with his pail and shovel. He'd fill the pail with sand, dump it out and start all over again.

"Dr. Johnston is waiting," the nurse said impatiently. "Exam room one."

Laura flushed and got to her feet. She wrapped the thin hospital gown around her and followed the nurse. "I - I'm sorry. I was just ..."

When the doctor had finished examining her, she sat up, fighting an odd sensation in her chest. She remembered so clearly the day this same doctor had told her she was pregnant with Todd.

"I hope you've been well, Laura."

She gave him a tremulous smile. "Thank you for writing to me about Todd," she said. "Those little anecdotes made him come alive."

She got dressed and waited in his office, pleating and re-pleating her skirt between her fingers. A few minutes later he joined her, his expression businesslike. She leaned forward, waiting for his answer.

"You're six weeks pregnant, Laura. The baby is due on May fifteen next year."

She leaned back in her chair with a whoosh of air, unsure of exactly how she felt. Pregnant? But ...

"Are you all right, Laura?"

She nodded briefly, then smiled as realization raced through her. Yes, she was all right. She was pregnant. With Erich's baby.

"I'll write you a prescription for prenatal vitamins and see you next month." He tapped his pencil on his prescription pad, thinking. "Did you have any problems with the vitamins when you were carrying ..."

"Todd," Laura offered, shaking her head slightly. "Don't be afraid to say his name. When I talk about him I feel closer to him. That's why I loved the stories you wrote about him in your notes. Remember the one about you trying to give him a shot and him trying to pull his diaper up?"

"He's an independent little guy."

"Probably even more now that he's entered the terrible twos. I try to imagine what he's like these days, but it's getting harder."

Doctor Johnston stood up and nodded, all efficiency again. "Well, now you're going to have another beautiful baby. Soon Todd will be home and you'll be a whole family again. Mr. Austin is a lucky man."

She said nothing. She couldn't tell him Phillip wasn't the father. A couple of minutes later she left the doctor's office and stepped onto the sidewalk. A man smiled at her and she smiled back, thinking he reminded her of her father. As she walked, she went through an exercise she'd been using lately. One feature at a time, she assembled Todd's likeness in her head, rebuilding his face so she wouldn't forget. Even so, he slipped farther away each day. Her greatest fear was one day he'd become nothing more than a faded daguerreotype of a little boy who had died a long time before.

When she got home, Laura sat at her kitchen table, sipping a glass of water and staring sightlessly out her window. She needed time to get used to the idea of a new baby. She also had to figure out what she was going to do. She wanted nothing more than to pick up the phone and share the news with Erich. He would be thrilled. This baby should bring them both so much joy.

But the situation was impossible. If she told him she was pregnant, he would come back to her in a heartbeat. That would fix nothing. Somehow she had to keep him from finding out.

She drew herself a bubble bath, hot enough that steam rose over the tub and fogged the mirror. She undressed and eased into the tub, squeezing in tight so she could be crowded by bubbles. At Willow Pond the tub was sunken and twice the size of this one. She missed the luxuriant space. Nevertheless, the lavender scented bubbles tickling her skin worked their magic and she relaxed a bit, letting the tensions of the day fade into the background. She closed her eyes, breathed in deeply and dreamed about the baby.

Would it be a boy? A boy who looked just like Erich? She smiled fondly, picturing Erich. He was so handsome. Then again, Todd hadn't looked at all like his father. Maybe this baby wouldn't either. What about a girl? Erich would love a daughter. A girl who looked like she did. Chuckling at the fantasy, she imagined boy and girl twins. *In this apartment? They'd never fit.*

Despite everything, Laura was happy about the baby. She just couldn't tell anyone yet. There would be questions to answer eventually, but for now they could wait. Laura sighed, thinking of her aunt. Virginia wouldn't be afraid to voice her opinion. She wouldn't want Laura to raise a child on her own, which Laura thought was ironic. Despite Virginia's lifestyle, she could be conventional when it came to certain things. This was one of them. It was almost unheard of for a single woman to have a child in 1930, then raise it on her own. The poor little thing would be marked a bastard. Laura didn't want that, either.

It had to be Laura's decision based on what she thought was best for herself and her children. Yes, she thought stubbornly, *children.* Todd *would* be home one day.

A few minutes after she got out of the tub, the phone rang. It was Phillip. He called almost every day now. As she wrapped a thick white towel around her hair, she couldn't help thinking he had the worst timing in the world. At this precise moment, Phillip was the last person she wanted to talk to.

"You took so long to answer I thought you weren't home," he said, sounding hurt.

She bit her tongue before saying something she'd regret. She wished he would stop calling her. "I was just getting out of the tub," she muttered.

"Really? In the afternoon? As I recall, you only take afternoon baths when you aren't feeling well. Are you all right?" he asked. She didn't say anything so he continued. "I'm not surprised you're worn out after everything that happened in

Miami. I wish I could have spared you that ordeal, Laura. I'm sorry."

For once she knew he was being honest. "I don't blame you for any of this, Phillip. Not anymore. When Todd was first kidnapped I did, but blame doesn't solve anything."

"Thank you, Laura. I appreciate you understanding. I'm waiting to hear from the private eye I hired. If he doesn't bring in something soon I'll fire him and hire someone else. Five months and only one false lead? Not a great record."

"Doesn't Detective Wilson have an appointment with Gabrielle Madigan's doctor next week?" Laura asked.

"Yes," Phillip said, sounding vaguely hopeful. "Maybe he'll be able to tell us something after that."

"We have to keep hoping."

Chapter Forty-One

The clatter of milk bottles interrupted Maggie's thoughts as she walked home from work. She watched the milkman climb back into his truck and chug down the street, then stop at another house and repeat the ritual.

The hours just after dawn were Maggie's favorite time of day. Despite her exhaustion, she always made certain she noticed nature's gifts: the sun rising over the horizon, the flowers in a neighbor's garden. Sometimes she'd pick a few violets or black-eyed susans and bring them home to set in a vase.

Things were going well. She'd been living in Vandalia for two months, but had heard winters in Ohio were frigid. She intended to be gone by then, and she'd saved over half the money she needed for the fare home.

She and the little boy enjoyed each other. She absolutely adored him. He had needed a name, so she decided on Andrew, or Andy, and he was beginning to respond to that name. On rare occasions he called her Mommy, but most of the time he didn't address her at all. He just stared with those pleading green eyes in much the same way he had from the beginning.

Yawning, Maggie climbed the front steps to the boarding house, craving her bed. But a light in the main sitting room surprised her. There was never a light on at 5:00 a.m. Maggie's heart plunged. Something must have happened. Concerned, she rushed in the front door and was met by Mary Flay, who had apparently been waiting for her.

Over Mary's shoulder, Maggie caught a flash of light hair, which she recognized as the top of Andrew's head.

"Oh hello, Maggie. Why didn't you tell me you had a child?" Mary asked, smiling sweetly.

Maggie trembled. She didn't want to have this conversation. "It wasn't any of your business."

"But dear, he was crying. He seemed so frightened, the poor little thing. I couldn't leave him there by himself, could I? That would have been crueler than old Mr. Simms from across town." She narrowed her eyes and glared at Maggie. "He was arrested for letting his dogs starve to death, you know." Mary set her fists on her hips, looking incredulous. "What on earth possessed you to do such a thing? Don't you know how dangerous it is to leave a child alone?"

Maggie sniffed, standing straighter. This woman had no right to question her. "I had no choice. I took every precaution."

Mary frowned and shook her head. "No choice? We always have choices, dear. All you had to do was ask for help. You're too proud, that's all."

Maggie pushed past her and scooped the little boy off the sofa. He opened his eyes and smiled at her. "This isn't your problem," Maggie muttered. "I'll have to figure out something else."

"He's a beautiful child," Mary said. "And so good. I fed him soup and he drank a little juice, then climbed onto the couch and fell asleep right where you found him."

"I'm glad he was no problem."

Mary followed her to the door. "Bring him to me tomorrow when you leave for work and I'll be happy to take care of him."

"Thank you for offering," Maggie said, and headed up to her second floor room. By the time she'd closed the door behind them, the child had woken all the way up and was whining. When she put him down, he toddled to the icebox and pulled the door open.

"What's the matter, Andrew?" she asked.

"I hungwy!"

"What would you like to eat?"

He clapped his hands. "Cookie."

"I'll get one for you straight away."

She opened the cookie tin that she kept on one of the shelves he couldn't reach, and handed him his favorite cookie: chocolate chip. Satisfied, he wandered into the living area, plunked onto the floor and began to play with his blocks.

She went into the bedroom, removed the two suitcases from under the bed and began packing. Something she had seen in Mary Flay's eyes tonight had disturbed Maggie, and she knew they couldn't stay. She was folding one of her blouses and laying it into the suitcase when Andrew arrived in the room. She couldn't help smiling at the mess of cookie crumbs smeared all over his face and hands.

"I'll have to clean you up before we leave."

He studied the clothes strewn on the bed, then looked searchingly at her. "Go bye-bye?"

"Yes, we are, my smart boy. Why don't you help Mommy and bring your toys in here."

"No."

His favorite word. He left and she went back to packing, her smile fading as she worked. By the time she had him cleaned up and everything in the suitcases, it was after six. She tiptoed downstairs, lifted everything into the trunk of the car and came back to get Andy, praying Mary Flay didn't hear anything. It was time to leave Vandalia, Ohio, and find somewhere new.

***

Two days later Detective Wilson had a meeting with Gabrielle Madigan's doctor. Afterwards, he called Laura and Phillip separately and asked them to come to the second precinct in Manhattan. The same place they'd taken Virginia after she was arrested.

Wilson was waiting for them at the precinct.

"Did you see the doctor?" Phillip asked.

The detective nodded briefly. "Let's go into another room and talk. It's not very private in here. Too much noise."

They followed him down the hall. This time they entered a room that was painted institutional gray instead of institutional green. Without some hint of color, Laura thought it must be a horrible place to work. The three of them pulled out chairs and sat at the old table, which had been dented and scratched from years of interrogations.

"What's going on?" Laura asked.

Wilson's lips pulled tight and he squinted at Laura and Phillip, as if deciding how to tell them something. "Gabrielle Madigan is schizophrenic," he declared.

Laura's hand went to her throat. "Is she dangerous?"

"You could say so. She tried to kill her little sister when she was five. When that happened, her parents brought her to Doctor Chandler. Two years later they committed her to the state hospital and moved away. They've had no contact with her since then."

"How old was her sister when she tried to kill her?"

"She was around two."

"Oh dear God. That can't be."

"Why isn't she still in there?" Phillip asked. "You would think someone so ill—"

"I asked the doctor the same thing. He said she was in voluntarily, which means she can sign herself out any time she wants."

Laura was aghast. "But she tried to kill her sister!"

"My hands are tied," Wilson said. "She's been in and out of the hospital over the years. The doctor said at times schizophrenics seem normal, and it was during one of those periods that she met and married Madigan."

"Did anyone warn this guy about what he was getting into?" Phillip asked.

Wilson shrugged.

"Does the doctor have any idea where they might be?"

"The last he heard, Madigan was working for you."

"Does he think she could have kidnapped my baby?" Laura asked.

Wilson couldn't answer yes or no. "It's been a long time since she was capable of doing such a thing, but her condition could have changed overnight."

"We have to find her."

"Doctor Chandler promised to contact me if he hears from either one of them. In the meantime, we've issued an APB in all forty-eight states.

Chapter Forty-Two

Originally, Virginia hadn't wanted Laura to have anything to do with Erich Muller. Now, whenever she saw her niece, she looked so miserable Virginia would do anything to bring them back together. She tried to speak with Laura about what was going on, but Laura always cut her off. One day she decided to give it another try. She picked up the phone and was pleased when Laura answered.

"Let's go for lunch," Virginia said. "You pick the restaurant."

"It doesn't make any difference to me," Laura said. "I'll go wherever you want."

"Marta's a nice place, and I know how much you like Italian food. It's not far from where you live, is it?"

"Not that place."

Virginia understood immediately. Laura must have been there with Erich Muller. "I'll find a place. Maybe you'd enjoy a good American cheeseburger and a malted milk? I bet you'd feel better after one of those. Remember how much you loved them when you were a little girl?"

"Hmm," Laura said. "I don't think I'm in the mood for anything so ... fattening. But a hamburger might be nice. Plain with no cheese. Don't they make dynamite hamburgers at *Bacchanal*? I could meet you there for dinner tomorrow night."

The tone of Laura's voice had Virginia feeling optimistic. "Sounds great. Cab Calloway is appearing there for the next three nights, so we'll have a great time."

When she got off the phone, Virginia wondered if it might be a good idea to call Erich Muller and suggest he meet them at *Bacchanal*. She knew she was interfering in her niece's life, and Laura had admonished her before about doing that, but she hated seeing her so unhappy.

She dialed the Herald Tribune's number, fully expecting Erich to refuse to speak with her. When she heard his voice she was taken slightly aback. "Thank you for taking my call, Mr. Muller."

"Well, well, well," he said, carrying more than a note of surprise in his voice. "What can I do for you, Miss Kingsley? Are you calling to see if I might write a retraction to the article?"

"No, no," Virginia said. "I'm sure you won't do any such thing. No. I'm calling about Laura."

She heard someone call his name in the background. When the caller persisted, she could tell by Erich's muffled voice that he'd put his hand over the phone. "Not now," she heard him say. He returned to Virginia. "What about Laura?" he asked.

"She's miserable. What happened between the two of you? I don't understand."

"If she's miserable it's her own fault," Erich said. "She won't see me and she won't speak to me. Whenever I call she hangs up on me, so I don't call anymore."

"I thought the two of you … Never mind. I want you to come to *Bacchanal* tomorrow night around nine. Laura and I should be finished dinner by then."

Erich laughed. "Are you trying to play matchmaker? It won't work. She doesn't want to have anything to do with me. Anyway, I thought you hated me. Thought you didn't want me anywhere near Laura."

"Hate is a strong word, Mr. Muller. Anyway, I'm not thinking of myself right now. I'm thinking of my niece. I've come around to thinking you might just be good for her. I don't necessarily approve of you, but right now I think she needs you. Do you still love her?"

His voice was a whisper. "Of course I do."

"See you tomorrow night," Virginia said.

***

All the usual characters were at *Bacchanal* the following night. Many of the women, including Laura, were wearing flapper attire, complete with jewel encrusted headbands. Others wore floor-length gowns in silk or satin. Some of the men were in tuxedos, while others wore their best suits. Every time Laura came to *Bacchanal* she was struck by how funny it was that people got so dressed up just to get drunk.

Harry Davis saw her first and waved her toward the bar. She settled into the chair he indicated and ordered a glass of wine. She intended to drink little tonight.

A man in a dark blue suit sat next to her and smiled suggestively. She looked at her drink.

"I haven't seen you here before," he said. She glanced at him, noticing with distaste how his eyes traveled over her body. "I would certainly remember you if I had."

Laura glanced at Harry and they both laughed. The two of them looked at the newcomer. "Is this the first time you've been here?" she asked.

"No, it's the second. What's your name?"

"My name is Laura. I'm Virginia Kingsley's niece. I want you to leave me alone."

Harry nodded approvingly.

The man sat straighter. "Hey. You're the one whose kid was kidnapped. Have you—"

Laura stood abruptly and went in search of her aunt. Virginia was in her office finishing the week's payroll. While Virginia worked, Laura wandered around the room looking at pictures of her parents on their wedding day.

"Were they really as happy as I think they were?" Laura asked.

Virginia glanced up from her desk. "They were happier and more in love than any couple I ever knew." She closed the checkbook and gazed at her niece.

"I like hearing you say that," Laura said. "Sometimes I get angry with myself because I can't remember them they way I'd like to. I try, but it's hard sometimes. Then I think of Todd and wonder if he'll remember me at all."

"I had the chef make your favorite meal tonight," Virginia said, changing topics.

"What's that?" Laura asked, a little afraid to ask. Morning sickness had plagued her during the morning, afternoon and even at night. She wasn't in the mood for eating anything and had brought a dozen crackers with her to ease the nausea.

"Lobster Newburgh," Virginia announced.

At the mere thought of the rich food, Laura's stomach rolled. "Actually, I'm not that hungry. How about a bowl of chicken soup?"

"Not tonight. Tonight we are going to celebrate and do our best to forget our problems." Virginia took her niece's face in her hands. "I know how much pain you're in, and I'm here for you."

"Nothing is going to help me. Nothing but time."

"Why?" Virginia asked. "I don't understand about you and Erich. He means so much to you and yet you refuse to see him. What happened?"

Laura breathed deeply, trying to stay calm. "Is that what this is about? Why can't you treat me like an adult and allow me to make my own decisions? Must you always have something to say about everything I do?"

"I want to be there when you need me," Virginia said.

"Right now what I need is to be on my own. I need to figure out my life."

Virginia led Laura to their table toward the back of the room, and the waiter brought their dinner to the table. Laura barely touched her meal, managing only to eat a bit of rice. Her aunt watched closely throughout. Laura saw the concern in her eyes and found that both touching and annoying.

When she was younger she hadn't minded Virginia's tendency to be overprotective. She behaved that way because she'd felt she had to protect her after Laura's parents died. Apparently some of those old feelings had returned after Todd had been kidnapped. But Laura felt strongly that if she didn't learn to handle her own problems now, she never would.

Being alone and pregnant would be the hardest problem she'd ever faced. She knew Erich would find out one day, but she couldn't deal with that now. She needed time to think about what would be best for all of them. She wanted Erich to be with her because he couldn't live without her, not because he felt trapped. Besides, they would have to find a solution to their problems before they could have any kind of life together.

Since they'd sat, not a word had passed between her and Virginia. Their dishes were removed from the table and replaced by a creamer, sugar bowl and two coffee cups.

"I'd rather have a cup of tea," Laura said.

"You've hardly eaten anything," Virginia said. "Aren't you feeling well?"

"I'm just not hungry."

Laura was stirring her tea when she sensed someone standing next to her. She turned to her left and gazed up into the bluest eyes she had ever seen. Erich. For just a moment she forgot herself and wanted nothing more than to leap to her feet and fall into his arms. Then she remembered. Being with him was no good. They loved each other, but it could never work.

How wonderful it was to see him, though. God, she'd missed him. It was like he'd taken a part of her when he'd left. She saw the love in his eyes and hated him for putting her through this. Why hadn't he stayed away like she'd asked? What was he doing here? She glanced at her aunt and saw the truth. Virginia was a good liar. She could lie to anyone but Laura. From the expression on Virginia's face, Laura could tell she had invited him.

Virginia had set this up and uprooted all the pain Laura had been trying to bury. She glared at her aunt, her eyes slits of rage. "How could you do this to me? Don't you know what I've been through?"

Virginia covered Laura's hand with hers, but Laura slid hers away and glared up at Erich. He stood without saying a word, his eyes filled with such longing it made her uncomfortable. She looked back at Virginia.

"I asked you not to interfere in my life and yet you continue to do so. How can I make you understand?" she asked Virginia, then shifted her gaze to Erich. "How can I make you *both* understand? I need to be by myself right now."

"If that's what you want," Erich said. Laura felt a warm current pass through her at the sound of his voice. "If it makes you happy. Are you happy, Laura?"

"I don't even know what 'happy' is. All I know is that this is the way things have to be right now."

Before she could move, Erich touched her face lightly with his fingertips, then turned and walked away. Laura was overwhelmed by confusion and almost burst into tears at the sight of his receding back. His touch had sealed it for her. She would never love anyone else. Someday, somehow, they would have to be together. Otherwise she would lose her mind.

Chapter Forty-Three

The hunt for Todd's kidnapper hit a snag toward the end of the year. New leads were rare, and the ones which came in made Detective Wilson laugh. First there was the woman who claimed to have dreamed about the kidnapping. Then there was the old man who brought in a picture of his grandson. He'd said it was Todd, and he was hiding in the woods somewhere in New Jersey.

It was frustrating. Wilson felt powerless. Laura Austin called every day, and every day he had to tell her the same thing: there were no leads but they were investigating every tidbit that came into the department, no matter how silly. Phillip Austin called too, though not as often. Maybe two or three times a week.

Virginia Kingsley never called. He knew she was in the middle of her own investigation and that her lover, Police Commissioner Jaeger, had sanctioned her activities. Wilson didn't approve, but he couldn't do anything about it. If she came up with the solution to the crime he wouldn't have a problem, except he doubted she would. Good old-fashioned police work would eventually solve the Austin kidnapping. He just hoped it didn't have a tragic ending.

He removed a soggy tuna sandwich from a brown paper bag in his desk drawer and tossed it into the garbage. The phone rang and he grudgingly picked it up, knowing it would be Laura Austin. Whenever he spoke to her he wished he had something tell her.

"I know," she said. "You don't have any news."

"I wish I did."

"I know you do," Laura said. She paused. "Maybe I have something for you."

That stopped him. "Do you have a lead? What is it?"

"Now, I know this sounds strange, but hear me out. I went to a psychic the other day and she told me ..."

His heart sank. He'd seen this so many times, desperate people hanging onto the last shred of hope. He had thought Laura Austin would be different. Sure, she was young, but she was smarter than a lot of people. Educated, too.

"Those people are charlatans, Mrs. Austin. They take advantage of people's misery. You can't pay any attention to them."

"Aren't you even going to listen to me?"

His voice was gentle. He might as well listen. He had nothing else to go on. These predictions were usually fairly entertaining. "Of course. Tell me what she told you."

"She said Todd was in southern state, in a town that begins with the letter V."

"Did she call him by name?"

"No, that's just it. I'm certain she didn't recognize me. If she had I wouldn't have paid any attention to what she told me because I'd figure she just read it in the newspaper. I got the feeling she lived in her own little world and didn't pay much attention to what went on outside of it."

"You could be right. Those people always sound crazy to me. Very little contact with reality."

"I can see you don't believe me," she said, sounding annoyed. "But look. She knew things I hadn't told her. Things she couldn't possibly know. She described a picture of me and some friends down to the smallest detail. She even knew my friend was pregnant, even though my friend herself barely knew. I'm begging you to look into this. See if a child matching Todd's description was seen down south recently. Please, Detective."

"I'll put one of my men on it tomorrow."

He heard a choked sob from the other end of the line. "Thank you."

***

She hung up the phone, relieved that at least he had listened to her, even if he hadn't taken her seriously. She wished she could go looking for Todd herself, but she didn't know where to start. If Erich were still a part of her life he would have been a help, but right now that was impossible. What had happened at *Bacchanal* had made things worse.

How could she explain to anyone that for the first time in her life she felt as if she had to finally make her own decisions? That was so important to her. All her life someone else had been in control of her life. First her parents, then Virginia, then Phillip. He was the worst of all, insisting on knowing everywhere she went and everyone she saw. Erich wasn't like that, but still. She needed this time to herself, though someday she would have to tell him about the baby. No. She didn't *have* to. That wasn't right. She *wanted* to.

She knew she was being selfish, not letting him know. This was Erich's child she was carrying. He had the right to share this pregnancy, to watch her belly grow, to share in the first flutter of life. She remembered feeling those first movements with Todd and how incredible they had been. No one had been there to share that with her either. Phillip had either been off on some movie set or with another woman. This time was different. This time the father of her child was the man she loved. So why was she doing this to them?

The truth was she was being stubborn. She wanted him to be with her because he wanted to, not because she was pregnant. It was going to be difficult to hide this pregnancy much longer. She would start showing soon. Then what? It wasn't just Erich she needed to worry about. How would she keep it from Virginia?

The phone rang and she picked it up reflexively. Erich. When she heard his voice tears welled up in her eyes.

"I want to see you," he said, his voice gruff. "We can't go on this way any longer. If I knew what I'd done to make you so angry I would fix it, but I don't."

"What do you mean you don't know? You accused Virginia of kidnapping my son. How could you even think such a thing might be true?"

"Laura," he said, sighing deeply. "Listen. The truth is, there's a lot of circumstantial evidence against her. It might not hold up in a court of law, but the police *should* be investigating her. The trouble is her relationship with the police commissioner has made that impossible. No one in the department will touch her."

"You know that for a fact?"

"If anyone even tried to investigate her, he'd answer to Commissioner Jaeger."

Laura fought back tears. She didn't believe him, but she didn't want him to know how much it hurt to hear his voice. It reminded her of how much she still loved him.

He changed topics. "Peter told me you and Dorothy have become good friends."

"Yes, she's a wonderful person. I enjoy her company." She didn't tell him that she had plans to meet Dorothy for lunch later that day.

After an awkward pause, Erich let out an exasperated breath. "Laura, why won't you see me? I can't believe what I said about your aunt has destroyed our relationship. That's not right. I won't believe it."

"Believe whatever you want," Laura snapped. She hung up the phone and burst into tears.

A couple of hours later, she walked down the steep flight of stairs leading to the *Village Vanguard*. The Vanguard had opened about six years earlier as a small theatre. Over the years it had gained a reputation for serving some of the best coffee and sandwiches in the city. She loved their taleggio cheese with heirloom tomatoes on a Kaiser roll. Laura was tremendously relieved to be at the end of her first trimester. She'd really missed eating.

During the evening the Vanguard often hosted up-and-coming singers, and the owners were gaining the reputation of discovering some amazing talent. When they were first married, she and Phillip had gone there, but he'd said everyone was too scruffy for his taste. Because of that, she didn't have to worry about seeing him there, which was a relief. He still called her a few times a week to talk about the investigation, but he had stopped asking her to come back to him.

She found a table and waved at Dorothy when she saw her by the door. It was the first time they'd seen each other in weeks. Dorothy was so far along in her pregnancy she looked as if she had a basketball in front of her. Laura grinned.

"Yes, I know," Dorothy said wryly. "And I still have two months before my due date. Peter swears I'm carrying twins."

Laura watched her friend squeeze into the seat.

"Don't you dare laugh at me, Laura Kingsley!"

"I'm not laughing. Really I'm not." *I'll be in the same boat pretty soon,* she thought. "What does the doctor say? Does he think it's twins?"

"No, he only hears one heartbeat. I didn't feel this way the first time, though. I'm constantly tired, my back hurts and I have no patience with either my husband or my son."

Laura wanted to commiserate but caught herself in time. "Peter should understand and try to help you as much as he can."

"You know how men are," Dorothy said, then paused and gazed at Laura. "Laura, Erich is miserable without you. He's a broken man. Don't you know how much he loves you? Peter and I are worried about him. Why won't you see him? Talk to him. If you do I just know the two of you can straighten things out."

"I can't. I'm not ready. He has to stop saying things about my aunt."

Dorothy glanced over the menu then put it down. "But what if he's right about her?"

"Oh no. Not you, too. I'm telling you he's wrong. I know her and I know she's no angel, but she'd never do anything to hurt either me or Todd. She loves us both too much. No. What it comes down to is Erich and I don't understand each other. I wish we did, but we don't. He refuses to see my point of view and I've already been married to one man like that. I won't make that mistake again."

Chapter Forty-Four

A few days before Easter, Virginia sat at her desk in the living room of her brownstone, finalizing plans for *Bacchanal*'s annual New Years Eve party. She glanced up when someone knocked on the door, but when she opened it, no one was there. They'd left an envelope in the mailbox, though. She stepped back inside and used her letter opener to slice it open and reveal a note. She'd received quite a few of these little anonymous nuggets recently.

Whoever had written it claimed to know who had kidnapped Todd and where he was. This time they'd included a lock of what they claimed was the little boy's hair. She doubted it was important, but she'd take it to the police so they could compare it to the lock Laura had. Then again, she didn't know why she should bother. The whole police investigation was little more than a farce. That inept detective, Ben Wilson, didn't have any idea what he was doing.

She hadn't seen her niece in nearly two months, and she missed her very much. Every time Virginia called, Laura didn't want to talk. If she suggested they get together for lunch or something, Laura came up with one excuse after another. Many of the excuses were so ridiculous Virginia wondered if Laura were trying to hide something from her. She'd made it very clear she didn't want to see her. Virginia had even gone unannounced to her apartment once, but Laura had refused to let her inside.

She'd had enough of Laura's nonsense. Whatever was going on, Virginia needed to know. She showered quickly, changed into black slacks and a white blouse and headed out to her Packard. The traffic was terrible. Forty-five minutes later she pulled up in front of 12 Patchin Place, pleased she had been able to find a parking space.

When she rang the doorbell, no one answered for several minutes. She waited, wondering if Laura were even home. Then the door opened, revealing a hugely pregnant Laura, who stared open-mouthed at her aunt. Suddenly everything fell into place. Especially Laura's reluctance to see her and Erich. She wondered briefly if the baby were Phillip's or Erich's but quickly dismissed the idea. It had to be Erich's.

Laura's lips were pursed tight, her brow drawn down in a furious scowl. "You should have respected my wishes."

"I couldn't, honey," she said, trying to disguise her shock. "I missed you too much. Let me come in?"

Grudgingly, Laura opened the door the rest of the way and let her inside. They headed into the living room and sat on the flowered chintz sofa. Virginia faced her niece, staring at her anguished profile. Laura stared straight ahead, studying a painting on the wall which her mother had commissioned when Laura and her sister were little girls.

"Laura, what's wrong? What's going on? Erich called me last week, you know. He wanted to know how you were. He's all torn up."

Laura glared at her. "Why can't you mind your own business?"

"Oh, Laura. This is so unlike you. Please talk to me. When's the baby due?"

Laura sighed and the armor holding her together melted away. "In a few weeks. Did you know tomorrow is the first anniversary of Todd's kidnapping? What do you expect from me? That everything should be just fine? Well, it's not. I'm terrified for this baby I'm carrying. I'm terrified that someday, when he's smiling and toddling around and loving me, he'll be kidnapped. What happens if he disappears, too?" Tears streamed down her cheeks. "I can't go through that again."

"Laura, come on. The likelihood of that happening is almost nonexistent."

"How can you be so sure? Oh, everything seems so wrong. I don't know what to do."

"That's because you've been trying to cope with everything all by yourself. Why don't you put your feet up? Get some rest. I'll fix us some lunch. What are you in the mood for?"

"Tomato soup and grilled cheese. It's what I crave all the time," Laura said, lying back on the couch.

Virginia covered Laura with a light blanket then went into the kitchen, chuckling to herself. It had been so long since she'd prepared a meal for anyone she didn't know if she'd be able to. But she managed to find the ingredients she needed. Before too long, soup simmered on the stove and sandwiches sizzled in the frying pan.

If she had known Laura was pregnant she would never have agreed to stay away. She was certain Erich never would have, either. That was a dilemma. Erich was about to unknowingly become a father. He had the right to know. But Virginia didn't want to go against Laura's wishes even though the way she was acting made no sense. Laura and Erich loved each other. They belonged together.

"Laura," she said, sitting beside her on the sofa. "What are your plans for the baby? Are you planning to keep it?"

Laura stared at her in shock. "What? Why would you even ask that? Of course I'm keeping the baby. Why wouldn't I?"

"Have you thought about how much trouble you're going to have raising a child as an unmarried woman?"

Laura frowned, looking puzzled. "A little. I wonder if it will affect the baby. That's what I should be worried about, isn't it?" Her frown hardened. "But I will absolutely not be forced into going back to Phillip."

"Laura. I can't believe this. How thickheaded can you be? Unless the baby is his, which we both know it isn't, the only consideration you should give Phillip is to ask him for a divorce. Is the baby Phillip's?"

Laura's silence gave Virginia the answer she'd expected. "Laura, I'm going to tell you something about myself that I've never told anyone. The only people who knew this story were my parents." She took a deep breath. "When I was sixteen I met a man who was ten years older than I was. We fell in love. Everything was fine until I discovered I was pregnant. Soon after that, I learned the man I loved was married."

Laura stared at her, not knowing what to say.

"My father, your grandfather, treated me like a pariah. He sent me away to one of those unwed mothers' homes. You know, the ones run by the cruelest nuns in the world. Anyway, after I gave birth to my son I ran away, determined to make a life for the two of us."

"Were you planning to raise him on your own?" Laura asked.

"Yes, but that was impossible."

"How can you compare your situation to mine? You were a child and I'm an adult," Laura said, sounding annoyed. "They are two completely different situations."

"No, they aren't. You'll suffer and so will the baby. Why do you want to do this to yourself and your baby when you have a man who loves you and who will love the baby? I had no choice. I had to give up my baby. It was the most difficult thing I've ever had to do."

"Virginia, I can't talk to Erich right now. And the baby isn't the reason."

"I don't understand."

Laura sighed deeply. "He believes you're behind Todd's kidnapping. I can't live with that. I don't think I'll ever be able to live with him thinking that way."

"What? That's why?" Virginia asked, incredulous. She shook her head. "No. I won't stand for you giving up your happiness for my sake. That's ridiculous. Call him right now. Tell him about the baby."

"I need time to think. I'm just not sure we're right for each other. And I won't make that mistake again." She got up and left the room, then returned moments later with an envelope which she placed in her aunt's hands. "It's the divorce papers. I signed them earlier and will mail them to the lawyer tomorrow. My divorce from Phillip is almost final."

Virginia grinned a little. "And how did that go? Did Phillip treat you well?"

Laura chuckled. "Very well. Better than I thought he would, actually. Let's see ... well, my favorite part is he let me have Willow Pond. He kept the ranch in California and the apartment in New York, but I never cared about either one of those places anyway."

"Are you happy he gave you Willow Pond?"

"I am. After we find Todd I'm going to take him back there. I know he was only a baby the last time he was there, but I hope he remembers the place somehow."

Virginia put her arm around Laura's shoulder. "I like how confident you are about finding him, how you refuse to give up."

"I'll never stop searching for him. My life won't be complete until I find him."

Chapter Forty-Five

Virginia sat on the edge of the bed and gazed down at the tiny baby nestled in Laura's arms, all pink and white. Her downy cap of flaxen hair had gathered all the early morning light in the room.

"She is beautiful," she said quietly. "Though I had little doubt she would be."

Laura smiled up at her aunt. "She is, isn't she? Thank you for being here for me, Virginia. It would have been so much harder if you hadn't been."

"Laura, Erich Muller has the right to know he has a daughter."

Laura smiled down at the baby in her arms. She touched the perfect nose with her fingertip. "In time he will."

Virginia lifted the baby from her mother's arms and walked to the window. The sun had begun to rise, and the baby's dainty reaction to the light was comical.

"You still want to name her Rachel?" Virginia asked.

"Yes. Rachel Amanda after my mother and grandmother."

"I know how much that would mean to them."

Laura's eyes shifted from her baby to Virginia. "I'm starved. Can you make me something to eat?"

"What would you like?"

Laura grinned. "Let's see. How about a cheese omelet with bacon, toast and a pot of tea? Then we'll see."

"You *are* hungry," Virginia said.

Virginia cradled the baby, remembering the night Todd had been born. It seemed a lifetime ago. "Are you disappointed you didn't have a boy?" Virginia asked.

"No. A boy would remind me too much of what I lost." She sighed. "I can't believe it's been a year since he was kidnapped." Tears filled Laura's eyes and she brushed them away with an impatient swipe. "No. I won't cry. She deserves a happy mother."

"You'll be a wonderful mother to her. Here," Virginia said, setting the baby back in her mother's waiting arms. "I'll get your food ready."

"Rachel Amanda." Laura touched the baby's cheek with her fingertip and she smiled when the tiny face turned instinctively toward her.

"Oh, you're going to be something, aren't you, Rachel? Pretty little thing. You look just like your daddy, don't you?"

The next day Virginia dialed Harry's extension. "Bring me Rudy's personnel records, would you? I've got a little time to look them over."

"Might be a few minutes, boss. I'm meeting with a couple of Owney Madden's boys and I just heard them walk in the door. I don't want to keep them waiting."

"How's the new kid working out?"

"He's young and has a lot to learn, but he's smart. I wondered at first if you'd just hired him to piss off that reporter, but you've got an eye for talent. He may be a real asset to you someday."

"Good. When you're done come to my office. Don't bring those two, okay? I can't stand them."

"Who can? Don't worry. I'll make the meeting short and sweet."

She was on the phone when Harry walked in the door half an hour later. He laid the requested folder on the desk in front of her and opened it.

"Hang on, Paul," she said into the phone, then motioned toward the door. "Lock it, Harry. I don't want to take any chances." Her attention went back to the phone for a few moments. When she hung up, the look on Harry's face made her smile.

"Paul O'Malley?" He grinned. "Are you two picking up where you left off?"

Virginia laughed. "Twenty years later? Not a chance. Just getting the location of a warehouse in Chicago where we're supposed to meet in three days."

"What do you need from me?"

"Pour yourself a drink while I take a look at Strauss's folder."

He dropped a couple of ice cubes into a glass and filled it with gin. "Some for you, Virginia?"

She didn't look up, but shook her head. "I gave up Gordon water months ago. Ginger ale instead."

After a few more minutes of reading she put the folder down and glanced at Harry, looking pleased. "You are thorough."

"I do things the way you tell me to do them. So where the hell is Strauss? No one's heard from him in months."

"That's what I want to know. The rat kidnapped Todd and I've got enough evidence to hang him. I think he may also be responsible for two murders."

Harry didn't seem surprised. "There's one thing I didn't put in that folder because it didn't seem important at the time. A couple of months before the kidnapping I walked in on Rudy scrounging around my desk. When I asked what he was doing, he said he was looking for a set of keys."

She frowned. "What are you talking about? Keys to what?"

"One of the storage cabinets in the basement." He sipped his drink. "I told him he was too damn nosey."

"The keys are all here in my office. But he knew that, because he'd helped Pinella put away a couple of deliveries."

"Should I call a locksmith and have the locks changed in case he shows up?"

"No, he won't come here. But you may have hit on something. Maybe he was looking for cash and when he didn't find any he came up with the plan to kidnap Todd. I wish he'd robbed me instead."

She was aware there had been talk about her and Rudy. She knew people wondered if she'd gone soft. She and Harry had argued about it once, and she had even considered firing him because she thought he was being disloyal. She changed her mind when she realized he was concerned with her wellbeing. One thing Rudy had taught her through all this was to question people and their motives all the time. No one would ever take advantage of her again.

"What are we going to do about the bastard?" asked Harry.

"The file says he has a cousin or an uncle in the San Francisco area. Did he ever mention anything to you about them?"

"Strauss and I never talked much. I remember hearing something about Berkley, but I don't know if it had anything to do with Strauss. Want me to ask around?"

"No. I don't want to arouse suspicion. I'll have to get the answers I need from Paul."

There were no flights to Chicago until the following week, which meant Virginia had to drive. The trip, with stops only when necessary, left her so exhausted she checked into the first hotel she could find. She slept for nine straight hours and would have slept longer if a hotel maid hadn't woken her up, wanting to clean the room.

The next morning she drove to the address of the warehouse Paul O'Malley had given her. He was going to meet her there. She knocked three times. Another round of knocking produced no response, so she tried the door and discovered it was unlocked.

She reached into her purse and fumbled for her gun but came up empty-handed. Just then a figure emerged from the shadows and raced past her, running so fast she couldn't be certain of what she'd seen. She ran back to the car to look for her gun, then remembered she'd left it at the hotel. *How could I be so stupid?*

She pulled a flashlight from her glovebox and walked cautiously back into the warehouse. Clicking it on, she shone a pale circle of yellow light into the darkness. Something moved on the ground in front of her, and she gasped when she recognized it was a body. Then she saw who it was. Virginia ran toward him and knelt at his side, trying not to cry. Paul lay in a pool of blood, making awful gurgling noises. His eyes fluttered, then opened wide one last time. Whatever he'd wanted to tell her died with him.

Chapter Forty-Six

For several weeks, Erich heard nothing. Then he got a lead from a friend of his, Tim Scanlon, a crime reporter at the *Chicago Tribune*. Tim told him Paul O'Malley, the former fiancé of Virginia Kingsley, had been found dead in a warehouse in Chicago.

The first place Erich went when he arrived in Chicago was the offices of the *Chicago Tribune*. He, Peter Bergen and Tim Scanlon had worked together at a community newspaper in the Bronx before they'd moved on to dailies.

"I hear you're socializing with the elite," Scanlon said, lifting one eyebrow.

"That's yesterday's news," Erich said. "Back to business, gentlemen. What else do you have on O'Malley?"

"He was one of Torrio's drivers. He was liked by everyone: Capone's people and Torrio's, which is unusual in this town. Everyone I've spoken to thinks an outsider was responsible."

"Who told you this?"

Tim Scanlon handed Erich a piece of paper. "You need to see this guy."

Erich found the North Side speakeasy which Tim had scribbled on the paper, and parked his rental on a side street. He didn't like the neighborhood or the look of the speakeasy, but he followed Scanlon's directions and knocked on the door three times. The door was opened by a big guy who looked more interested in chewing on a chicken drumstick than in asking Erich any questions.

"I'm here for Rossi," Erich said.

The doorman continued to chomp on a chicken leg, pointing toward the back of the place with his chin.

"Sorry if I disturbed you," Erich said, then walked to the back of the room. There he was confronted with two doors: one straight ahead and one to the right. He glanced back to ask for direction, but the doorman was no longer in sight. Probably gone out for more chicken, he thought. On impulse, Erich tried the door to the right. It swung open and he saw a guy hunched over a large round table, sleeping.

"Are you Rossi?"

The man's eyes popped open. "Who the fuck are you?"

Erich closed the door behind him and locked it. Rossi sat up straight.

"We need to talk," Erich said.

"Says who?"

"A mutual friend."

The man narrowed his eyes, suspicious. "You haven't told me who you are."

Erich folded his arms, trying to look tougher than he felt. "The friend of a friend of a friend of a friend of yours. How's that?"

"That's horse shit. Either give me a name or I'll call my friend in here."

"Who, the big guy out front? Oh, I wouldn't bother with him. He loves his chicken leg and I'm gonna bet he doesn't care about anything else. In answer to your question, I'm Erich Muller from the *Herald Tribune*. I don't think you'll do anything dumb, because you Chicago gangsters are still answering questions about the Lengle murder."

"State your business and get the hell out."

"I need information about a guy named Paul O'Malley. And also about some pretty boy."

"You on Virginia Kingsley's payroll?"

That was unexpected. "What?"

"Don't play dumb. She sent you here to see what else I know. Guess the guy in Texas wasn't much help to her."

"Think whatever you want, pal. What do you know that you didn't tell Virginia Kingsley?"

"Not a damn thing."

"How would you like me to tell her you're keeping secrets from her? Bet you know what that'll get you."

Sweat bubbled on Rossi's brow. "You need to see someone at the Lexington Hotel. Room 235."

"Thanks. Oh, and if you're hungry, your buddy might still have a little chicken to share."

Erich drove to the Lexington Hotel and climbed to the second floor. No one answered the door of Room 235, so he went to the front desk. The hotel manager told him the woman who'd been living there for more than three weeks might have had a child with her, but she had checked out that morning and left no forwarding address. The clerk wrote the woman's name on a piece of paper and gave it to Erich.

***

Virginia arrived in San Francisco in time for the biggest rainstorm to hit the city in twenty years. Rain streamed down the windows and pounded the hotel roof. She ordered room service and tried to read the newspaper, but the image of Paul O'Malley with a bullet in his brain kept popping into her head. Only the good die young.

The rain eased up on the third morning. This time, before leaving, Virginia made sure she had her gun with her. She drove through puddles, parked the car near the address Harry had given her on Jones Street, then set off on foot. Jones Street was only two blocks long. It had three houses on the first block and four on the second. Now Virginia had to play a game of elimination. She watched a woman came out of one of the houses along with two young children and an elderly woman, so she eliminated that house. A car pulled up the driveway of the last house on the second block and a middle-aged couple got out. Not that one, either.

With its overgrown grass and weeds, one of the five remaining houses caught her eye. She hoisted herself onto the sill of a broken window on the main floor, cleared away a few stray shards of glass and landed with a thud on the wood floor of what turned out to be the kitchen.

The stove and icebox were caked with dirt and something smelled rank. The next room was empty apart from a box of tissues. She picked up the box and examined a smudge. Could it be blood? She found nothing of interest upstairs and was checking to see if any of the doors would open from the inside when heard something that sounded like a muffled sneeze.

She headed in the direction from which the sound seemed to have come and discovered a door ajar to the basement. Sliding the gun from the pocket of her coat, she started down the stairs, stopping on each step to listen. When she reached the bottom step, enough light peeked through the window that she saw she was alone in the room. At the other end was a door to another room.

She eased the second door open and was met by the impressive image of bottle after bottle of wine lined up against the wall. A man half sat, half lay against the wall, and he didn't appear to be awake. Rudy. Rudy in pretty rough shape. Blood seeped from his left arm and bloody tissues were strewn all over the floor.

"Get up, you bum."

He raised his head. "Who's there?"

He yelped when she yanked him to his feet. "Oh, Jesus. I need help. I've been shot."

"Help? You want me to *help* you? You're out of your mind."

"Virginia?" He peered at her in the faint light. "Is that you, Virginia? Thank God. I need a doctor."

She shoved him onto the floor, and he landed on his left side, groaning loudly. She prodded him hard with her foot, as if she shoved a sack of garbage. "Don't you pass out on me, you lousy piece of shit."

"Please. I can't stand it anymore."

She knelt in front of him and brought her face as close to his as she could bear. She felt repulsed by the familiar face. She was disgusted with him, disgusted with herself for ever having been with him. "Where's Todd?"

"I don't know."

"Liar." The sound of her slap across his face was like a whip in the tiny room. "What have you done with my nephew? Is he dead?"

"Don't know."

She grabbed his left arm and twisted it as hard as she could. "Tell me where he is."

He made a pathetic mewling sound and his breath came in gulps. She eased up just enough so he could speak.

"I'm telling you the truth. I have no idea."

She held the gun to his head. "Stand up like a man when you talk to me."

It took him a few minutes, but he managed to struggle to his feet. "How long have you known?" he asked.

"Since the beginning, you bastard. Start talking."

"It was for the money. I was going to give him back. I swear."

"More lies." She twisted his left arm and his nose began to run. "Out with it."

"When I got back from picking up the ransom, Nancy and the kid were gone."

"Some girlfriend of yours has Todd?"

He wiped his nose with the back of his hand and slumped against the wall. "I guess. But I swear. I have no idea where they are."

She let him go, then watched him slide down the wall until he lay in a heap at her feet. Her stomach rolled with nausea. How had she allowed such a man near her?

"Are you stupid enough to kidnap my nephew and think I wouldn't come after you? Did you actually think I wouldn't find you?" She shook her head. "I'm very unhappy with you, Rudy. You'd better come up with something quick."

"Maybe they're in England. Nancy's English. She used to live in London."

"Nancy. Last name?"

"Evans."

"And the money?"

"It's all gone. You think I'd be here if I still had any of it? Please, Virginia, get a doctor for me. I can't stand the pain anymore. Please."

Ice replaced the nausea as she tightened her grip on the gun. "Oh, I can take care of the pain for you."

She pulled the trigger twice then stood over his body, wishing she could kill him again.

"God damn your black soul to hell, Rudy Strauss."

Chapter Forty-Seven

Maggie was so proud of her little Andy. All the time they'd spent traveling because she'd been afraid to stay in one place for too long had left no marks on him. She couldn't say the same thing about herself. He was stronger than she was. She loved him so much. And yet sometimes when she looked at him she was filled with such guilt she didn't know what to do.

The weeks after they left Flay's's Boarding House were terrible. They'd traveled from town to town, sometimes sleeping in the car, trying all the while as if everything were perfectly normal. Maggie was a pretty girl, used to being looked at. She had always enjoyed the attention. Now that she needed to be invisible, she didn't know how to do it. Every stray glance or word seemed suspicious, every encounter threatening. She spent her days watching and her nights worrying, trying to figure out where to go next, how to stretch what little money she had, how to keep them both clean.

The nappies drove her crazy. She only had four. Washing them in the sinks of public bathrooms was difficult enough, but getting them to dry was impossible. More than once she scolded him for soiling one right after she'd put it on. Afterwards, she felt awful. He was so sweet. He never complained, just studied her face and watched. He had a habit of putting his little hand on her face as if to comfort her. That's what it seemed like, anyway.

It wasn't supposed to be this way.

One night while he lay sleeping in her arms, she was so hungry she ate the remains of his apple, core, seeds and all, flavored by the salt of the tears running down her face. She knew there was an escape for her, and it was easy. All she had to do was call Laura Austin and tell her where to find him. Then she'd be free of the worry and bother, the smell of nappies, the frantic need to keep moving. But what would she have then? Nothing. Just like before.

The money ran out in Chicago. She had to leave Andy alone so she could clean offices at night and return every morning, afraid he'd be gone. She knew firsthand how easy it was for a child to disappear. Once she started bringing in a tiny income, she guarded every penny.

Only when an ocean stretched between them and his parents was she able to sleep through the night again.

They stepped onto British soil then moved into a four room flat in South Kensington in February 1931. She got a job at a jewelry store, and after more than a year of being on the road and living in boarding houses, Maggie was delighted to have a home of her own. It gave her a sense of security. Also, now they were living in London she no longer worried someone would find them and take Andy away.

She decorated the large sitting room with furniture she'd bought at yard sales. The combination gave the room an eclectic look, which had received many compliments. Her new friend, Terri, gave her a bed and a dresser for Andy that her youngest son had outgrown. Maggie slept on a mattress and box spring, but that didn't matter. She and Andy were together and happy. That was all she cared about.

She was in the kitchen putting away groceries when she heard his laughter coming from outside, where he'd been playing with the little girl who lived in the downstairs flat. A moment later she heard his footsteps on the carpeted hallway. He walked into the kitchen and proceeded directly to the cookie jar.

"Hi, Mommy."

"Hi, Andy. Did you have fun with Janie today?"

"Yep." He began to sing, "London bridge is falling down, falling down," then plunked down on his little rear. He was a beautiful boy. She still kept his hair short so his curls didn't grow, but had stopped dyeing it. Now it was its natural golden shade. The other mothers in the neighborhood were always quick to compliment her on his sweet looks and nature. She never told anyone she couldn't take credit for either.

"Don't hurt yourself."

He got up and climbed on a stool, trying to reach the biscuit jar, but he couldn't quite make it. She helped him down from the stool and put the biscuit jar on the table.

He peeked inside and sighed. "No more bickies."

She pointed at the two shopping bags on the table. "I bought some today."

He opened the icebox door and reached for a bottle of milk, but she was there in a second, ready to help him. In recent days he'd wanted to do everything by himself. Even things she knew were difficult for him. He prided himself on being a "big boy" and got angry whenever she babied him, which was her natural instinct.

"It's too heavy for you. I'll pour it for you straight away."

"No, Mommy. I want to. I want chocoly milk."

"You know where the chocolate syrup is. Not too much, though."

He put his pudgy hand over his mouth when he laughed. "I want lots of chocoly."

He started to sit across from her but when she patted her lap, he crawled into it. He looked inside one of the shopping bags again and pulled out a party favor.

"Mine."

"Put them back." She rested her chin on top of his head and a wave of tenderness engulfed her as the silkiness of his hair brushed her skin. "They're for Steve's party tomorrow. Put the biscuits in the biscuit jar and stop snooping."

He took another biscuit and held it between his teeth. When the rest of them were in the jar, he began nibbling around the edges the way he always did.

"I like peanut butter bickies best. Is Auntie going to have cake and ice cream?"

"Yes. Now you must be a big boy and remember you can't say anything to Steve because it's a surprise. Mommy is going to help her get ready for the party."

"I want to help."

She kissed the top of his head. "If you're a good boy maybe you can help. Now go back out and play. I'll call you when tea's ready. I'm making your favorite, bangers and mash."

She bent over to tie his shoes. When he looked up, the sunlight hit his face just right and Maggie's heart raced. He looked just like the picture of Laura Kingsley on the dust jacket of her novel. He had her eyes and that magical golden hair.

***

Maggie kept her eye on the kitchen clock and listened to Terri drone on about her ex-husband, who never paid his child support on time. Maggie had no one to help her with the expenses of raising a child, so she especially hated hearing Terri complain. It also made her think of Rudy and the half million dollars he'd collected from the Austins.

Maggie almost never thought about Rudy. When she did, she wondered if he were alive and looking for her.

To celebrate Maggie's twenty-fifth birthday, her new boyfriend, Dennis Collins, took her to *Picassos*, her favorite Italian restaurant. Terri had offered to keep Andy in her flat, saying he could spend the night with Steve. The two little boys loved nothing more than to play with their trucks in the sitting room and try to see who could scream the loudest.

Maggie and Dennis had met when he'd come into the jewelry store where she worked, looking to buy a gold cigarette case. They didn't sell such things at her store, so she told him to try Harrods instead. They somehow got into a conversation about tennis, a sport they both loved, and wound up promising to attend a match at Wimbledon together. She gave him her telephone number and he called the next night. They had been seeing each other since then, making it almost six weeks now.

His biggest problem was he was unemployed. He barely managed to pay his month's rent. He'd worked in construction for years but hadn't been able to find anything recently. He had decided to go back to bar-tending, something he hadn't done for years. He constantly complained about not having any money, so Maggie had trouble understanding how he could afford to take her out to dinner for her birthday.

Dennis had one habit which Maggie couldn't stand. He was always late. Always. Tonight was no exception. At six-fifteen he rang the bell, more than twenty minutes past the time they'd set. Maggie kissed Andy.

"Now you be a good boy, Andy. Make sure you listen to Terri and do what she says. Oh, and make sure you use the potty whenever you need to. Mommy's so proud of you for learning how to use the potty! Goodnight, sweet boy. I'll see you tomorrow."

Maggie followed Dennis to his car. "I hope you made reservations," she said. "Otherwise we'll have to wait an hour for a table."

"Of course I did."

As promised, a table was waiting for them when they arrived at Picassos. By the time their waiter brought their food to the table, they'd devoured an entire loaf of Italian bread.

"I don't even like Italian grub," Dennis said. "See what I do for you, Maggie?"

Maggie smiled at him. "Any luck on the job hunt?"

"I've got applications at every pub and club in the city and not one interview yet. I even sent an application to that new club. What's it called?"

"I have no idea."

"*Kingsleys*, that's it. The place that American lady gangster opened. A couple of my mates told me it's quite the place. We should go there sometime."

Maggie wondered if she had gone as pale as she suddenly felt. Virginia Kingsley? In London? That was too much of a coincidence. She tried to keep the conversation casual, since she obviously couldn't explain to Dennis why her hands were shaking. "We can't go there. How could you afford to eat at a place like that?"

He shifted slightly in his seat. "I can't right now, that's for sure. But I'll be on my feet again soon."

"Not me. I'm not going there."

"It would be a lark. Virginia Kingsley is something else. They say she has guys like Dutch Schultz and Al Capone scared to death. A lot of people are wondering why she's over here. There are rumors it has something to do with her nephew's kidnapping, but I don't see how. I thought they'd found the kidnapper's body months ago."

Maggie sipped at her wine, trying to disguise her expression. She managed to look slightly disgusted at the idea. "I don't know how you could even think about working for a woman like her. A gangster."

"I wouldn't worry about it, Maggie. I won't be working for her, I'm sure."

He filled her wine glass and she stared suspiciously at him. Where had this talk of Virginia Kingsley come from? Had he done it innocently, or was there more to it?

Chapter Forty-Eight

About fifteen minutes after receiving an anonymous phone call, two policemen arrived at 31 Jones Street in San Francisco. The caller said it was in regard to a terrible stench emanating from that house. During the time between the phone call and the arrival of the first police car, the entire neighborhood congregated outside the house. They separated so the police car could park, then gathered around again. As he got out of the car, the first cop searched the crowd, asking which one of them had made the call.

They told the cop the house had been deserted for at least eight months. The owner, George Strauss, had an odd, but harmless reputation with his neighbors. The grass was waist high and the shrubbery so overgrown the first cop had to shove it out of the way with his nightstick as he and his partner made their way to the front door. They knocked, just in case, but no one answered. When they tried the door knob they weren't surprised find it was locked. They gave it a few good kicks, then heard a loud crack as the door gave way. They stepped over the splintered door and found themselves standing in the middle of a dusty living room, its walls laced with filthy cobwebs.

The second they stepped inside they were hit by the putrid stench. The first cop gagged and clamped his hand over his nose and mouth in an attempt to dilute the stink. It seemed to be coming from the kitchen, but when he walked into the room, he realized it was coming from the basement. Fighting natural instincts, he followed the smell down the stairs and discovered the decomposed body of what appeared to be an adult male. It lay on the floor, the head a pulpy mess and the skin black with rot.

The cop took the stairs back up two at a time. In the kitchen he found his young partner vomiting into the dirty sink.

"Is there a dead body down there?" asked the second cop, wiping a sleeve over his mouth.

"How did you guess?" the first cop snarled. He pushed his partner toward the outside, needing to escape the smell. They stepped back over the wrecked door and into the sunlight, not meeting the curious eyes of the neighborhood. He turned his back to the crowd and spoke quietly to the younger cop. "Go back to the station house and tell them we need the medical examiner. Could be a homicide."

The crowd stepped aside for the younger cop as he backed his car out of the space and drove away. The first cop faced the onlookers.

"No one goes in, you get it? This is now an official police crime site."

The people immediately buzzed with words like "murder" and "dead body", though none of them had seen anything yet. The reek spoke for itself. It was so thick, even outside in the fresh air, the cop felt like he'd never be able to wash the stink off. He walked to the corner of the building, looking for any kind of clues and breathing in relatively clean air.

On his way back he heard a commotion coming from the west side of the house and headed toward it. Could it be vandals? At first the only thing he saw was a birds' nest on the ground, holding three dead baby birds. The mother bird was nowhere in sight. She'd obviously abandoned her babies a while back.

Then he heard a scream from inside the house. He ran inside, braving the smell again. Downstairs he discovered two teenage boys standing over the body. One of them looked as if he'd been about to search the corpse's pockets, but had stopped short when some sort of liquid oozed out of the blackened mouth.

"One move and you're both under arrest."

The boys ran for the stairs, but the cop was too fast for them. He tripped the first boy, who fell flat on his face, and grabbed the other one around the waist, then handcuffed them together and pushed them to the floor. They were still there half an hour later, looking slightly green, when the medical examiner arrived.

"What are they doing here?" the M.E. asked as he bent down to examine the body.

"Learning a lesson I hope they never forget." Lesson taught, he unlocked the handcuffs, grabbed both boys and dragged them upstairs. As he left, he heard the examiner sigh with resignation.

"It'll be tough to identify this one," he said.

***

After spending three days checking for a fingerprint match and looking through photographs of John Does that had gone missing during the last six months, the corpse discovered at 31 Jones Street remained unidentified. He became John Doe #67 for the year 1931.

The owner of the house, sixty-three-year-old George Strauss, was located at a veteran's hospital in Colorado. He suffered from both alcoholism and diabetes. The first cop was able to speak to him by telephone.

"Do you know anything about the body we found at your house on Jones Street?"

"Nope."

"Did anyone have a key to your house?"

"No. No one."

"Why did you abandon it?"

"No money, no mortgage payments. It belongs to the bank. Maybe you should call them."

"How long have you been in the hospital?"

"August 13 last year."

"And you haven't been inside the house since then?"

"Haven't gone anywhere near it."

The medical examiner estimated the corpse had been in the house for two months. George Strauss hadn't been there in nine months, so he obviously hadn't had anything to do with the murder. And based on how weak his voice sounded over the phone, the cop doubted the old man would have had the strength to harm anyone even if he had been around. They were back to square one.

"Tell you what, Sergeant," said the old man. "You need to find my nephew, but I'll be damned if I remember his name. Rudy ... no, I think it's Randy. Yeah, that's it. Randy."

"Randy Strauss."

"No, he hated his father. Took his mother's name instead. Damn it, I can't remember what that name is. Give me some time and I'll come up with it."

"I'm sure you will."

"Randy no-last-name" wasn't much help at all. The cop said he'd keep in touch with George Strauss in case he remembered his nephew's last name.

***

Laura walked into the baby's nursery and her tiny daughter turned her head. She peered into the crib and saw the baby was awake. She reached in and wrapped her fingers around the warm little body, then lifted her up and snuggled her against her chest. Rachel cooed and her little head wobbled slightly when she tried to look up at her mother.

Laura was convinced this tiny girl was the most beautiful baby girl she'd ever seen, with her mother's gold hair and her father's blue eyes. At times Laura couldn't believe how much she looked like Erich. Even though she was only two weeks old, Laura could tell Rachel had a more willful personality than Todd ever had. When she wanted something, she cried until she got it. Laura tried to be a firm parent, but most of the time all Rachel had to do was stare at her with those beautiful blue eyes, her father's eyes, and she gave in. If she felt as if she were spoiling the baby, she made herself think of Todd, and it no longer mattered.

The baby seemed content in her mother's arms, so Laura carried her out while she went to look for Mrs. Nickerson, who was helping her take care of Rachel a few days a week. She found her in the kitchen rearranging the shelves. Mrs. Nickerson smiled when she saw them, then reached for Rachel's tiny fist.

"There, there. Let's get that out of your mouth, shall we?"

Laura looked down and laughed. She hadn't noticed Rachel had gotten a hold of a handful of Laura's hair and was chewing on it. "Oh, you funny girl. That's right. Get that out of your mouth." She pulled the little fist of hair from Rachel's toothless gums, then chuckled at the baby's startled expression. "Will you just look at her?"

"I guess you've forgotten that Todd did the same thing," Mrs. Nickerson said, smiling fondly.

"When he was this young?" She sighed and glanced at the nanny. "Oh, Iris. I'm only twenty-three years old and my memory's already shot. Oh well. Iris, would you mind helping me bring up Todd's old bassinet from storage?"

"No trouble at all. Why don't we do it while she's napping?" Iris suggested. "What are you going to use it for?"

"I'd like to keep her with me during the day as much as I can. She seems much happier when she isn't by herself."

Mother and daughter spent the remainder of the morning together while Laura worked on her memoirs and her second novel. Afterwards Laura read out loud what she'd written, then realized her audience had fallen asleep. So she continued to work until Rachel woke up, needing to be fed and changed. Once she was finished doing that, she went into the kitchen to make her own lunch.

"I was just coming to look for you," Mrs. Nickerson said. "Here. Let me take the baby so you can have some time to yourself."

Laura put her hand on the nanny's arm and kissed the top of Rachel's velvet-soft head. "When she's out of my sight I can't help thinking of her brother. But you can take her now. After I finish what I'm doing I'm meeting my aunt at her house. We're going to do a little shopping. I hope you don't mind staying here alone with the baby."

"Of course not." Iris Nickerson paused, then frowned at Laura. "I'm sorry, Laura. This may be none of my business, but well, I think you and I have known each other long enough for me to speak my mind."

"Of course. You can say whatever you want to me, Iris. You know that."

"When are you going to let the baby's father know he has a child? He calls here several times a week, and you refuse to speak to him. He's miserable without you, and you're miserable without him. Why do you insist on punishing both him and yourself?"

Chapter Forty-Nine

As much as he longed to be with Laura, Erich had to get on with his life. When he received an anonymous invitation to a dinner party, he decided to go. Peter and Dorothy, both of whom had been worried about him, were delighted to hear he was going.

He dressed in his best navy blue and white pinstriped suit and wore a red tie, thinking the color made him look more festive. He didn't want anyone to know how miserable he felt. Peter and Dorothy were right; it was time he enjoyed life again.

Instead of driving, he took the subway to the Upper East Side townhouse. A maid showed him inside, reminding him of the first time he'd gone to Willow Pond to interview Phillip and Laura. The thought bothered him, and he shook his head like a dog, needing to get Laura out of his mind and heart.

When he walked into the dining room he couldn't help admiring the natural wood floor and the oval shaped dining room table. An elaborate chandelier hung from the ceiling, illuminating the entire room. The twenty dinner party guests had already arrived, and he was embarrassed when he realized they were waiting for him. He was directed to his seat beside a pretty young woman named Jenny Abbott, who smiled at him when he sat down. He smiled back.

"My father says you're the best journalist in the country."

He hadn't expected that. Whether it were true or not, it was definitely good for his suffering ego. "And what do you say?"

She threw back her head and laughed. "Oh, I always agree with my father. Most people do."

"Good grief. Who is he?"

"Preston Abbott."

"The producer? *That* Preston Abbott?"

"Oh, you know him?" Jenny smiled, nodding. "Not that I'm surprised. Most everyone does."

"I don't actually know him. I just know he produced Phillip Austin's last three movies."

Phillip Austin again. Erich barely managed not to roll his eyes at his own words. This was one of the few times he'd been out socially since the breakup with Laura. No matter where he went, something always seemed to come up to remind him of her. He wondered if she'd haunt him for the rest of his life. The woman next to him was different from Laura. Lovely though, with her slender figure and large brown eyes.

"Isn't this delicious?" she said, sipping at her soup.

He found himself admiring the slow grace with which Jenny lifted the spoon to her lips and took a tiny taste.

He dipped his spoon into the thick soup. "I'm not sure if I've ever had it before. I don't even know what it is, for that matter."

"It's shrimp bisque. Taste it. It's delicious."

"Shrimp bisque? That explains it. A reporter doesn't make enough money to—"

"My father says having a lot of money can be annoying at times."

"I wouldn't mind being annoyed that way."

Jenny blushed. "I'm sorry. I must sound like a spoiled, overindulged little rich girl."

"No. Yes. But that's okay. When you do it, it's charming. Fresh and natural." It was true. She was enchanting.

Two waiters came to take their soup plates away, then brought the second course: stuffed artichokes. Erich was glad he knew what the food was this time and how to eat it. He hated the thought of making a fool of himself in front of all these people.

"Tell me about your work, Mr. Muller. Is it as exciting as everyone imagines it is?"

"Oh, you know. A fire here, a murder there. No big deal."

"That's not what I hear. Daddy says you're out to destroy the mob one-handedly."

Erich lifted one eyebrow. Daddy seemed to have something to say about everything.

"Does he? Well, he's giving me more credit than I deserve. One man could never take on the mob and live to talk about it."

"I expect you're right." She nodded. "I expect they'd find you floating in the East River one day. Are you working on anything interesting now?"

"I just got back from Oklahoma a couple of days ago. I went down there to interview some farmers. They weren't in the mood to talk at first but before long they opened up and couldn't stop talking."

"I read about that in the newspaper. They call it the Dust Bowl. It sounds awful. All those poor people need help."

Erich finished his last artichoke leaf and wiped his mouth with his napkin. He nodded, frowning. "Yeah. It's a bad scene. They've been forced to leave their farms and move to the big cities in droves. But they can't find work. The dust is so bad I still don't feel I've washed it all off me yet. Kansas, Oklahoma - it's awful."

The waiter refilled their glasses and another waiter took their appetizer plates away.

"This is some party." He glanced up and down the table, taking in the different, unfamiliar faces. "Somehow I missed meeting the Masons before we sat down. Do you know them?"

"Yes, I've known them all my life. She was my mother's maid of honor and my godmother."

"Well, that explains how you got invited. I have no idea what I'm doing here."

"Oh, that's easy. This dinner party is for literary types and writers." She leaned closer and lowered her voice. "You may not know who the Masons are, but they know who you are."

"So which ones are they?"

"Oh, they never come to their own dinner parties. They're on their yacht somewhere."

That was a surprise. "You're not serious."

"I am." She smiled. "Cross my heart and hope to die."

After they finished the main course, and coffee and dessert were brought to the table, Erich turned to Jenny. "Do you think we'd offend our host and hostess if we went for a walk?"

She took his arm and they strolled down a path covered in small pebbles which which seemed to glow in the moonlight. The moist night air carried the scent of the boxwoods bordering the path. And he smelled lavender coming from somewhere. It was hard to believe they were in the heart of Manhattan.

"I ate too much," Jenny said. "I'd better stick to salad tomorrow or I'll get as big as a house."

"Do you know what you make me think of? A sparrow."

She punched his arm playfully. "I may look frail, but I'm strong."

"Do you want to go back to the party?"

She looked sideways at him, blinking shyly. "No. Since you asked, what I'd really like would be to go someplace where you and I could talk and listen to music."

"I know the perfect place."

***

They were married on July 29, 1931 in the landscaped gardens of the Abbot mansion in Greenwich, Connecticut. A cloudy morning gave way to a sun-filled afternoon, and a balmy, early autumn breeze filled the air with a perfumed fragrance from the rose garden. Jenny's simple but elegant vanilla satin gown complimented her slender figure. She looked stunning.

Erich saw her walking toward him on the arm of her father and hoped he was doing the right thing. He tried to keep his mind off Laura but couldn't. She intruded on his thoughts almost constantly, no matter what he did.

After two weeks honeymooning in the Bahamas, he carried Jenny over the threshold of his apartment in the Bronx, which had become their apartment.

Her pretty face made him smile. If he could just get the other one out of his heart they'd have a chance to be happy. But he was doomed, and he knew it. Who was he trying to kid? He was still in love with Laura. Jenny, sweet Jenny, deserved better. She stood on tiptoe and wound her arms around his neck. He pulled her close and they kissed. She smelled soft and floral, like jasmine and roses.

Erich went back down to get the suitcases, leaving her to explore the apartment. When he returned, Jenny stood at the door of the kitchen holding a wooden spoon.

"I've got the headline for tomorrow's paper: 'Bride finds spoon but nothing to stir.'"

He winked at her. "We'll go out to eat."

She walked to the window and looked out, arms folded across her chest.

"This must be a real letdown for you," he said. He came up from behind and put his arms around her. "We'll look for a bigger place. I promise."

"Good." She turned in his arms and kissed him. "There are some houses for sale in Yonkers."

"I can't afford a house now. In another year or two we'll be able to, but not now."

"*You* can't, but *we* can. My parents will help us."

"We talked about that, remember? We decided we'd make it on our own. Dan knows a couple that are moving out of their apartment in the village next month. The rooms are big, not the usual closet size." He grabbed her hand. "Come on. Let's go get something to eat."

Chapter Fifty

On his way to work the following Monday morning, Erich was held up by a terrible accident on Boston Post Road. He was certain he'd be late. Dan had called him twice on Sunday, begging him to come in early. He figured that was the real reason he was going to be late. What did they call it? Karma? This wasn't exactly the way he'd planned to start his first day back at the newsroom after a two week vacation. Dan had told him there were at least fifty messages waiting for him.

At last the police let cars pass through. When it was his turn he couldn't help glancing at the two mangled cars and wondering if anyone had been killed. He got his answer when he saw someone pull a sheet over one of the bodies. He was grateful he hadn't been able to see much.

Dan was waiting for him by his desk when he walked into the newsroom. "You're late."

Erich grimaced at the stack of messages piled on his desk. "It's twenty to nine. I'm twenty minutes early."

"I expected you here by eight. Sorry I missed the wedding."

Erich laughed. "I'll bet you're glad you had to go to the editors' conference."

"Go ahead and rub it in." Dan walked away, retracing his steps. "Oh, we may be sending you over to London for a while. Our bureau chief is retiring next year and we want you to take over."

"I'm not moving to London."

"Not for good. You'd be a temporary replacement."

"I'll have to talk to Jenny about it."

Ten minutes later Dan came back to his desk, accompanied by a tall, thin woman about fifty years old. Erich was on the phone with one of his sources and didn't pay much attention to them at first. The woman sat in a chair, waiting, and Dan watched Erich until he finished the call.

"Mrs. Flay came in to see you last week. She has something important to tell you. I asked her what it was and she wouldn't say."

She shook her head. "It's important that I tell him," Mary Flay said and pointed at Erich. Dan nodded and walked away.

Erich turned away from all the paper on his desk and gave Mary Flay his undivided attention. "What can I do for you, Mrs. Flay?"

She smiled sweetly. "Oh, please call me Mary. I suppose I could have told the other gentleman what I have to say, but I really think this is information I should only share with you."

"Okay. What is it?"

"When I was a young girl I knew a man who worked at our local paper. He made up half the things he wrote about. I found that out when he interviewed my cousin's father. My uncle was a fireman and saved three people from a fire. The story he wrote said a lot of things that hadn't been said in the interview. You don't do that, do you?"

"Make things up? That's called fiction and no, I don't do that."

He tried not to look impatient, but he wished she'd say what she came to say. He had to tackle the mountain of messages.

"Well, all right. The thing is, when I visited my sister in the spring, I read all the articles you wrote about the Austin kidnapping. You made it come alive for me."

Austin kidnapping? That got his attention. He let the phone messages slide a bit lower on his list of priorities.

"I need to tell you about a young woman who lived at my boarding house in Vandalia, Ohio for a few months. But it's not actually the woman I want to tell you about. It was the child. I didn't even know she had a child until the last night she was there. I was cleaning the hallway outside her room when I heard him cry. You should have seen the look on her face when I confronted her."

A copy editor placed a couple of articles on his desk and Erich nodded thanks at him. Mary opened her handbag and removed something that he recognized as being the dust jacket of Laura's memoir *A Life*, which had just been published. She laid the paper on his desk and pushed it toward him. He found himself staring at Laura and couldn't look away. She grew more beautiful all the time.

"Have you read this? It's wonderful."

"No, I haven't had a chance. Look, I'm sorry, Mary but could you please finish telling me about the little boy? I've been away, as you know, and I have a ton of work to catch up on."

"Yes, I'm sorry. I should have known you'd be busy. It's just that I wanted to see you face to face and tell you what I think might be important. There's not much to tell about the little boy, except for the eyes. When I saw this picture I knew what it was that grabbed my attention. The little boy had Laura Austin's eyes. Not just the color and the shape, but also the same dreamy expression."

Erich pulled a photograph out of one of his desk drawers and handed it to her. "Is this the child you saw?"

She stared hard at the photo, but shook her head. "I'm not sure. The hair was short and mousy brown, not blond and curly. But I can't get those eyes out of my mind."

"What did you say this woman's name was?"

"I didn't. It's Maggie Pierce. She looks a bit like the actress. You know. The one they call the 'it' girl." Mary got up and took a couple of steps away from Erich's desk. "Oh, and she has an English accent."

***

Within two weeks of finding and killing Rudy, Virginia had closed up her brownstone, packed her bags and was on her way to London. She'd told Laura she was going to open a new club and hoped she believed her. It wasn't really a lie. She did plan to open a new club there. She figured in that type of environment she might meet people who had information about Todd.

It took her eight days to find a suitable location in London. Then she left her new assistant in charge of renovations and began her search for Nancy Evans. She started with the telephone directory. Listings for Nancy Evans and N. A. Evans led to four people: the son of a woman who had died seven weeks earlier at ninety-seven, a vacuum cleaner salesman, a foul-mouthed mother of six, and an enormous middle-aged woman who spoke a lilting but almost incomprehensible combination of Jamaican and English. In other words, nothing.

For the next couple of months Virginia spent mornings canvassing playgrounds. At first she made herself as inconspicuous as possible, but one day one of the mothers asked her why she kept staring at the children. Since she didn't have a suitable answer, she stopped going to playgrounds.

One afternoon in the middle of September she visited a nursery school in South Kensington. The bell rang and the children lined up. Virginia looked at all the blond-haired children carefully, but none of them were Todd. As she was about to leave, a mother dropped off her little boy.

"Do you have a minute?" Virginia asked.

"That's about all I have."

"How old is your son?"

"He's almost three."

"Do you know if any of the children in his class are named Evans?"

"No, no one by that name."

It had been more than a year since Todd had been kidnapped. Virginia wasn't any closer to finding him than she'd been on the first day. Her nephew was growing up in a strange country without his family, and it was all her fault.

***

Laura stared at the engraved invitation she held in her hand.

Miss Virginia Kingsley
cordially requests your attendance
at the opening of her new supper club,
KINGSLEY'S
Saturday September 17, 1931 at 8:00 PM
Formal attire required.

Virginia had added a little note that read, "I can't wait to see you. I hope you and Rachel are both well."

Could she possibly go? If she did, she'd have to leave Rachel. The baby would be barely four months old, and the thought of leaving her made Laura's heart race. She had once left Todd, too. And had never seen him again. She knew Mrs. Nickerson would take good care of Rachel, but still …

For days she couldn't decide what to do. One morning she found Mrs. Nickerson in the kitchen preparing Rachel's bottle. She sat at the table, folded her arms in front of her and sighed.

"What's the matter, Laura? You've had something on your mind for days. What is it?"

Laura handed her the invitation and watched Mrs. Nickerson's expression as she read it. "What's the problem? You'll have a wonderful time. I've heard your aunt knows how to throw a great party."

"Yes, she does, but I can't go."

"Why not?"

"You know why. I can't leave Rachel. The last time I left my baby …"

Mrs. Nickerson sat beside her and took her hand. "Laura, don't do this to yourself. You're a good mother. You're a good mother to Rachel and you're a good mother to Todd. And you will be again when he comes home."

Laura gazed at Mrs. Nickerson and a little smile played at the corners of her lips. "Do you really believe he's going to come home, Iris? I try to hang onto that, but sometimes it's so hard. It's been a long time."

Mrs. Nickerson shook her head decisively. "I don't *believe* he's going to come home. I *know* he is."

Laura took the nanny's hand. "Thank you."

"Now you go to your aunt's party and have a wonderful time. That little angel asleep in the nursery will be safe, I promise you. I won't let her out of my sight, and I won't let anyone else near her, either."

Chapter Fifty-One

Kingsley's opened in London on September 17th, 1931. At a quarter to nine, a white Rolls Royce pulled up to the curb. Laura stepped out and made her way into the club.

Once inside, she slipped out of her full-length ermine mink coat and looked around. Two of *Kingsley's* walls were painted white, and the other two were black. The dance floor was black and white marble and the tables and chairs alternated in black and white. The decorator had even gone so far as to ensure the black tables had white accessories and vice versa.

Every eye went to Laura. Her strapless red velvet evening gown was a sharp contrast to the stark decor of the club, and the lights shone on the curve of her golden chignon, sparking off the tasteful diamond earrings and matching pendant hanging around her slender neck.

All Laura saw was Erich. Their eyes met and in that second there was no one in the room but the two of them. She wanted more than anything to be alone with him, just to see him, talk to him, touch him. Then his beautiful young wife said something and he looked away from Laura. She'd known Erich had gotten married, but … Seeing them together made her feel ill with regret. She'd lost him forever, and it was her own fault for being so stupid, for refusing to see him for so long. What a fool she had been. A stubborn, stupid fool.

The band began to play "Night and Day" and Erich got up to dance with his wife. Laura couldn't take her eyes off them. Every so often Erich glanced over at Laura, squeezing anguish through her heart. After three dances, the couple went back to their table and Virginia appeared, pouring champagne for herself and Laura.

"It's wonderful to see you, Laura," Virginia said. She followed Laura's gaze and took a deep breath, then let the air out slowly. "Why don't you go over and say something to him? It's obvious he still has feelings for you."

"Aunt Virginia, he's a married man, and I know it's my fault he married her. I've lost him, and there's nothing I can do about it."

"Oh, yes there is. You could tell him about Rachel. Don't you think that would make a difference to him?"

Laura studied her aunt. "I'm curious. What is he doing here?"

"He's working in London and I—"

"You did this on purpose, didn't you? You did it again." Laura shook her head. "You planned for the two of us to be here so we could reunite. Well, I'm telling you it isn't going to work."

Virginia grinned. "We'll see about that. Speaking of which, did you bring any pictures of the baby?"

Laura nodded and handed her two photographs of four-month-old Rachel.

Virginia smiled fondly at the pictures. "She looks just like him, Laura. Especially her eyes. They're so blue. You won't be able to keep the secret from him much longer. As soon as he sees her, he'll know. Everyone will know."

Laura glanced over at Erich. "Rachel also has a lot of Todd's sweetness."

"Too bad you didn't bring her with you," Virginia said, grinning. "I have gifts for her."

Laura chuckled. "I bet you do. I just thought she'd be better off at home with Mrs. Nickerson, though I've been terribly nervous about leaving her. I call home two or three times a day just to check that she's okay."

The film director, Richard Hamilton, who had worked with Phillip in the past, came by her table and greeted her with a kiss.

Laura turned and noticed Erich's wife, Jenny, walking toward their table. Erich was right behind his wife, his blue eyes focused on Laura. Laura couldn't look away. Her heart raced. Jenny chatted happily with Richard, who had also worked with her father. She was oblivious to her husband's distracted gaze.

"You don't mind if I dance with your wife, do you, Erich?" Richard asked.

"Oh, no. Go ahead."

Jenny and Richard headed for the dance floor. A moment later Erich came toward Laura and she rose from her chair as if in a dream. He took her hand and without a word he led her to the dance floor.

***

Being in each other's arms seemed like the most natural thing in the world. By the time the dance ended they'd agreed to meet in the street just outside her hotel later that evening.

When the time came, they sat in his car, gazing at each other.

When Erich finally spoke, his voice was harsh with regret. "I can't do this to my wife. It isn't right."

"Do you love Jenny?"

At the mention of her name, Erich closed his eyes, searching his emotions. Did he love her? No. But he had married her with the intention of making a life with her. Maybe he had even thought he would learn to love her. He did care about her. How could he do this to her? He hated himself for it. And it only felt worse when Erich remembered the shabby way his father had treated his mother. It was important that he not hurt Jenny, but that seemed unavoidable.

He looked at Laura, who was watching him closely. As he gazed into her intense green eyes he thought he saw something new. Something had changed in her life and it was as if she carried whatever it was with her. Whatever it was, he was drawn even more to her now. He could never leave her again. He couldn't even be separated from her.

He hung his head. "Love her? No, I never have. I never should have married her. It was wrong. I just needed ... Oh, I don't know what I needed. Truth is, I've never stopped loving you."

"I can't be the cause of your marriage ending. You have to be sure."

"I am sure. I may never forgive myself for breaking Jenny's heart, but I'm sure about you and me. I've always been sure."

They headed south to Kent, checked into the White Lion Inn and spent the next five days holding hands, bathing together, feeding each other, and sleeping in a tangle of arms and legs. They made love frantically at first, then moved more slowly, but with no less urgency, as if their hunger for each other would never be satisfied.

Laura tried a few times to talk about Jenny, about what they were going to do, but Erich refused to discuss it. He put his finger to her lips as he'd done that first time on the boat, and wiped away her tears until she gave herself up to the joy of loving and being loved.

On the second night, Laura couldn't sleep. Erich was curled up next to her, sleeping soundly with a look of utter contentment on his face. She didn't think she had ever seen him as happy as he had been that day. Laura didn't feel as light with happiness, weighted down as she was beneath a heavy secret. A secret with golden hair and blue eyes like her father's. And Laura was afraid that when she told him, he would hate her.

Rachel was Erich's child, his flesh and blood, yet he didn't even know she existed. What would he say if she told him about her? Would he be filled with joy or would he lash out at her? He had every right to be angry, but if he left her, Laura would be destroyed.

She sat up in bed, wide awake. It would be impossible for her to sleep tonight. She went into the small sitting room and looked out the window, staring at the stars. Laura turned her arguments over in her mind, trying to make excuses for her behavior, but it was no good. No matter how hard she tried, Laura knew she was wrong. She had made a mistake in not telling Erich about Rachel. Now she had to do what she could to make it up to him. She was going to have to tell him about his daughter.

The next day the couple took a leisurely walk down one of the country roads, enjoying the bright, sunny weather. Erich picked a bunch of daisies and tucked one of the flowers into her blonde ponytail. But Laura was distracted. She couldn't carry the guilt any longer. She squeezed his hand and stopped walking.

"I have something to tell you."

He frowned. "What is it?"

"Oh, God, Erich, I don't know how to tell you this." She chewed on her lower lip, hoping for courage. "All right. I'll just say it. You and I have a baby, a little girl named Rachel. She's four months old."

His jaw dropped. "What? We have …" He goggled at her, speechless. Then his cheeks flushed with anger. "What are you telling me?"

"I was pregnant when you and I split up, but I didn't know it. I didn't go running back to you because, well, because I didn't want you to come back out of duty. I wanted you to … Oh, never mind. I just couldn't tell you. Oh, Erich. Please try to understand."

He walked a few feet away and stood by a small pond. Picking up a couple of stones, he tossed them into widening circles in the water. Laura wrung her hands as she watched, desperate for him to say something.

He didn't turn to look at her. "Where is she?" he asked quietly.

"She's in New York with Mrs. Nickerson. I hated to leave her, but she's too young to make such a long trip."

"Do you have any pictures of her?"

She had one in the pocket of her dress. She'd put it there that morning, knowing he would ask. For several minutes he stared at the picture and said nothing. Then he took a deep breath and any sort of anger melted away.

"My God. She's so beautiful," he said. "I've never seen anything so beautiful."

Laura took a cautious step toward him. "She looks just like you," she said. "Even Virginia thinks so."

He spun to face her. "I have to see her, Laura. I'll be back in New York next week. My God. I have a daughter. It's killing me that I can't see her this minute."

"So ..." she said carefully. "So you don't hate me?"

He laid his warm palm against her cheek and she leaned into it, closing her eyes with relief. "I could never hate you, Laura. Never. But I'd be lying if I didn't say I was confused. You have to tell me this. Why did you give up on us even after you knew about the baby?"

She sighed. "Maybe it wasn't you. Maybe it was me. Todd had been kidnapped, my marriage was over, then you came along. It was all too much."

"Then can I assume you've forgiven me for what I said about Virginia?"

"I don't know. She has, and she's told me I should. I guess she's pretty open to you these days. Otherwise, why would she have invited you to the opening of her new club? Unless ..."

Erich smiled. "Unless what?"

"Unless she knew exactly what she was doing. She wanted us to see each other because she knew what would happen." Laura looked deeply into his blue eyes and saw herself reflected in them. "What about your wife? I hate to think of anyone being hurt this way. She seems so nice and genuine. That's a huge accomplishment, considering her background."

The corner of his mouth curled in a gentle smile. "Yes, Jenny's terrific. A lot of her friends and family think I married her for her money - or, should I say, her father's money, but I didn't. I never loved her the way I love you, but I did care for her. I thought that was enough. We wanted the same thing: a home, children, but now ..."

She moved closer, planting a soft, gentle kiss on his lips. "At least it wasn't the disaster my marriage to Phillip was."

Chapter Fifty-Two

Five days later Erich dropped Laura off at the Mayfair Hotel and continued on to the townhouse he and Jenny rented on Oakley Street, in Chelsea. Jenny felt at home among the mink-coated women walking poodles in Cheyne Park; Erich felt like a man with two left feet. The place was far too expensive for him to afford. The only reason they were living there was the *New York Herald Tribune* was footing the bill. Erich missed New York and was glad his London assignment would be over in another month.

He drove slowly, feeling horrible. Jenny deserved a reasonable explanation, and he didn't have one for her. Was their marriage over? He pulled in the driveway, walked through the back door and found her sitting at the kitchen table, staring at a cup of tea.

"You're back," Jenny said, her voice flat.

He sat across the table from her but didn't say anything.

"Aren't you going to talk to me?" she said, her tone lowered to a vicious whisper.

He swallowed. "I don't know what to say."

"I think you'd better come up with something."

He'd never heard her use that tone. It was sharp with fury. "I'm sorry," he said.

She leaned back in her chair, fiddling with the handle of her teacup. She looked away from Erich and stared at her cup. "Are you in love with her, Erich? Is she in love with you?"

He didn't say a word. Didn't have to.

"When you make love to me do you think of her? Is that how you can stand being with me?"

"That's not it at all."

She shook her head slowly, staring at him with an incredulous expression in her big brown eyes. "You and I have nothing compared to what's between you and Laura Austin."

"Jenny—"

"How do you think I felt, watching the two of you dance? The look in your eyes - I wanted the floor to swallow me up."

He got up and put the tea kettle on the stove. "Is your tea cold? I'll make you another cup."

"I don't want anything. I'm nauseous."

"Are you sick?"

"No, damn you." She glared at him. "It's morning sickness. I'm pregnant."

He dumped the spoonful of sugar he was holding onto the table and stared at her. "My God."

She dropped her head into her hands and began to cry. Erich felt wretched. After a moment she raised her tearstained face and looked deep into his eyes. "I wish I'd never met you, Erich Muller. I had this fantasy about telling you about the baby, how you'd take me into your arms and tell me you'd never loved another woman the way you loved me, then talk about how much you were going to love our baby ..."

"Jenny—"

"Well, that's what I get. I wanted a baby for so long and now I'm going to have one. Lucky me."

"It'll be okay, Jenny. We'll work things out."

"I don't think so."

"I'll make it up to you. I promise."

She shuddered. "When I think of you and her ... Give me the car keys." She walked toward the door. "I have to get away from here for a while."

"Where are you going?"

She looked back over her shoulder at him and shot him a look of disgust. "Don't you dare question me about anything."

***

The following afternoon he went to meet Laura at *The Serpentine* in Hyde Park. While he waited, he watched people drift by in rowboats and remembered the boat ride he and Laura had taken so long before. When he saw her walking toward him, he knew he couldn't give her up. But everything was such a mess. What could they do?

They embraced and kissed, then sat on a bench, pressed closely together.

"I'm going to Paris for a few days," Laura said. "I'd love for you to come with me."

"Jenny's pregnant. I've got to try and work things out with her." He swallowed hard, seeing Laura's eyes fill with tears. "Please try and understand, Laura. I can't desert her and the child."

"I know you can't."

He took her hand in his. "God, Laura. This is killing me."

"I can't give you up."

He put his arm around her and she snuggled her head into his chest. They sat that way for a few moments, listening to nature.

"What are we going to do?" Laura asked.

He said nothing but followed her gaze to the boaters. He knew she was thinking the same thing he was. He took her hand and they stood up.

"A boat ride," he said. "How about it?"

"It's the perfect day for one."

Chapter Fifty-Three

Two days later Laura called Erich and told him she wanted to see him. He considered telling her they shouldn't see each other, but he couldn't. Jenny was so busy shopping for baby clothes he didn't think she even heard him when he told her he'd be late and not to wait up.

He took the subway to Eighth Street, then walked the few remaining blocks to Laura's apartment on Patchin Place. Rain had begun to come down heavily and the sidewalk was slick with fallen leaves. It was the kind of day people should stay inside. But Erich had decided to go to Laura, and when Erich made up his mind to do something nothing could stop him.

Jenny was eight weeks pregnant, which meant she must have conceived right after their honeymoon. He'd always wanted children but never imagined it like this. Jenny's parents were thrilled. She insisted on visiting them every Sunday and he didn't have the heart to refuse her. In her parents' company she was much happier, but he thought his in-laws behaved more coldly towards him lately. In the past they'd treated him like the son they'd always wanted. Then again, maybe it was just his imagination. Jenny was too proud a woman to tell them her marriage was failing.

He rang Laura's bell, remembering the first time he'd ever seen her. She came to the door, lovelier than ever, and put her arms around his neck. She kissed him, filling him with strength, and he kissed her back, loving the smell of her, the feel of her, the reality of her.

"I'm glad you came," she said. "I've missed you."

"Me, too," Erich said and kissed her again.

She nuzzled his neck. "Mmm. What kind of aftershave are you wearing?"

"Don't remember."

She took his hand and led him into the house, then closed the door behind them. As soon as they were inside they were in each other's arms again, kissing hungrily.

***

Jenny stood at the floor-to-ceiling windows of her parents' living room in Connecticut, watching her husband. Erich had been riding for almost two hours and didn't seem to be tiring. He had so much energy she found it difficult to keep up with him, now that she was pregnant. The morning sickness she suffered with all day hadn't gotten any better. Despite her difficult pregnancy, Jenny loved her unborn baby more than she'd ever had anyone. She couldn't wait to hold him in her arms.

She heard the front door close, and a moment later her father stood in the doorway. He held his suitcase in one hand and the *Sunday New York Times* in the other. Preston Abbott kissed both his daughter's cheeks, then stood back and stared at her.

"You're too pale. I don't like it. Something's not right."

"I'm fine, Daddy." She put both hands on her abdomen. "I just can't fit into any of my clothes anymore. I didn't expect you back today. Where's Mother?"

"Still at your sister's, helping her get settled. I have a meeting tomorrow morning at eight so I couldn't stay."

She turned her back to him and he took a few steps toward her. "What's so interesting out there?" he asked.

She glanced at him, then back out the window, but didn't say anything.

Her father nodded. "Erich's riding again. He enjoys it very much, doesn't he? He's a good man, Jenny. I asked him to come to work for me, but he turned me down. Can you imagine?"

"He'll never give up being a journalist. It's in his blood."

Preston watched his daughter as she gazed at her husband. "I have to admire his independence. Why aren't you out there with him?"

"I'm not in the mood to go riding. Besides, the doctor told me it isn't good for me or the baby."

He grinned. "How is that grandson of mine doing?"

"He's fine, Daddy."

"Those doctors don't know what they're talking about." He took her hand. "Come on, I'll help you saddle your horse. You know how much you love to ride."

"I don't feel like it."

He stopped, staring at her with concern. "Are those tears, baby girl?"

"I'm not your baby girl anymore, Daddy, but I wish I were. I'm a married woman who's expecting a baby and has a terrible problem that I don't want to talk about."

He pulled her close against him and she snuggled in, wishing she could disappear. "I'm always here for you, Jenny. So is your mother."

"I know you are. But this is something I have to take care of on my own."

The next day, Jenny and Erich returned to their Greenwich Village apartment. As soon as they walked in the door, she strode into the bedroom and shut the door behind her. When they were with her parents they tried to put on a good front, but as soon as they left the façade collapsed.

Since their return from London she'd been fighting the truth about their marriage. Now she had to face up to it. The marriage was over, though she hated that fact. Despite what had happened between Erich and Laura Austin, she wanted to forgive him. She wanted to do it for herself, and for the baby. But in her heart she knew she couldn't.

Days after their return, Erich was named the *Herald Tribune*'s Washington D.C. bureau chief. He spent so much time traveling between Washington and New York they were able to spend little time together. When he was home they either didn't speak or they fought.

Yesterday, like on most other days, he had passed up the chance to spend time with her and had gone horseback riding instead. Even her parents had commented on it. He always seemed distracted when she mentioned the baby, and Jenny had begun to wonder if he cared about her or the baby at all.

This time, Erich opened the bedroom door and peered inside. "We should talk."

She followed him into the kitchen where he had prepared steaming cups of tea. It was served in the Lenox china they had received as a wedding gift from her parents, and when she looked at it she was struck with the realization that her marriage had been a lie from the first day.

"You never loved me," she said calmly. She stood by the kitchen counter, bracing herself against its edge. "You married me because Laura Austin wouldn't have you."

"That isn't true. I did love you. I still do." He took a bottle of milk out of the icebox and poured some into a creamer, then looked at her pale face. "Please sit down."

"What can you say to me that will change anything?"

"I vowed once that we'd always be together."

"You aren't going to be able to keep that promise."

He stared at the cup of tea, then looked up at her. "I've made a mess out of everything."

She hesitated, wanting to say exactly what she felt in that moment. "Do you know what hurts the most?" she asked. "Your lack of interest in our baby. I've seen the pride in your eyes whenever you mention Rachel, but it's not there when we talk about our child. You seem almost … bored with the subject. That hurts."

"I want our child very much. I will love him with all my heart and soul. But that doesn't mean I can't love my daughter, too."

"My God, Erich. I wish I could believe you. You say one thing, but your actions tell me something else." She shrugged. "Maybe you'll love our baby, but you certainly don't love me. I can't live with that."

"I care about you. Very much."

"*Care* about me? That's a laugh. I want to be loved. I want someone to love me the way I love you or the way you love Laura Austin. I saw it in your eyes when you looked at her. I want that. I don't want to share you with anyone, and as long as she's on the face of this earth, you'll always belong to her."

"What are you saying?"

"We need time apart."

He reached for her hand. "Can't we at least try?"

"Why are you making this harder than it already is? You know as well as I do that it's over between us. There was never anything there to begin with. At least not on your part."

"You're wrong."

"Oh, Erich. No more. I can never trust you again. You belong to Laura, not me. I'll move out as soon as I pack my things."

"There's no need for you to go anywhere. I'll find a place."

"No. I don't want to live here. I can move into my parents' house. They have plenty of room for me and the baby."

He looked at her, his eyes so incredibly blue she wanted to cry. If only they had made it. If only there had been no Laura Austin. If only. If only.

"I never wanted to end up this way," he said. "Please believe me when I say I want to be a part of our child's life. A father."

"I'd never take him away from you. I know what my father has always meant to me."

She glanced critically around the kitchen. "I don't want to be in this apartment anymore. It's never felt like a home to me. Then again, you never wanted to have a home with me, did you? Your heart's always been elsewhere."

"Jenny, I'm sorry I disappointed you."

She finished her tea and put the cup in the sink. Without a word she left him alone and headed back to the guest bedroom, where she spent the night crying. In the morning Erich got up 6:00 a.m. and left for Washington D.C. before Jenny was awake. When he returned three days later, she'd moved out.

***

The day after he returned from Washington D.C., Erich called Laura. He told her Jenny had left him and had called that morning to tell him she planned to file for divorce as soon as the baby was born. When Laura heard him say the words she wanted to laugh with relief, but she detected a note of sadness in his voice. Just because her marriage to Phillip had been a nightmare, there was no reason to believe his marriage to Jenny had also been that way. They'd been married such a short time, and she was expecting a baby. Laura sensed he was fond of her. No, none of this could be easy for a man as sensitive as Erich.

"I never thought things would end this way," Erich said quietly. "Do you feel as miserable as I do?"

"My marriage was over before I met you. I've just let it drag on out of habit. It's different for you. I don't think you would have married Jenny unless you'd thought it would work out."

"You're too easy on me. I knew how I felt about you. I never should have married her." He reached for a cigarette then tossed the pack onto the table. "I hurt her more than she could ever deserve. That makes me feel like the biggest louse that ever walked the earth. Then there's the baby ..."

"How can I help? Maybe I had told you about Rachel none of this would have happened."

"I've got the next three days off. I'd really love it if you and the baby could come here and stay with me. There's an art expo in Washington Square Park tomorrow and Sunday, and I know how much you enjoyed the one last year."

"Sounds like fun." She laughed. "I'll be there as soon as I can."

Chapter Fifty-Four

Erich leaned down and brushed his lips against the baby's soft, round cheek. Rachel gurgled and smiled up at him and he kissed her again. Beside him, Laura beamed. He kissed her, too, then took the suitcase.

"There are a couple of other bags out in the car," she said. He headed for the door and she called out, "I'm parked on the corner."

She watched him walk out the door, then realized she hadn't told him which corner, but he was back within minutes. Without saying a word, he marched past her into the bedroom. In the next moment he'd wheeled out a brand new baby carriage filled with stuffed animals and other baby toys. He handed Rachel a white teddy bear and she grinned at him. Laura let him take the baby out of her arms as tears streamed down her cheeks.

"Laura? What did I do?"

She sniffed, wiping her face with the back of her hand. "I'm sorry, Erich. It isn't you. This is so sweet. It just made me think of Todd's first teddy bear and how happy he was when he got it."

Rachel squeezed the teddy bear and smiled up at both of them.

"You're a big hit," Laura said.

Erich ran his fingers through the baby's flaxen hair. "It's like silk, you know? Does she need a nap or anything?"

"She slept on the way here. I'll change her diaper and she should be fine." Laura smiled at the vague expression of disgust on his face. "Unless, of course, you want to do it."

"Uh ... maybe next time."

Once Rachel was changed, Erich took the carriage outside and they walked toward Washington Square Park. The late summer sun cast a pinkish glow over the streets of Greenwich Village.

"I'm going to start reading to her soon. Like I did with Todd. It's never too early to start reading to a child."

He nodded. "I've got some books to give you."

When they reached the park, Laura spread a blanket on the grass. She set Rachel on it and the baby immediately rolled onto all fours and started crawling around. Laura sat next to her and handed her a bottle. A couple of teenage boys tossed a soccer ball at Erich and he threw it back to them with ease. Peter had told her one time that Erich had been both a champion soccer player and swimmer in Germany, but whenever she asked him about that time in his life he always changed topics.

"If you want to join the game, go ahead. Rachel and I will wait for you."

He took her hand and kissed it, then kissed the baby's pudgy hand. "I'd much rather be here with my two girls. Besides, Peter and I have a game planned for next weekend."

For the next half hour they sat on the blanket talking about Rachel and drinking lemonade from the thermos he'd brought. The baby had just fallen asleep when they noticed a man staring at them. Erich got up and faced him.

"Can I do something for you?" Erich asked.

"Yes, actually. I know I was staring, and I'm sorry if I disturbed you. I'm a portrait artist and I'd like to paint you and your wife and baby. The three of you have an almost ... surreal beauty."

"We have no time to pose at a studio," Erich said.

"No, no. Right here, right now. All I need is my sketch pad and some charcoal and I have both of them with me."

He sat on a park bench and Erich joined Laura and Rachel on the blanket. They continued to talk, not feeling the least bit self-conscious, while Rachel slept and the artist sketched. Laura's favorite thing about it was the fact that the artist seemed not to recognize her. He didn't want to sketch her because she was Phillip Austin's wife, but because he found her interesting. In just over an hour he finished the sketch and handed it to them. Erich gave him a couple of dollars, but the artist handed the money back.

"No thank you, sir. I do this because I love to do it. I don't need the money."

Laura and Erich watched him walk away, then turned their attention to the portrait.

"Do you realize this is the first image of the three of us together?" Laura asked. "One day soon, when we're all living together, we'll buy a frame and hang it in our home."

Erich stared hard at the picture.

"What?" she asked.

He shook his head incredulously. "I just can't believe how much I love our little girl. Just look at her! I never thought I could love anyone so much."

Laura chuckled and lay back on the blanket. "I guess I'm going to have to play second fiddle. Is that the way you want things to be?"

"Of course not." He lay beside her and searched her face. The breeze stirred a few golden strands of hair across her face and he tucked them behind her ear. "Since Jenny has filed for divorce it won't be long before we're both free. Then there will be nothing standing in our way."

"You know," she said, "when I first met you, I didn't think I had the right to be happy."

"I knew someday you'd realize our being together or not being together had nothing to do with what happened to Todd," said Erich.

She sighed, sad again. "Everything I've been through since the day he was kidnapped has made me a stronger person, but it hasn't made me miss him any less." Erich pulled her to him and kissed the side of her face. "We *have* to find him, Erich. I can't live without him."

"All I ever wanted to do was spare you the pain."

She leaned back and touched his cheek with her fingertips. "That's sweet, but you can't do that. No one can. For years other people took care of things for me, fought all my battles. Now I realize no one else can do that except me."

Back at Erich's apartment that night, he cooked steak and mushrooms for supper. Afterwards, they put the baby to bed and carried their glasses of red wine into the living room. The flower arrangement in the living room, the candles in the bedroom, and the pastel shades of bath salts in the bathroom were proof that another woman had once lived there. Laura wondered why Jenny had left those things behind. She picked up a copy of *Reader's Digest* from the coffee table, and the first article she turned to was one about Phillip's desperate search for Todd.

She snorted. "He's not doing a thing to find him. It's all publicity."

"I know he's not. But …" he said, clinking his glass against hers, "I have new information."

He told her about Mary Flay and Maggie Pierce, though he seemed concerned at first, as if she'd be angry he hadn't told her before. She wasn't.

In the corner of the room hung a painting of a young girl with long red hair. She wore a white dress from the early 1900s, and Laura stared at it, mesmerized.

"My grandmother had red hair like that," she said quietly. "I always wished I'd inherited it. When I was little I loved to watch her unpin it and see it fall in waves down her back. It was so luxurious."

"I love your hair. It's like gold. Rachel's is going to be the same."

"My grandmother died a few months after my parents did, but I remember her telling me that love was the only reason to marry. She said if you married for any other reason the marriage would fail." She sipped her coffee. "Phillip and I never loved each other. Now our son is paying for a marriage that never should have been."

"Laura, you're too smart to believe anything like that."

"Maybe. But in my heart sometimes I wonder. So based on what you told me, do you think Todd could be in England?"

"I'm not sure. All I know is what Mary Flay told me about Maggie Pierce and her little boy."

"Maggie Pierce." She thought for a moment "The name means nothing to me. Did you look into it while you were over there?"

"I did, and I came up with nothing."

She frowned. "Wait a minute. Erich, why did Virginia move to London so suddenly? She gave me some excuse about wanting to open a club, and she did that. It's just that never made sense to me. She loves New York and her brownstone. She could have sent Harry or Vince to London if she were really interested. I also know it must be killing her to be separated from the baby and me. She adored Todd and would absolutely want to be a big part of Rachel's life."

He shrugged. "Well, there's one thing I can do. I'll go to Ohio and talk to Mary Flay, see if there's anything she forgot to tell me."

"I'm going with you. I need to do something to help find my son. Phillip insisted on protecting me from everything, but I won't let you do that."

***

Difficult economic times were making themselves known in Vandalia, Ohio. Laura insisted on stopping every time they saw another hobo so she could give him money. Within a mile radius they saw more than a dozen soup kitchens, each one serving a long line of defeated people. Cardboard shacks lined the streets, and Laura was hard pressed not to weep as they drove by. Despite her problems, she knew she was a lucky woman. She had more than she deserved and felt obligated to do something for these people.

Erich parked in front of the Tudor house, went around the car and opened Laura's door for her. They climbed the long flight of stairs to the front door, then he rang the bell. A few moments later Mary Flay appeared, holding a bowl of dough in her hands. When she saw Laura her mouth dropped open.

"Please come in." She held the door for them. "I'm sorry I'm such a mess. I'm making peach pies for Sunday dinner. Oh, I'm so pleased you've come over. Come and sit down. Coffee? Iced tea?"

They declined her offer, but sat at the dining room table across from their host. Mary stared at Laura for some time, which made Laura slightly uncomfortable.

"No doubt about it," Mary finally said.

"What are you talking about?"

"The little boy with Maggie Pierce. He is your son. He had such a strong resemblance to you. Especially around the eyes." She leaned back in her chair and crossed her arms. "It would be impossible for him not to be your child. Of course the hair color was different, but that doesn't matter."

"You're sure."

"Yes." She beamed at them both. "As sure as I am that my peach pie is the best in the state of Ohio. Speaking of which, I've got one cooling on the windowsill." She smiled coyly at Erich. "Would you like a piece?"

"Sure. If it's not any trouble."

"What about you, dear?" Mary asked Laura.

"It smells so good. Yes, I'd love to have a small piece. Thank you," Laura said.

Within moments Mary returned with two of the biggest slices of pie either Laura or Erich had ever seen. Laura was certain that she never be able to finish it. She changed her mind when she'd taken her first bite. It was delicious.

"Is there anything you forgot to tell me when we met before, Mary?"

"No, but I did find something in her room you might be interested in."

She went to the hutch, opened the top draw and extracted a small, heart-shaped locket. She handed it to Erich, who turned it over in his hand.

"There's an inscription," he said. "To N. With love G."

"I wonder who N and G are," Laura said. "I also wonder why she left it here."

Erich cleaned his mouth with a napkin. "Maybe she wants to be found and this is a clue."

"I don't think so," Mary said, shaking her head. "Maggie kept very much to herself. She was very secretive. She did her best to make sure no one found out anything about her. I imagine what must have happened is that she was in such a hurry to get out of here she left this behind by accident. She probably hasn't even noticed it's missing yet. Do you have any idea where she is now?"

"Nothing definite. England's a good possibility. Maybe London," Erich said.

"Do you think that because I told you she had an English accent?"

"That and other things," Erich said, getting to his feet.

Erich reached to shake Mary's hand and Laura leaned in to give her a kiss on the cheek.

"You've been a big help to us, Mary. I feel more confident than ever that we'll be able to find my son. When we do, you have an open invitation to come and see him and our new baby girl," Laura said.

Mary looked puzzled for a moment as she glanced between the two of them. "You and him?" she said, pointing at Erich. "Why, I never knew! I'd read about your split from Phillip Austin, but ..."

"Do you mean you came to see me and didn't know I was involved with Laura?" Erich asked, looking impressed. "Huh. An honest citizen who actually just wants to help. Don't see that too often these days."

Mary grinned, then waved a hand at him. "Oh, it's nothing. But I'm not much for gossip, so I guess that's why I didn't know about the two of you. Now when are you going to show me a picture of this new baby of yours?"

They were laughing when they got back into the car, both feeling optimistic. Erich drove another way back into town, hoping to avoid the soup kitchens. Laura wasn't paying much attention anyway. She was too busy figuring out when they'd be able to go to London.

Chapter Fifty-Five

A few days later, Laura and Phillip received word that the private eye had found Gabrielle Madigan. She had been living in a small house in the woods just outside of Springfield, Massachusetts. He gave them directions then told them he and the Massachusetts State Police would meet them there.

Phillip picked her up in his new Rolls a half hour later. She climbed in next to him, barely glancing his way. He didn't greet her, only motioned with a wave of his hand for the chauffeur to keep going. Laura ignored him. Instead, she gazed out the window, fantasizing about what it would be like to see Todd. She loved imagining his first reaction to his baby sister. He was three years old now. No longer a baby. He'd be able to dress himself and tie his own shoes and maybe even read, since Laura had planned on teaching him by now. Would he remember her? They'd been apart for half his life already.

Erich had wanted to come with her and she had wanted him there, but realized how awkward it would be for him and Phillip to be in the same place. It was uncomfortable enough just for her to be with him. They'd been on the road for twenty minutes before they spoke to each other.

"Is he sure it's her?" Laura asked.

"Yes. Why do you ask?"

"I've been disappointed enough times. I'll be damned if I'll let it happen again," Laura said.

She ignored his snide expression and went back to focusing on the possibility that in a few hours she could possibly be reunited with Todd.

Seven hours later they drove up a dirt road lined with police cars, and the private eye jogged over to meet them. Laura wondered if all the police cars parked outside of the house would make Gabrielle Madigan, or whoever was in the house, suspicious, but the cops didn't think so. Apparently no one had left the house since they'd arrived.

"Is there a back door?" Phillip asked. "Maybe they went out that way."

"No back door. Only the front door and a side door, and we have clear views of both."

Laura stared at the house, letting the conversation between Phillip and the private eye fade into the background. Could Todd be in there, just a few feet away from her? Doubt crept into her mind. For so long she'd been sure the Madigans were the kidnappers, but she saw no sign of a child anywhere. A little boy Todd's age might have a tricycle or a pair of roller skates. She didn't see anything like that.

"You're sure she's in there?" Laura asked.

"We saw her through the window about ten minutes ago."

"Have you seen anyone else?"

"No."

***

After a while, Gabrielle got bored with the game the men in the cars were playing with her. When more cars arrived she considered going outside and telling them to leave, but Brian told her not to.

She stopped, her hand on the doorknob. "What should I do?" she asked.

"Wait."

She backed away from the door. "But I don't like them."

"They can't do anything to you," Brian said. "Don't worry. I'm here to protect you."

She glared suspiciously at him. "You better not be handing me one of your bullshit stories. I'll kill you if you are."

He yawned dramatically. "Yeah, yeah. I'd like to see you try. Shut up and stay away from the window. Do you want them to see you or something?"

She looked outside anyway and saw a man in a uniform get out of his car and walk to another car. Then they all strode toward her front door.

"Brian?"

He didn't answer. Typical. Whenever she needed him, he disappeared.

"Who are you and what are you doing at my house?" Gabrielle demanded when she opened the door.

"Massachusetts State Police, Miss. We need to ask you and your husband a few questions. Is he around?"

"Do you see him anywhere?"

"No, I don't. Do you have any idea when he'll be home?"

"I talked to him a few minutes ago, but I haven't seen him in ages."

"What are you talking about?" Phillip asked, stepping forward. "You mean on the phone?"

Gabrielle opened her eyes, wide and mysterious, and put a finger to her lips. "Shh. Brian's like a magician. Poof! He disappears."

Laura shoved through the policemen in the front. "We're here about my son. If you have our little boy, tell us where he is. His name is Todd and we miss him very much. Please tell us if you know anything."

"Todd, Todd, Todd," Gabrielle mused, her voice rising and falling in a singsong pattern. "Where are you, Todd?" She giggled, then the sound grew into a full-throated laugh. She didn't stop until she collapsed on the floor.

The police turned back and called Doctor Chandler, who stepped into the house and spoke to Gabrielle for a few moments. When he was done, he turned and spoke quietly to Laura.

"If she knows anything she may tell you, or she may not. Mrs. Austin, I know you're in the middle of a terrible ordeal, but this woman needs to be hospitalized."

"Mrs. Madigan, where's your husband?" The private eye asked, peering around the police. "Do you know when he'll be home?"

"I don't have a husband. He's gone."

"You won't mind if we come in and take a look around then?"

They didn't wait for her answer, but pressed into the house, walking around her and into the various rooms. They found Brian Madigan's clothes hanging in his closet and folded neatly in his dresser drawers.

"Where is he?"

"In the garden," she said, smiling calmly.

They looked outside, but it was empty.

"Where? I don't see him."

She grinned. "I planted him."

***

Laura handed Phillip a glass of lemonade from Gabrielle's refrigerator. They grabbed a couple of chairs, which they carried out to the porch. Gabrielle had fallen asleep on the couch and a cop sat across from her, on guard. The rest of them had headed into the extensive garden and had begun to dig.

"Did you call Muller and tell him what's happened?" Phillip asked.

"I did, but I told him not to come. There's nothing he can do here. Besides, it would be too uncomfortable for all of us."

"But what if—"

"Then I'll need him."

Five hours passed, then six, then seven. Digging was heavy work, but they kept at it. They had to stop when the light got too dim, but at dawn they began again. Phillip went with them and Laura wanted to, but they wouldn't let her. She was just as glad they didn't.

A few hours later she heard yelling and saw Phillip running toward the house. *Not Todd. Please God, don't let it be Todd.*

"Phillip! Did they find him?"

He grabbed her hands. "Her husband, yes. Not Todd."

Laura felt all the tension from the past two days melt from her shoulders. At least she knew that much. "Are they sure?"

"It's the remains of an adult."

A couple of hours later the medical examiner came and took Brian Madigan's remains away. Throughout the day the police continued to dig. By nightfall they'd discovered nothing. The next morning it all started again. By early afternoon they'd dug up the entire property six feet deep and still found no sign of Todd. By that point, Gabrielle had fallen into a catatonic state and didn't respond to anything.

Laura stared at the woman, shaking her head. "She could have done anything to him and will never be able to tell us," she said.

They brought Gabrielle Madigan to police headquarters and booked her on suspicion of murder. The following morning Doctor Chandler arrived. He tried to reach Gabrielle, to talk to her, but couldn't.

"There's nothing more I can do," he told Laura and Phillip. "They'll commit her to the state hospital and try to bring her out of this so she can stand trial, but they may never be able to."

"Do you think she kidnapped my son?" Laura asked.

"No, as a matter of fact. I doubt that she did."

After he left, Laura and Phillip stared at each other over their coffee cups.

"I have to be back in L.A. in the morning," Phillip said.

Laura shook her head, trying to control her quivering chin, but it was no good. Tears squeezed from her eyes. "How could we have been so wrong? We were so sure Brian Madigan was the kidnapper that we ignored other leads. Now he's dead and his wife's insane and we may never know what happened."

"I'd rather be wrong and have Todd alive." For once, Phillip made sense.

Laura sniffed. "She could have killed him and buried him anywhere. We wasted so much time looking for the Madigans and now we have nothing. I can't think of any other connection to us, can you? I mean, if someone were just going for a ransom, they'd have grabbed one by now. This is more personal. Almost like they were teaching someone a lesson." She paused, thinking hard, trying to see through the confusion in her head. "Maybe I should have paid attention to Erich. I just didn't want to believe him. Have I been fooling myself all this time?"

***

Erich awoke to the aroma of fresh coffee. He reached for Laura, but her side of the bed was cool and empty. He forced his eyes open and noticed her peach satin dressing gown wasn't where she'd left it the night before. He put his robe on and went downstairs, where he found her in the kitchen, mixing pancake batter.

"I was just coming upstairs to wake you," she said when he kissed her neck from behind.

"What time is it?"

"After nine."

He put his arm around her and stuck his finger into the pancake batter. "Mmmm, delicious."

She slapped his hand. "Stop it."

"Didn't know you liked to cook."

"I love to cook. Phillip never wanted me to. I think he felt it was beneath him to have his wife cook. You know, like if I cooked I was some kind of servant."

"Hey, if I could find a maid who looked like you I'd hire her in a second."

"Funny. Very funny. As a matter of fact, I'm thinking of taking a culinary class at Southampton College."

"Sounds like a good plan." He turned the volume up on the radio and frowned at the news. "Looks like that hurricane is going to pound the New England coast."

"It's not coming here, is it?"

"They don't think so, but we'll keep the radio on today, just in case."

Erich looked out the kitchen window, eyebrows raised. The grounds of Willow Pond looked back at him. "You've got a delivery from Country Furnishings."

"They're early." Smiling, she put the spoon down and headed for the front door.

Erich was right behind her. "What are they delivering?"

"A new dining room set."

"Oh."

He turned and saw Mrs. Nickerson standing behind them with Rachel in her arms. The baby held out her arms to Erich and he was happy to bundle her in his arms.

"The cook isn't feeling well again this morning. I'll set the table and start breakfast," Mrs. Nickerson said.

Laura smiled at her. "Set the table, yes, but there's no need to start breakfast. I already have. Just watch the pancakes for me, would you?"

"She's trying to show us she's a gourmet cook," said Erich.

Mrs. Nickerson winked and headed into the kitchen.

"What's wrong with your old dining room set?" Erich asked. "Hey!"

Laura giggled, seeing Rachel had grabbed hold of his nose and wouldn't let go. "Nothing," she said, "but it's Phillip's taste and I hate it. Since he and I aren't together anymore, I'm going to have what I want. That's not a problem for you, is it?"

Erich grimaced. His nose was reddening under the little girl's grip. "Not at all. What are you going to do with the old set?"

"Sell it. For now I'll have them put it in the garage."

Rachel had such a firm grip on his nose he was beginning to find it difficult to breathe. Laura gave him the baby's bottle and he tried to distract her with it, but she was fixated on his nose. Finally he had enough and unclamped her hand. Rachel began to wail.

"Well, you do have a nice nose," Laura said, trying to contain her laughter. "If I didn't have other things to do, I'd grab it, too."

"She hurt me, tiny little thing that she is." He looked into his daughter's moist blue eyes and she stuck out her bottom lip.

Laura grinned at them both. "Put her in the high chair and give her some peaches. She loves them."

After the new, solid oak, art deco dining room set was in place, they sat down to a breakfast of pancakes, juice and coffee while they waited for the movers to carry the old dining room set into the garage.

"She loves those peaches. She's almost finished the whole jar."

"Something else she has in common with Todd. You better get some cereal into her before she's full."

He managed to get a half dozen spoonfuls of Gerber's barley cereal into her before she pushed the dish away.

"Let's take a walk after the movers finish," said Laura. "I want you to see the rest of the property. It's beautiful."

He drained his coffee cup. "Let's see who can get dressed the fastest."

Chapter Fifty-Six

Later that afternoon, Erich and Laura arrived at the East Hampton police station where they were met by Detective Wilson. Laura handed Wilson a single white child's sock and a gray rubber mouse, and remembered the last time she'd seen Todd playing with the mouse. It had been in the bathtub of their Patchin Place apartment. For a moment she could practically hear him splashing in the water.

"Where did you find it?" Wilson asked.

"On the West side of Willow Pond about an hour ago," said Laura.

"It was covered with dirt and leaves. I was about to throw it away when Laura grabbed it out of my hand," said Erich. "I didn't understand her reaction at first until she told me what it was."

"Mrs. Austin, can you positively identify this as having belonged to your son?"

"Yes. Mrs. Nickerson told me he was playing with it in the pond that day. She repeated the story when I spoke to her a while ago."

"We'll have to dust it for prints."

"I hope we didn't destroy any evidence."

"I doubt it," Detective Wilson said. "After all this time, who knows what we'll find. What I don't understand is how it could have been on the property all this time without anyone seeing it."

"Animals," Erich said. "Animals could have dragged it from one place to the other. There are teeth marks on it."

"The West side of the property is pretty woodsy," Laura admitted. She shuddered at the thought of Todd lost in those woods. "I rarely go there."

"Let's see what we can find," Wilson said. He carried the sock and toy into another room and returned a few minutes later.

"Well?" Laura asked.

"Nothing great, but we did get some prints. Now it's a question of finding a match."

"How long will that take?"

Wilson shook his head. "There's no way to tell. It could happen tomorrow, or it could take a year. Or more."

***

Two days later, just before five o'clock, the phone call they'd been waiting for finally arrived. Erich had been at the *Herald Tribune*'s offices in Washington when it came in. Another five minutes and he would have been out the door on his way to catch a train back to New York.

Wilson was succinct. The sock had yielded no results, but they'd found a match on the toy mouse. The guy's name was Rudy Strauss, a small time hood with a record of petty theft who'd spent four years behind bars. His record dated back to the 1920s. His last arrest had been in June of 1929, for which he was put on probation.

Erich decided to wait until he saw Laura to tell her. This wasn't something he wanted to explain over the phone. She had come into the city so they could spend some time together, away from the baby, and was meeting him at his apartment in the village.

Erich grabbed a cab at Penn Station and arrived at the apartment twenty minutes later. When he walked in the door he did a double take at the trail of rose petals leading from the living room into the bedroom. Erich left his jacket at the door, loosened his tie and happily followed the trail. At its end he found Laura lying on the bed, clad only in a black lace bra and matching panties.

He sighed, smiling broadly. "This is what every man dreams of coming home to." He shook his head, incredulous. "You're so beautiful."

"Well, why are you just standing there?" she purred.

He sat on the bed and she took his hand, drawing him toward her. Bad timing, he thought, but he had to tell her now.

"Laura, we have to talk."

She sat bolt upright. "Something's happened. What is it?"

"Wilson called me. They found a match."

She climbed out of bed and put her robe on. "Why didn't he call me?"

"He tried but got no answer at Willow Pond. He didn't know where you were so he called me."

"So who do the fingerprints belong to?"

"Rudy Strauss. Is the name familiar?"

"No."

"I was wondering if your aunt might have mentioned him to you."

Laura frowned. "She rarely discussed that part of her life with me. Why? Does he have something to do with her?"

"I think we need to talk to Harry Davis."

Laura hadn't been to *Bacchanal* since Harry had become the manager. She knocked and the peephole opened, allowing Laura to show her card and give the password, which she hoped was still the right one. Someone unlocked the door and she and Erich went right in.

A few people were at the bar, drinking openly. They found Harry in his office, which had once been Virginia's office. It felt strange, seeing him at her aunt's desk. When he saw Laura he got up and kissed her cheek.

"Laura, my dear. What brings you here?" Then he noticed Erich and gave him a polite but cool smile. "And you, Mr. Muller?"

"We need to ask you about a man named Rudy Strauss. Do you know who he is?"

"Can't say that I do. Why do you ask?"

Laura told him what had happened

"Wish I could say that I knew who Rudy Strauss is, but I don't."

"Are you sure about this, Mr. Davis?" Erich asked, flicking one eyebrow.

Harry set his feet apart and crossed his arms. "Mr. Muller, I never liked you or your attitude. But I'd never do anything to hurt Laura. If Virginia ever found out that I had, it would be too damn bad for me."

***

Five minutes after Laura and Erich walked out of *Bacchanal*, Harry dialed the overseas operator. Virginia picked up the phone on the other end.

"We were just going to have a can-can contest, Harry." He could hear laughter in the background. "Think of what you're missing."

"We may have a problem," he said.

"Like what?"

He told her about Laura and Erich's visit.

"You did the right thing. They can't know. Not yet."

"He's a damn good reporter. He'll find out. You can't keep them in the dark forever."

"I can and I will. And you're going to help."

"How?"

"By destroying anything that connects us in any way to Strauss. Understand? They can't know anything until I find Todd."

"Any leads?"

"I'm working on it."

Chapter Fifty-Seven

Where was Rudy Strauss? That was the question weighing on Ben Wilson's mind in the days following the discovery of Rudy's fingerprints on Todd Austin's toy. Was Rudy the kidnapper? To answer the second question, he'd have to answer the first. And right now answering either one seemed impossible.

Working out of the second precinct in Manhattan, Ben spent days going through missing person's files, and each time he came up empty. He decided to go under the assumption that Strauss was the kidnapper and tried to put himself in Rudy's shoes. The file on Strauss wasn't big, but he knew enough about him to know he was a punk whose main goal in life was to make a quick buck. To a guy like Strauss, half a million dollars was the jackpot. Wilson assumed Strauss had spent it as fast as he'd gotten it. By now he wouldn't have much left. He'd be looking for his next big touch.

Virginia Kingsley's people denied it, but Ben had the feeling Strauss was tied to organized crime. At first he'd planned to subpoena their records, then decided he didn't want to make them suspicious. But how else could he get the information about Strauss that he needed? He tapped his fingers on his desk, thinking. He could think of one person who might be able to help. He dialed Willow Pond. The maid told him Mrs. Austin was staying with a friend, and gave him Muller's phone number.

Laura answered the phone on the second ring.

"Mrs. Austin, it's Wilson here. I hope I'm not disturbing you."

"Not at all."

"Good. I need you to do a favor for me. This might seem strange, but I feel it's important. It's connected to your son's case. Do you have access to your aunt's office at *Bacchanal*?"

"Yes, I have a set of keys."

"Is anyone else there at this hour?"

"No. Harry opens the place between 2:00 and 3:00 in the afternoon. Why?"

"I want you to get over there as fast as you can and look for any information on Rudy Strauss. Do you understand? You have to be quick and thorough. Can you do that?"

Laura started to put her shoes on. "Do you think Rudy Strauss kidnapped my son?" She flipped through her address book, searching for the car service she always used. "Wait a minute. The baby. I'll have to bring her with me."

"I'll send a man over and you can give him the keys, if it's too much trouble. But it's imperative we find out more about Strauss."

"No, I can do it. It will be fine."

For the next hour and half, Wilson kept himself busy going through more missing person's files. Ate half a pound cake and drank three cups of coffee. By 11:30 he was ready to go to *Bacchanal* himself, fearing he'd made a mistake sending a woman on a man's errand. By 11:45 he was headed out for a squad car when a taxi pulled up in front of the station house. Laura Kingsley held her wailing baby in one arm and carried a manila folder under the other.

"I have to get this back by tomorrow morning," she said.

They went inside and he showed her where she could change the baby. He made a fresh pot of coffee then flipped through Strauss's folder while she tended to the baby. He didn't have to read much to learn Strauss was from the San Francisco area.

Laura wrapped the baby in a blanket, then sat down and gave her a bottle. The infant drank a little and fell asleep in her mother's arms.

"You know," Ben said, "you'd make a good cop, Laura."

She grinned mischievously. "I don't know about that, but it was kind of fun. Did you find the information you were looking for?"

"We'll find out soon."

He picked up the phone and dialed the S.F.P.D. The call was transferred to the squad commander, and Wilson told him about finding Rudy's fingerprints on Todd Austin's toy. He heard an audible gasp on the other end of the phone.

"I'm not sure," said the squad commander, "but I think Rudy Strauss was murdered."

"What?"

"About six weeks ago we found the badly decomposed body of a thirty, thirty-five-year-old male at a house on Jones Street. Turns out the house belonged to one George Strauss, whose nephew, Rudy or Randy Strauss, had been missing for a few months. I bet if you send me a copy of the fingerprints there'll be a match."

"I'll send them to you. Did the medical examiner take any photographs of the corpse?"

"Yeah, but it's not a pretty sight."

"Send them. I've got some good mug shots of Strauss. Maybe someone will be able to give a positive ID."

"You think he kidnapped the Austin kid?"

"Could be. But you've got your own crime to solve."

"I do?"

Wilson couldn't believe how dense the man was. "Yeah. You have to find out who killed Strauss."

***

When Erich got home that night, Laura told him what had happened that morning. She was noticeably upset about the fact that Rudy Strauss, a known criminal, seemed to have some connection to her aunt.

Erich was bothered by something else. He picked up the phone and dialed the second precinct. Within seconds Wilson picked up the phone.

"What the hell are you doing sending Laura to do a cop's job?" Erich demanded. "Are you trying to get her killed?"

"Take it easy, Muller. We figured if someone came in and caught her she'd be able to make up some excuse about why she was there. We had a man watching the place the whole time."

"You're a liar."

"Think what you want." Wilson glanced down at the post mortem photographs of Rudy Strauss. "That girl has more guts than you do. Tell her again that I said she did a great job."

Erich's voice rose. "Don't you dare use her again, do you hear?"

He slammed the phone down and turned around, coming face to face with a furious Laura. She clutched a can of spaghetti sauce in one hand and looked as if she wanted to throw it at him.

"Why did you have to make such a big deal out of it?"

"Because it *is* a big deal, that's why. Wilson did a stupid thing, putting you in danger that way."

"I wasn't in any danger. I'd never have taken Rachel with me if I thought I was. Harry knew Virginia had given me keys to the place and if he'd found me there I already had an excuse made up."

"The baby was *with* you?"

"Yes, she was. And we both did fine. You have to start trusting that I know what I'm doing."

Erich squeezed his hands against his head and held them there for a moment before lowering them and forcing himself to relax. "I'm sorry, Laura. It's just that I love you and Rachel so much I can't stand the thought—" He took her hand. "I'm sorry. Really. So what did you find out?"

"It looks like Rudy Strauss was murdered. Wilson is trying to make a positive ID. The worst part is that he had some connection to Virginia. Because of that, we have to go to London as soon as we can. I want Virginia to tell me what she knows about Rudy and about Todd's kidnapping, if anything. And Erich, when we're through with all this, if you were right all along, you can go ahead and say 'I told you so'."

Chapter Fifty-Eight

Four days later they left for London. Erich managed to get a month's leave of absence by making the excuse that he was chasing down some important leads in the Austin kidnapping and by promising the *Herald Tribune* daily updates. Both he and Laura were brokenhearted about having to leave Rachel at home, but chasing down a kidnapper's accomplice wasn't the sort of thing a six-month-old baby could be part of. Besides, Laura knew Rachel would be safe in Iris Nickerson's care. As an added security measure, Ben Wilson assigned cops to guard Willow Pond twenty-four hours a day.

Their plane landed at just after 3:00 in the afternoon and a taxi dropped them off at their hotel. The flight had been long and bumpy and they both were exhausted, but Laura didn't want to waste any time. She wanted to see her aunt immediately.

They left their suitcases at the hotel and settled into another of London's spacious taxis, then headed to *Kingsley's*. She had wanted to call Virginia and tell her they were coming, but Erich didn't think it was a good idea to give her advance notice.

The door was unlocked. When they went inside they saw Virginia speaking to a man they didn't recognize. She turned and glanced at them, but didn't seem to recognize them. She turned back and went behind the bar where she began counting bottles. When they approached the bar, she looked at them again. This time her eyes widened with surprise.

"I thought my eyes were fooling me," she said, smiling. "But it really *is* you. Didn't you get enough of rainy London when you were here before?"

Her voice didn't sound right. 'Guarded' was the word Laura would have chosen. She felt suddenly uncomfortable in front of the woman who had raised her. The one woman she had always trusted above everyone else. But there was no way to avoid this conversation.

"We need to talk about Rudy Strauss," Laura said bluntly.

Virginia couldn't look at her, and Laura feared what that meant. She was relieved when Erich took her hand and told Virginia they needed privacy. Virginia nodded shortly and led them to her office. Laura had never seen her aunt look apprehensive before. It was a disturbing thing to see. It didn't last long, however. By the time they'd walked into her office, Virginia was her old self: calm, confident and serene.

"Tell us what you know about Strauss," Laura said.

Virginia's brow creased and she rolled her eyes toward the ceiling as if trying to remember. "Rudy Strauss. The name's sort of familiar," she said, returning her gaze to Laura's, "but I don't know who he is."

Erich removed his notepad from his jacket pocket and jotted a few things down. Virginia glared at him. "What is this? Are you here to interview me, Mr. Muller?"

Erich glanced up at her but kept writing. "Can you tell us why you had a personnel file on Strauss at *Bacchanal*?"

She shrugged. "He must have applied for a job there." She turned to Laura, frowning. "I'm curious about how he found that information."

"Actually, he didn't. I did," Laura said.

Before Virginia could object, they told her about finding Todd's sock and toy mouse on Willow Pond, and about the matching fingerprints. Then they told her about the corpse found on Jones Street in San Francisco and Wilson's belief that it was Rudy.

Virginia clicked her tongue dismissively. "Wilson has no idea what he's doing. It could be anyone."

"The age and size fit the description we have of Strauss."

"Did you ever meet him?" Laura asked.

The phone rang, but Virginia made no move to answer. "Whoever that is can call back. Did I meet him? I don't know if I ever did. I might have, but if I did I don't remember him. Maybe Harry would know. Have you spoken to him?"

Laura nodded, feeling increasingly uneasy. "Yes. He told us he had no idea who he was."

Erich glanced around the room. "This office is nicer than the one you have in New York. You do know how to live. You always have."

"Thanks for the backhanded compliment."

"You're welcome. Okay. Well, there are three things we know for sure," Erich said. "One is that Rudy Strauss was at *Bacchanal* at some time, because we found his signature on a piece of paper in your office. The second is that his fingerprints were on Todd's toy. The third is that Todd was playing with that toy the day he was kidnapped. Now you tell me, Virginia. What you think that means?"

"I don't know."

"Maybe you just don't want to say."

Virginia's smile was demure. "Think whatever you want." She turned to Laura and touched her arm, back to the caring aunt Laura had always known. "It's wonderful to see you, Laura. Under any circumstances. Now I don't mean to be rude, but I have a large party coming in tonight and I have to make some preparations in advance. Why don't you stop by later on, and we'll have dinner together?"

Laura smiled, desperate to believe her aunt, but unable to stop wondering about her possible connection to Rudy Strauss. She decided it might be a good idea to meet up with Virginia a little later on. She might have come up with new information by then. "I'd love to, but I'm tired. I just want to get back to the hotel and relax this evening. How about tomorrow? Maybe we could have lunch."

"That sounds fine. You're welcome to tag along, Mr. Muller. That is, if you can tolerate my company for an entire meal."

On their way outside they argued about Virginia. Erich hailed a cab and held the door open for Laura, then climbed in the other side. All they way back to the hotel they argued about what Virginia's connection to Rudy might or might not be.

They ordered tea and scones from room service and headed upstairs to their suite. Laura slipped her high heels off and put on a pair of slippers, and Erich removed his jacket and tie. By the time room service arrived they were both relaxing on the couch, arguments pushed to the side for now. Moments later they were sipping tea and munching on scones with cream and strawberry jam.

"We didn't really come here about Virginia," Laura said. "At least I didn't. We came here to find Maggie Pierce."

"Yes. That's right. And we'll go to the police tomorrow."

Chapter Fifty-Nine

Maggie worked late on Tuesdays, so Dennis walked the two miles to Terri's place to pick up Andy. Maggie had asked him to bring the boy back to their flat. She'd also asked him to start dinner. He'd had to sell his car because he was so low on cash, and he wasn't in the best mood, but he knew Maggie needed help and he liked her too much to refuse.

It started to rain a couple of blocks from her house, so he was glad to see the kid already waiting outside, wearing a slicker and rain hat. Terri stood beside him, holding his hand.

"Tell Maggie I'll ring her tomorrow," she said as Dennis departed with Andy.

They walked three blocks to the bus stop, and Dennis was glad he'd listened to the weather report before he'd left. He'd brought an umbrella with him and kept telling Andy to stay under it with him, but the child kept dancing around him, playing with the red and yellow yo-yo Terri had bought him.

The bus finally pulled up, and Dennis breathed a sigh of relief. He handed the driver a three-pence and the driver smiled down at Andy, who was still mostly interested in the yo-yo.

"Where's your mate Andrew?" asked the driver.

"Home with his mommy."

"Where's your mommy?"

The little boy frowned. "Working."

By the time they got home it had stopped raining, so Dennis helped Andy change clothes and sent him outside to play. Dennis lit the cooker and put chicken and potatoes into a roasting pan, then slid it all into the cooker. When he was done, he carried the newspaper with him to the living room couch.

The headlines were all about Winston Churchill having been elected prime minister. Dennis wasn't interested in politics. He turned a few more pages and stopped at an article about a movie star named Phillip Austin.

"The actor is no stranger to tragedy," it said. "It has been nearly a year and a half since Austin's only son, nineteen-month-old Todd, was kidnapped from his estate on Long Island, New York. He and the boy's mother, Laura Kingsley, from whom he is recently divorced, have never given up hope of finding their son. The actor's publicist says the memory of their little boy remains painfully clear in their minds."

Dennis and a couple of friends had actually talked about the Austin kidnapping a few days before. They all figured the baby was dead or else he'd have been found by now. They also felt certain the crime was connected in some way to Virginia Kingsley's bootlegging activities. But as long as the child remained missing, the case would stay open.

A few minutes later he went into the kitchen to check dinner and heard the apartment door close. It was too early for Maggie to be home, so it had to be Andy. When Dennis finished in the kitchen he went back into the living room. There he found Andy sitting on the floor, holding the newspaper he'd just been reading. The little boy was staring intently at Laura Kingsley's picture. Dennis knelt down next to him.

"Is something wrong, lad?"

Andy jabbed his finger at the photograph, but didn't say anything. Dennis studied the photograph, then looked at the little boy.

"What is it? What's wrong?" The boy's eyes were creased with concern. Something about them looked amazingly familiar. A thought suddenly struck him and he stared at the paper, then the boy. Could there possibly be a resemblance? No. It couldn't be.

Or could it?

***

Three days later, on a Saturday, Maggie had to work. Dennis dropped Andy off at his little friend Steve's, then came back to Maggie's flat to tend to the tomato plants in their tiny garden.

He'd forgotten his work gloves and thought he'd borrow hers, so he opened the bottom draw of her dresser where he knew she kept them. They were underneath some scarves, which he dug through. As he was about to close the drawer, an envelope caught his eye. It was marked *Medical Diagnosis* and was slightly yellowed with age. Dennis pulled the envelope out of the drawer, feeling a guilty curiosity. He didn't want to snoop, but what if Maggie were sick? What if, God forbid, she were dying? He had to know. He sat on the bed and removed a single sheet of paper from the envelope.

"Re: Nancy M. Evans," it read.

Who was Nancy M. Evans? Why did Maggie have a letter about her in her dresser? He read the letter, which was from one doctor to the other.

"The patient has been in a severe depression since the stillborn birth of her infant son on January 31, 1928," the document said. *"She has twice attempted suicide. Her depressed state has been compounded by the knowledge that the complete hysterectomy I had to perform following the infant's birth has made it impossible for her to bear another child. She has been unable to accept this and I am referring her to you for treatment. She ..."*

Another small piece of crumpled paper had fallen onto the floor when Dennis had pulled out the first sheet. He leaned down and picked it up, then studied the signature at the bottom. Very strange. The signature looked just like Maggie's writing, except she'd signed it "Nancy Evans." Dennis had never been more puzzled. If Maggie were Nancy Evans and she'd had a dead baby more than eight months before Andy had been born, then how could she be Andy's mother? Maybe the boy had been adopted.

He heard shuffling footsteps coming down the hall and stuffed the letter into his pocket. A moment later Andy stood by the door, keen eyes intent on Dennis.

"Why are you in Mommy's room?"

"I came in here to get gloves for gardening. Do you want to help me with the tomato plants?"

"Yep. I want to eat them."

"If any of them are ripe you can have one. I bet they're bloody delicious."

Andy giggled when he heard the word 'bloody'. Maggie had asked Dennis many times not to swear around the child.

They walked outside to water the tomato plant, but Andy lost interest when his friend Janie called him. Dennis followed him to make sure they were busy playing, then went back into the flat with the letter still in his pocket.

He headed back into Maggie's room and read the letter again, feeling utterly confused. What did it mean? Maybe Nancy M. Evans was Maggie's sister. Then again, Maggie had never mentioned a sister. In fact, she had told him many times that she was an only child. Maggie had kept the letter well hidden, or so she'd thought, so he obviously wasn't supposed to know about it. He couldn't ask her what it meant, but someone must know.

What should he do? She'd be home in half an hour. He had to decide quickly. Should he put the letter back or keep it and take the chance that she might discover it missing? He didn't have enough time to get to the doctor's office and back before she got home. He decided if Maggie had to work the following Saturday, he could go see the doctor then. Otherwise he'd have to wait until the next opportunity presented itself, and he had no idea when that might be. Before he put the letter back into Maggie's dresser drawer, Dennis copied down the name and address of the doctor and tucked it safely away.

***

The doctor's office was in Knightsbridge, a short bus ride away. He'd checked the date before he'd set off, so Dennis knew the letter was only three years old. Because of that, he was optimistic the doctor would still have the same office. The office was three blocks from the bus stop. When he arrived, he was pleased to see the same doctor's name on the shingle.

The nurse looked startled when Dennis walked up to the desk. She regarded him strangely then asked if he had an appointment. He told her he didn't, wondering at her reaction. Then he glanced around the office. When he saw all the pregnant women, he realized it was an obstetrician's office. He should have known, and he felt like a fool.

"I need to see the doctor," he said quietly to the nurse.

"Is your wife a patient?"

"No. Well, she was once a patient of his. I have to see him. It's important."

"I'll see what I can do. Why don't you have a seat?"

Over two hours later, the doctor's last patient left. The doctor emerged from his office and handed a stack of manila folders to the nurse.

"Please put these away, Miss Simmons. I have to get over to hospital. The Donnelly baby is on its way."

"Yes, sir. But before you go, this gentlemen would like to speak to you. He's been waiting quite a long time. It's about his wife."

"What's the problem, Mister …? I don't have much time."

"Collins. Can we talk in your office?"

The doctor frowned, thinking. "Collins? Never had a patient by that name. I'm sorry. I don't have time, anyway. You'll have to come back next week."

"No. It has to be now."

"You can walk me to my car then. It's the best I can do."

When they got outside, Dennis handed him a picture of Maggie. "Was this woman ever a patient of yours?"

The doctor studied the picture for a moment then handed it back to him. "She looks familiar, but I can't be sure. Why do you ask?"

"She's my wife, and I'm worried about her. She's been acting strangely lately."

"In what way?"

"She's been telling crazy stories about a dead baby who she can hear crying at night. I'm afraid she's losing her mind."

"What's her name?"

"Nancy Evans."

"Ah, yes. I believe she was one of my father's patients. I took over his practice when he retired two years ago."

"Where is he? Can I talk to him?"

"I'm afraid not. He's suffering from dementia. He doesn't even know who I am."

"I'm sorry to hear that. But you recognized her, right?"

The doctor stood by his car, thinking. "When I have time I'll check my father's records, but I'm pretty sure she was a patient of his. If I remember correctly it was a tragic case. Poor soul. You need to get help for her soon."

"I will. I promise."

Dennis walked into the nearest pub and ordered a pint of ale. He stared at the drink, thinking hard and getting nowhere. He'd hoped the doctor would have had been able to tell him more. Was Maggie Pierce actually Nancy Evans? Was she really Andy's mother? Because if she'd lost a baby eight months previously ... Most importantly, as incredible as it seemed, could Andy possibly be the famous kidnapped boy, Todd Austin?

After he finished his beer, Dennis headed down the street, still thinking. He walked past a few little shops, then stopped dead outside the window of a book store. Displayed up front was the bestselling autobiography, *A Life,* by Laura Austin.

Dennis rushed inside and grabbed the first copy he could get his hands on. He turned the book over and studied at the photograph on the back cover. Andy really did look a lot like Laura Kingsley, with the same green eyes and the same mouth. Could it be possible that dear, quiet Maggie had been involved in the kidnapping? He walked toward the till, gripping the book tightly in his hands.

The clerk took it and looked at the price. "This should be interesting. Her aunt, Virginia Kingsley, lives in London now. She comes in here occasionally."

Dennis paid for the book then walked quickly home, eager to start reading. He was expected at Maggie's for dinner around seven. He grabbed a beer, laid down on the sofa, and opened the book to the first page.

"I was born in San Francisco two years after the earthquake of 1906," it began.

Laura Kingsley went on to describe a happy childhood torn apart by the death of her parents. He read through her growing-up years quickly, even though he found it interesting. He especially enjoyed reading about all the boyfriends she'd had before she met Phillip Austin. He flipped through a few pictures, becoming more convinced all the time of her resemblance to Andy. She was gorgeous at age sixteen, wearing flapper garb and standing in front of Virginia Kingsley's speakeasy, *Bacchanal*. Dennis sighed. Women like her never gave him a second glance.

She and Phillip Austin were married on October 11, 1927. Their son, Todd, was born the following September 7.

Dennis thought back, remembering. He and Maggie had celebrated Andy's birthday on September 17. Andy Evans and Todd Austin were exactly the same age.

He flipped forward and read a couple of paragraphs about a place called *Bacchanal*. Then he skipped to another page and read some more.

"Iris Nickerson, Todd's nanny, didn't see the kidnapper's face because he was wearing a clown's mask, but she did her best to describe him to the police ..."

Dennis felt slightly ill. A few months earlier he and Maggie had taken Andy to the circus. When the boy had seen the clowns he'd kicked and screamed with terror. He had made such a commotion it had been impossible for them to stay. When he'd asked Maggie what was wrong, she avoided answering him. It wasn't until he pressed her that she admitted she thought Andy was afraid of clowns, but she never said why. Could he possibly have a vague memory of his kidnapping?

He read on. *"Todd was a good baby. I loved him more than I'd ever loved anyone. I couldn't bear to be separated from him, even for an hour. My favorite time with him was after his bath. When he was a tiny infant, I cradled him in my arms and rocked him to sleep. As he got older, he wanted a bedtime story. When I finished reading the story, he still wanted me to rock him to sleep. To this day I still feel the soft weight of him snuggled against me. Part of me died the day Todd disappeared."*

Maggie told him often that Andy loved being read to, especially the *Winnie the Pooh* books. He remembered a poem the little boy liked, one he could recite himself, word-for-word.

It must have been awful for Laura Austin to lose her baby and never see him again. He recalled the bottomless look of love Maggie wore whenever she watched Andy play. Dennis counted from September 1928 to April 1930, nineteen months. Far too long for a mother to be without her child.

What should he do? As much as he liked Maggie, Laura Kingsley had the right to know what had happened to her son. Also, maybe, just maybe, there'd be some kind of finder's fee in it for him.

Chapter Sixty

Dennis sat on the front stoop watching an old orange tabby chase a fly. The cat belonged to the bloke in the flat next to Maggie's and was old and slow. The stupid thing fell over every time he went to swat the fly. Finally the cat gave up, curled into an orange ball and went to sleep on the ledge. The fly disappeared with the wind. Dennis wished human dilemmas could be solved by sleep, but all sleeping did was delay facing the problems, like he was doing now.

He went back inside the flat and found Maggie sitting at the kitchen table, hunched over a ledger book.

"Why don't you come sit outside with me, Maggie?" Dennis asked. "It's such a beautiful night."

"Maybe later. I'm going over the books for Mr. Hendler."

"This can't wait."

Maggie glanced up from the ledger book, frowning. "What could be so important that it can't wait until I'm finished?"

Maybe it was her tone, maybe it was his need to understand, but Dennis couldn't help himself. "Where do I start?" he asked. "Let's see. How about with all those people who are looking for you? Like Virginia Kingsley?"

She swallowed hard. "What are you talking about?"

He gazed into her brown eyes. "You look like a scared little rabbit. Where's Andy?"

"At Steve's."

"Good. Just wanted to be sure he's not here."

"Why?"

"Take it easy, Nancy."

She narrowed her eyes at him, but he saw her lips tremble. "My name's Maggie."

"Bosh. It's Nancy Evans. To be more precise, it's Nancy Margaret Evans Pierce. Smart of you to change your name but keep it legal. I thought it would take me a long time to find out your real name, but it only took a few days."

"What's this all about?"

He grabbed her arm and pulled her down onto the couch next to him. "Tell me about Andy's father, Nancy."

"I already told you about him."

"You told me about someone, but I doubt he's Andy's father." He thrust a piece of paper at her, one marked *Medical Diagnosis*. "Smashing reading, this."

She grabbed it from him and her eyes widened. "Where did you find this?"

"You aren't Andy's mother. You can't be."

"What of it? He's adopted. When he's older I plan to tell him. Until then, keep your mouth shut."

"I was amazed when I found this." He opened the book he'd been hiding under a cushion in the couch and pointed to a picture of Laura and Phillip. "He looks so much like these people."

He put the book into her hands and she glanced at the picture. "Please—"

"Does anyone else know he's Todd Austin?"

"Don't do this to me."

"I won't tell anyone your little secret if you do me a favor."

"Tell me what you want, then get out of here. I never want to see you again."

"Now, now, Nancy," he said with a wink. "Don't spoil my fun."

She glared at him. "Stop playing games and get out."

Dennis hesitated a moment before he said what was on his mind. "You and your boyfriend came into a lot of dough, didn't you? Well, that's where I come in."

"I didn't get a cent."

"What about the ransom?"

"Rudy got it all. I have no idea where he is or if he's even alive. Andy and I live on what I make at the jewelry shop. If you came here looking for money you came to the wrong place."

He frowned. "Not again. Not another—"

"Scheme gone bad?"

"But you have the golden child," he said, shaking his head. "He must be worth something."

"Are you threatening my son?"

Dennis laughed. "He's not your son, and if I went to the bobbies and told them about the little tyke, you'd spend the rest of your life in jail. Is that what you want?"

"Leave me and my son alone."

"Sure I will, if you get me what I want. You'll do that, won't you, Maggie? You don't want the poor kid to get hurt."

She sobbed. "No."

"Twenty-five thousand is a nice round figure."

"Where the hell do you expect me to get that kind of money?"

"That's your problem. Just keep in mind your precious boy isn't safe until you do."

"I'll kill you if you lay a hand on him."

The door opened and Andy, Steve and Terri walked in. "It's ten of two and I thought you were picking Andy up at one," Terri said. "Steve's got a three o'clock dental appointment."

Maggie quickly wiped tears off her cheeks. "I lost track of time."

Dennis smiled at Maggie. "You hit the jackpot with this one, Maggie. That face is worth a million." He patted her on the back and headed into the kitchen.

"I have to go," Terri said. "Walk me outside." Once they stood by Terri's car, she frowned at Maggie. "What's going on? You're acting odd."

"Everything's fine. We had a disagreement, that's all."

Terri patted her arm. "He's an odd fish, luv. Be careful. I'll ring you later."

***

Maggie worked until nine o'clock every Tuesday night. Some Tuesdays her boss stayed until closing and other times he left at seven. He told her he planned to start keeping the shop open late on Friday nights, too, but he didn't expect her to work late two nights a week.

He'd had a cold for over a week, and by Tuesday he was so tired he left at four o'clock. She was busy until nearly seven-thirty with two couples coming in for engagement rings and an elderly man looking for a necklace to give his wife for their fiftieth wedding anniversary. From the bits of information the old man told her, Maggie was almost certain his wife had been in the previous week to buy a gold watch for him.

After more than half an hour, the gentleman found a necklace he liked and bought it, along with a pair of gold, heart-shaped earrings. Maggie waited another half an hour after he left and when no more customers came, she locked the door and pulled down the shade.

She took the key, went to one of the display cases and opened it. Then she removed two rings. One was an emerald surrounded by diamond chips. The other, the most valuable ring in the store, was a three and a half carat teardrop-shaped diamond. She dropped them into her purse and went to another display case. From it she removed a diamond and emerald bracelet.

She stood motionless, looking at the jewelry and thinking about what she was doing. If she got caught, she'd go to prison. Then what would happen to Andy? The authorities would probably find out the truth about him, and she'd lose him forever. She couldn't risk that. She returned the jewelry to the display cases, locked up the store and went home.

Andy was spending the night at Steve's again. When she got home she saw Dennis' car parked outside. He'd made her give him a key and would be waiting inside. This wasn't going to be a happy homecoming, since she hadn't brought him any money. She took a deep breath for courage and opened the front door.

The first thing Maggie noticed when she stepped into the foyer of 74 Onslow Gardens was that someone had thrown her mail on the floor. Every day the housekeeper put all the first floor tenants' mail in neat piles on a table in the foyer. On nights that she worked late, Dennis usually took hers in, or else her neighbor slid it under the door.

She checked her watch. 8:45 p.m. Dennis had said he'd be there by 6:00 p.m. after picking up Andy at her friend Terri's house. She'd been terrified he might have done something to the boy, but reasoned that he wouldn't. He was good with the child. Besides, he couldn't expect any money if he did anything.

She slid the key in the lock, then frowned when she discovered it had been broken. Her heart pounded. What if whoever had broken the lock was still inside? But what about Andy? Was he all right?

She eased the door open and peered around. She heard nothing. Stepping inside, she almost tripped over one of the living room chairs. For a brief second she thought of going for help, but she knew she had to go through this alone. She walked across the carpeted hallway, then turned to the right and found the living room in disarray. The curtains had been torn from the windows and the couch was toppled to the side. She saw no sign of either Andy or Dennis.

She stepped carefully over the mess, heading to the kitchen, where she found Dennis in front of the cooker, lying on his side in a widening pool of blood. His body was still warm to the touch. After she placed her fingers to his cheek, she vomited everything she'd eaten that day. Then she scrambled up and screamed Andy's name over and over, racing through the rooms, throwing furniture over, looking in closets and under beds, sofas and chairs until every inch of the house had been searched. The child was nowhere to be found.

Shaking convulsively, she returned to the kitchen and stared at Dennis' dead body. Something white gleamed among all the red: a sheet of paper propped up on the stove. She grabbed at it and barely managed to keep her stomach down when her skirt brushed Dennis' face. With trembling hands she unfolded the paper and read the words: *"Todd's gone again. Goodbye!"*

Rudy had found her. He'd taken the boy again. But how? She thought she'd covered her tracks well, and it made no sense for him to just show up here now. If he'd been hunting for her, he should have found her long before.

She glanced at the note again and noticed something familiar about the handwriting, even though it was obviously disguised. The large loop in the capital letter G on the word 'Gone' was what caught her eye, and she remembered back, years before. She shook her head. No. It couldn't be. Not *him*. It couldn't be his handwriting. He never would have been involved in such a thing. Besides, he and Rudy didn't even know each other, she didn't think. Still, she'd seen him write the capital letter G in his name that way.

There was one person she had to contact before she called the police. In the hall closet she found the telephone directory and quickly located the listing she wanted. A woman answered the phone on the second ring.

"Virginia Kingsley?"

"Who is this?"

"I'm Nancy Evans. I need you to come right away." She recited her address. "Don't delay. It's a matter of life and death."

Chapter Sixty-One

Virginia stood in front of Maggie's door, trying to remain calm. This woman had kept Todd from his family for a year and a half. When Nancy Evans opened the door Virginia would have to restrain herself from putting her hands around the woman's neck and choking the life out of her. That wouldn't do anyone any good, especially Todd. The thought of the little boy sent a little thrill through her. Was he behind that door right now? She put her hand up to knock and the door flung open. She looked into the face of Nancy Evans and saw fear in the woman's brown eyes. Virginia took a few steps inside and saw the condition of the living room. Something was very wrong.

Nancy's voice trembled. "You've got to help me."

"Why should I do anything for you?" Virginia glared at the woman, looking her up and down. "Is Todd here?"

Tears spilled from Nancy's eyes. "No."

Virginia took three steps toward her and stopped. Nancy kept repeating, "I'm so sorry, so very, very sorry."

"Is Todd all right?"

"I don't know. Oh my God! I don't know!" She handed Virginia the note. "I need your help. Rudy broke in here, murdered my friend and kidnapped him again."

Virginia raised her eyebrows "That's impossible. What friend are you talking about? Where is he?"

Virginia followed Nancy into the kitchen and was soon looking into the frozen face of a man she didn't know. He'd been dead for at least a couple of hours. Nancy stood in the kitchen doorway, too squeamish to look at the corpse. Cool as a cucumber, Virginia thought. Couldn't handle a dead body, but capable of keeping a child away from his mother.

"So you called me and not the police, thinking I'd help you? Maybe you killed this guy. I know one thing for certain: Rudy didn't. So maybe it was you. You're capable of anything, aren't you, Miss Evans?"

"How do you know Rudy didn't do this?"

"He's dead, that's how I know. Somebody put a bullet in his black heart months ago."

She went to pick up the telephone but Nancy put her hand out to stop her. She waited while Nancy went into the bedroom, returning moments later. She handed Virginia a photograph of a long-nosed, brown haired man.

"I think it might be my ex-husband, Geoffrey Pierce."

They sat on the sofa and Virginia stared at the picture. She'd seen this man, this Geoffrey Pierce before, but couldn't remember where. Suddenly it came to her. The poker game. The one where Rudy had lost big. He'd been the dealer. Didn't say much, but she couldn't forget those probing eyes.

"Was he involved in my nephew's kidnapping?"

"I don't think so. I don't think he and Rudy even knew each other."

Virginia stared at Nancy, trying to discern was what going on in the woman's mind. Most of the time Virginia found it easy to read people, but not this time. Nancy was either shrewd or not too bright. She had the feeling it was the latter. No woman of average intelligence would get involved with not one, but three losers. Not only that, but the woman would soon find herself facing jail time for a crime she probably went along with just because she was told to.

"Do you know where he is?" asked Virginia.

"I have no idea," said Nancy. "The last time I heard from him was almost four years ago and he was living in New Zealand. He's Australian."

"You think he has Todd? Where would he have taken him?"

Nancy hung her head and sniffed. "I didn't want to lose him. Now I've lost him for good."

"He was never yours to lose. Trust me. I intend to see to it you pay for what you've done."

The phone rang and Nancy grabbed it.

"Mommy!"

"Andy?"

"Mommy! Help me!"

The line went dead.

Chapter Sixty-Two

It was drizzling when the cab pulled away from the curb. Laura gripped Erich's sleeve tight, terrified by what the detective had said. Todd had been found, but Todd was missing again.

The police were holding Maggie Pierce, whose real name was Nancy Evans, at the South Kensington police station. She and Erich were told to get there as quickly as they could.

When they arrived, Erich held the door for her and they walked into the police station, where she found themselves in a crowded room. Erich took her arm, maneuvered them through the people and soon came face to face with Virginia. She stood by the detective's desk, and when they approached he stood to greet them. Beside Virginia, with her back to them, stood a dark-haired woman in handcuffs.

Laura was still trying to cope with the anger she felt toward her aunt. After four days in London, they'd learned nothing new.

Virginia blinked at Laura, speechless, then looked away. At that moment, as if she'd sensed their presence, the woman beside Virginia turned and looked directly at Laura.

Laura's eyes popped open. "You! You're Nancy Evans, aren't you? Where is he? What have you done with my son? Damn you! Where is he?"

The woman's face was almost green with remorse. Her eyes pleaded with Laura, but this was something she could never forgive. Never.

"I swear, I don't know," Nancy said. "Please believe me. You've got to believe me."

"I don't have to believe anything," Laura hissed. Her whole body was shaking by this point. Erich took hold of her shoulders and squeezed gently. "Where is he?" she demanded. "What's happened to my son now?"

The detective stepped in, only slightly diffusing Laura's rage. "Detective Joe McStravick," he said, his Scottish accent strong. "O'Toole, get chairs for Mrs. Austin and Mr. Muller."

"What's happened to Todd?" Laura asked. She saw desolation in Virginia's eyes. "He's dead, isn't he?"

"No," said the detective, and told her what had happened, including the phone call, though he omitted Todd's plea. "All we know is he's been abducted again."

Tears filled Laura's eyes. She wanted to hit Nancy, wanted to slap her so hard she'd knock her over. She stepped toward her, but Erich held her back. "How?" she shouted. "How could you have kept my little boy from me all this time?"

Nancy hung her head.

The detective told them what had happened at 74 Onslow Gardens earlier, then showed them the note Nancy had found. Laura glanced from her aunt to Nancy Evans, waiting for one of them to say something, but they sat like two lumps. It was very unlike Virginia.

Laura shook her head at her aunt and spoke through clenched teeth, tears of rage spilling over. "How could you have done this to me, Virginia? How? I've always defended you to everyone, even Erich, but he was right about you, wasn't he? Wasn't he? Answer me, damn it!"

Nancy spoke first. "Your aunt had nothing to do with your son's kidnapping. You've got to believe me."

"Then explain to me why she kept the truth from me."

Erich patted Laura's hand, bringing her back to the present. "We need to hear what Detective McStravick has to say, sweetheart. I know how upset you are, but we need to listen to him."

The detective cleared his throat and handed a piece of paper to Erich. "I think you should look at this before we go any further."

It was a picture of Geoffrey Pierce, and both he and Laura had the same reaction. Geoffrey Pierce was unquestionably the portrait artist they'd met at Washington Square Park a few weeks before. The one who had insisted on painting their portrait. Laura remembered thinking he was odd, but never could have imagined he'd have any connection to Todd's kidnapping. Suddenly she and Erich had the same thought. Rachel! What if he—

"Detective McStravick, I need to make an immediate overseas call to Detective Ben Wilson at the East Hampton police station," Erich said.

Laura leaned against him for reassurance. "It can't wait."

"I'll get the detective for you straight away," McStravick replied with a nod.

Erich reported to Ben Wilson that Todd had been kidnapped again. He told him they had no idea where he was and both he and Laura felt Rachel might be in danger. He asked for twenty-four hour a day protection for her. Wilson agreed and asked to be kept informed of developments. Erich gave the phone to Detective McStravick, and the two policemen exchanged a few words. When McStravick hung up, he stared pointedly at Nancy.

"What's going on?" Erich asked, catching the look.

"Geoffrey Pierce is my ex-husband," Nancy explained.

McStravick cleared his throat again. "I think it's time we looked at some mugshots." Another officer brought an enormous book to the detective's desk and placed it on front of them. "This could take days. Mr. Muller, I suggest you take Mrs. Austin home. Miss Kingsley, you may leave if you want, though we will want to talk to you again later."

"No," Virginia said. "I don't want to leave. I know Laura doesn't either. But she and I need to talk. Is there some place where we can have some privacy?"

***

The women and Erich followed Sergeant O'Toole down a steep flight of cement steps then through a long corridor, until they found themselves standing in a long, narrow room. It was where, the sergeant told them, prisoners had once come to exercise. Giving them a nod, he left them alone.

In reality, the three people left in the room would have preferred anything to being left alone together. Virginia had wanted to speak with Laura alone, but Laura had insisted Erich be there. She told Virginia that Erich was the only person she could trust.

Laura faced her aunt, trying to contain her rage. She was angry and hurt and didn't know what she might do if she gave in to the need to strike someone. "You know I don't believe Nancy Evans, or whatever her name is. I think you were either involved in Todd's kidnapping, or you knew something and didn't want to tell me. Whatever the truth, I can never trust you again."

Virginia leaned against the wall and sighed. "If it makes you feel better to hate me, then that's what you must do, though if I were you I wouldn't waste energy on me. I'd save it all for Todd."

A mouse scooted up the wall and they all recoiled.

Laura shuddered. "I'm leaving if I see another one of those," she said. "Couldn't they have found a better place for us to talk?"

Erich lit a cigarette and blew the smoke straight up to the ceiling. "It took half the police force to keep the press from following us. They did the best they could."

"You should have stayed there with them," Virginia said, glaring at him. "I wanted to talk to Laura alone. But wherever she goes you go, right?"

"I understand that you don't want me around. That way you can fill her head with more lies. Come on, Virginia. Why don't you tell her the truth for a change?"

Virginia took a step toward Laura, but Laura backed away. "I always thought you loved me," Laura said, shaking her head. "I thought you loved Todd, too. I know Todd loved his auntie. You know, before this I would have trusted you with his life. I thought you were kind and loving, despite your chosen lifestyle. Now I see that lifestyle is who you really are."

Virginia turned her back to Laura and Laura heard a sound she'd never heard before. Her aunt was sobbing. Virginia's shoulders shook and she kept crying, but Laura didn't make a move toward her. She wanted to believe her aunt's tears were genuine, not a ploy for sympathy, but that wasn't easy to do.

"If I tell you I wasn't involved, you won't believe me," said Virginia, "so I need to prove it to you, and that will take time."

They heard rapid footsteps slapping down the stone corridor toward them. Sergeant O'Toole was out of breath when he stepped into the room.

"Detective McStravick sent me to get you. Something important."

Within two hours they were on a plane headed back to New York. A meek Nancy Evans, still in handcuffs, was seated with Detective McStravick. She had decided not to fight extradition and to plead guilty to a charge of accessory to kidnapping. Her sentence would be left up to the judge and could be as much as ten years or as little as eighteen months.

Laura and Erich sat across from them, still stunned. When they'd returned to his office, McStravick had told them Australian Geoffrey Pierce was actually an American, and the son of Herb and Gladys Pierce. Herb and Gladys were the owners of the farmhouse where Todd had been held when he'd been kidnapped the first time.

Laura took a sip of water. "Wine would be better than this." She looked at Erich, who had been jotting things down on his notepad since they boarded the plane. "Or maybe straight scotch." She frowned at Erich's notes. "Did Wilson ever question the Pierces? He never said anything about them that I can recall. How could the police have overlooked the fact that the Pierce's son had a record in two countries going back almost fifteen years?"

"That's what I intend to find out," said Erich. "I don't remember Wilson ever mentioning the Pierces either, but that doesn't mean he didn't speak to them. He never wanted to tell me anything. He's got a lot to answer for, otherwise he'll make more trouble for himself than he can handle."

"He bungled the case from the start and now look." Laura turned and glanced at Virginia, who was sitting alone in the last row of seats with her head in her hands. "Do you know Geoffrey Pierce, Virginia?" she asked.

Virginia shook her head, but didn't look up.

Chapter Sixty-Three

Virginia had been unable to stop thinking about the confrontation she would have with Ben Wilson in a few hours. From the very beginning he had wanted to pin Todd's kidnapping on her. She would never forgive him for that. She would never forgive him for locking her in jail for no reason, either. She might have been just as angry with Erich Muller as she was with Wilson, except she realized how much Erich loved Laura. Everything he'd done had been with her best interests in mind.

Virginia had thought about seeking retribution against Wilson, but decided that would be overkill. It would be enough to see him proven incompetent. The most important thing now, as it had been all along, was finding Todd.

The plane landed a few minutes after three in the afternoon, and Phillip was waiting for them in a long, white Rolls Royce. No one would ever accuse the man of not knowing how to live in style. When Virginia realized she, Laura, Erich and Phillip would all be sitting in the back seat together, she almost offered to sit in front, then realized that might make things even more awkward. They all climbed into the car and sat in silence while they headed to the second precinct on Greenwich Street, the same place Wilson had interrogated her after Todd's kidnapping. Two police cars followed, sirens wailing. One contained Detective McStravick and Nancy Evans, who would be arraigned the next day.

Virginia's hope for an uneventful trip was dashed the moment Phillip opened his mouth.

"The more I think about it," he said, glaring out the window, "the more convinced I am that Todd was kidnapped by an irate fan. Maybe a woman who fantasized about being with me. Has anyone checked into Nancy Evans' background?"

Erich stared at Phillip and started to laugh, loud enough that Phillip glanced suspiciously at him. "Yes. Sorry to disappoint you, but they didn't find a single photograph of you in her apartment. I thought you were a horse's ass the first time I met you, Austin, and I still do. I know Laura's said this to you before, but I think it's time you realized the world doesn't revolve around you."

Laura nodded. "Erich has never seen Todd, you know. Except in pictures. And yet he's shown more concern for his welfare than you have. I think you're upset because you haven't gotten the chance to play the hero and bring your son home yourself. That would be your greatest role yet, wouldn't it?"

"Don't try to make a fool of me, Laura," Phillip said, sounding slightly hurt. "You and I discussed the possibility of some crazed fan kidnapping Todd, and you agreed it was a possibility. But obviously now that you and your lover are playing detective, you no longer take my opinions seriously."

Laura sighed and shook her head sadly at Phillip. "I know deep down you care about Todd, but you don't always show it."

"All actors are vain and self-centered," he said, lifting his chin defensively. "And I'm no different ... except when it comes to my son. He's my future."

The conversation dropped, as did the level of tension Virginia had sensed earlier in the car.

***

So many reporters and photographers surrounded the second precinct, the group wondered if they'd make it inside in one piece. The reporters shouted questions and the photographers snapped pictures as they made their way inside the police station. There they came face to face with a shamefaced Ben Wilson.

"I just got off the phone with San Francisco P.D.," he said. "They're checking the prints found in Nancy Evans' flat with the one discovered in the house with Rudy Strauss' body to see if there's a match." He glanced at the group. "Where's Miss Evans?"

"McStravick took her to Riverhead where she'll be booked. She'll spend the night in the clink," Erich said. "Why don't we find a room where we can talk?"

"Yes," Virginia said. "How about the one where you gave me the third degree? It had such a lovely ambiance. Ah, I remember the shade of green on the walls so well."

"I suppose you refuse to accept that even cops make mistakes," said Wilson.

"Find Todd, and we'll talk. Until then if you even look at me the wrong way you'll be in trouble," Virginia said.

"Fine. Come with me, please. There are a few things we need to discuss before the Pierces get here. We don't have much time."

They followed Detective Wilson down a short flight of stairs and into a large office where two other police officers waited with a stack of photographs. They divided the stack into four, giving a pile to Laura, Erich, Phillip, and Virginia. Fifteen minutes went by without a sound, apart from the occasional shuffling of papers.

Finally Erich looked up. "Are you sure these pictures are all of Pierce?"

"Quite a chameleon, isn't he? The guy's got so many disguises it's hard to keep up with them."

"Look at this," Laura said, passing one of the photographs to Erich. "That looks like the man who was driving the car the night you were beaten up."

"Didn't you say he looked like Vince?" Virginia got up and peered over Erich's shoulder at the picture. "You were right. It does look like Vince. Except it's not him." She looked up at the detective. "What are we dealing with here, Wilson?"

"Maybe you should tell us, Miss Kingsley. He seems to know quite a lot about you and your gang. Did you ever get the feeling that you were being watched?"

Virginia chuckled. "No more than usual." She sat back down in the chair and glanced at Phillip, who hadn't said a word. She frowned at the others, thinking out loud. "Geoffrey Pierce may or may not be connected with the Purple Gang in Detroit. Even if he isn't, he's sat in on their poker game at least once, so he knows them. They're dangerous. Pierce is obviously an expert at using disguises, so he could even have decided he'd be a photographer today. He could be outside with the rest of them."

"What else?" Wilson asked.

"You are lazy, Detective, getting everyone else to do your work. This guy has murdered at least one person, maybe more, and he has Todd."

A few moments later, Herb and Gladys Pierce, both in their seventies, arrived at the police station. Though he was starting to stoop with age, Herb was about six foot three and all arms and legs. Gladys was barely five feet tall and was dressed in pink from head to toe. Gladys' eyes went directly to Laura, and the woman's look of awe made Laura smile reflexively.

"You're even more beautiful in person, dear," Gladys said to Laura and took both of her hands. "Oh, I hope they find that precious little boy of yours soon." Gladys' eyes darted to the side and fell upon Virginia. Her eyes widened. "You!"

"Sit down, Glad," Herb said, guiding his wife into a chair. "Take it easy. The police want to talk to us, remember?" He turned to Detective Wilson. "What can we do for you?"

"I'd like to ask you some questions about your son, Geoffrey."

Herb shook his head. "Maybe you can tell us where he is. Last we heard he was in Houston. The Missus and I have been planning to retire to Arizona for two years, but that boy of ours can't stay put long enough for us to discuss what's to be done with the farmhouse."

"Do you know that house was used as a hideout in the Austin kidnapping?" Virginia asked

Herb frowned. "Detective Wilson mentioned something to us about that, but we thought if it were true, we'd have heard more about it."

"We have reason to believe that your son Geoffrey was involved in the kidnapping," Wilson said. "He's most likely also responsible for a homicide that took place in London last night. We need to find him. We're certain he has Todd Austin." Wilson glanced at Laura, then back to the couple. "The child could be in danger."

The couple stared with disbelief at Wilson, then at each other. Tears rolled down Gladys Pierce's pale cheeks while her husband grasped her hand and tried to comfort her. "Oh, dear, dear, dear. Anything but this," she sobbed.

Herb looked around the room, looking for inspiration. "The last we heard he was in Houston. Other than that we don't know. If there's anything—"

The phone rang. Detective Wilson said a few brief words to the caller then put the receiver down.

"The prints from London and the prints from San Francisco are a match. Pierce was in both places. We've got to find him."

"What about searching the farmhouse again?" Laura asked.

Chapter Sixty-Four

Today's disguise consisted of a curly gray wig, a padded, flowered housedress, and glasses. From a distance, Geoffrey Pierce resembled his mother. Geoff opened the basement window and carefully lowered himself inside. After he dusted off the dress, he stood quietly, listening. The kid was singing to himself somewhere nearby. It was a sweet sound that made Geoff feel a little more calm. Strauss had told him that even a year and a half ago the child had a knack for comforting himself and others.

Geoff knew he was taking a chance by visiting the farmhouse, because the cops might be staking out the place, but he'd had to go. He couldn't let the kid starve, though he didn't dare stay there himself. The whole thing would be finished in a couple of days, anyway. He'd found a couple in Vancouver who were willing to buy the kid. The only thing left to do was visit the plastic surgeon Rossi had lined up, who would change the kid's appearance enough so the Vancouver couple wouldn't recognize him.

Geoff headed down the hall toward the little voice. The boy continued to sing the nursery rhyme, even though he must have heard the footsteps. At the exact moment Geoff checked his watch, Todd ran by. Before he could react, the child had climbed onto a chair and was trying in vain to reach the window.

"I want to go outside! I don't like it in here!"

"I told you we'd go out later. Now come on. I've brought some food for you."

"I don't want to eat. I want Mommy! I want to go home!"

Geoff smiled, but Todd glared furiously at him. "You'll be going home to Mommy soon, but for now you have to be patient."

"No! I want Mommy!"

Geoff didn't know if the kid was talking about Nancy Evans or Laura Austin, but it didn't matter. He'd never see either one of them again. Geoff figured the boy was young enough to forget both of them eventually and live a happy rest of his life. That was the beauty of the whole thing. In time they'd all get on with the rest of their lives. Everyone except Rudy and the guy Geoff had found at Nancy's place. And that O'Malley fellow with the horses. Those guys he'd had to bump off.

Geoff tried to take Todd's hand, but the child yanked it away and stomped back into the main room. Geoff set up the hot plate and warmed up the spaghetti and meatball dinner he'd brought for them. When it was done, he called the little boy, but the kid didn't budge from the dark corner where he sat, sulking. Geoff put some food on a plate and brought it to him. Todd glanced at Geoff, then at the food, and knocked the plate out of Geoff's hand.

Geoff stepped back, grinning wryly. "You must get your feistiness from Virginia Kingsley."

"I don't like you. I want my mommy."

"Eat some food and I'll take you to see Mommy soon."

Geoff cleaned up the mess and brought Todd more food. The boy grudgingly ate, crying all the time for his mommy. When he was done he curled up on the floor and fell asleep with his thumb in his mouth. Geoff covered him with a blanket and watched him for a while. He could almost have felt sorry for the kid if it weren't for the cool half million the couple were willing to pay for a healthy son.

He considered tying the kid up. He would have if he'd thought the little guy could have escaped. But he couldn't. He was too small and too helpless. To make certain the cops didn't find him, Geoff gently lifted Todd and moved him to a secret room no one would ever be able to find.

Chapter Sixty-Five

For thirty-six hours the police staked out the farmhouse in Bayside without seeing any activity. Laura and Erich stayed at Erich's apartment in the village, Virginia at her West 77th Street brownstone and Phillip in his penthouse, waiting for word. They had stopped talking to each other and only communicated through Ben Wilson, whom none of them trusted.

Virginia made a quick trip to Houston where she saw Mike at the racetrack, and Mike confirmed Herb and Gladys Pierce's story that their son had been in Houston until about three weeks earlier. Geoffrey Pierce's whereabouts since then were a mystery. Virginia knew she could have handled this over the phone but had a feeling the cops had tapped her line.

On the afternoon that she returned from Houston, Virginia stopped at *Bacchanal*. Harry had done a good job with the place in her absence, and she was thinking about selling it to him. She sat at the bar, nursing a glass of orange juice, trying to decide what she wanted to do. She no longer cared about socializing with people she didn't know, and she didn't want to be forced to make idle conversation. She'd lost Laura's love and respect, and nothing seemed to matter anymore. If they found Todd alive, she and Laura would probably go their separate ways. If they didn't find him or found him dead, Virginia dreaded the future. Either way she might as well sell the place to Harry. He and Vince could make a go of it.

She thought she heard a soft knock on the door, but ignored it, thinking it was just the wind. She poured herself more orange juice, then hesitated, hearing the sound again. This time someone was rattling the door handle, too.

She pulled the door open and stared at the friendly face of Erich Muller. Confused, she glanced around to see if Laura was with him, but she didn't see her. Virginia looked back at Erich and stared at him for a moment. She had never noticed how gentle Erich Muller's blue eyes were. She'd always noticed how handsome he was, but never his kindness. Animosity had blinded her to his good qualities.

"I never expected to see you here, Mr. Muller. Has something happened to Laura?"

He shook his head. He looked exhausted. "She's waiting, like the rest of us, and getting tired of it like I'm sure you are. She knows I'm here, though, and why. The police are doing nothing, which is what they've done from the first day. I think it's time we do something, don't you? You and I can search the farmhouse ourselves."

"Don't we need a search warrant?" Virginia said.

"Yes, and the Pierces could press charges, but I doubt they will," Erich said.

Feeling suddenly optimistic, she led Erich inside and poured him a glass of orange juice. "How come it took us this long to find out we could trust each other?" Virginia asked. "I mean it only makes sense. We both love Laura and we both have her best interests at heart."

"Then you're with me?" Erich asked. Virginia nodded. "Good," he said. "Now here's what we're going to do."

Armed with flashlights, Virginia and Erich arrived at the farmhouse a few minutes after eight o'clock that evening. The night was pitch black. It was so dark neither one of them could see their hands in front of their faces. It was a good thing Erich had suggested the flashlights. As they started to head toward the house they heard a car, followed by the crunch of tires on gravel. The car stopped, a door slammed, and their flashlights found Laura as she walked toward them.

"I couldn't let you do this alone," she said. "I'm so sick of waiting and doing nothing. I thought if I came here I might find something."

Erich and Laura kissed and Virginia couldn't help smiling. They were a gorgeous couple, and she could see how much they needed each other.

"Let me take a look around," Erich said. "Laura, you and your aunt should go across the road and crouch down in those bushes."

Virginia took Laura's arm. "I suggest you take this, Erich," she said and handed him a small revolver. "Just in case."

"Smart woman," he said and took the gun from her. "It seems pretty quiet around here, but I still want to be sure. The cops are going to be angry enough as is."

A few minutes later Erich finished his inspection and walked across the road. "There aren't any cops around, that's for sure, and unless Pierce is hiding underground he isn't here, either."

Laura raised her eyebrows. "He could be inside the house."

"We won't find that out until we get inside," Virginia said.

The three of them headed for the front door and, to no one's surprise, found it locked. Erich tried to break the lock, but it wouldn't budge. Virginia chuckled, teasing him that he'd never make it as a thief. The only way in was through one of the first floor windows. Erich set off, looking for something with which he could break the window, and Virginia's mind filled with memories of when she'd found Rudy in San Francisco. Did she feel remorse for what she'd done? She wasn't sure, though she had no doubt he'd gotten what he'd deserved.

"I guess my fist will have to do," Erich said when he returned empty-handed.

"You'll hurt yourself," Laura said.

"A few cuts—"

Virginia laughed, interrupting them. Obviously neither one had ever broken into any place, and she hoped they never would. She returned a moment later dragging a large tree branch. With one shove she shattered the glass of what appeared to be the living room window. Erich nodded, admiring her handiwork, then cleaned away the shards of glass before they climbed in the window. He cut his hand in a couple of places, but reached back to help Laura get through.

"Watch where you walk," Erich said.

"Don't you think if Pierce were here he'd have come after us the second he heard the glass shatter?" Laura asked.

Virginia put her finger to her lips. "We need to keep our voices down to a whisper."

Laura nodded. They crept through the first floor rooms, then went upstairs. Laura paused and stared into the crib where Todd had slept all those months before. She picked up the pillow, buried her face in it, then gently set it back down.

"Don't do this to yourself," Erich said.

"It comforts me in a way."

After searching everywhere upstairs, they went downstairs and looked through every inch of space, but found no sign of either Todd or Geoffrey Pierce. Once again, it was a dead end. Virginia took Laura into her arms and let her sob.

"Maybe it's time we called the cops and let them take over," Erich said.

They looked at each other at the same time, and Virginia mouthed the name "Wilson". They all shook their heads, knowing they had a better chance of solving this then he did.

Laura rested in an armchair covered with cat hairs. Virginia ran her fingers through her hair, wondering what the next move should be. Should she go back to Houston and see if Mike had heard anything during the last couple of days?

Chapter Sixty-Six

Erich froze, his eyes slightly unfocused. "Wait," he whispered. "Listen."

"What is it?" Laura asked, frowning at his eager face.

"Shh."

The sound came again. All three heard it distinctly this time, though no one could figure out what it was. Laura got up, walked to the fireplace and put her ear to the wall above, but the sound wasn't coming from there.

"Here," Virginia said. She walked toward a wall and pushed a rocking chair out of the way.

They waited for ten minutes but heard nothing. With each disappearing moment their hope, so briefly stirred, faded. Laura straightened and looked at Erich, her expression miserable. Just as they were about to give up, the sound grabbed them again. Laura's eyes popped open wide, and she began to tremble. With a mother's instinct, she knew.

"It's a child's voice. It's Todd."

"Do you understand what he's saying?"

She smiled. "Just one word. Mommy."

Virginia's hands went to her throat. "How do we get to him?"

Erich didn't miss a beat. "There's just one way I can see. We have to break down the wall, because he's right behind it."

Erich and Virginia ran outside to the garage, which had been almost completely hidden by ivy and overgrowth. Laura stayed behind and spoke to the unseen child behind the wall. At first he was quiet, but within seconds he'd responded to the soothing sound of her voice.

Erich and Virginia returned with a couple of hammers and a claw hammer. They pummeled the wall, breaking through to the drywall, which gave way easily. Suddenly the words the child was speaking became clear.

"James James
Morrison, Morrison
Weatherby George Dupree
Took great
Care of his mother
Though he was only three."

Laura swayed. Erich reached out to catch her, but she caught herself, determined to stay strong. When the dust cleared from the demolition, they walked a few steps into the tiny room. A curly haired, wide-eyed little boy huddled against the wall, pressing as far away from the noise as he could get. On his lap trembled a kitten. The child stared up at them in confusion. Then his eyes found Laura. He dropped the kitten, leapt to his feet and ran to her.

"Mommy! Three!"

"Todd!" Laura didn't remember running to him, dropping onto her knees and gathering her little boy against her. All she knew was the solid warmth of his little body, the fingers clutching at her back, the smell, oh, the sweet familiar smell of him. She sobbed, saying his name over and over, running her hands over his back and hair, then pulling away just enough so she could see his face.

Erich stood back, unable to move. Tears streamed down his cheeks. Virginia stood like a statue, staring at the miracle happening right in front of her.

***

After Phillip was reunited with Todd at his apartment in Manhattan, they all set off for Willow Pond in his Rolls Royce. Somehow the media found out, and cars filled with reporters and photographers followed them like a caravan. People lined the streets of Manhattan shouting well wishes as the Rolls sped by. Phillip opened the window and waved like a king, and the crowd went wild.

"I don't think that's a good idea, Austin," Erich said.

Phillip turned toward the back seat. "Huh? Why not?"

"Never know what kind of nut could be in that crowd."

Phillip quickly rolled up the window.

Laura didn't care about the noise or the people or the confusion. All she cared about was that her little boy was nestled safely in her arms, sleeping in peace, maybe for the first time in ages. She ran her hands through his blond curls, pleased that Nancy hadn't cut them off. Laura was relieved to see the woman had taken good care of him, and though she would never be able to forgive Nancy for what she'd done, she was at least grateful for that.

Every time she thought of what her baby had been through she wanted to cry. She held him closer and hoped that because he was only three he was young enough to forget everything that had happened. He sighed in his sleep and she brushed her lips against his forehead, swearing she would spend every day of the rest of her life knowing how much he meant to her. Erich, sitting beside her, took her hand and they smiled at each other.

"You were right, he is quite a little guy."

"I don't think he knew what he was doing when he started singing that song, but I hate to think of what might have happened if he hadn't."

"He'd still be there at the mercy of that madman," Phillip said.

Virginia put her hand on the little boy's arm. "That's too awful to even think about."

Laura pushed her aunt's hand away. "I don't want you to wake him up. Can't you see he's exhausted? I doubt that he's gotten much sleep in days."

Virginia smiled despite Laura's rebuff. "There's no better place for him to sleep than in his mother's arms."

Todd awoke when the car parked in front of Willow Pond. He sat up and looked around, then turned to Laura with an expression of puzzlement on his face. He clearly didn't remember the place. Maybe his mind was protecting him from the memory of his abduction, but whatever the reason, Laura was grateful. She sighed with relief.

"I want to go home," he said.

"This is home, sweetheart. We're home," Laura said.

The front door flew open and Iris ran out with Rachel in her arms. Erich got out of the car and took the baby from her so Iris could take his seat. The nanny sobbed, repeating his name and alternating between laughing and crying. Todd took one look at her and clambered into her arms.

"I wonder if he remembers you," Laura said.

Iris' cheeks shone with tears. "We've dreamed about this day, haven't we, Laura? I was so afraid it would never happen, and here it is." The two women smiled when Todd climbed back into Laura's arms. "He has a mind of his own, doesn't he?"

"Erich, let him see the baby," Laura said.

"I think it's time you got out of the car before those reporters catch up to us. They're not too far behind," Erich said.

"In a minute."

Erich gave Rachel back to Iris. Todd studied her and touched her blonde hair. "Baby."

"She's your baby sister, and her name is Rachel."

Todd gave her a final passing glance and wriggled out of Laura's arms. Before anyone realized it, he had gotten out of the car and was racing toward the house. Virginia caught him halfway there and tossed him up in the air.

"You aren't going to get away from us any time soon," she said.

She set him on the ground and tickled him under the chin. He giggled, his laughter like medicine for Laura's soul. Laura couldn't help smiling, seeing Virginia with Todd. She was still angry with her aunt, but watching them together made it difficult for her to believe Virginia ever could have done anything to hurt him.

Erich came up from behind her and put his arm around her waist. "You and Virginia need to talk," he said. "It's time."

"I'm afraid to hear what she has to say. I don't know if I'm ready."

At the sound of approaching cars they all headed for the house and managed to get inside before the first reporter reached the front door.

Laura laughed. "I thought they'd gotten lost."

"You mean you *hoped* they had," said Erich. "Why don't you and your aunt go into the solarium? We'll watch Todd. The two of you need some time alone."

***

Laura and Virginia walked into the kitchen and stood facing each other. They had once been as close as mother and daughter. Now they felt like strangers.

"Would you like a glass of soda?" Laura asked, trying to break the ice.

"Since I decided to curb my drinking I've developed a taste for Coca-Cola. If you have any, that would be great. Otherwise, water is fine."

"Erich drinks the stuff all the time, so I'm sure there's some in the refrigerator. Then we can go into the solarium and talk. It's my favorite room. It has such a beautiful view of the grounds."

"I remember. That's where you had Todd's first birthday party."

"If I'd known we were going to miss his second and third birthday I would have made even more of a fuss. But I suppose it's a good thing we can't see into the future sometimes."

They went into the solarium, Virginia sipping a bottle of Coke, Laura wondering what they could possibly say to each other. Laura had so many questions, but she didn't want to ask any of them. All she wanted was for things to be the same between her and her aunt as they'd once been.

"He's going to be fine, Laura," Virginia said, her voice smooth with reassurance. "Small children are resilient."

"How can you be sure?" asked Laura. "This is going to take getting used to. I don't want to smother him, but even now that I've been away from him for a couple of minutes I feel myself starting to panic."

"Give it time, Laura. Everything's going to be fine." Virginia had always known what was in her heart. "Laura, I know you have every reason to mistrust me, even hate me. But I want you to know I'd never do anything to hurt you or Todd. I've always loved both of you."

"Then why?"

A few minutes later they heard Todd squeal, "Mommy! Three!" again, followed by Erich's gentle voice. The women smiled at each other. Laura figured the words brought back some happy memory for him. A feeling of security.

No one had used the sunroom in some time and it felt stuffy, so she opened a couple of windows to let in some fresh air. The chirping of birds filled the room.

"The poem he's reciting is the one you told me about when he was first kidnapped, isn't it?" Virginia asked.

Laura cocked her head to one side. "I never thought you'd remember. You've seemed distracted for so long."

Virginia put her arms around Laura and hugged her. For the first time in a long time they both felt a sense of peace. "I'm so sorry for everything you've been through, Laura. If I could have done anything to prevent you from going through it all I would have."

Laura moved out of her aunt's arms. "Tell me about Rudy Strauss."

They heard footsteps, and Todd trotted into the room, munching a chocolate chip cookie, most of which had ended up on his face. Laura scooped him up and set him on her lap. He turned the cookie over and took another bite.

"He seems so ... normal," Laura said, looking at him with wonder. "You can't know how happy it makes me to see him do things most children his age do." She returned her gaze to Virginia. "Now. I have to know about Rudy Strauss."

Virginia told her everything, omitting nothing except her being responsible for Rudy's death. She hadn't expected to be so honest, but she couldn't lie to Laura. All she could hope for was that someday she'd understand.

When she was done, Laura stared incredulously at her. "You knew ... the whole time ... and yet you let me go on wondering? How could you?"

Todd glanced up at his mother, then at Virginia, his eyes round with concern.

"He senses something," Laura said.

"Of course he does. He's a sensitive child."

"I don't want him to hear this."

She called Iris then waited for Virginia to explain herself.

Virginia shrugged. "There is no explanation. I did what I did because I thought it was best for you and Todd. If I'd told you what I knew, you could have been in danger."

Laura stared at her in silence, then spoke quietly, her voice low. "Erich was right about you."

"I don't think he agrees with you anymore."

Laura shook her head slowly. "That doesn't matter." She got off the chair and glared down at her aunt. "I want you out of my house."

"Laura—"

"Now."

Chapter Sixty-Seven

Virginia left without a word to anyone. She didn't even stop when Erich went after her. He found Laura in the solarium standing by the window, watching a blue jay and listening to it caw to its family. He went to her side and wrapped an arm around her. She glanced up at him then looked back at the bird.

"Can you imagine anything as naturally beautiful as that bird?" she asked softly. "He's perfect."

"You and Virginia had a fight."

Laura shook her head. "I still can't believe it. She knew Strauss had kidnapped Todd almost from the beginning. I don't think she knew about Pierce, but I can't be sure because she lied about so much. You were right about her from the start. I don't know how I could have been so naïve. I knew the kind of life she led, and I still refused to listen to you. Because of her, you and I almost lost each other."

Erich took her hand in his. "When it counted, she told you the truth. I'm certain she was trying to spare you. You've been through so much, Laura. I want her at our wedding, and I know you do, too."

She grinned. "I promised we'd talk about that after Todd came home, didn't I? We need to pick a date."

Erich laughed. "With your ex-husband in the next room?"

"He's the next one I plan to throw out of here."

There was a knock on the door, and Iris opened it a crack. She peeked inside, looking nervous.

"I hope I'm not interrupting, but Todd ... well, he saw the pond and he wants to ... go swimming. Yes. If I don't find a pair of swimming trunks that fit him soon he'll go in his clothes."

"There aren't any swimming trunks in the house that will fit him. Oh, Iris. I don't think so. The whole idea of it terrifies me," Laura said.

"He can swim in his underwear," Erich said. Laura looked at him with pleading eyes, but his smile was calm and reassuring. He squeezed her against him. "Let him. We'll be there with him. You can't protect him from life forever."

Laura and Erich carried two lawn chairs outside. They sat and watched while Todd splashed in the pond. Beside them, Rachel slept soundly in her carriage. Iris, who had clear memories of the kidnapping and was still afraid to go near the pond, watched the little boy from a safe distance.

Erich handed Laura a calendar he'd carried outside with him. "How about the first weekend in December?"

She grinned. "Look at you, Mr. Planner. December? No. Too close to Thanksgiving and Christmas. I was thinking about next month," Laura said.

"Next month? I thought women needed ages to plan these things."

"You're right. I won't have enough time. December is better." She placed the calendar on the ground and turned her attention to her little boy, who was laughing and splashing in the water.

Erich reached across and held her hand. "The first time I interviewed you, you told me he loved the water most of all. I fell in love with you that day. Did you know that?"

Laura knew she should be paying more attention to Erich, but she couldn't get her mind off her aunt. Had she been too harsh? Thinking back, she realized Virginia could have lied to her, but she'd chosen not to, even though she'd had to know what Laura's reaction would be.

"Things will get better between you and Virginia in time," said Erich, reading her mind. "Not speaking to her isn't going to help, though."

"I know, I know. I'll call her tomorrow."

Phillip's voice travelled through the door and Erich got up, meeting him halfway between the house and the pond. When he returned he was smiling broadly.

"Looks like Geoffrey Pierce is not as smart as he thinks he is. The cops caught him trying to board a train to Houston, Texas," Erich said.

Laura sighed, finally feeling as if she could breathe. "It's finally over." She took off her shoes and pushed them to the side, then stood up and waded into the water. When Todd saw her he ran toward her, his arms outstretched.

About Carol Tibaldi

Carol Tibaldi was born and raised in Bayside, New York and attended Queens College of the City University of New York. She loves to travel and has lived in London and Los Angeles. For twenty five years she worked as a newspaper reporter and covered the crime beat. She is a history buff and loves to research different time periods having a special affinity of the prohibition era and the Civil War. Willow Pond is her first novel and she is hard at work on the sequel

Website: http://www.caroltibaldi.com

Blog: http://authorcaroltibaldi.blogspot.com

Twitter: https://twitter.com/#!/cat5149

Facebook: http://www.facebook.com/#!/pages/Willow-Pond-a-novel-by-Carol-Tibaldi/212483638798198

Made in the USA
Charleston, SC
22 March 2012